SOUTHERN BASTARDS

Volume 2

GRIDIRON

IMAGE COMICS, INC.

Robert Kirkman – Chief Operating Officer
Erik Larsen – Chief Financial Officer
Todd McFarlane – President
Marc Silvestri – Chief Executive Officer
Jim Valentino – Vice-President

Eric Stephenson – Publisher
Ron Richards – Director of Business Development
Kat Salazar – Director of PR & Marketing
Corey Murphy – Director of Retail Sales
Jeremy Sullivan – Director of Digital Sales
Randy Okamura – Marketing Production Designer
Emilio Bautista – Sales Assistant
Branwyn Bigglestone – Senior Accounts Manager
Emily Miller – Accounts Manager
Jessica Ambriz – Administrative Assistant
David Brothers – Content Manager
Jonathan Chan – Production Manager
Drew Gill – Art Director
Meredith Wallace – Print Manager
Addison Duke – Production Artist
Vincent Kukua – Production Artist
Sasha Head – Production Artist
Tricia Ramos – Production Assistant
IMAGECOMICS.COM

SOUTHERN BASTARDS, VOL 2: GRIDIRON. First printing. April 2015. Copyright © 2015 Golgonooza, Inc. and Jason Latour. All rights reserved. Published by Image Comics, Inc. Office of publication: 2001 Center Street, Sixth Floor, Berkeley, CA 94704. Originally published in single-magazine form as SOUTHERN BASTARDS #5-8. "Southern Bastards," the Southern Bastards logos, and the likenesses of all characters herein are trademarks of Golgonooza, Inc. and Jason Latour, unless otherwise noted. "Image" and the Image Comics logos are registered trademarks of Image Comics, Inc.
For information regarding the CPSIA on this printed material call: 203-595-3636 and provide reference #RICH– 615635. Representation: Law Offices of Harris M. Miller II, P.C. (rightsinquiries@gmail.com). ISBN: 978-1-63215-269-5

SOUTHERN BASTARDS

"GRIDIRON"

created by
JASON AARON & JASON LATOUR

JASON AARON writer
JASON LATOUR art & color

JARED K. FLETCHER letters
SEBASTIAN GIRNER editor

Introduction by
RYAN KALIL

Whenever I'm asked about living in the south, one thing comes to mind.

Football.

Southerners are a bit obsessive about their football. And if the good ol' alma mater has a head coach that wins?

He is king.

He is idolized, adored, never second-guessed and no one would dare challenge his authority. Well, except maybe an angry old man with a big stick (God rest his soul).

So it isn't any wonder why the villain of this story is the head football coach of the state champion Runnin' Rebs.

Or so I thought he was the villain.

After reading volume 2, I now find myself empathizing with the bastard.

I cringed every page I witnessed his troubled backstory, especially his days on the "Gridiron" trying to make the team as a middle linebacker.

In my opinion, middle linebacker is the hardest position in the game. Some would disagree with me but to them I say this:

What do you do when it's Cover 2, it's a 7 man box and you know the safeties aren't coming down for run support? Even if you mix in some stunts like a double pirate where the 3 technique and the 6 technique lateral step to the inside "a" and "b" gaps, you still have an extra gap that's open.

What do you think is harder for a middle linebacker? Having to run and cover the deep middle on any two vertical pass routes, essentially now becoming the deep third safety or playing downhill on a bounce "G" run out of slot formation where the guard and fullback both lead up on the sam and the mike?

I'm sure most middle linebackers will tell you how much they LOVE it when right before the snap the "H" back shifts to the other side of the QB in the gun and now you have a few seconds to decide: "Do I switch the side of the blitz?!"

Then there's this "no-huddle" nonsense (which Coach Boss shares my sentiment about). The hardest thing about it is lining up and making sure everyone is on the same page. The only time no-huddle is dangerous is if communication is poor. If they catch you in base personnel and they are in nickel personnel, you have poor match-ups in the slot. Oh, guess who's in charge of that?

Finally, there's the triple option. Arguably the hardest play in football to stop. They can hand it off, keep it or throw it to the TE. You're lined up in the "A" gap, the zone play action is heading weak away from you. Do you downhill step to maintain your "A" gap? Do you cheat to the TE to play the pass? Or, do you wait to see if the QB keeps it? It always looks the same!

Euless Boss had to be crazy to want to compete at that position. But then again, I suppose it makes sense. You have to be a little off upstairs to tolerate the complexity, pain and violence and keep signing up for more. That's why every team has a few wild cards on their roster. You may not want them coming to your next family cook-out, but they sure can wallop a back into the turf.

Aaron's writing and Latour's art are really remarkable and I didn't think they could humanize Coach Boss the way they did. I'm very fond of this story and I hope you are as eager as I am to see what Aaron and Latour fry up next.

In the meantime, enjoy the trip down memory lane with Euless Boss, that good-for-nothing, murder'n, Roll Tide worshiping, son of a bitch high school football coach from Craw County, Alabama!

That "Southern Bastard!"

Ryan Kalil is the All-Pro center for the Carolina Panthers of the National Football League. He was drafted in the second round of the 2007 NFL Draft after playing college football at the University of Southern California, where he won two national championships, was named a first-team All-American and won the 2006 Morris Trophy, which is given to the top offensive lineman in the Pac-12 Conference. Now in his 9th season in the NFL, Kalil has been to four Pro Bowls and was named All-Pro in 2011 and 2013. Ryan has long enjoyed sports and comics. He currently lives in Charlotte, North Carolina, with his wife, Natalie, and their three children, Cade, Kennadi and Chandler.

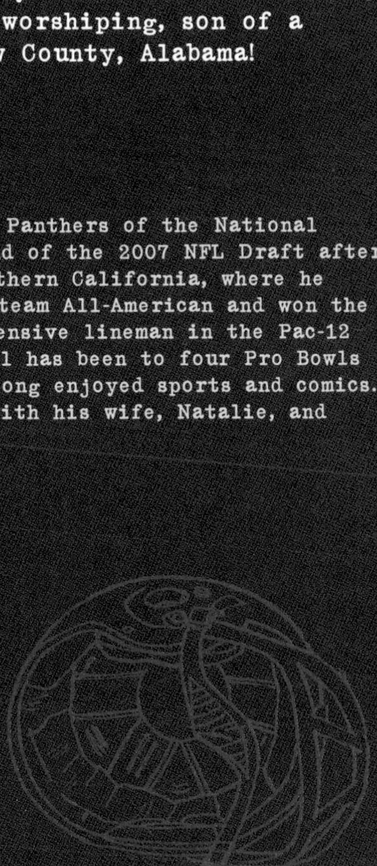

Chapter 5

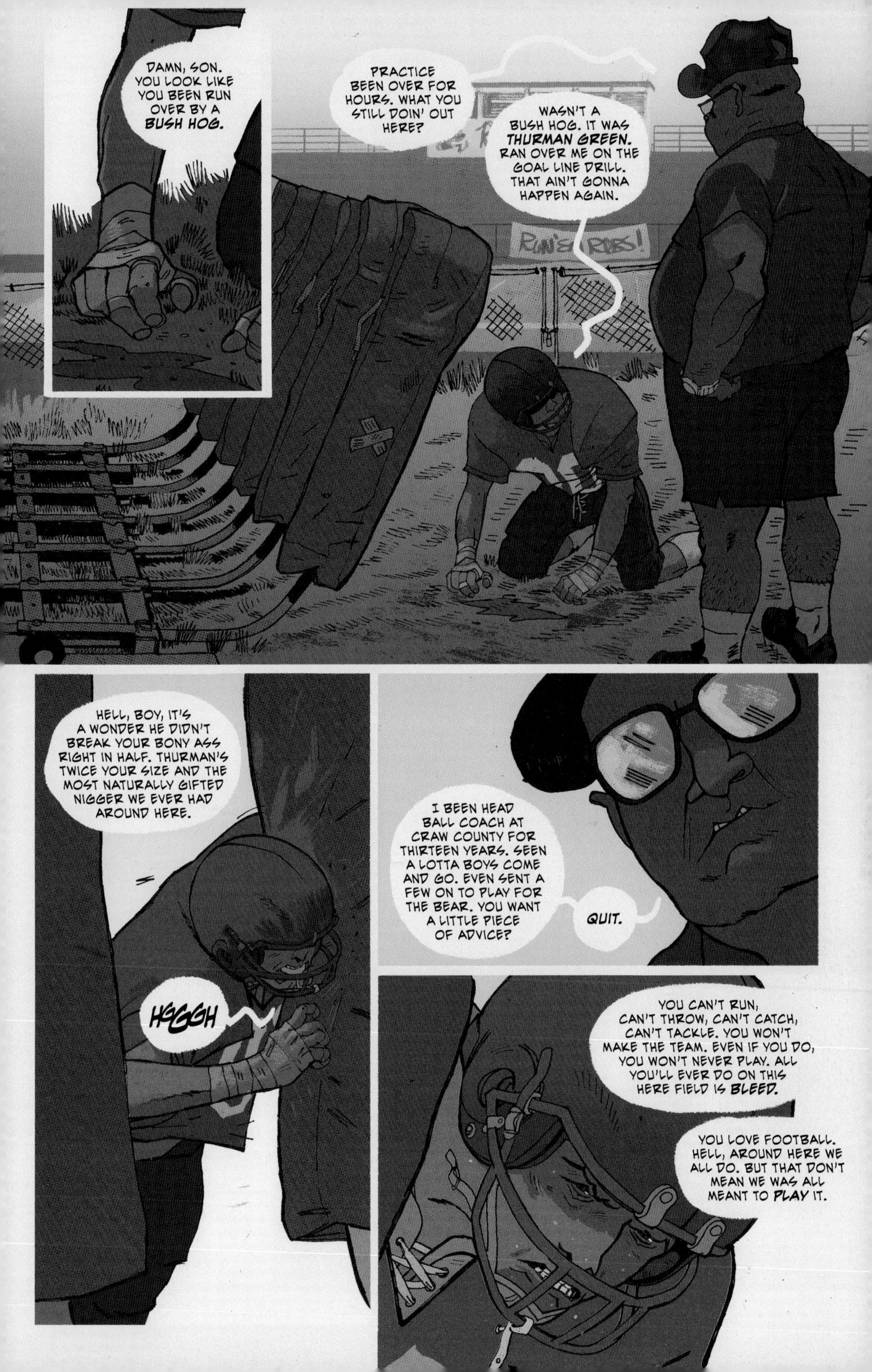
DAMN, SON. YOU LOOK LIKE YOU BEEN RUN OVER BY A **BUSH HOG.**
PRACTICE BEEN OVER FOR HOURS. WHAT YOU STILL DOIN' OUT HERE?
WASN'T A BUSH HOG. IT WAS **THURMAN GREEN.** RAN OVER ME ON THE GOAL LINE DRILL. THAT AIN'T GONNA HAPPEN AGAIN.
RUN'EM ROBS!
HELL, BOY, IT'S A WONDER HE DIDN'T BREAK YOUR BONY ASS RIGHT IN HALF. THURMAN'S TWICE YOUR SIZE AND THE MOST NATURALLY GIFTED NIGGER WE EVER HAD AROUND HERE.
HGGGH
I BEEN HEAD BALL COACH AT CRAW COUNTY FOR THIRTEEN YEARS. SEEN A LOTTA BOYS COME AND GO. EVEN SENT A FEW ON TO PLAY FOR THE BEAR. YOU WANT A LITTLE PIECE OF ADVICE?
QUIT.
YOU CAN'T RUN, CAN'T THROW, CAN'T CATCH, CAN'T TACKLE. YOU WON'T MAKE THE TEAM. EVEN IF YOU DO, YOU WON'T NEVER PLAY. ALL YOU'LL EVER DO ON THIS HERE FIELD IS **BLEED.**
YOU LOVE FOOTBALL. HELL, AROUND HERE WE ALL DO. BUT THAT DON'T MEAN WE WAS ALL MEANT TO **PLAY** IT.

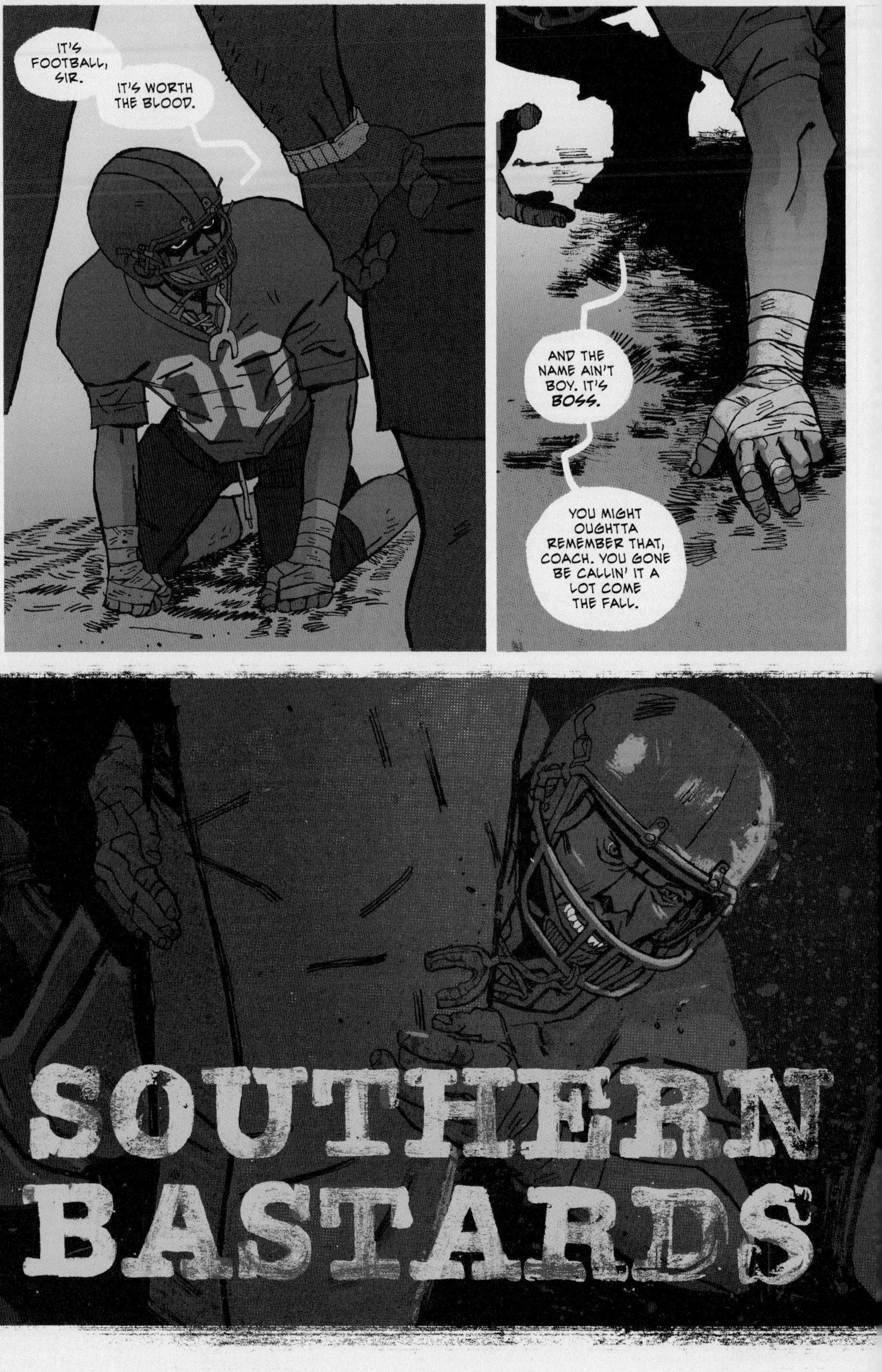
IT'S FOOTBALL, SIR.
IT'S WORTH THE BLOOD.
AND THE NAME AIN'T BOY. IT'S BOSS.
YOU MIGHT OUGHTTA REMEMBER THAT, COACH. YOU GONE BE CALLIN' IT A LOT COME THE FALL.
SOUTHERN BASTARDS

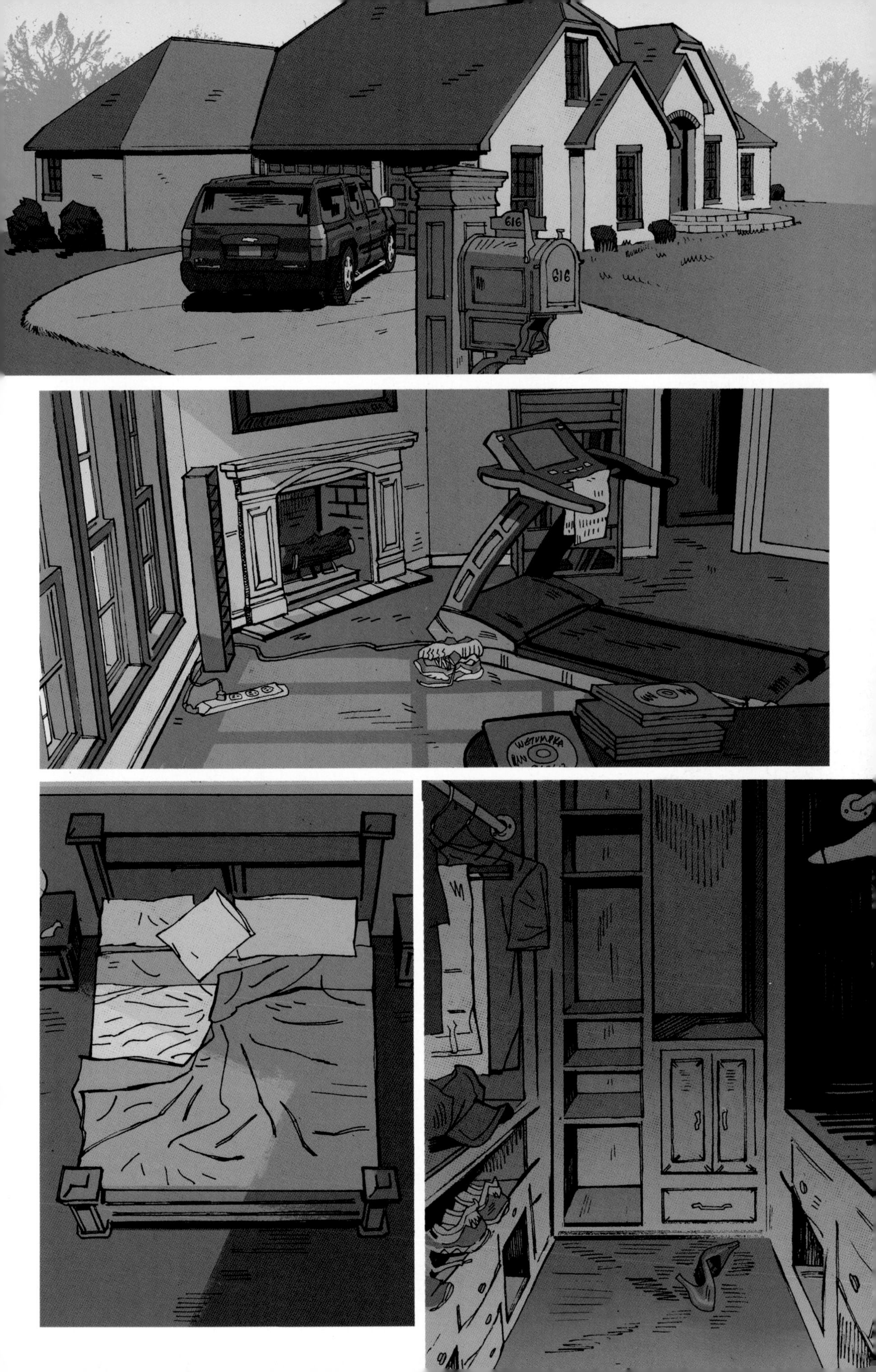
616
616
WETUMPKA

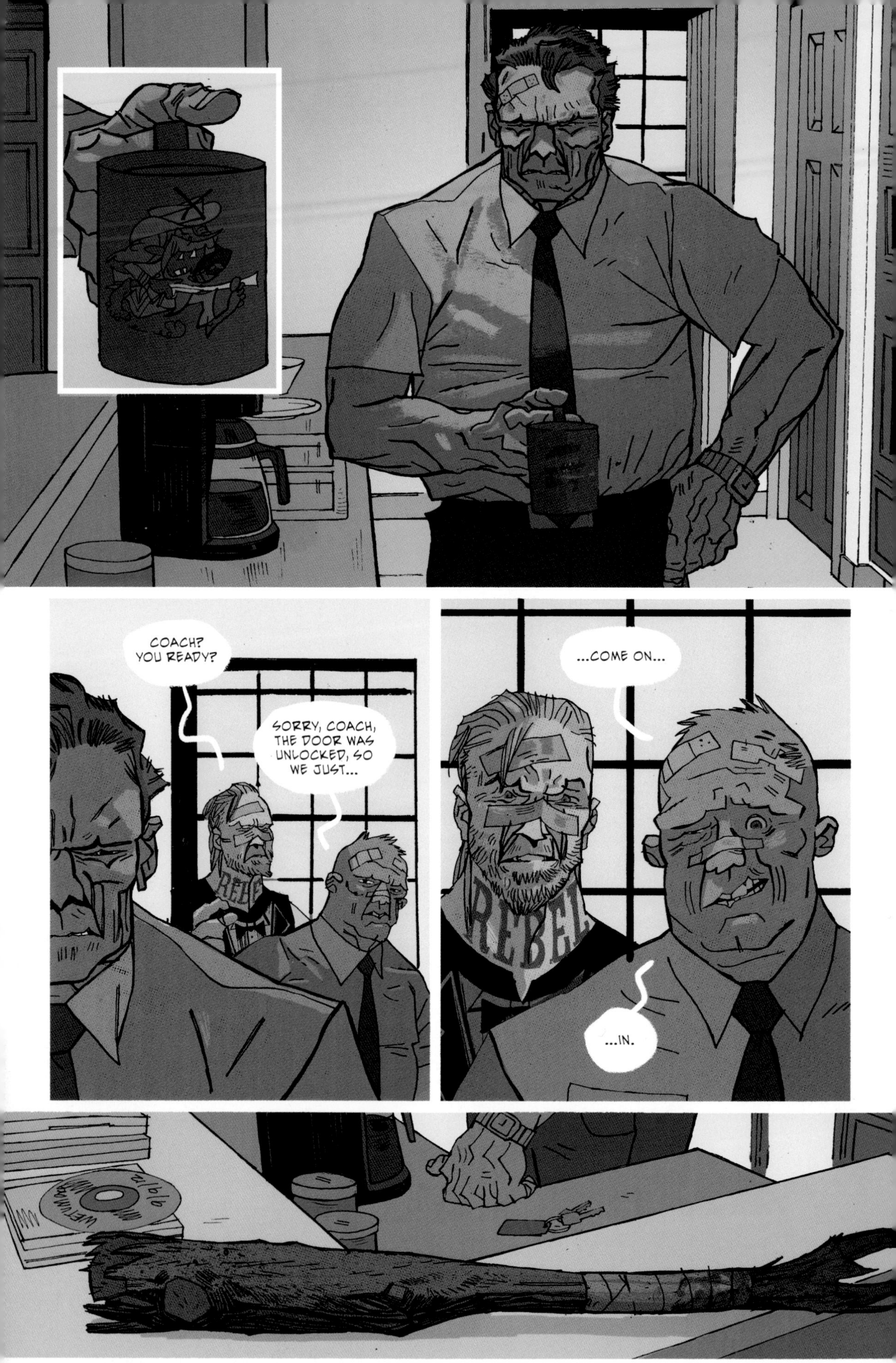
COACH? YOU READY?
SORRY, COACH, THE DOOR WAS UNLOCKED, SO WE JUST...
...COME ON...
...IN.

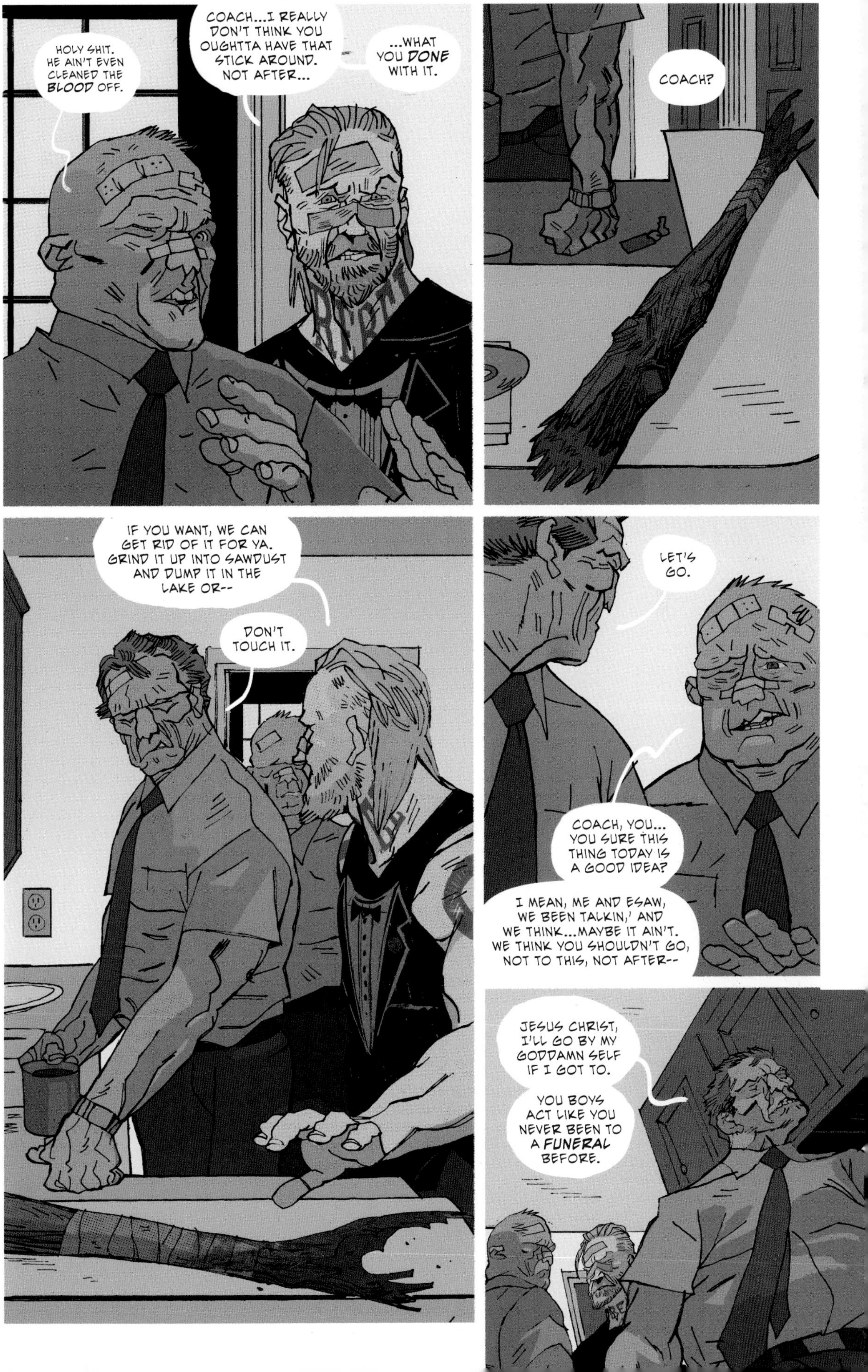
HOLY SHIT. HE AIN'T EVEN CLEANED THE BLOOD OFF.
COACH...I REALLY DON'T THINK YOU OUGHTTA HAVE THAT STICK AROUND. NOT AFTER...
...WHAT YOU DONE WITH IT.
COACH?
IF YOU WANT, WE CAN GET RID OF IT FOR YA. GRIND IT UP INTO SAWDUST AND DUMP IT IN THE LAKE OR--
DON'T TOUCH IT.
LET'S GO.
COACH, YOU... YOU SURE THIS THING TODAY IS A GOOD IDEA?
I MEAN, ME AND ESAW, WE BEEN TALKIN,' AND WE THINK...MAYBE IT AIN'T. WE THINK YOU SHOULDN'T GO, NOT TO THIS, NOT AFTER--
JESUS CHRIST, I'LL GO BY MY GODDAMN SELF IF I GOT TO.
YOU BOYS ACT LIKE YOU NEVER BEEN TO A FUNERAL BEFORE.

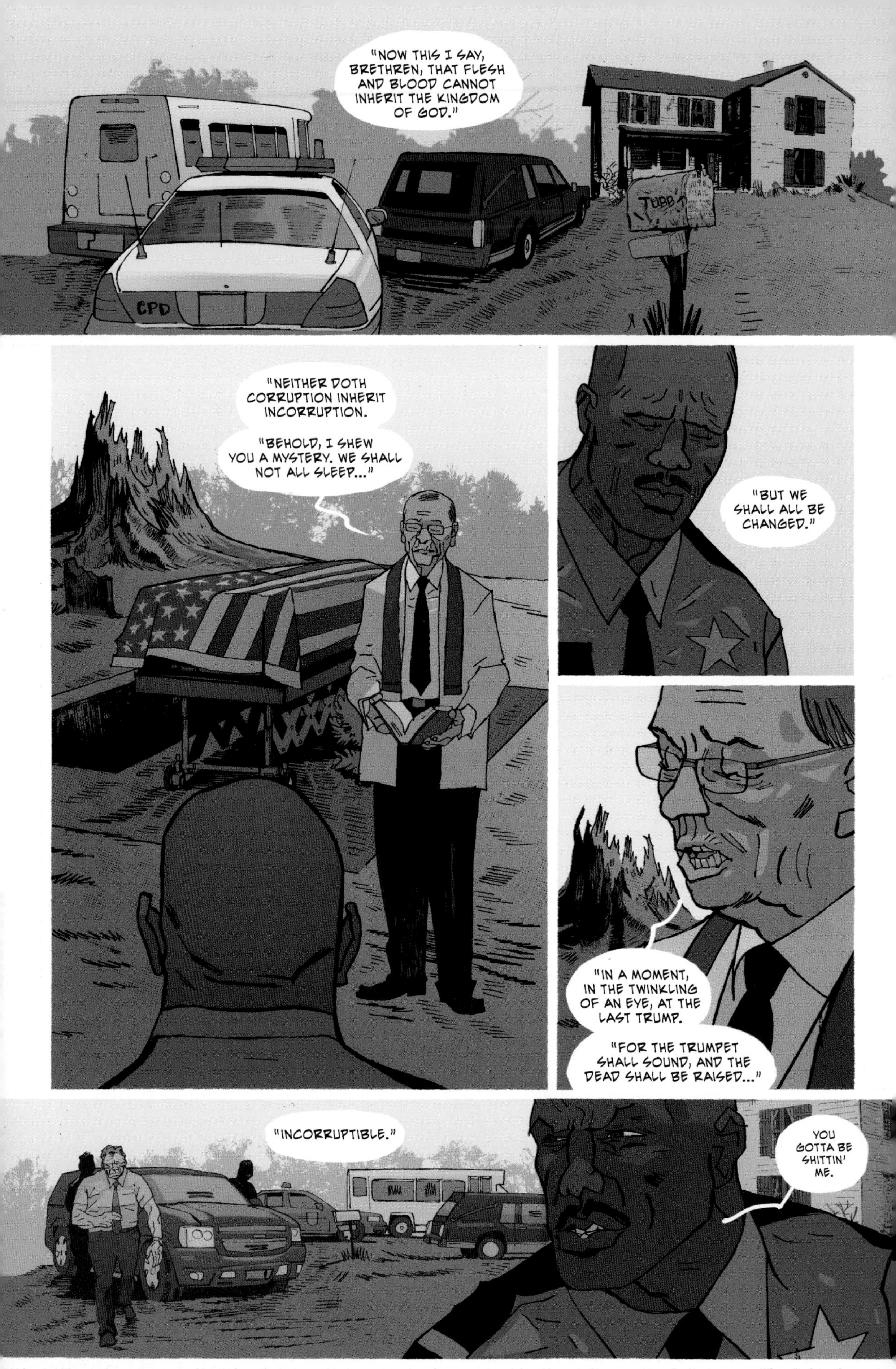
"NOW THIS I SAY, BRETHREN, THAT FLESH AND BLOOD CANNOT INHERIT THE KINGDOM OF GOD."
TUBB
CPD
"NEITHER DOTH CORRUPTION INHERIT INCORRUPTION.
"BEHOLD, I SHEW YOU A MYSTERY. WE SHALL NOT ALL SLEEP..."
"BUT WE SHALL ALL BE CHANGED."
"IN A MOMENT, IN THE TWINKLING OF AN EYE, AT THE LAST TRUMP.
"FOR THE TRUMPET SHALL SOUND, AND THE DEAD SHALL BE RAISED..."
"INCORRUPTIBLE."
YOU GOTTA BE SHITTIN' ME.

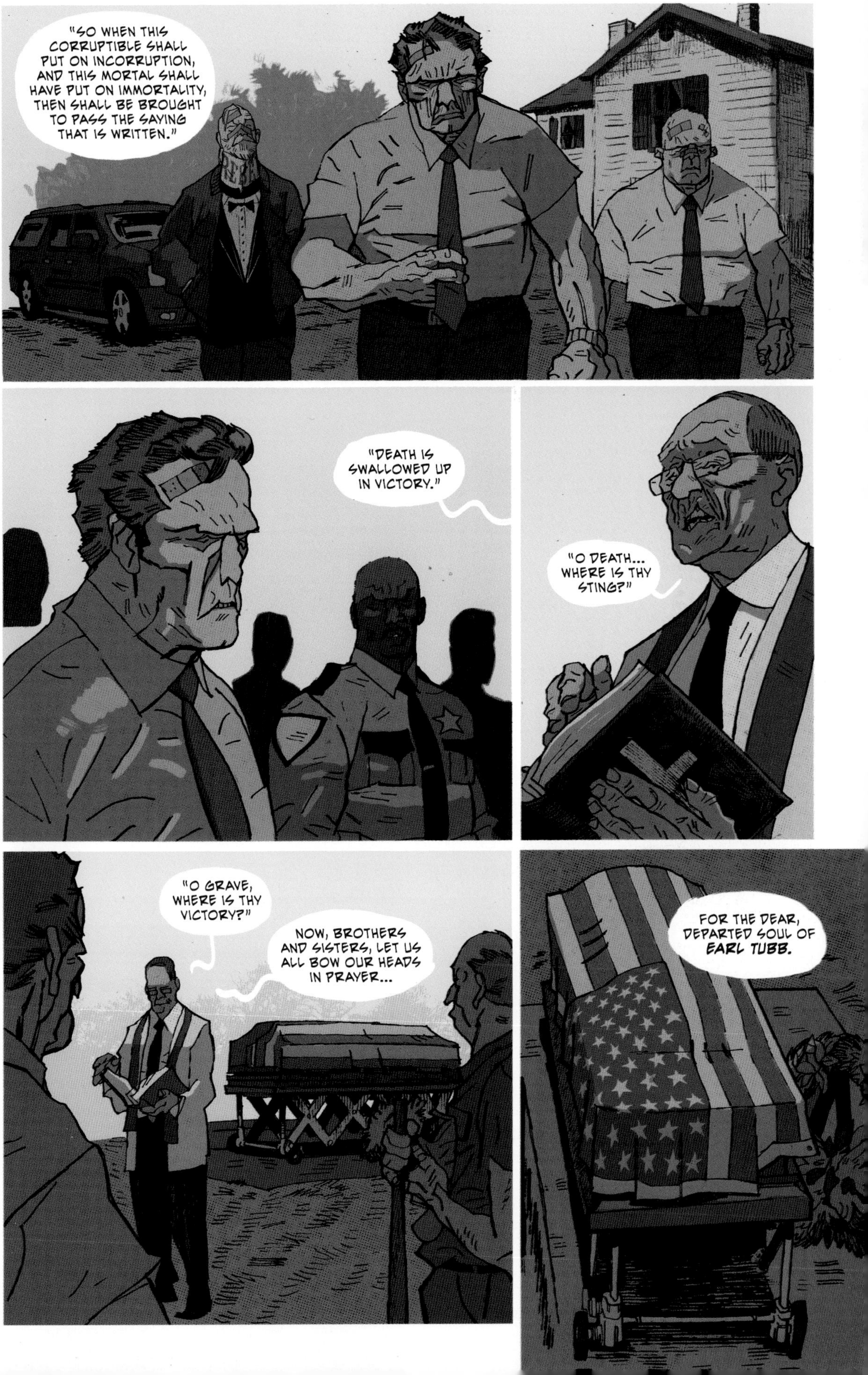
"SO WHEN THIS CORRUPTIBLE SHALL PUT ON INCORRUPTION, AND THIS MORTAL SHALL HAVE PUT ON IMMORTALITY, THEN SHALL BE BROUGHT TO PASS THE SAYING THAT IS WRITTEN."
"DEATH IS SWALLOWED UP IN VICTORY."
"O DEATH... WHERE IS THY STING?"
"O GRAVE, WHERE IS THY VICTORY?"
NOW, BROTHERS AND SISTERS, LET US ALL BOW OUR HEADS IN PRAYER...
FOR THE DEAR, DEPARTED SOUL OF **EARL TUBB.**

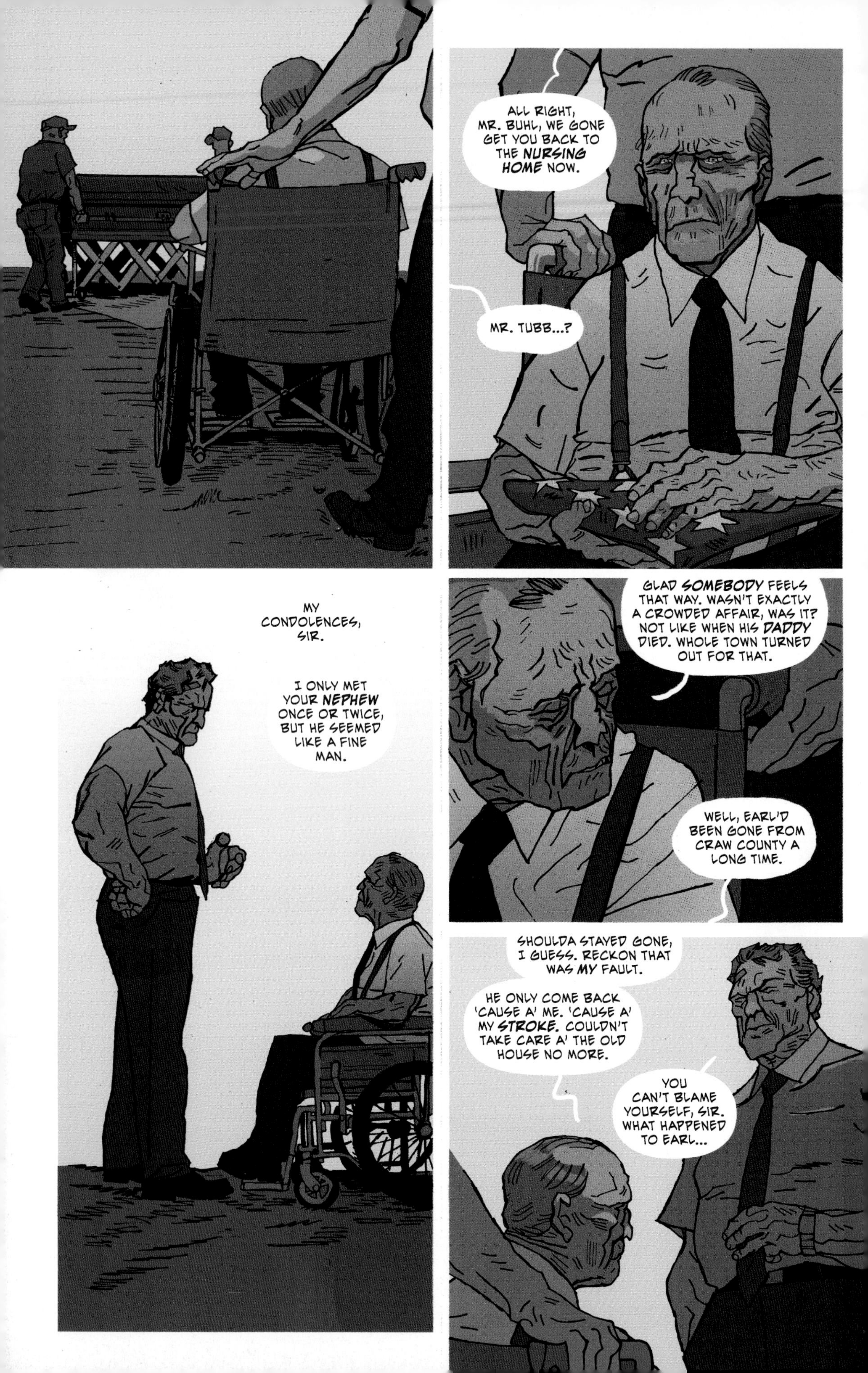
ALL RIGHT, MR. BUHL, WE GONE GET YOU BACK TO THE NURSING HOME NOW.
MR. TUBB...?
MY CONDOLENCES, SIR.
I ONLY MET YOUR NEPHEW ONCE OR TWICE, BUT HE SEEMED LIKE A FINE MAN.
GLAD SOMEBODY FEELS THAT WAY. WASN'T EXACTLY A CROWDED AFFAIR, WAS IT? NOT LIKE WHEN HIS DADDY DIED. WHOLE TOWN TURNED OUT FOR THAT.
WELL, EARL'D BEEN GONE FROM CRAW COUNTY A LONG TIME.
SHOULDA STAYED GONE, I GUESS. RECKON THAT WAS MY FAULT.
HE ONLY COME BACK 'CAUSE A' ME. 'CAUSE A' MY STROKE. COULDN'T TAKE CARE A' THE OLD HOUSE NO MORE.
YOU CAN'T BLAME YOURSELF, SIR. WHAT HAPPENED TO EARL...

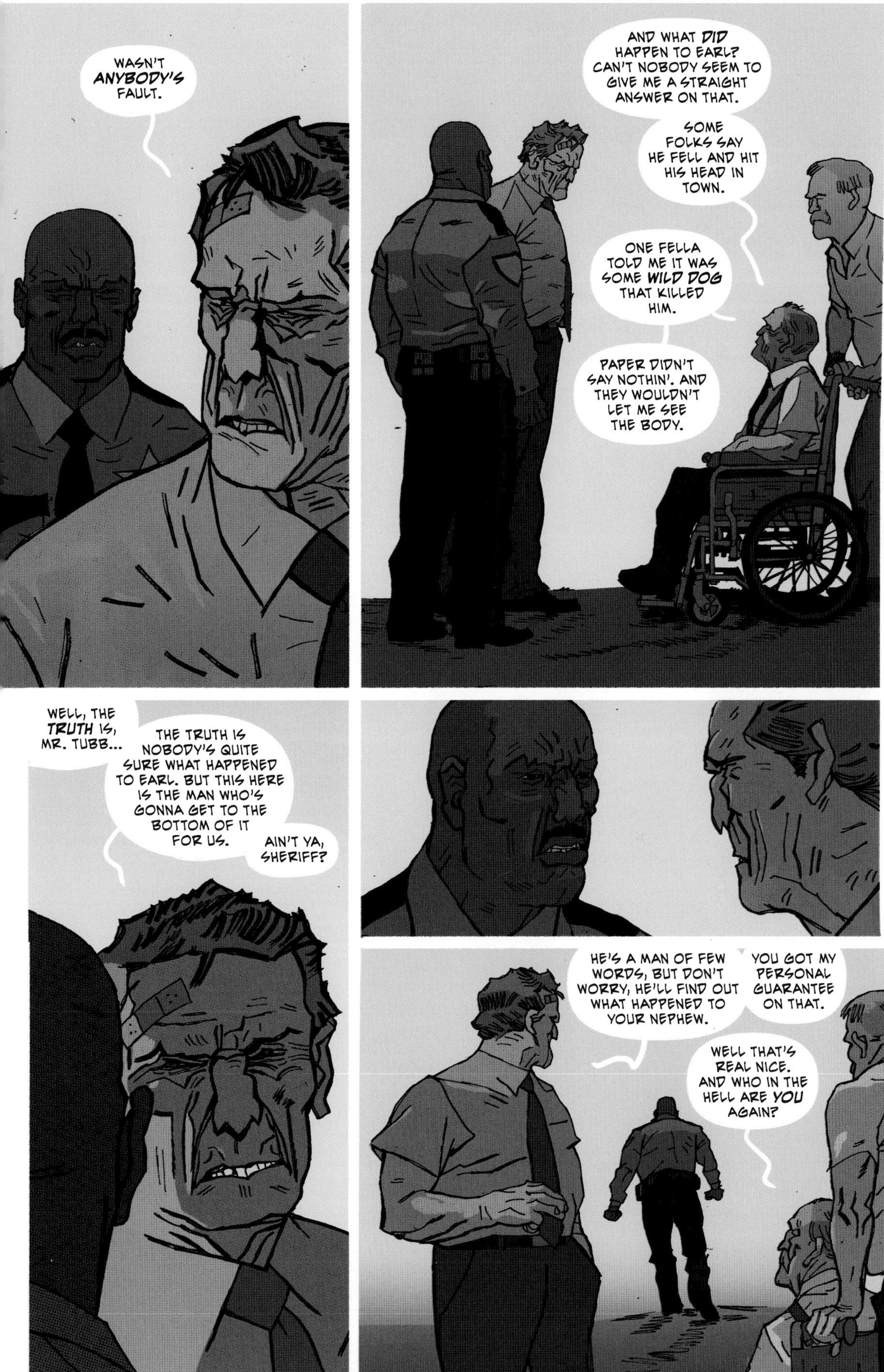
WASN'T ANYBODY'S FAULT.
AND WHAT DID HAPPEN TO EARL? CAN'T NOBODY SEEM TO GIVE ME A STRAIGHT ANSWER ON THAT.
SOME FOLKS SAY HE FELL AND HIT HIS HEAD IN TOWN.
ONE FELLA TOLD ME IT WAS SOME WILD DOG THAT KILLED HIM.
PAPER DIDN'T SAY NOTHIN'. AND THEY WOULDN'T LET ME SEE THE BODY.
WELL, THE TRUTH IS, MR. TUBB...
THE TRUTH IS NOBODY'S QUITE SURE WHAT HAPPENED TO EARL. BUT THIS HERE IS THE MAN WHO'S GONNA GET TO THE BOTTOM OF IT FOR US.
AIN'T YA, SHERIFF?
HE'S A MAN OF FEW WORDS, BUT DON'T WORRY, HE'LL FIND OUT WHAT HAPPENED TO YOUR NEPHEW.
YOU GOT MY PERSONAL GUARANTEE ON THAT.
WELL THAT'S REAL NICE. AND WHO IN THE HELL ARE YOU AGAIN?

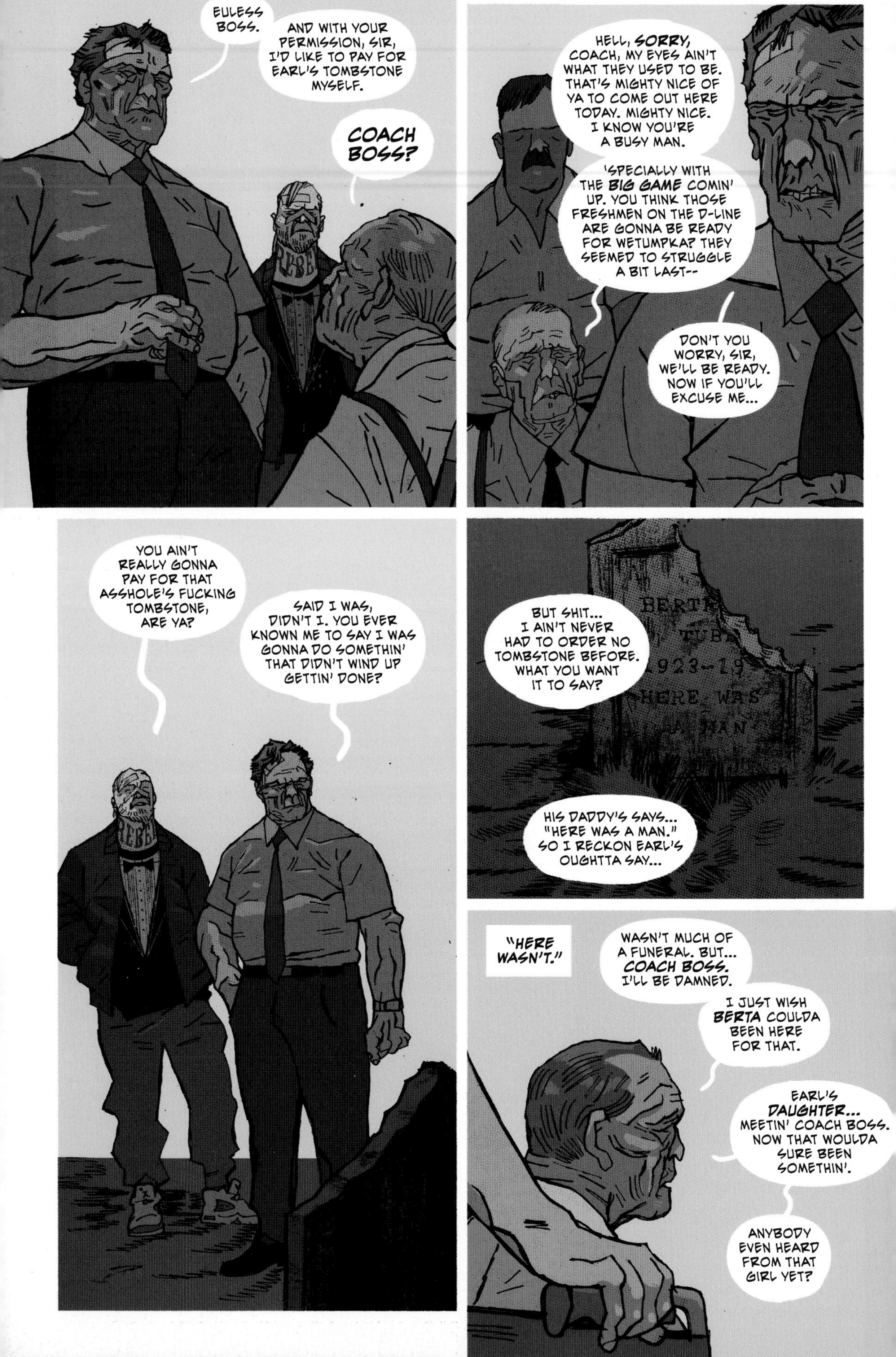
EULESS BOSS.
AND WITH YOUR PERMISSION, SIR, I'D LIKE TO PAY FOR EARL'S TOMBSTONE MYSELF.
COACH BOSS?
HELL, SORRY, COACH, MY EYES AIN'T WHAT THEY USED TO BE. THAT'S MIGHTY NICE OF YA TO COME OUT HERE TODAY. MIGHTY NICE. I KNOW YOU'RE A BUSY MAN.
'SPECIALLY WITH THE BIG GAME COMIN' UP. YOU THINK THOSE FRESHMEN ON THE D-LINE ARE GONNA BE READY FOR WETUMPKA? THEY SEEMED TO STRUGGLE A BIT LAST--
DON'T YOU WORRY, SIR, WE'LL BE READY. NOW IF YOU'LL EXCUSE ME...
YOU AIN'T REALLY GONNA PAY FOR THAT ASSHOLE'S FUCKING TOMBSTONE, ARE YA?
SAID I WAS, DIDN'T I. YOU EVER KNOWN ME TO SAY I WAS GONNA DO SOMETHIN' THAT DIDN'T WIND UP GETTIN' DONE?
BUT SHIT... I AIN'T NEVER HAD TO ORDER NO TOMBSTONE BEFORE. WHAT YOU WANT IT TO SAY?
HIS DADDY'S SAYS... "HERE WAS A MAN." SO I RECKON EARL'S OUGHTTA SAY...
"HERE WASN'T."
WASN'T MUCH OF A FUNERAL. BUT... COACH BOSS. I'LL BE DAMNED.
I JUST WISH BERTA COULDA BEEN HERE FOR THAT.
EARL'S DAUGHTER... MEETIN' COACH BOSS. NOW THAT WOULDA SURE BEEN SOMETHIN'.
ANYBODY EVEN HEARD FROM THAT GIRL YET?

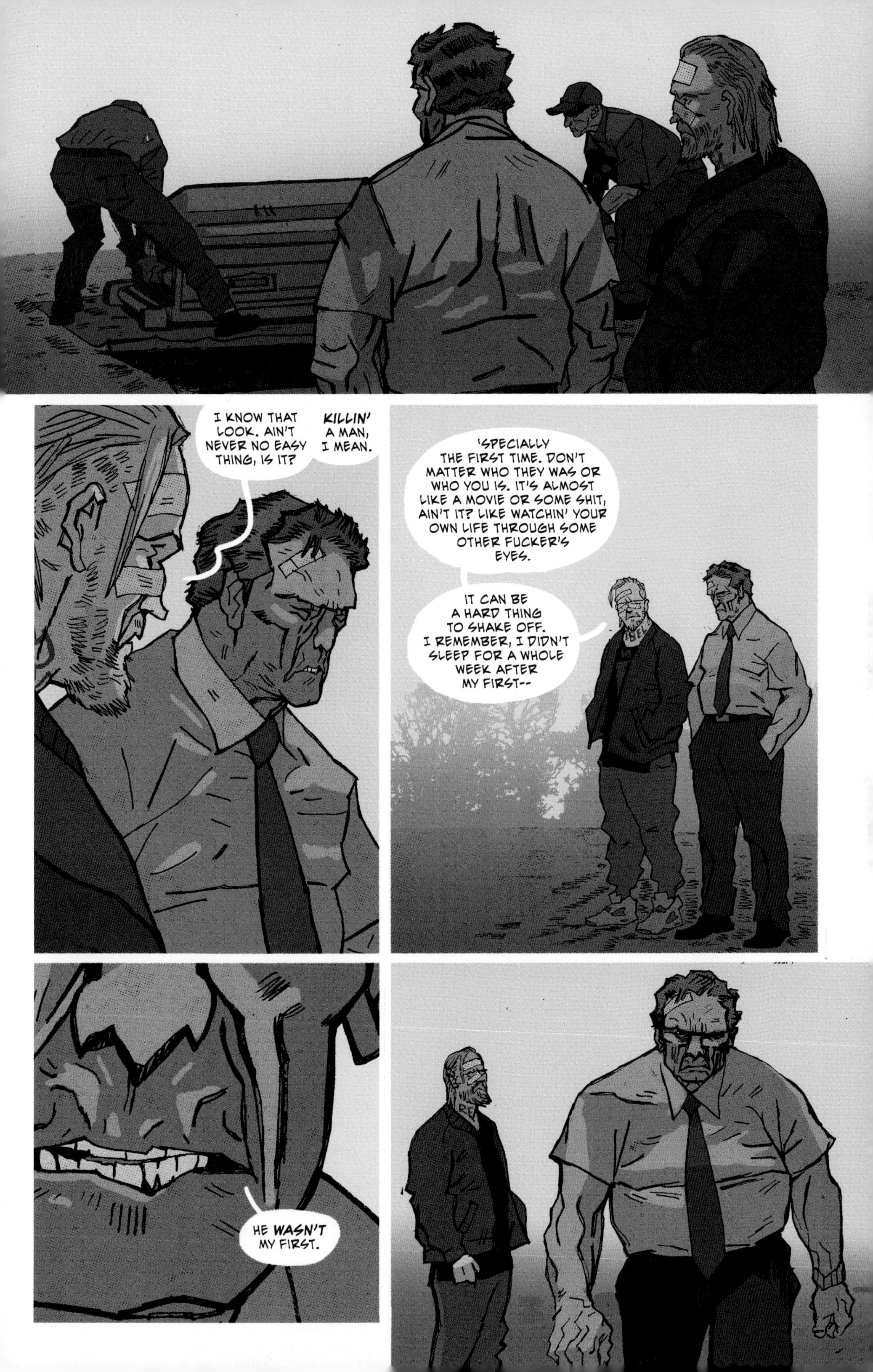
I KNOW THAT LOOK. AIN'T NEVER NO EASY THING, IS IT?
KILLIN' A MAN, I MEAN.
'SPECIALLY THE FIRST TIME. DON'T MATTER WHO THEY WAS OR WHO YOU IS. IT'S ALMOST LIKE A MOVIE OR SOME SHIT, AIN'T IT? LIKE WATCHIN' YOUR OWN LIFE THROUGH SOME OTHER FUCKER'S EYES.
IT CAN BE A HARD THING TO SHAKE OFF. I REMEMBER, I DIDN'T SLEEP FOR A WHOLE WEEK AFTER MY FIRST--
HE WASN'T MY FIRST.

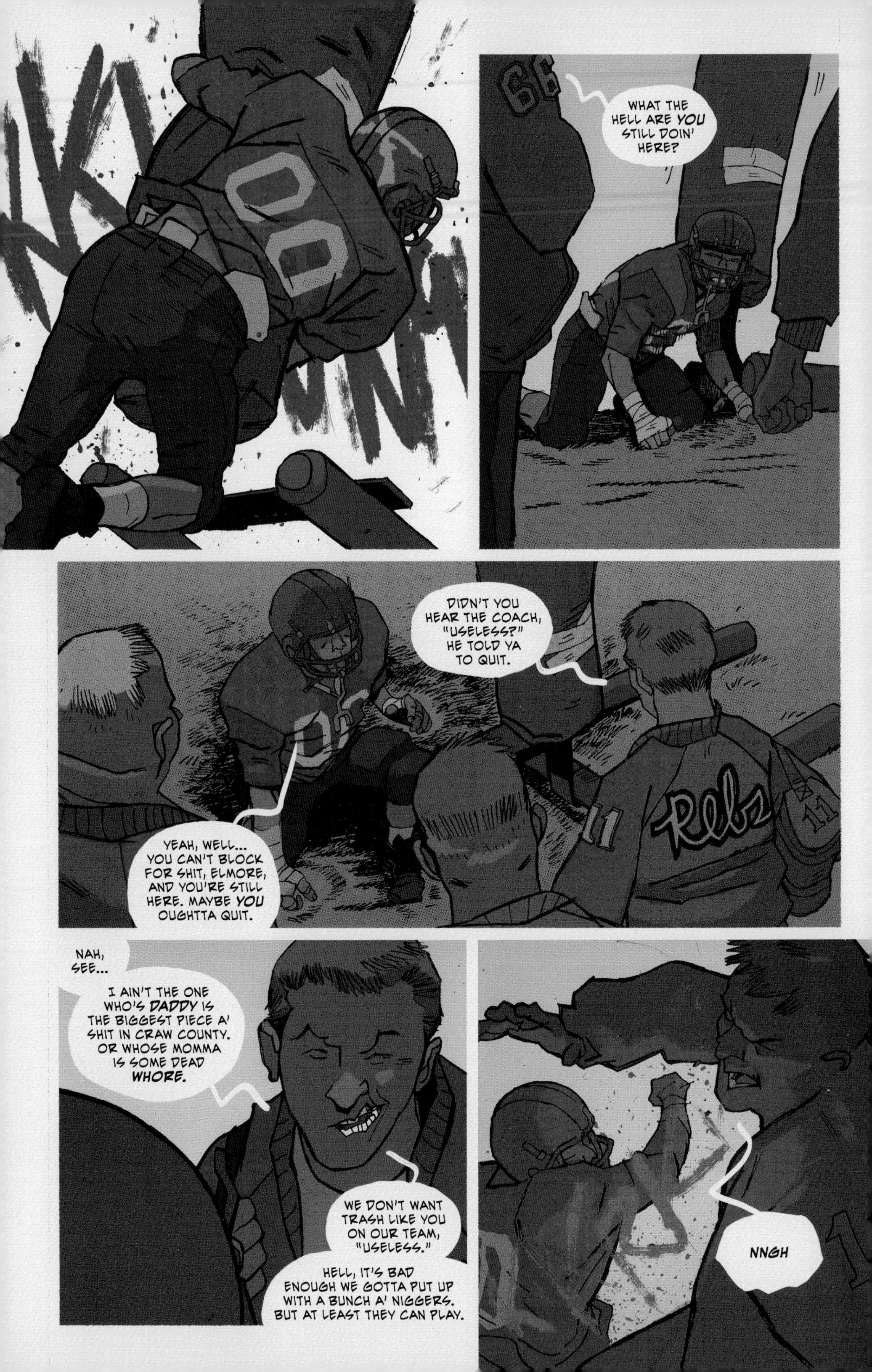
WHAT THE HELL ARE YOU STILL DOIN' HERE?
DIDN'T YOU HEAR THE COACH, "USELESS?" HE TOLD YA TO QUIT.
YEAH, WELL... YOU CAN'T BLOCK FOR SHIT, ELMORE, AND YOU'RE STILL HERE. MAYBE YOU OUGHTTA QUIT.
Rebs
11
NAH, SEE...
I AIN'T THE ONE WHO'S DADDY IS THE BIGGEST PIECE A' SHIT IN CRAW COUNTY. OR WHOSE MOMMA IS SOME DEAD WHORE.
WE DON'T WANT TRASH LIKE YOU ON OUR TEAM, "USELESS."
HELL, IT'S BAD ENOUGH WE GOTTA PUT UP WITH A BUNCH A' NIGGERS. BUT AT LEAST THEY CAN PLAY.
NNGH

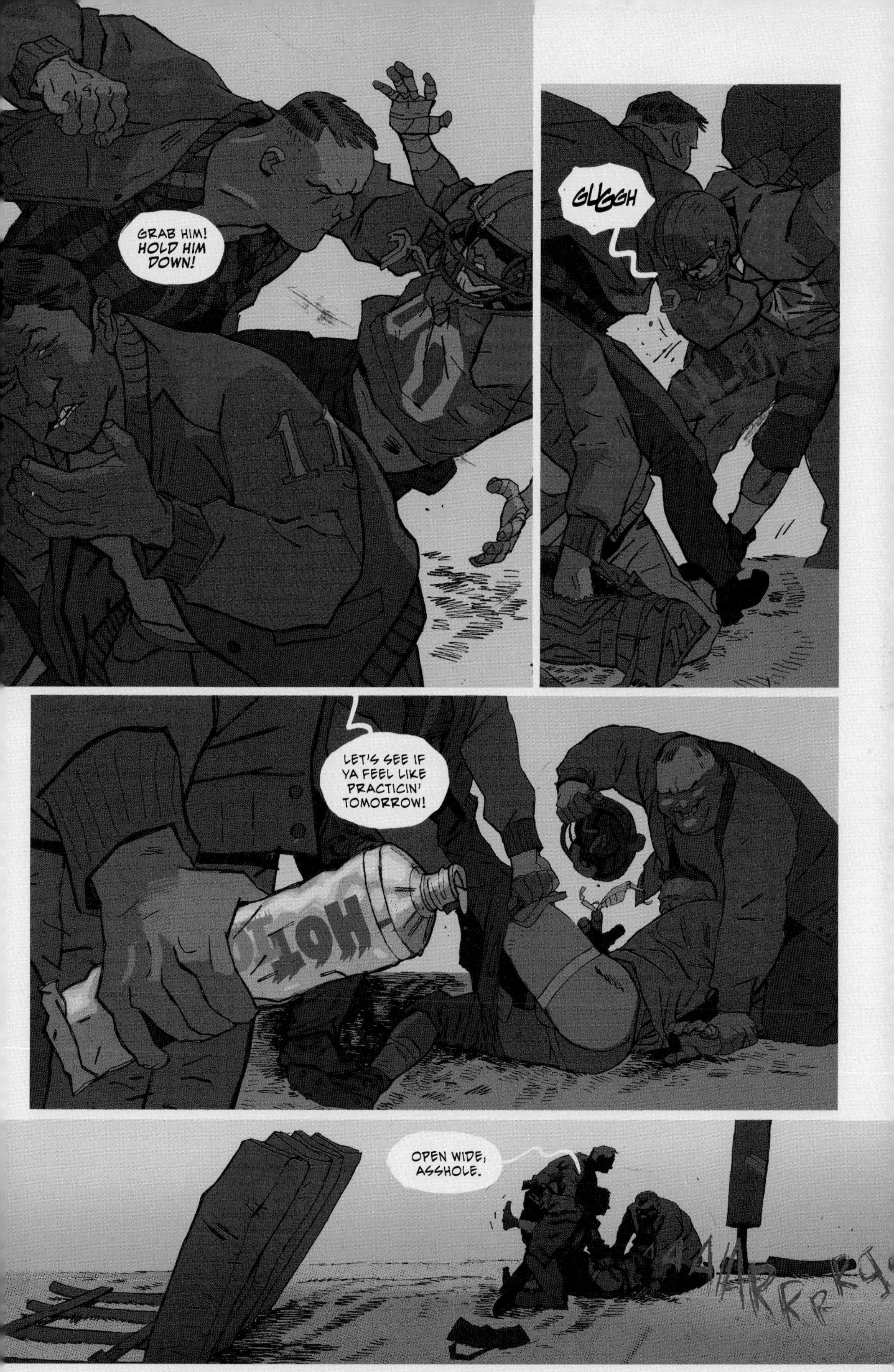
GRAB HIM! HOLD HIM DOWN!
GUGGH
LET'S SEE IF YA FEEL LIKE PRACTICIN' TOMORROW!
OPEN WIDE, ASSHOLE.

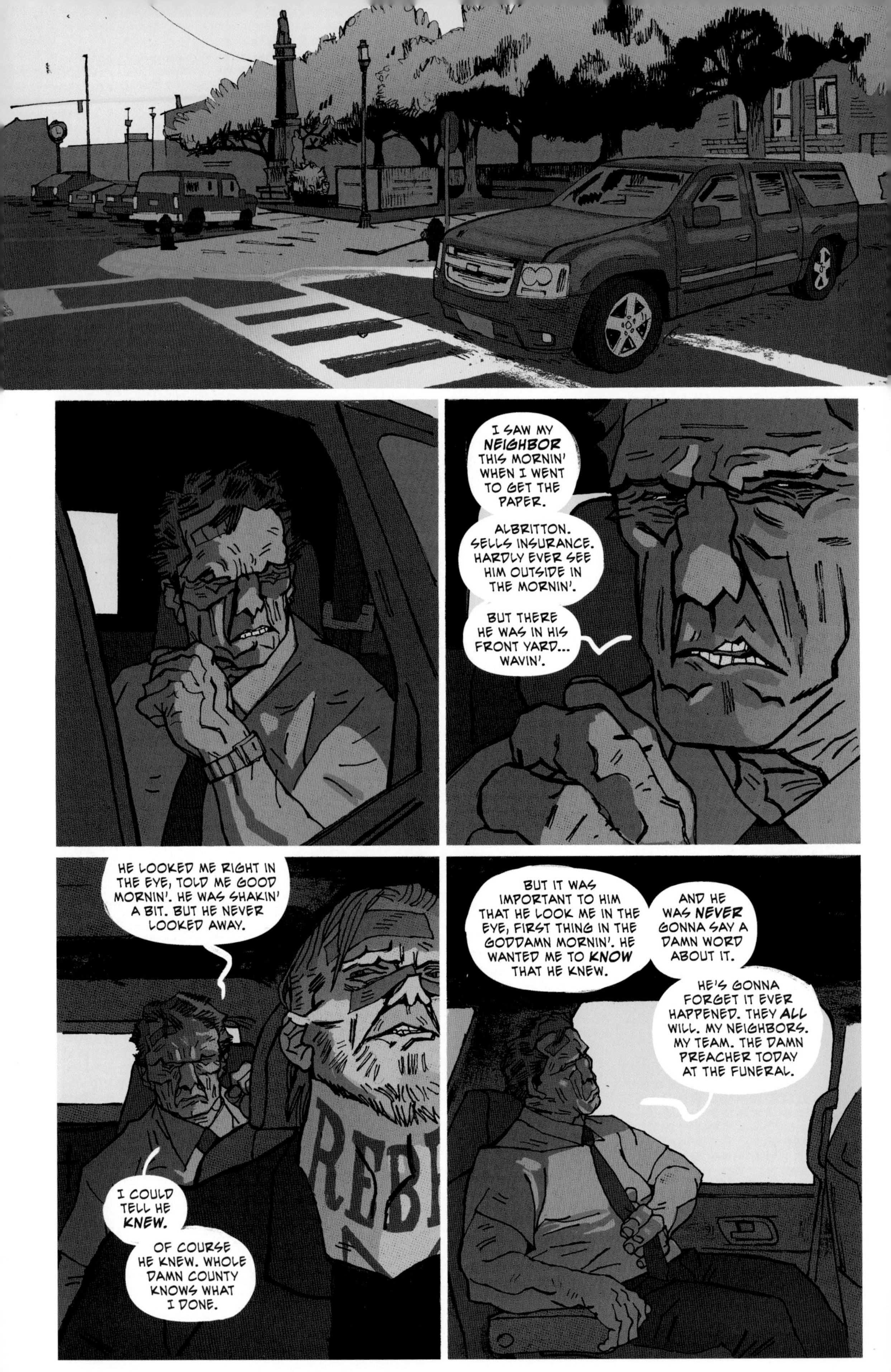

I SAW MY NEIGHBOR THIS MORNIN' WHEN I WENT TO GET THE PAPER.
ALBRITTON. SELLS INSURANCE. HARDLY EVER SEE HIM OUTSIDE IN THE MORNIN'.
BUT THERE HE WAS IN HIS FRONT YARD... WAVIN'.
HE LOOKED ME RIGHT IN THE EYE, TOLD ME GOOD MORNIN'. HE WAS SHAKIN' A BIT. BUT HE NEVER LOOKED AWAY.
I COULD TELL HE KNEW.
OF COURSE HE KNEW. WHOLE DAMN COUNTY KNOWS WHAT I DONE.
BUT IT WAS IMPORTANT TO HIM THAT HE LOOK ME IN THE EYE, FIRST THING IN THE GODDAMN MORNIN'. HE WANTED ME TO KNOW THAT HE KNEW.
AND HE WAS NEVER GONNA SAY A DAMN WORD ABOUT IT.
HE'S GONNA FORGET IT EVER HAPPENED. THEY ALL WILL. MY NEIGHBORS. MY TEAM. THE DAMN PREACHER TODAY AT THE FUNERAL.

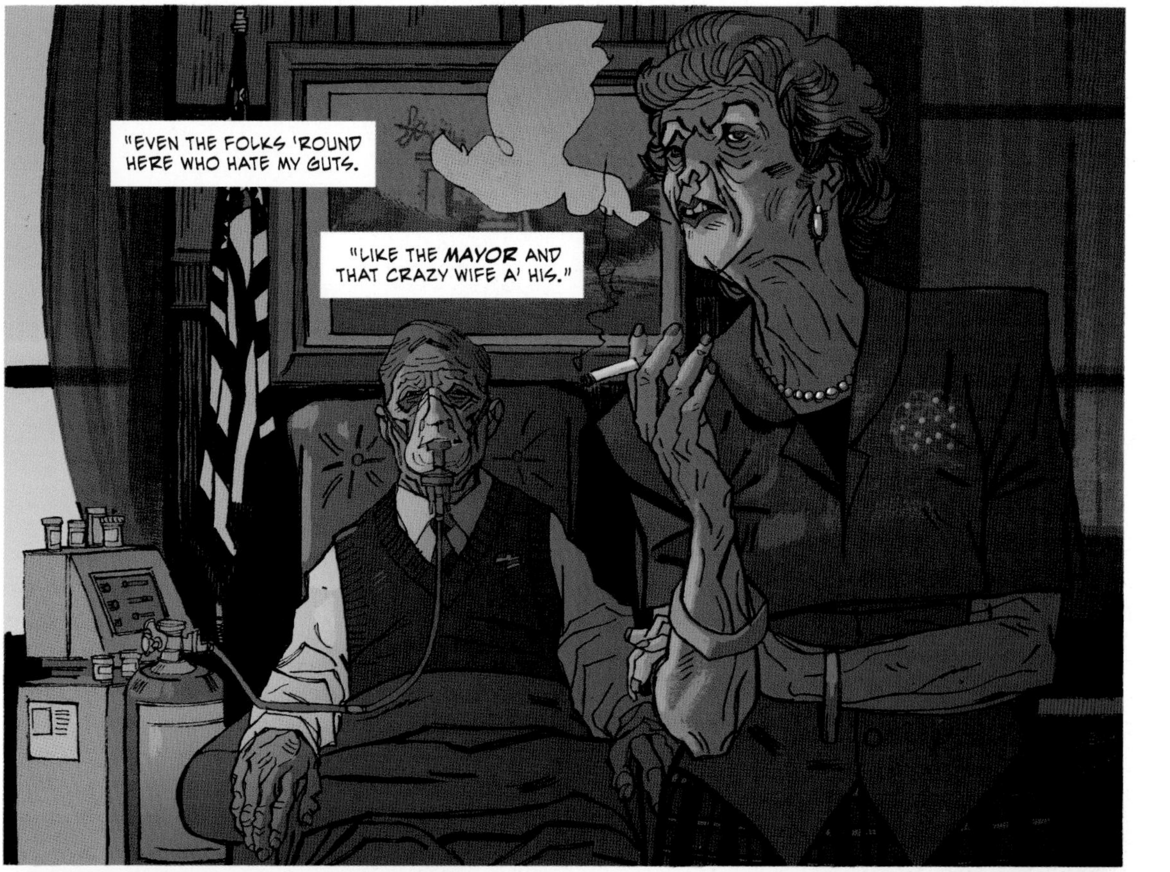
"EVEN THE FOLKS 'ROUND HERE WHO HATE MY GUTS.
"LIKE THE MAYOR AND THAT CRAZY WIFE A' HIS."

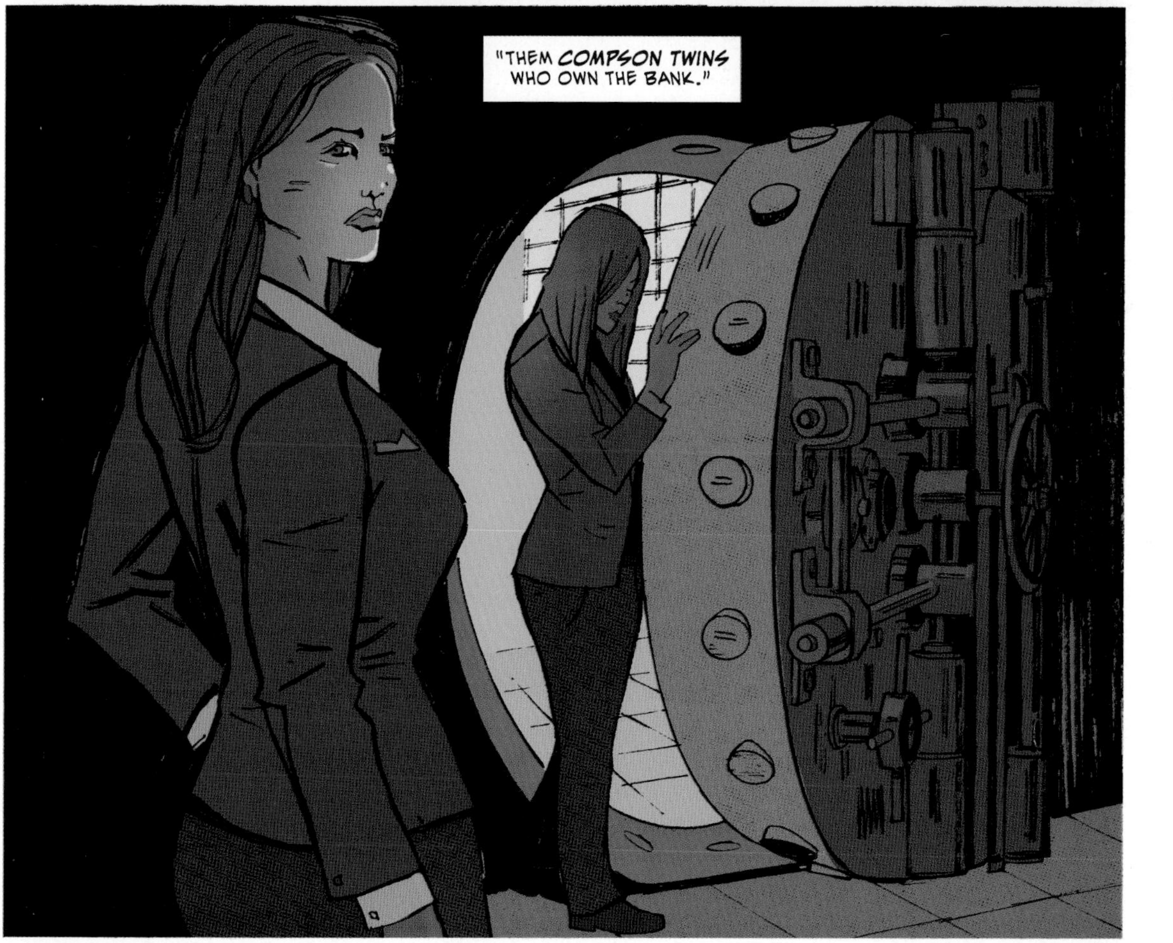
"THEM COMPSON TWINS WHO OWN THE BANK."

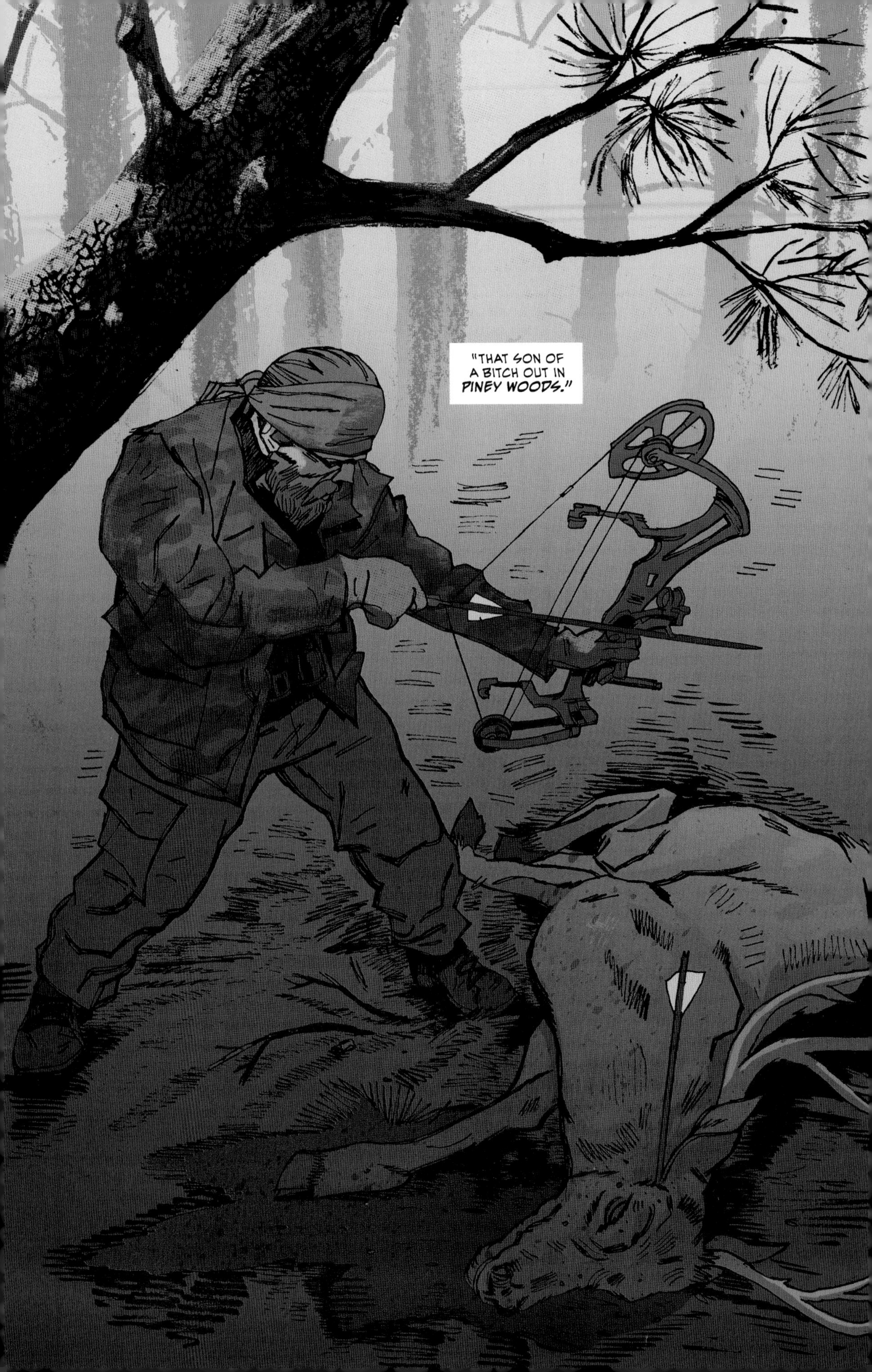
"THAT SON OF
A BITCH OUT IN
PINEY WOODS."

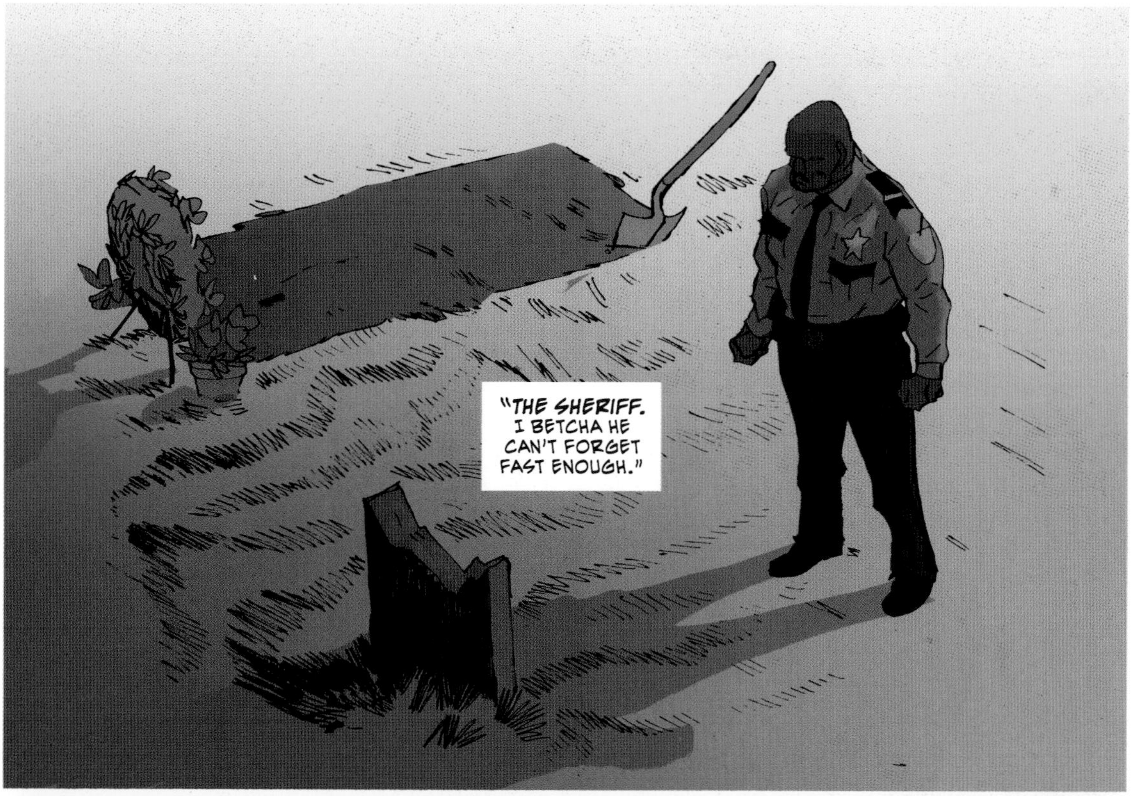
"THE SHERIFF. I BETCHA HE CAN'T FORGET FAST ENOUGH."

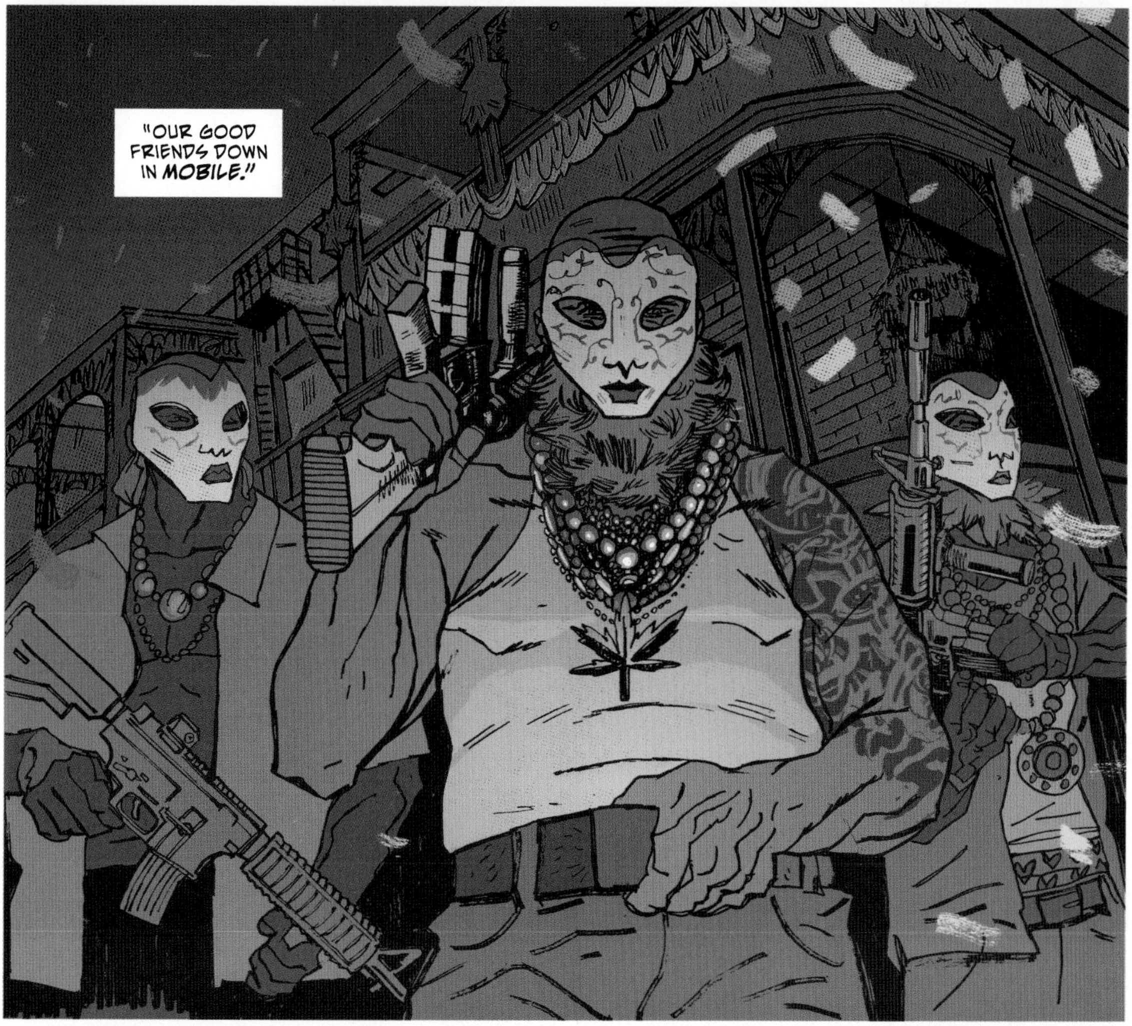
"OUR GOOD FRIENDS DOWN IN MOBILE."

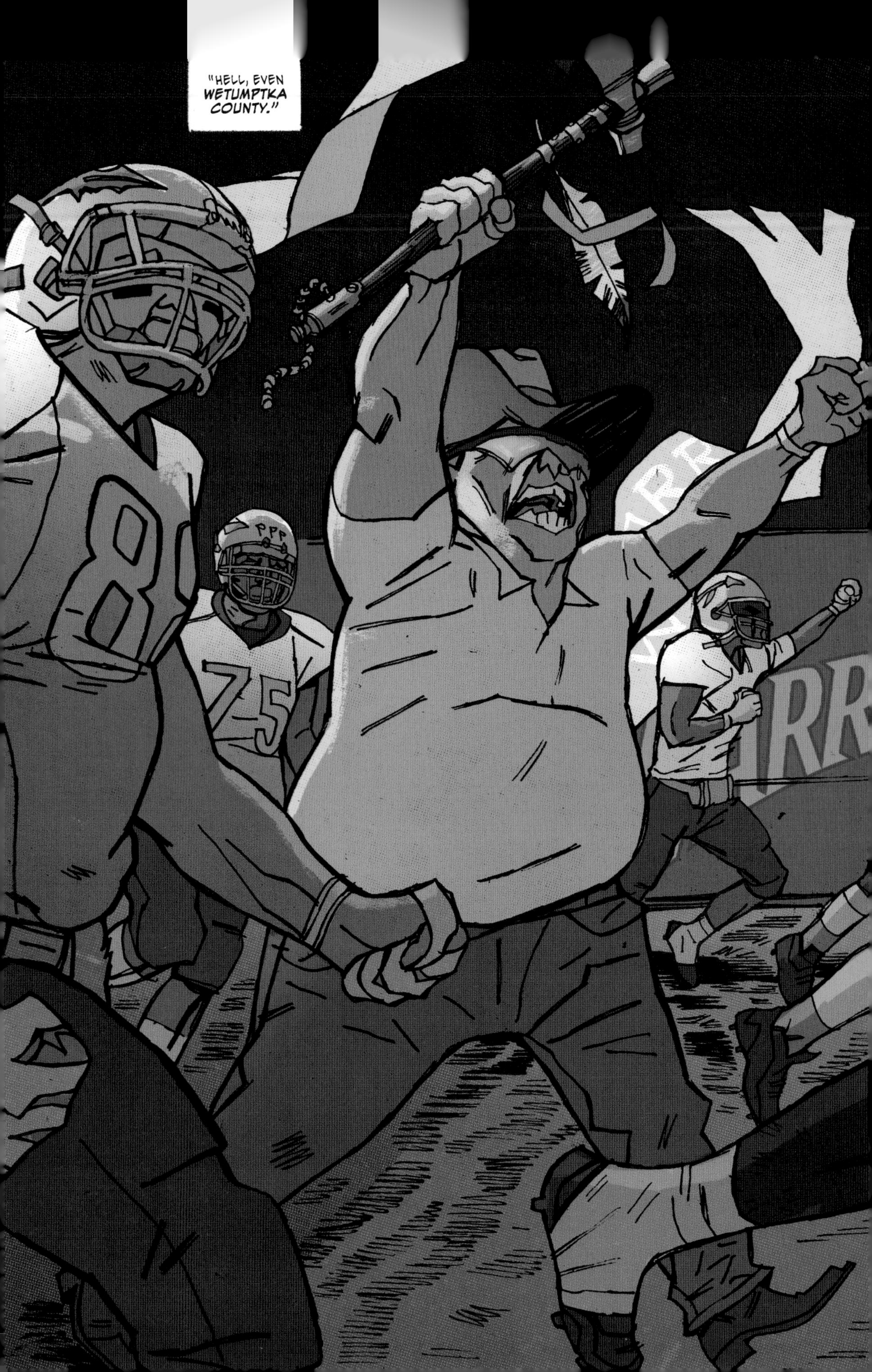
"HELL, EVEN WETUMPTKA COUNTY."

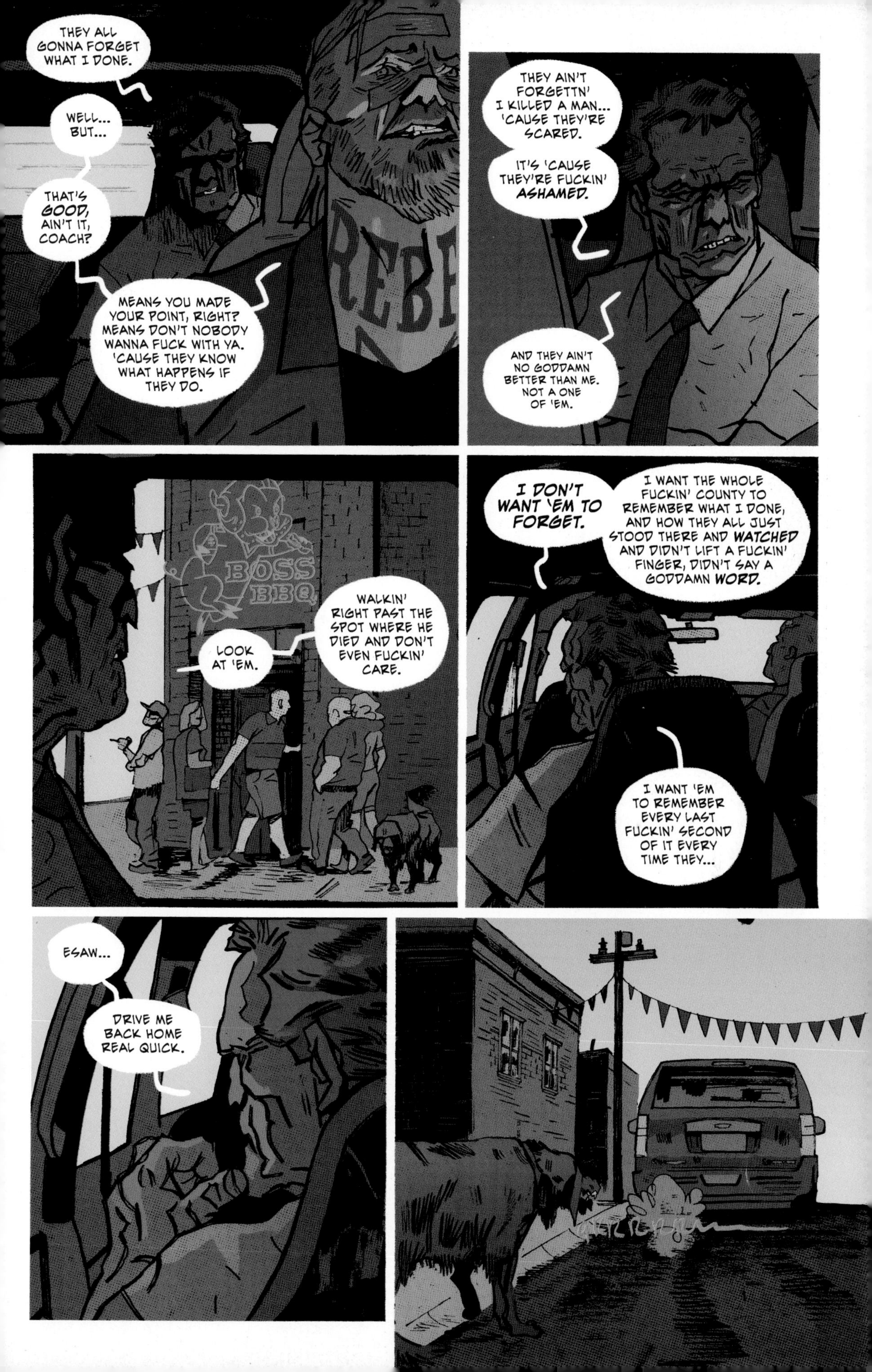
THEY ALL GONNA FORGET WHAT I DONE.
WELL... BUT...
THAT'S GOOD, AIN'T IT, COACH?
MEANS YOU MADE YOUR POINT, RIGHT? MEANS DON'T NOBODY WANNA FUCK WITH YA. 'CAUSE THEY KNOW WHAT HAPPENS IF THEY DO.
THEY AIN'T FORGETTN' I KILLED A MAN... 'CAUSE THEY'RE SCARED.
IT'S 'CAUSE THEY'RE FUCKIN' ASHAMED.
AND THEY AIN'T NO GODDAMN BETTER THAN ME. NOT A ONE OF 'EM.
BOSS BBQ
LOOK AT 'EM.
WALKIN' RIGHT PAST THE SPOT WHERE HE DIED AND DON'T EVEN FUCKIN' CARE.
I DON'T WANT 'EM TO FORGET.
I WANT THE WHOLE FUCKIN' COUNTY TO REMEMBER WHAT I DONE, AND HOW THEY ALL JUST STOOD THERE AND WATCHED AND DIDN'T LIFT A FUCKIN' FINGER, DIDN'T SAY A GODDAMN WORD.
I WANT 'EM TO REMEMBER EVERY LAST FUCKIN' SECOND OF IT EVERY TIME THEY...
ESAW...
DRIVE ME BACK HOME REAL QUICK.

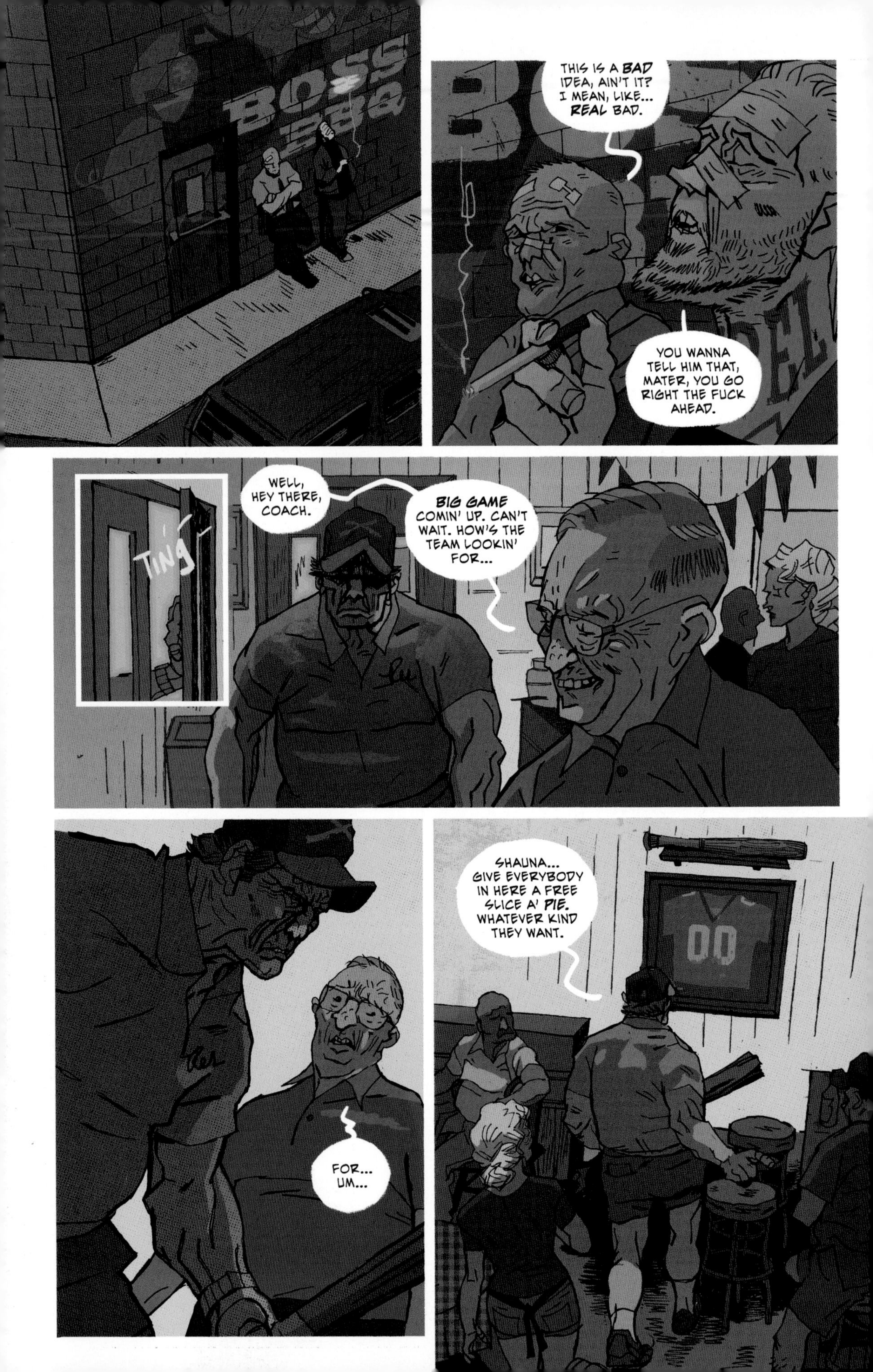
BOSS BBQ
THIS IS A BAD IDEA, AIN'T IT? I MEAN, LIKE... REAL BAD.
YOU WANNA TELL HIM THAT, MATER, YOU GO RIGHT THE FUCK AHEAD.
TING
WELL, HEY THERE, COACH.
BIG GAME COMIN' UP. CAN'T WAIT. HOW'S THE TEAM LOOKIN' FOR...
FOR... UM...
SHAUNA... GIVE EVERYBODY IN HERE A FREE SLICE A' PIE. WHATEVER KIND THEY WANT.
00

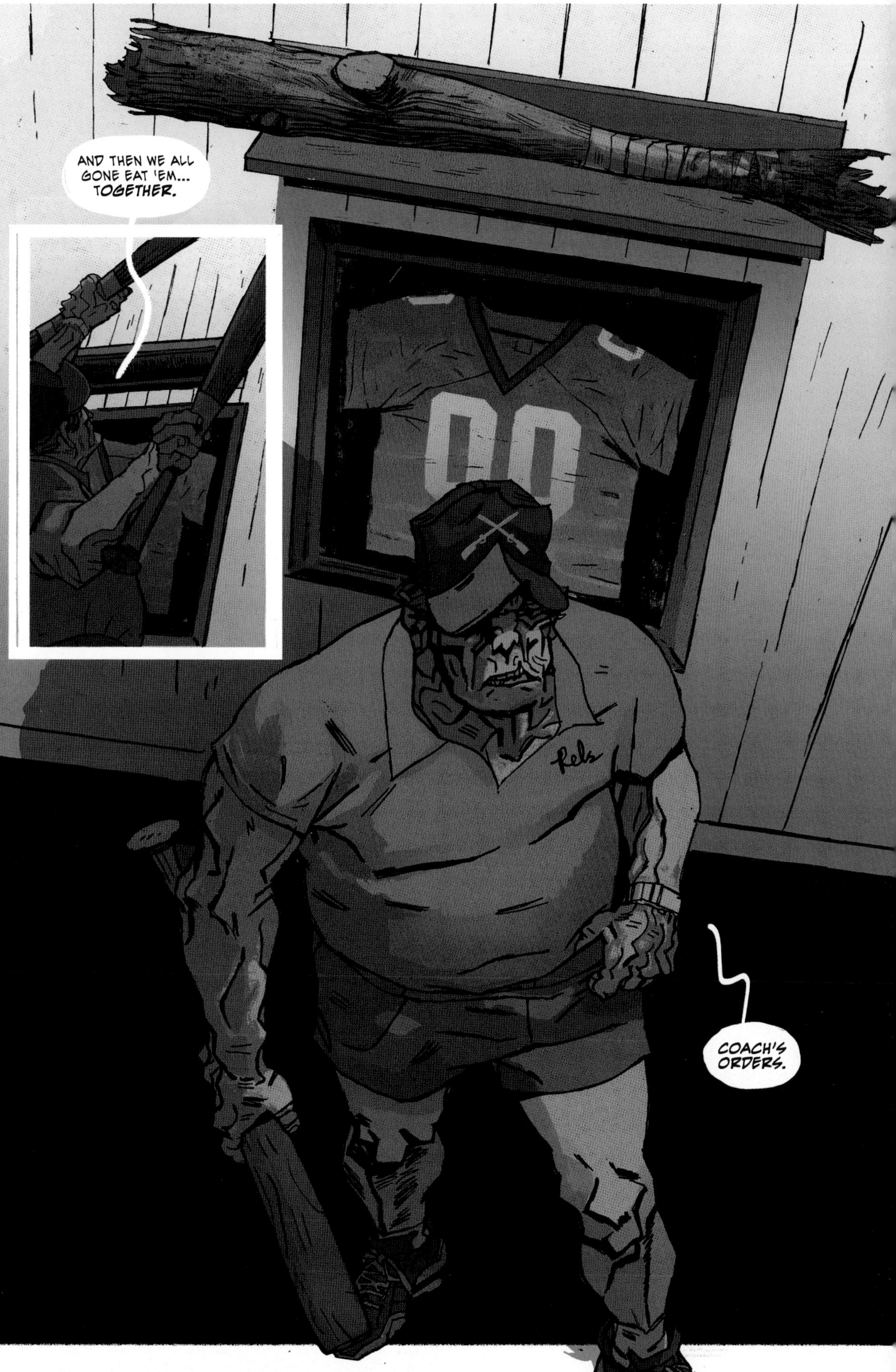
AND THEN WE ALL GONE EAT 'EM... TOGETHER.
00
Rels
COACH'S ORDERS.

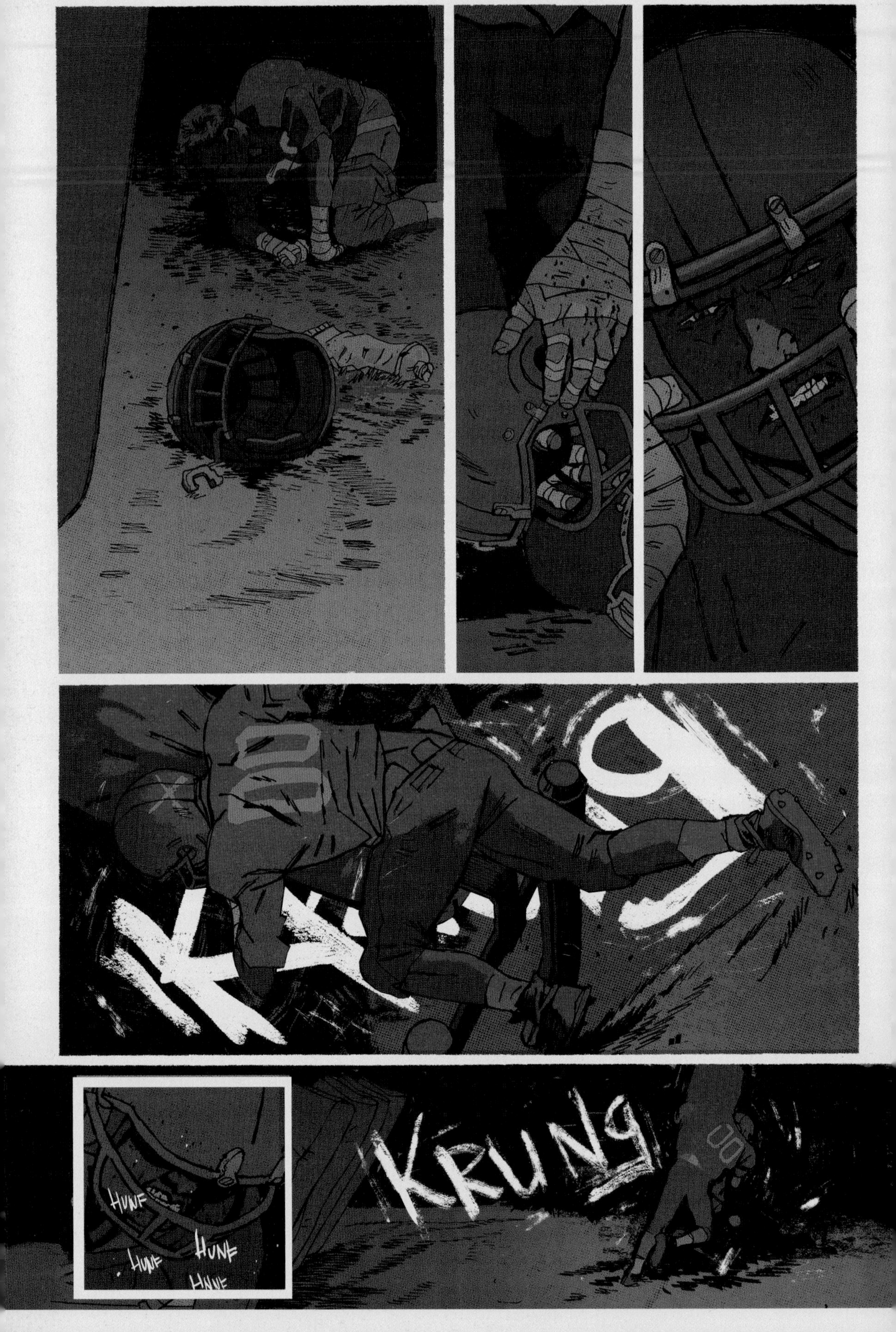
HUNF
HUNF
HUNF
HUNF
KRUNG

Chapter 6

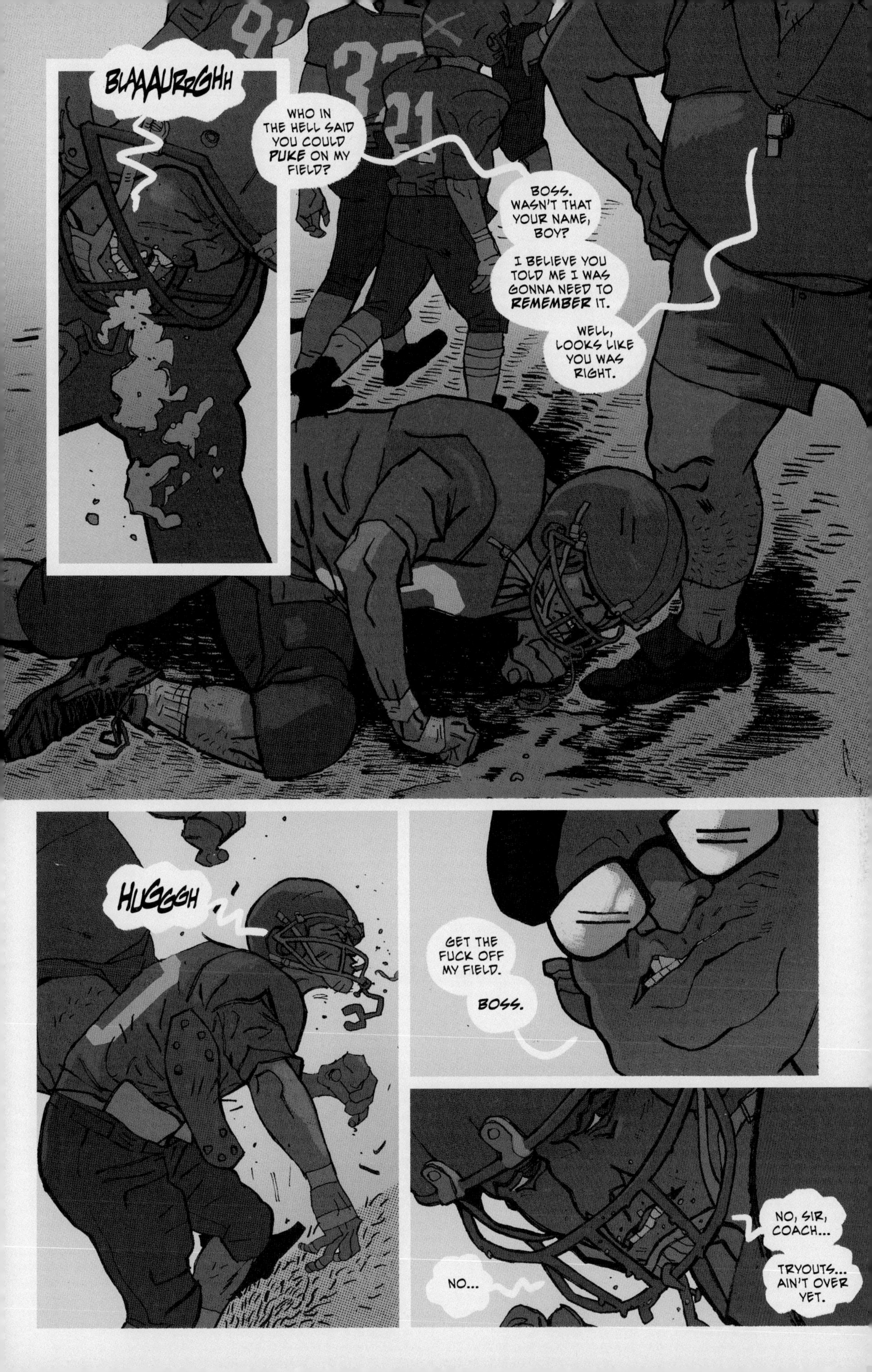
BLAAAURRGHH
WHO IN THE HELL SAID YOU COULD PUKE ON MY FIELD?
BOSS. WASN'T THAT YOUR NAME, BOY?
I BELIEVE YOU TOLD ME I WAS GONNA NEED TO REMEMBER IT.
WELL, LOOKS LIKE YOU WAS RIGHT.
HUGGGH
GET THE FUCK OFF MY FIELD.
BOSS.
NO, SIR, COACH...
TRYOUTS... AIN'T OVER YET.
NO...

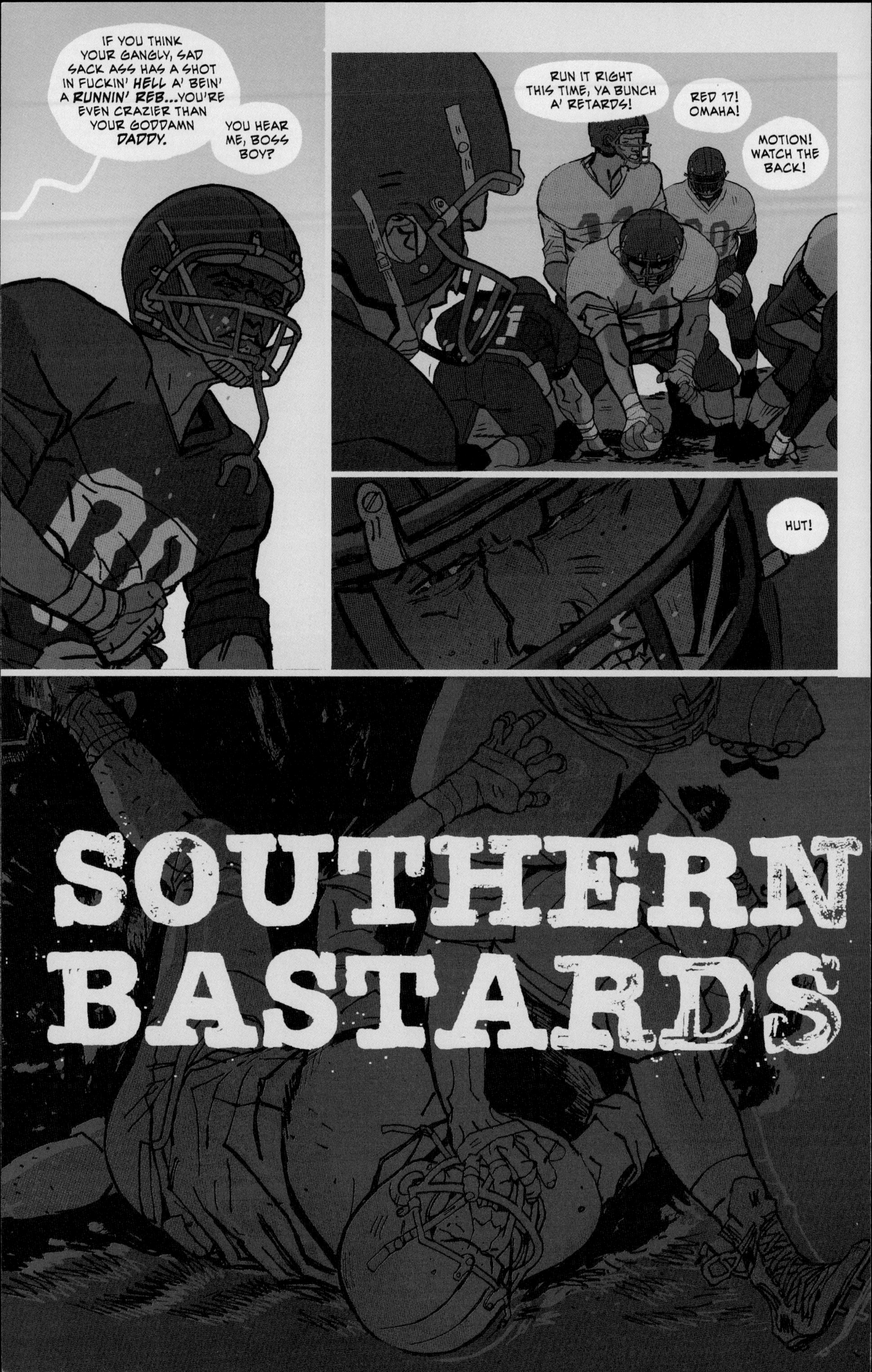
IF YOU THINK YOUR GANGLY, SAD SACK ASS HAS A SHOT IN FUCKIN' HELL A' BEIN' A RUNNIN' REB...YOU'RE EVEN CRAZIER THAN YOUR GODDAMN DADDY.
YOU HEAR ME, BOSS BOY?
RUN IT RIGHT THIS TIME, YA BUNCH A' RETARDS!
RED 17! OMAHA!
MOTION! WATCH THE BACK!
HUT!
SOUTHERN BASTARDS

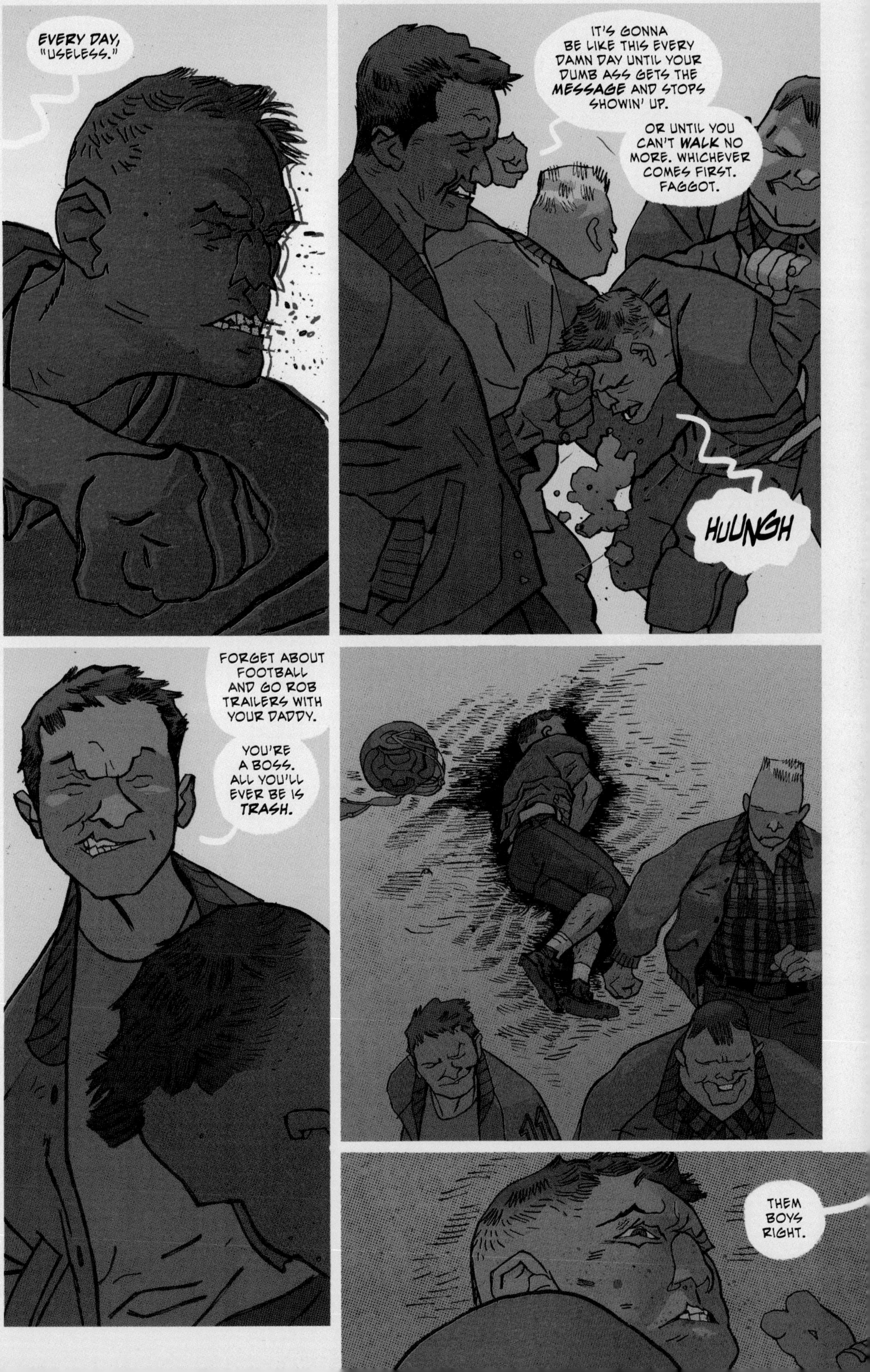
EVERY DAY, "USELESS."
IT'S GONNA BE LIKE THIS EVERY DAMN DAY UNTIL YOUR DUMB ASS GETS THE MESSAGE AND STOPS SHOWIN' UP.
OR UNTIL YOU CAN'T WALK NO MORE. WHICHEVER COMES FIRST. FAGGOT.
HUUNGH
FORGET ABOUT FOOTBALL AND GO ROB TRAILERS WITH YOUR DADDY.
YOU'RE A BOSS. ALL YOU'LL EVER BE IS TRASH.
THEM BOYS RIGHT.

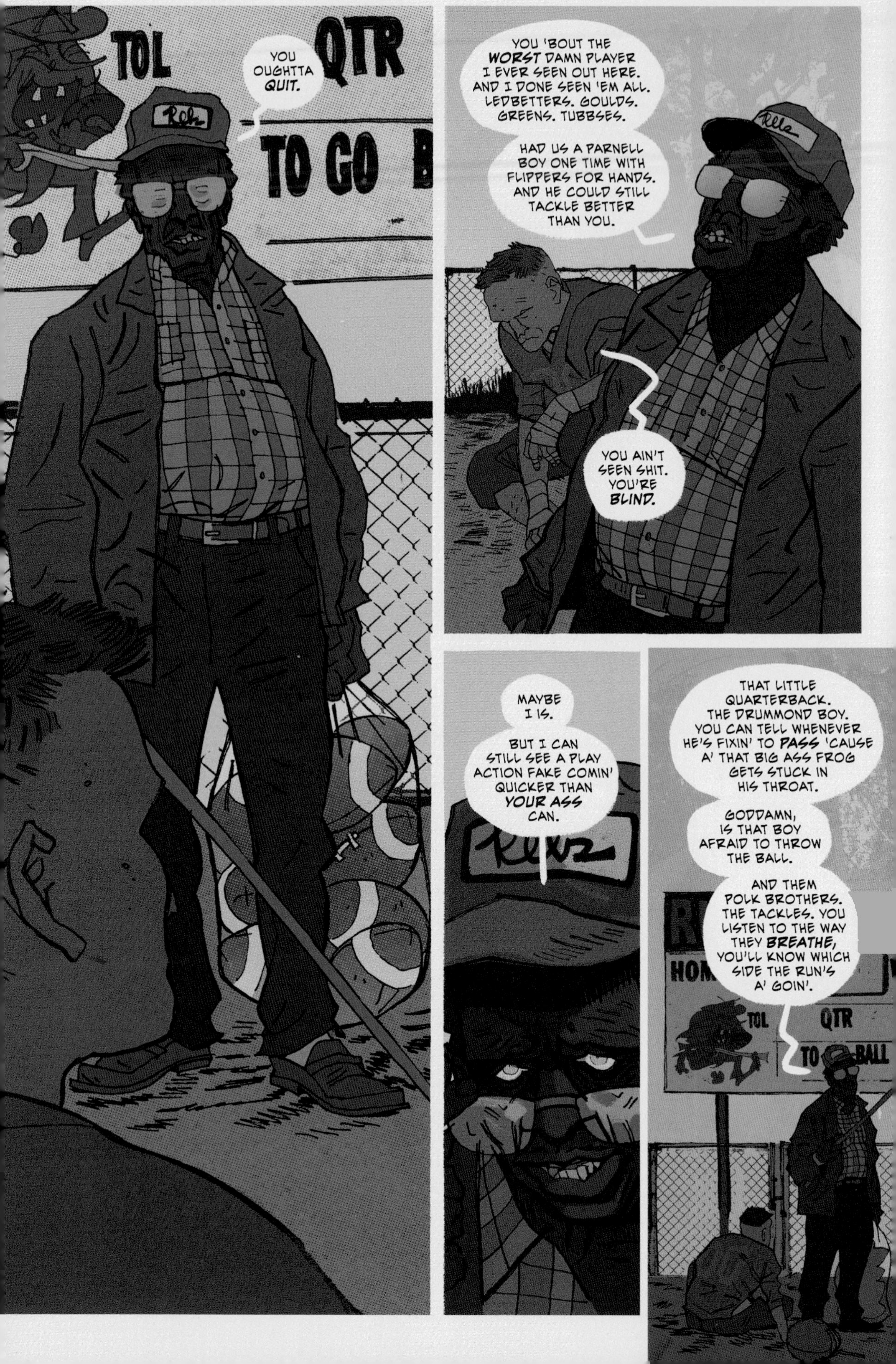
TOL
QTR
TO GO B
YOU OUGHTTA QUIT.
YOU 'BOUT THE WORST DAMN PLAYER I EVER SEEN OUT HERE. AND I DONE SEEN 'EM ALL. LEDBETTERS. GOULDS. GREENS. TUBBSES.
HAD US A PARNELL BOY ONE TIME WITH FLIPPERS FOR HANDS. AND HE COULD STILL TACKLE BETTER THAN YOU.
YOU AIN'T SEEN SHIT. YOU'RE BLIND.
MAYBE I IS.
BUT I CAN STILL SEE A PLAY ACTION FAKE COMIN' QUICKER THAN YOUR ASS CAN.
THAT LITTLE QUARTERBACK. THE DRUMMOND BOY. YOU CAN TELL WHENEVER HE'S FIXIN' TO PASS 'CAUSE A' THAT BIG ASS FROG GETS STUCK IN HIS THROAT.
GODDAMN, IS THAT BOY AFRAID TO THROW THE BALL.
AND THEM POLK BROTHERS. THE TACKLES. YOU LISTEN TO THE WAY THEY BREATHE, YOU'LL KNOW WHICH SIDE THE RUN'S A' GOIN'.
HOM
TOL
QTR
TO
BALL

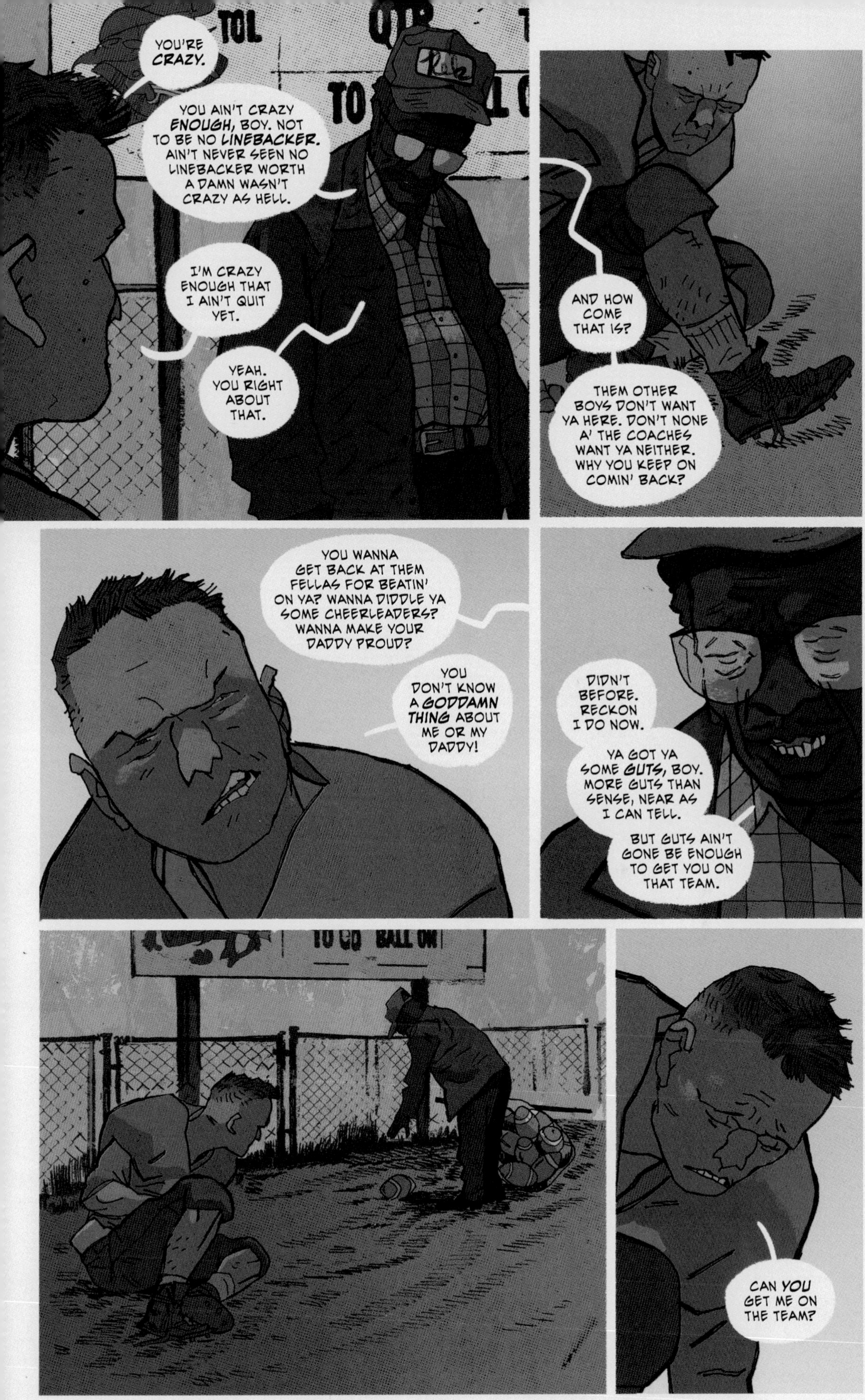
TOL
TO
YOU'RE CRAZY.
YOU AIN'T CRAZY ENOUGH, BOY. NOT TO BE NO LINEBACKER. AIN'T NEVER SEEN NO LINEBACKER WORTH A DAMN WASN'T CRAZY AS HELL.
I'M CRAZY ENOUGH THAT I AIN'T QUIT YET.
YEAH. YOU RIGHT ABOUT THAT.
AND HOW COME THAT IS?
THEM OTHER BOYS DON'T WANT YA HERE. DON'T NONE A' THE COACHES WANT YA NEITHER. WHY YOU KEEP ON COMIN' BACK?
YOU WANNA GET BACK AT THEM FELLAS FOR BEATIN' ON YA? WANNA DIDDLE YA SOME CHEERLEADERS? WANNA MAKE YOUR DADDY PROUD?
YOU DON'T KNOW A GODDAMN THING ABOUT ME OR MY DADDY!
DIDN'T BEFORE. RECKON I DO NOW.
YA GOT YA SOME GUTS, BOY. MORE GUTS THAN SENSE, NEAR AS I CAN TELL.
BUT GUTS AIN'T GONE BE ENOUGH TO GET YOU ON THAT TEAM.
TO GO BALL ON
CAN YOU GET ME ON THE TEAM?

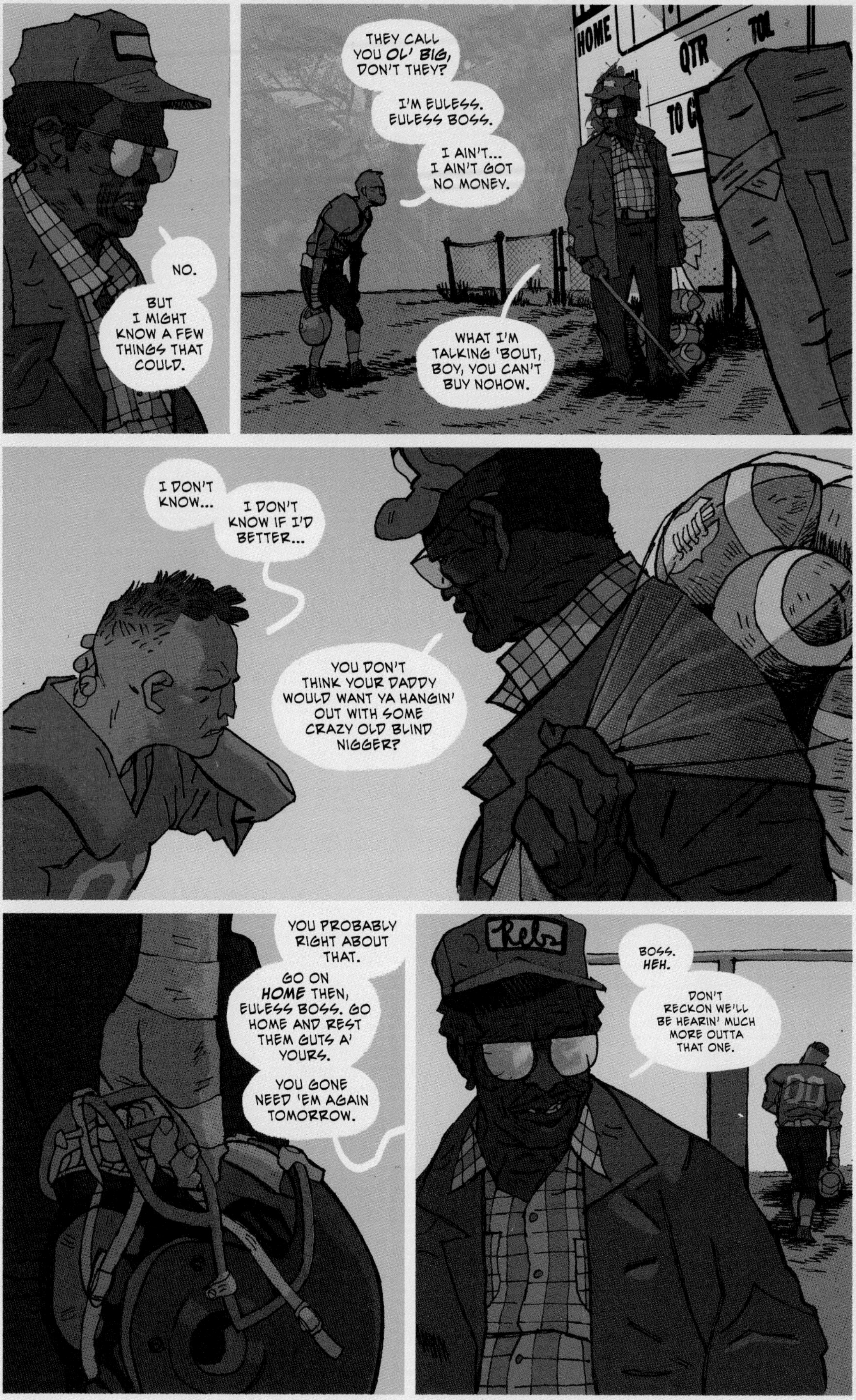
NO.
BUT I MIGHT KNOW A FEW THINGS THAT COULD.
THEY CALL YOU OL' BIG, DON'T THEY?
I'M EULESS. EULESS BOSS.
I AIN'T... I AIN'T GOT NO MONEY.
HOME
QTR
TOL
WHAT I'M TALKING 'BOUT, BOY, YOU CAN'T BUY NOHOW.
I DON'T KNOW...
I DON'T KNOW IF I'D BETTER...
YOU DON'T THINK YOUR DADDY WOULD WANT YA HANGIN' OUT WITH SOME CRAZY OLD BLIND NIGGER?
YOU PROBABLY RIGHT ABOUT THAT.
GO ON HOME THEN, EULESS BOSS. GO HOME AND REST THEM GUTS A' YOURS.
YOU GONE NEED 'EM AGAIN TOMORROW.
Rebs
BOSS. HEH.
DON'T RECKON WE'LL BE HEARIN' MUCH MORE OUTTA THAT ONE.

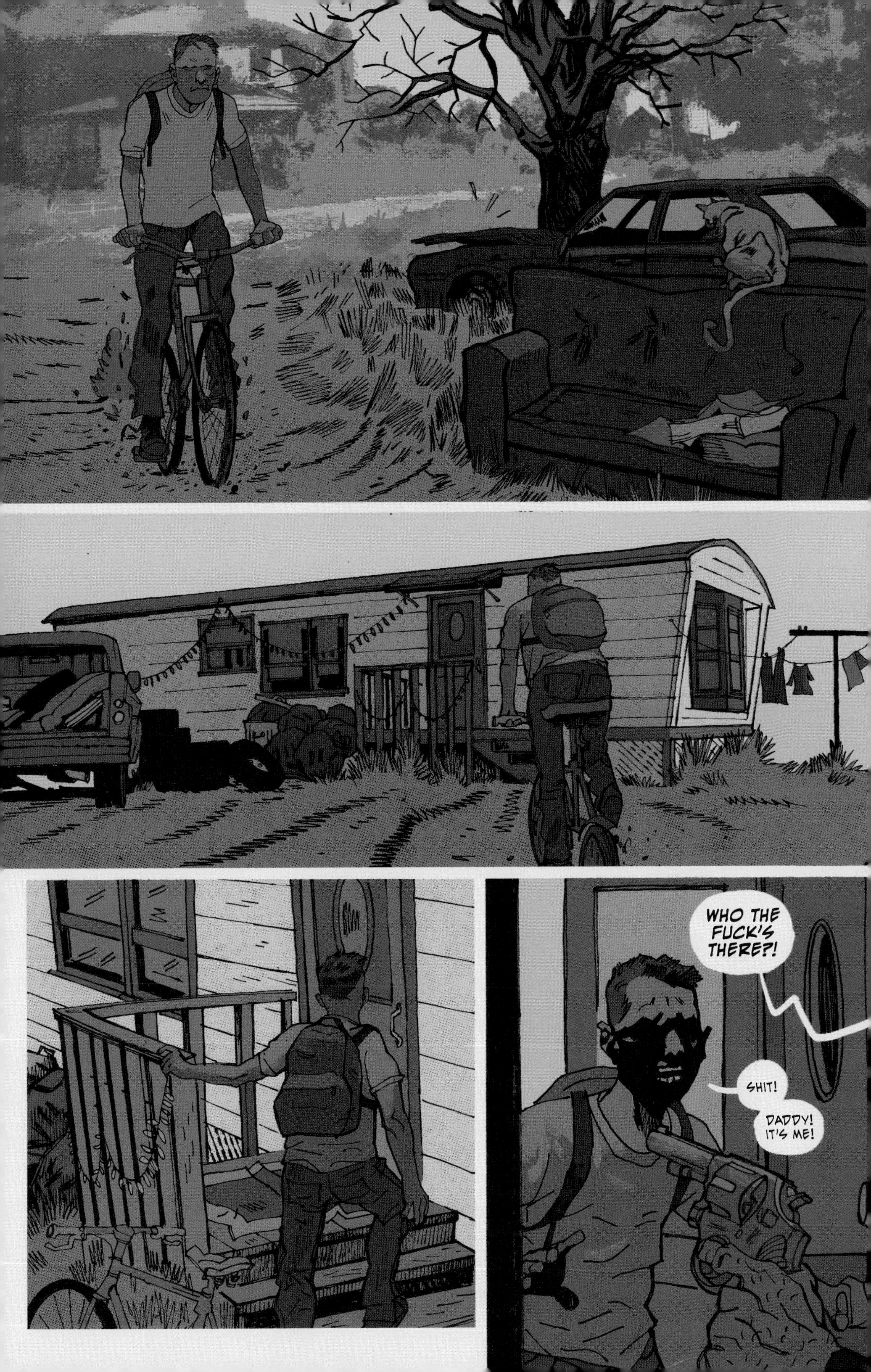
WHO THE FUCK'S THERE?!
SHIT!
DADDY! IT'S ME!

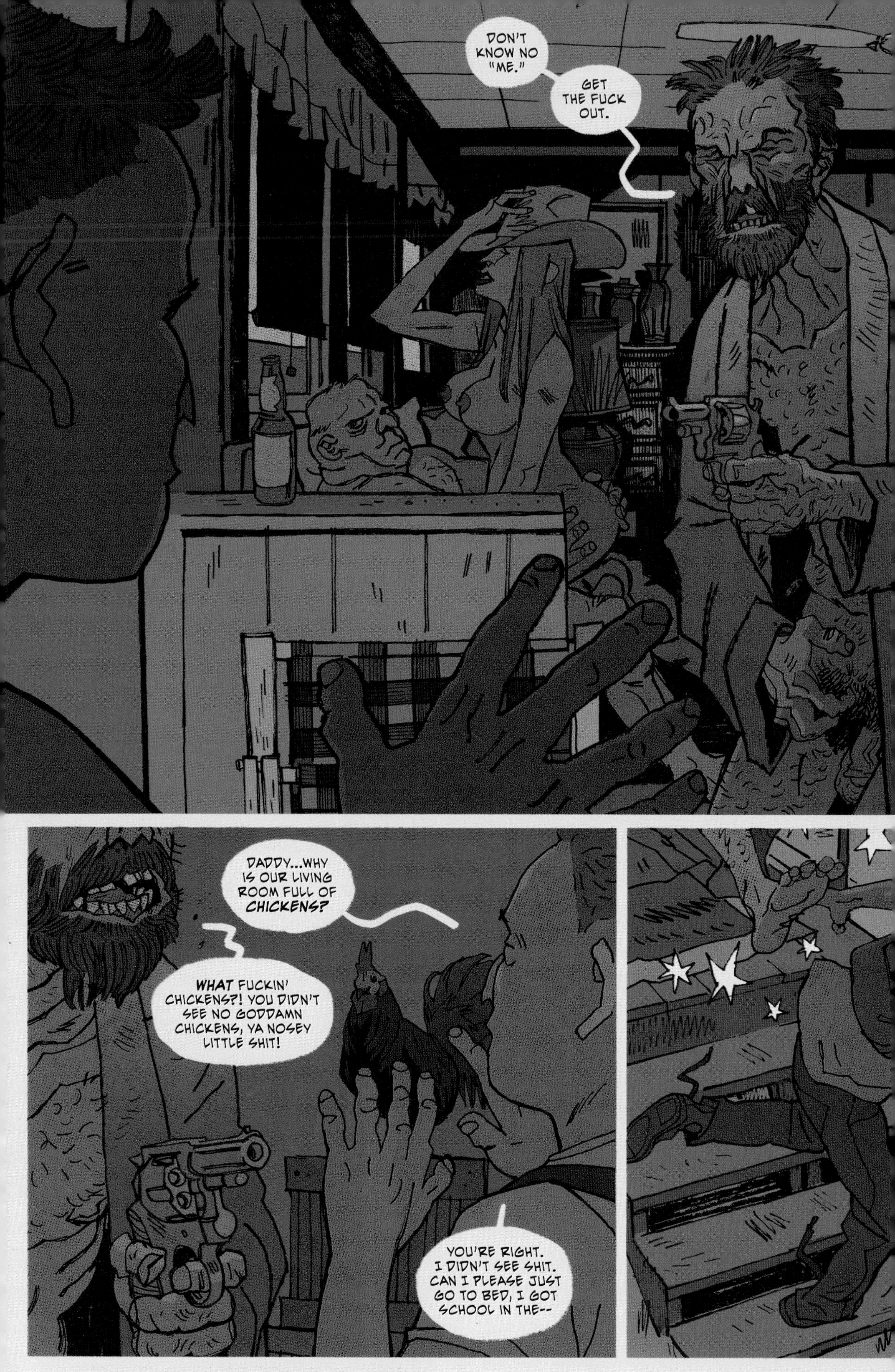
DON'T KNOW NO "ME."
GET THE FUCK OUT.
DADDY...WHY IS OUR LIVING ROOM FULL OF CHICKENS?
WHAT FUCKIN' CHICKENS?! YOU DIDN'T SEE NO GODDAMN CHICKENS, YA NOSEY LITTLE SHIT!
YOU'RE RIGHT. I DIDN'T SEE SHIT. CAN I PLEASE JUST GO TO BED, I GOT SCHOOL IN THE--

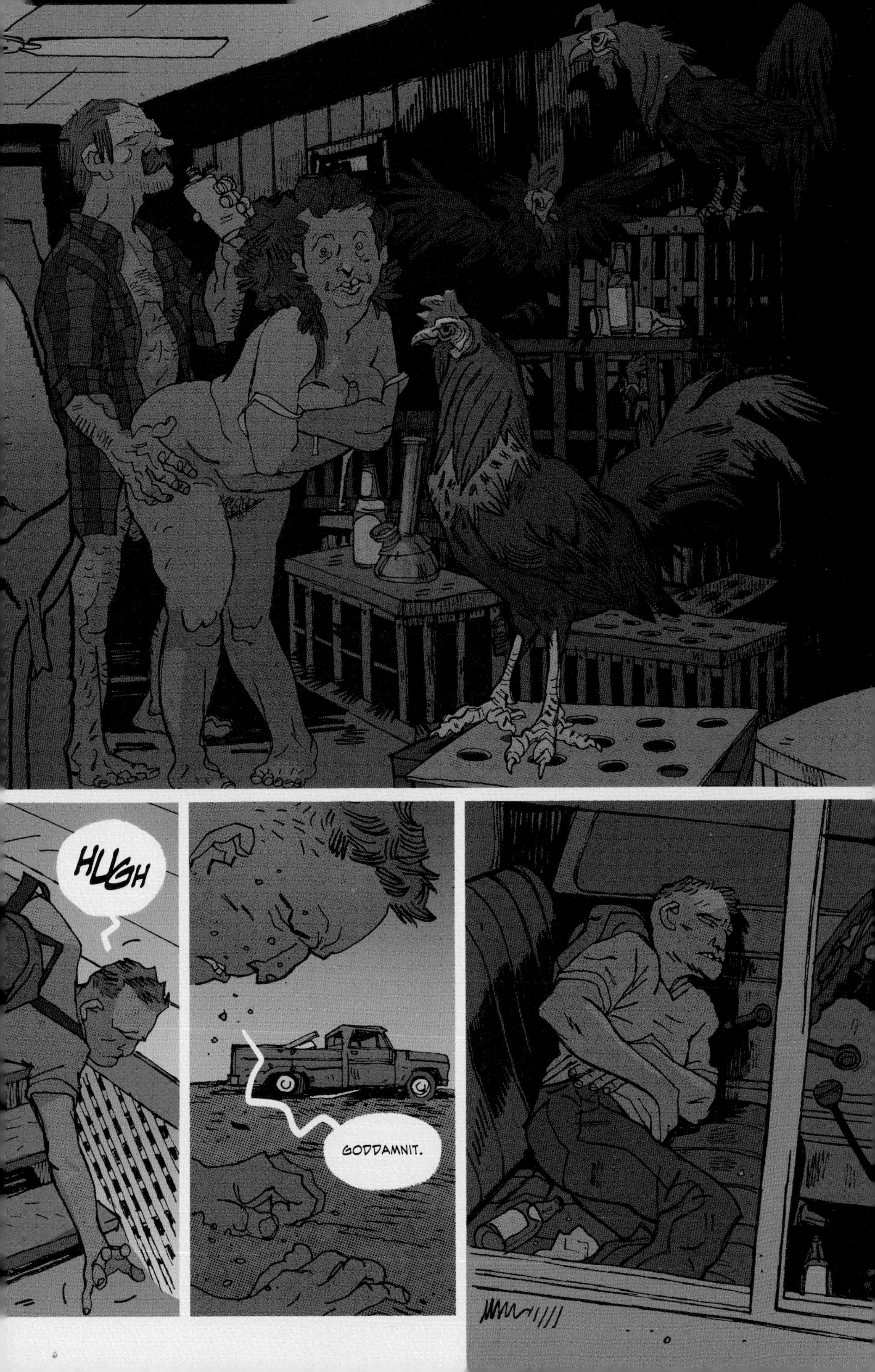
HUGH
GODDAMNIT.

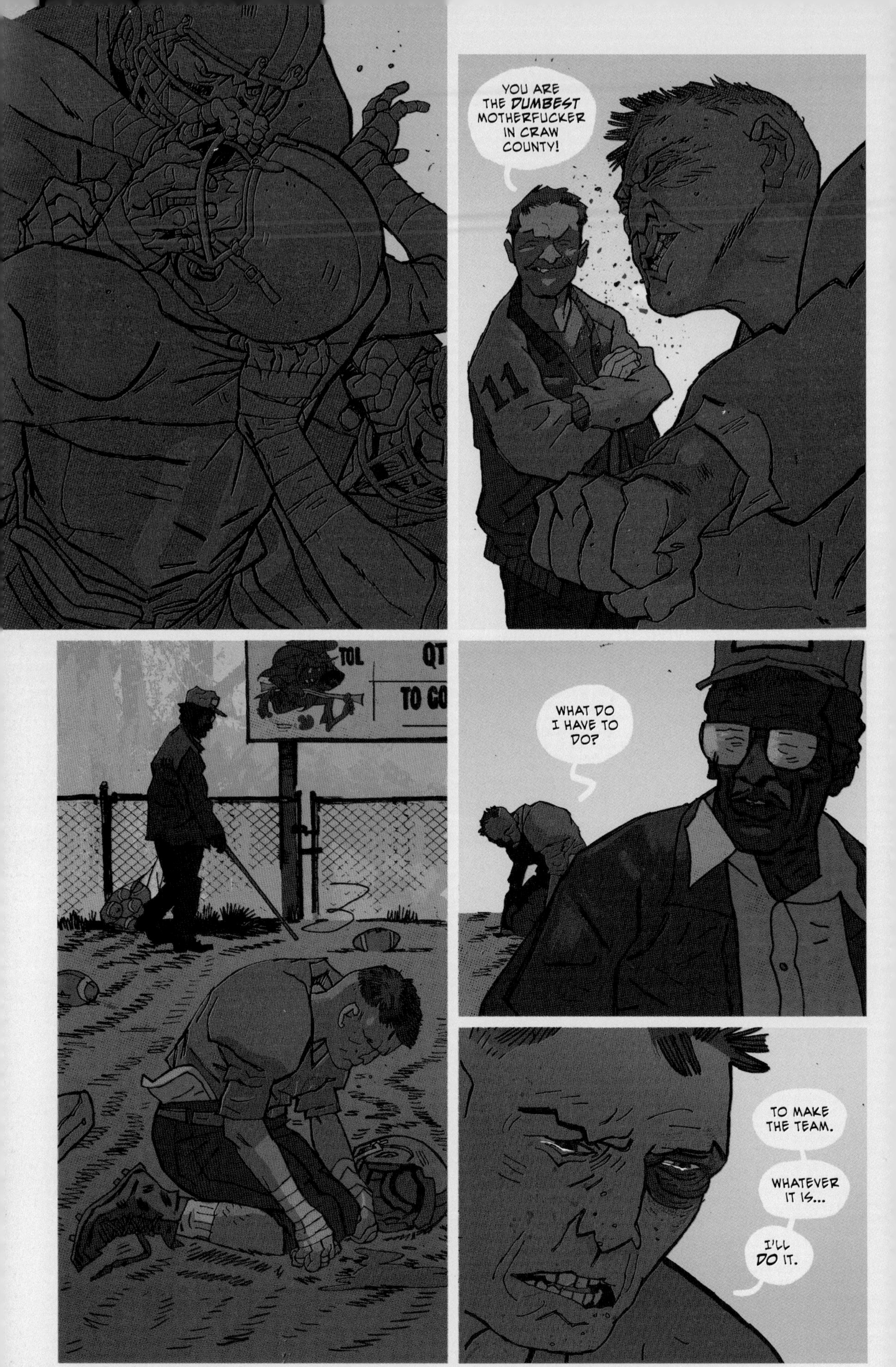
YOU ARE THE DUMBEST MOTHERFUCKER IN CRAW COUNTY!
TOL
QT
TO GO
WHAT DO I HAVE TO DO?
TO MAKE THE TEAM.
WHATEVER IT IS...
I'LL DO IT.

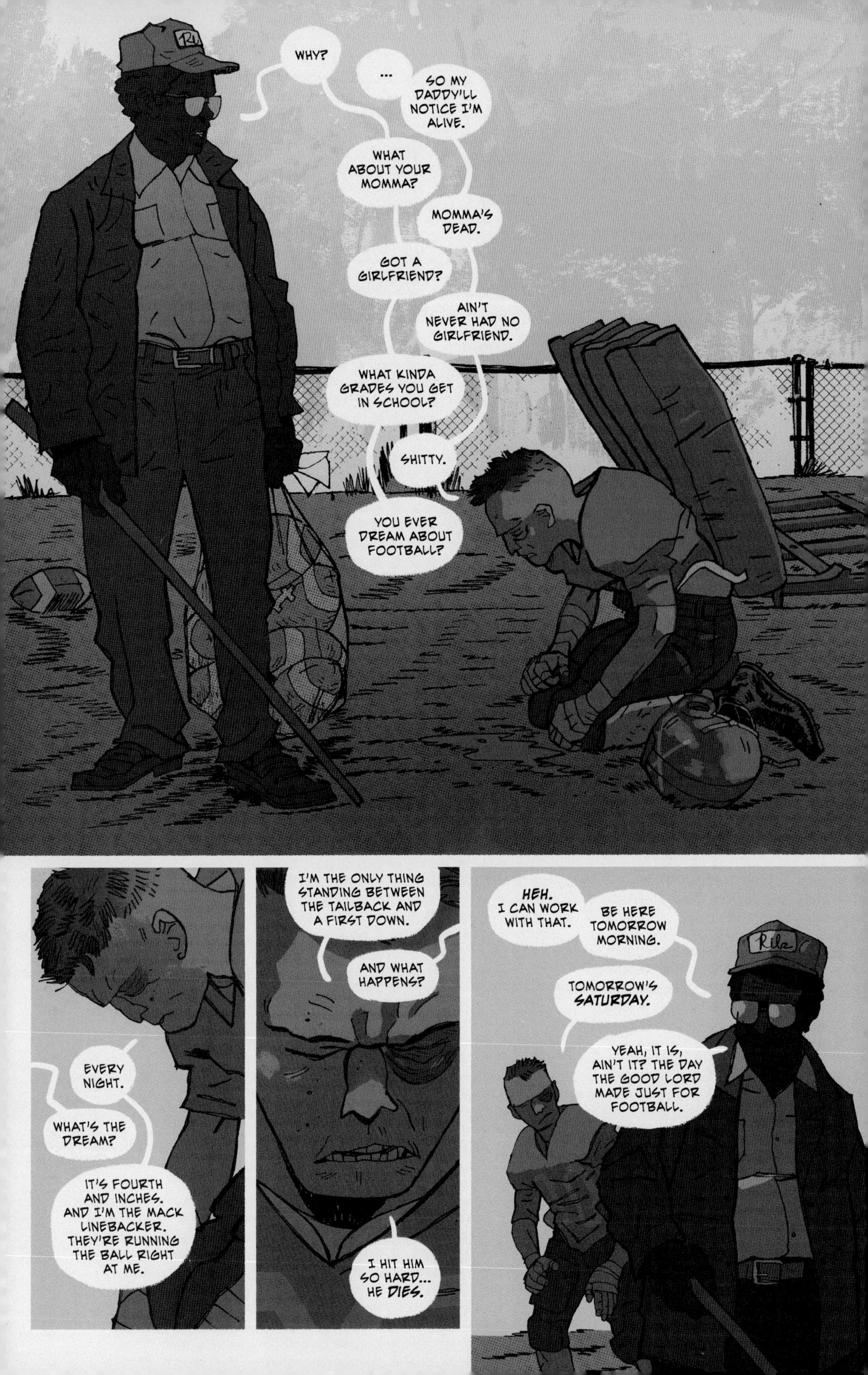
WHY?
...
SO MY DADDY'LL NOTICE I'M ALIVE.
WHAT ABOUT YOUR MOMMA?
MOMMA'S DEAD.
GOT A GIRLFRIEND?
AIN'T NEVER HAD NO GIRLFRIEND.
WHAT KINDA GRADES YOU GET IN SCHOOL?
SHITTY.
YOU EVER DREAM ABOUT FOOTBALL?
EVERY NIGHT.
WHAT'S THE DREAM?
IT'S FOURTH AND INCHES. AND I'M THE MACK LINEBACKER. THEY'RE RUNNING THE BALL RIGHT AT ME.
I'M THE ONLY THING STANDING BETWEEN THE TAILBACK AND A FIRST DOWN.
AND WHAT HAPPENS?
I HIT HIM SO HARD... HE *DIES*.
HEH. I CAN WORK WITH THAT.
BE HERE TOMORROW MORNING.
TOMORROW'S *SATURDAY.*
YEAH, IT IS, AIN'T IT? THE DAY THE GOOD LORD MADE JUST FOR FOOTBALL.

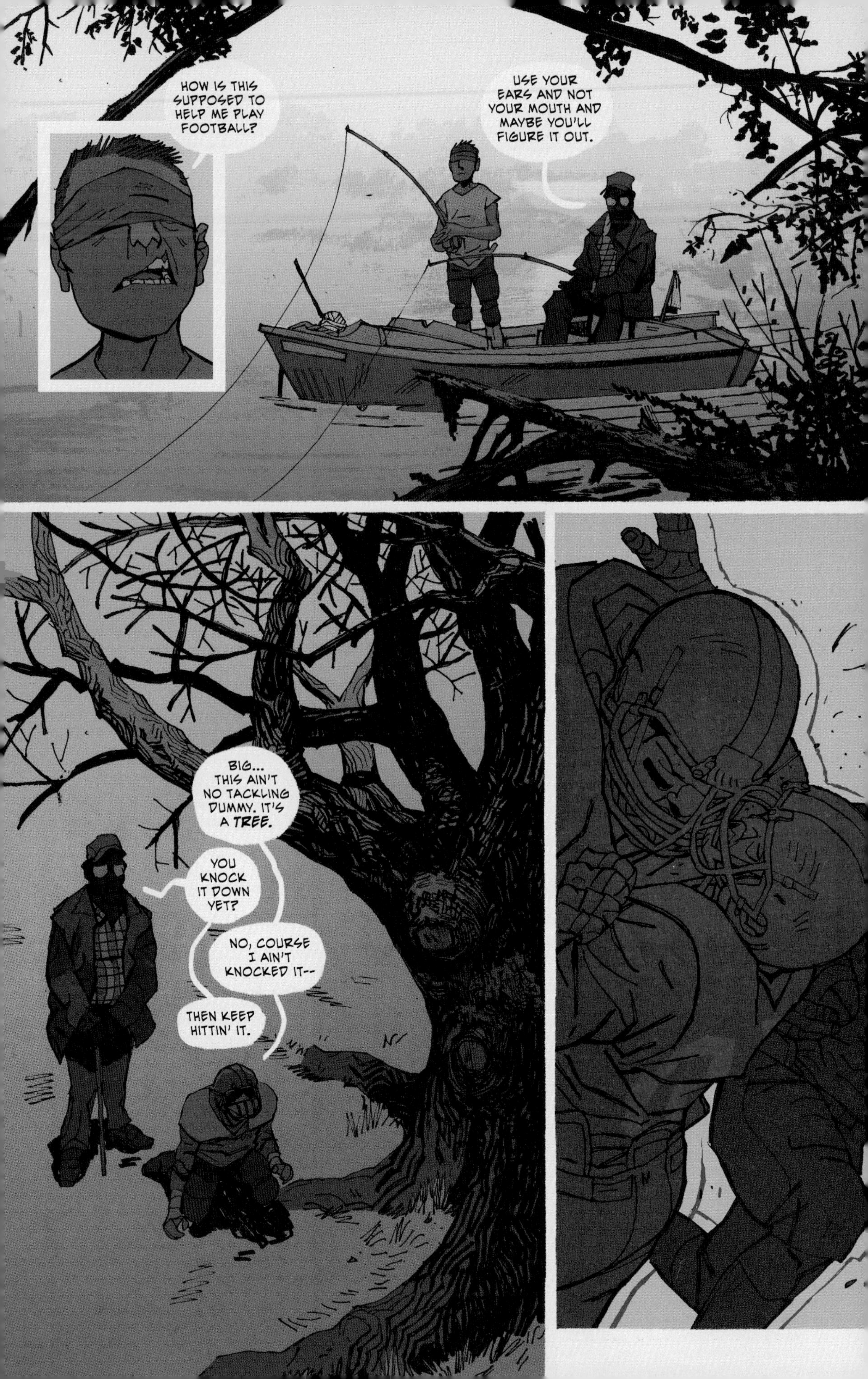
HOW IS THIS SUPPOSED TO HELP ME PLAY FOOTBALL?
USE YOUR EARS AND NOT YOUR MOUTH AND MAYBE YOU'LL FIGURE IT OUT.
BIG... THIS AIN'T NO TACKLING DUMMY. IT'S A TREE.
YOU KNOCK IT DOWN YET?
NO, COURSE I AIN'T KNOCKED IT--
THEN KEEP HITTIN' IT.

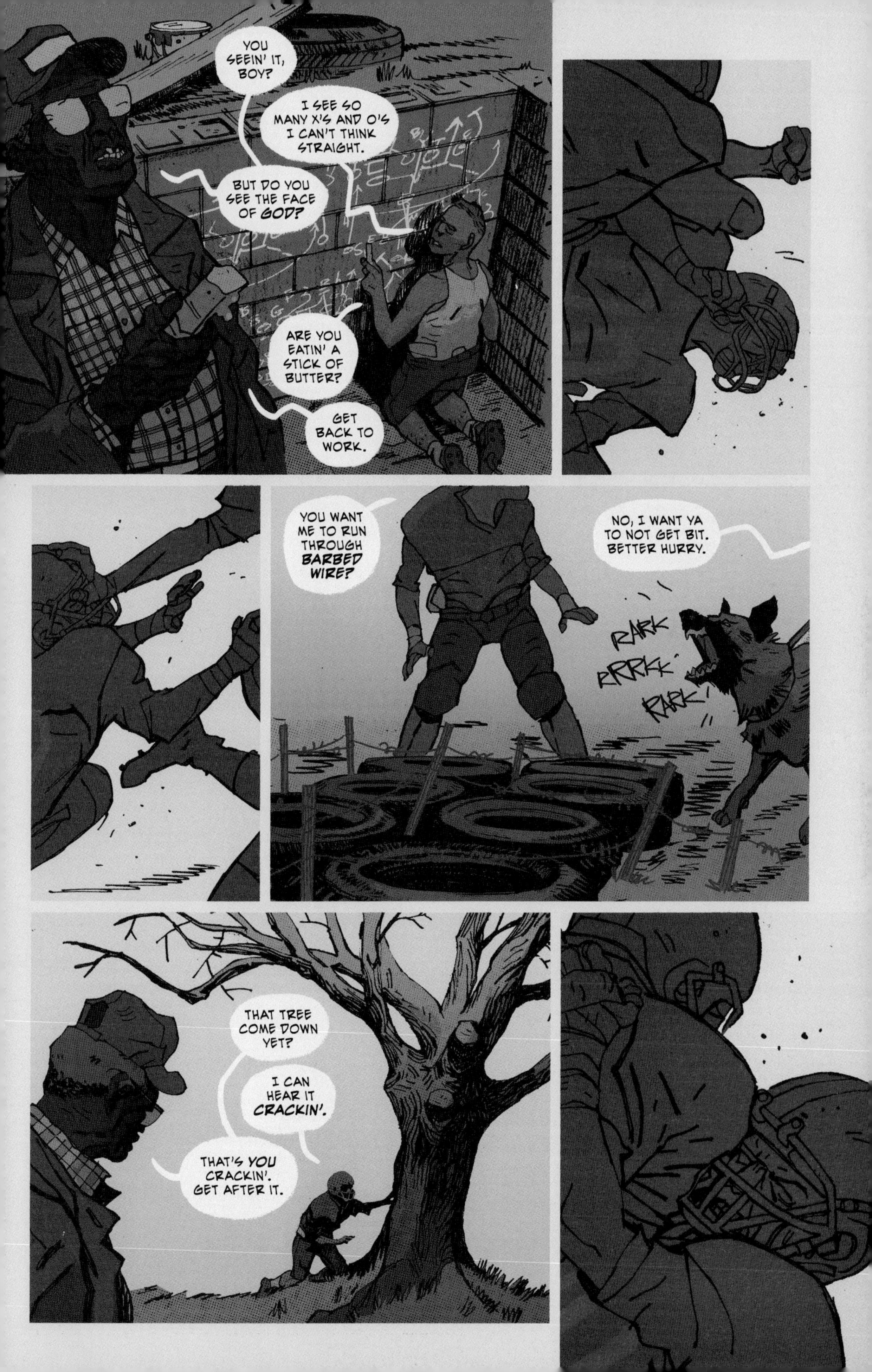
YOU SEEIN' IT, BOY?
I SEE SO MANY X'S AND O'S I CAN'T THINK STRAIGHT.
BUT DO YOU SEE THE FACE OF GOD?
ARE YOU EATIN' A STICK OF BUTTER?
GET BACK TO WORK.
YOU WANT ME TO RUN THROUGH BARBED WIRE?
NO, I WANT YA TO NOT GET BIT. BETTER HURRY.
RARK
RRRKK
RARK!
THAT TREE COME DOWN YET?
I CAN HEAR IT CRACKIN'.
THAT'S YOU CRACKIN'. GET AFTER IT.

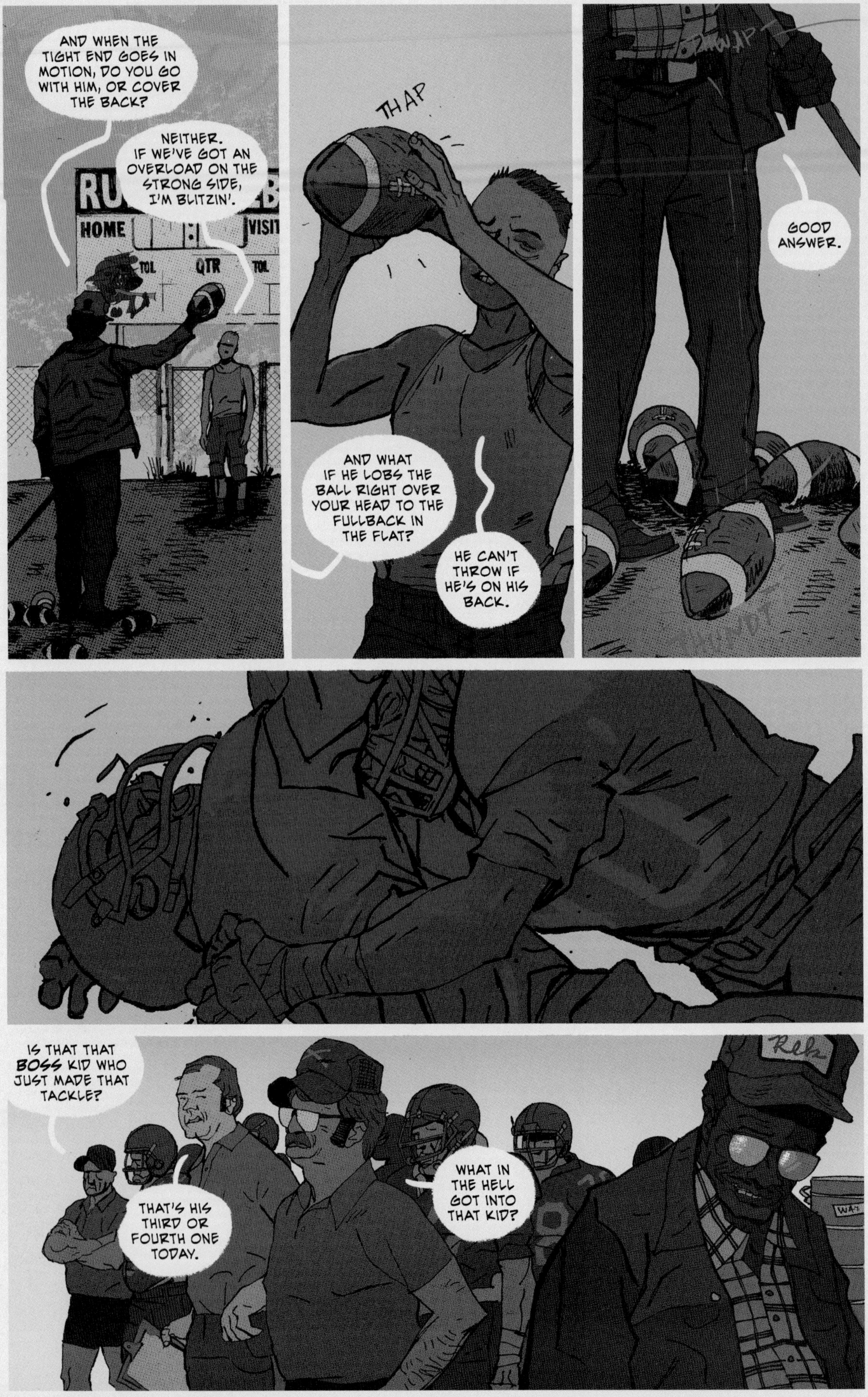
AND WHEN THE TIGHT END GOES IN MOTION, DO YOU GO WITH HIM, OR COVER THE BACK?
NEITHER. IF WE'VE GOT AN OVERLOAD ON THE STRONG SIDE, I'M BLITZIN'.
HOME
VISIT
TOL
QTR
TOL
THAP
AND WHAT IF HE LOBS THE BALL RIGHT OVER YOUR HEAD TO THE FULLBACK IN THE FLAT?
HE CAN'T THROW IF HE'S ON HIS BACK.
GOOD ANSWER.
IS THAT THAT BOSS KID WHO JUST MADE THAT TACKLE?
THAT'S HIS THIRD OR FOURTH ONE TODAY.
WHAT IN THE HELL GOT INTO THAT KID?

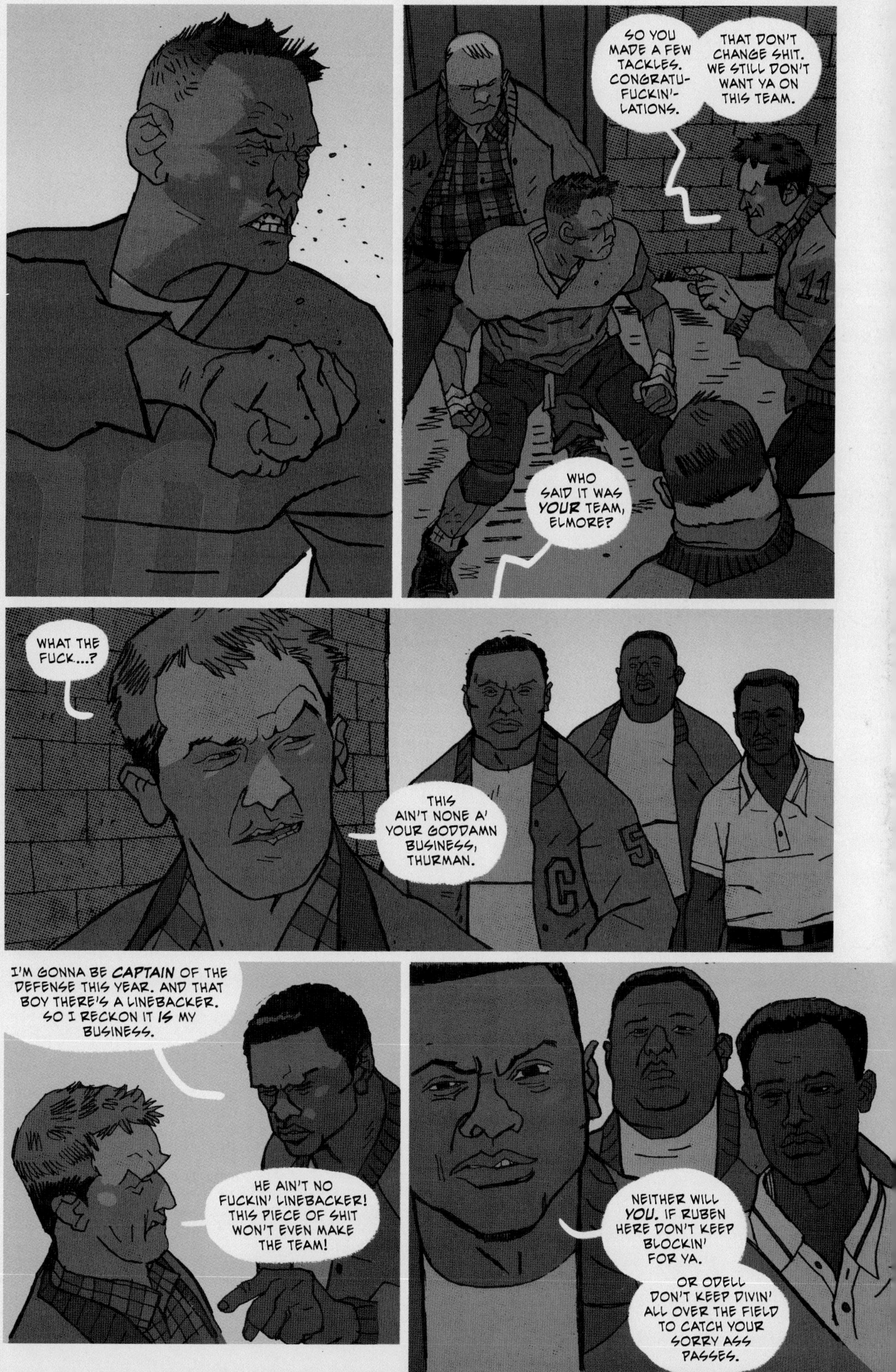
SO YOU MADE A FEW TACKLES. CONGRATU-FUCKIN'-LATIONS.
THAT DON'T CHANGE SHIT. WE STILL DON'T WANT YA ON THIS TEAM.
WHO SAID IT WAS YOUR TEAM, ELMORE?
WHAT THE FUCK...?
THIS AIN'T NONE A' YOUR GODDAMN BUSINESS, THURMAN.
I'M GONNA BE CAPTAIN OF THE DEFENSE THIS YEAR. AND THAT BOY THERE'S A LINEBACKER. SO I RECKON IT IS MY BUSINESS.
HE AIN'T NO FUCKIN' LINEBACKER! THIS PIECE OF SHIT WON'T EVEN MAKE THE TEAM!
NEITHER WILL YOU. IF RUBEN HERE DON'T KEEP BLOCKIN' FOR YA.
OR ODELL DON'T KEEP DIVIN' ALL OVER THE FIELD TO CATCH YOUR SORRY ASS PASSES.

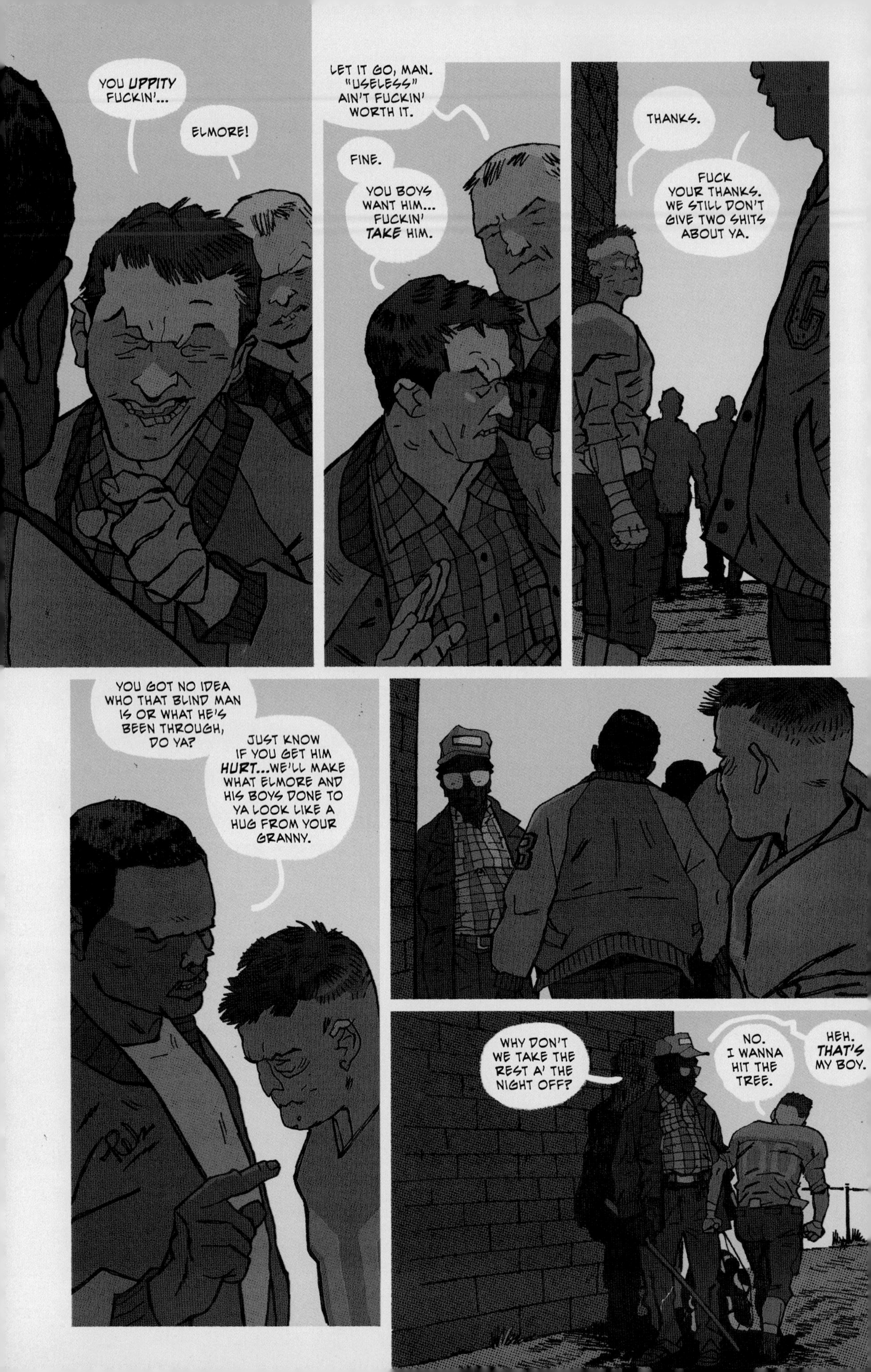
YOU UPPITY FUCKIN'...
ELMORE!
LET IT GO, MAN. "USELESS" AIN'T FUCKIN' WORTH IT.
FINE.
YOU BOYS WANT HIM... FUCKIN' TAKE HIM.
THANKS.
FUCK YOUR THANKS. WE STILL DON'T GIVE TWO SHITS ABOUT YA.
YOU GOT NO IDEA WHO THAT BLIND MAN IS OR WHAT HE'S BEEN THROUGH, DO YA?
JUST KNOW IF YOU GET HIM HURT...WE'LL MAKE WHAT ELMORE AND HIS BOYS DONE TO YA LOOK LIKE A HUG FROM YOUR GRANNY.
WHY DON'T WE TAKE THE REST A' THE NIGHT OFF?
NO. I WANNA HIT THE TREE.
HEH. THAT'S MY BOY.

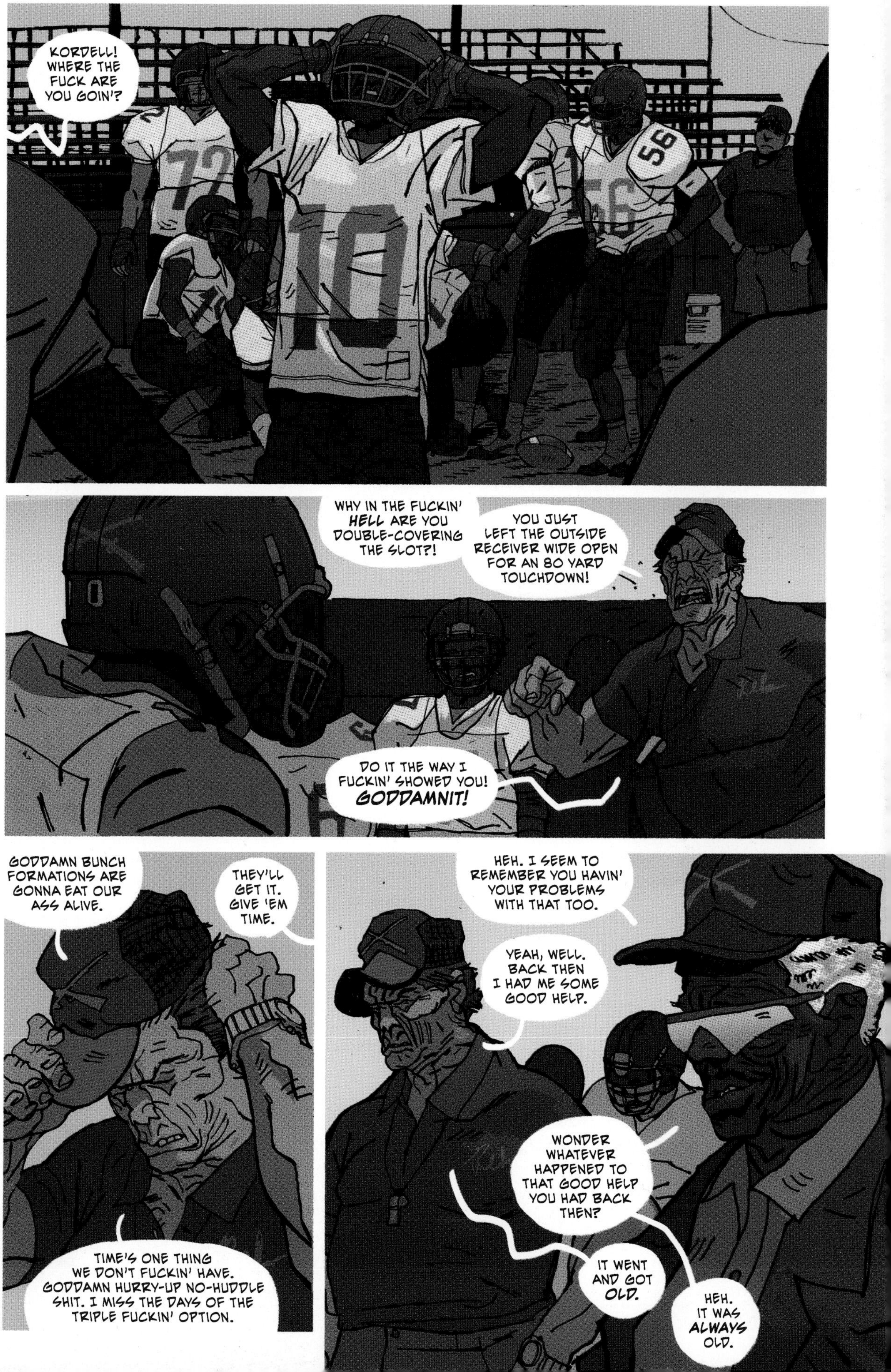
KORDELL! WHERE THE FUCK ARE YOU GOIN'?
WHY IN THE FUCKIN' HELL ARE YOU DOUBLE-COVERING THE SLOT?!
YOU JUST LEFT THE OUTSIDE RECEIVER WIDE OPEN FOR AN 80 YARD TOUCHDOWN!
DO IT THE WAY I FUCKIN' SHOWED YOU! GODDAMNIT!
GODDAMN BUNCH FORMATIONS ARE GONNA EAT OUR ASS ALIVE.
THEY'LL GET IT. GIVE 'EM TIME.
TIME'S ONE THING WE DON'T FUCKIN' HAVE. GODDAMN HURRY-UP NO-HUDDLE SHIT. I MISS THE DAYS OF THE TRIPLE FUCKIN' OPTION.
HEH. I SEEM TO REMEMBER YOU HAVIN' YOUR PROBLEMS WITH THAT TOO.
YEAH, WELL. BACK THEN I HAD ME SOME GOOD HELP.
WONDER WHATEVER HAPPENED TO THAT GOOD HELP YOU HAD BACK THEN?
IT WENT AND GOT OLD.
HEH. IT WAS ALWAYS OLD.

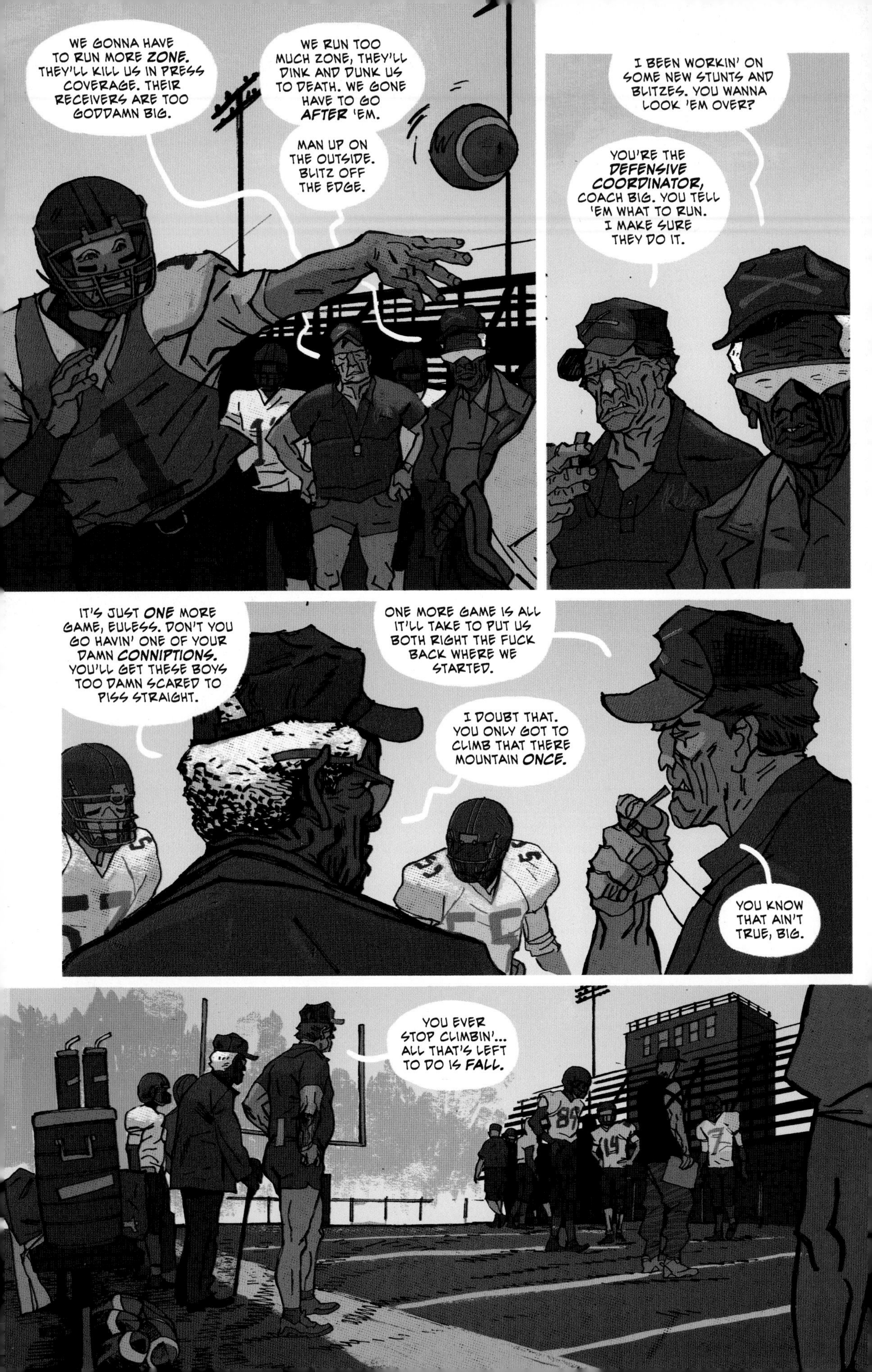
WE GONNA HAVE TO RUN MORE ZONE. THEY'LL KILL US IN PRESS COVERAGE. THEIR RECEIVERS ARE TOO GODDAMN BIG.
WE RUN TOO MUCH ZONE, THEY'LL DINK AND DUNK US TO DEATH. WE GONE HAVE TO GO AFTER 'EM.
MAN UP ON THE OUTSIDE. BLITZ OFF THE EDGE.
I BEEN WORKIN' ON SOME NEW STUNTS AND BLITZES. YOU WANNA LOOK 'EM OVER?
YOU'RE THE DEFENSIVE COORDINATOR, COACH BIG. YOU TELL 'EM WHAT TO RUN. I MAKE SURE THEY DO IT.
IT'S JUST ONE MORE GAME, EULESS. DON'T YOU GO HAVIN' ONE OF YOUR DAMN CONNIPTIONS. YOU'LL GET THESE BOYS TOO DAMN SCARED TO PISS STRAIGHT.
ONE MORE GAME IS ALL IT'LL TAKE TO PUT US BOTH RIGHT THE FUCK BACK WHERE WE STARTED.
I DOUBT THAT. YOU ONLY GOT TO CLIMB THAT THERE MOUNTAIN ONCE.
YOU KNOW THAT AIN'T TRUE, BIG.
YOU EVER STOP CLIMBIN'... ALL THAT'S LEFT TO DO IS FALL.

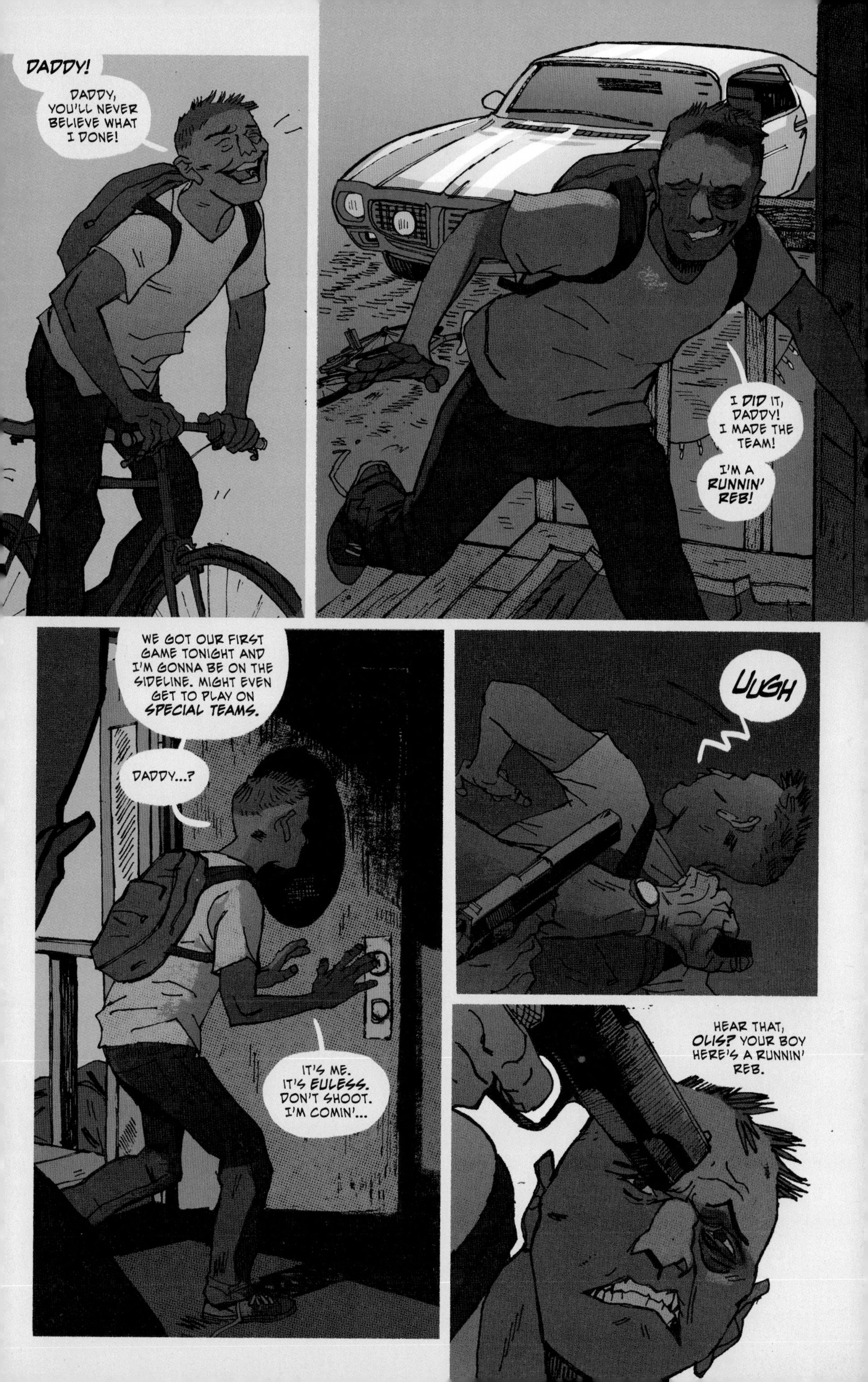
DADDY!
DADDY, YOU'LL NEVER BELIEVE WHAT I DONE!
I DID IT, DADDY! I MADE THE TEAM!
I'M A RUNNIN' REB!
WE GOT OUR FIRST GAME TONIGHT AND I'M GONNA BE ON THE SIDELINE. MIGHT EVEN GET TO PLAY ON SPECIAL TEAMS.
DADDY...?
IT'S ME. IT'S EULESS. DON'T SHOOT. I'M COMIN'...
UUGH
HEAR THAT, OLIS? YOUR BOY HERE'S A RUNNIN' REB.

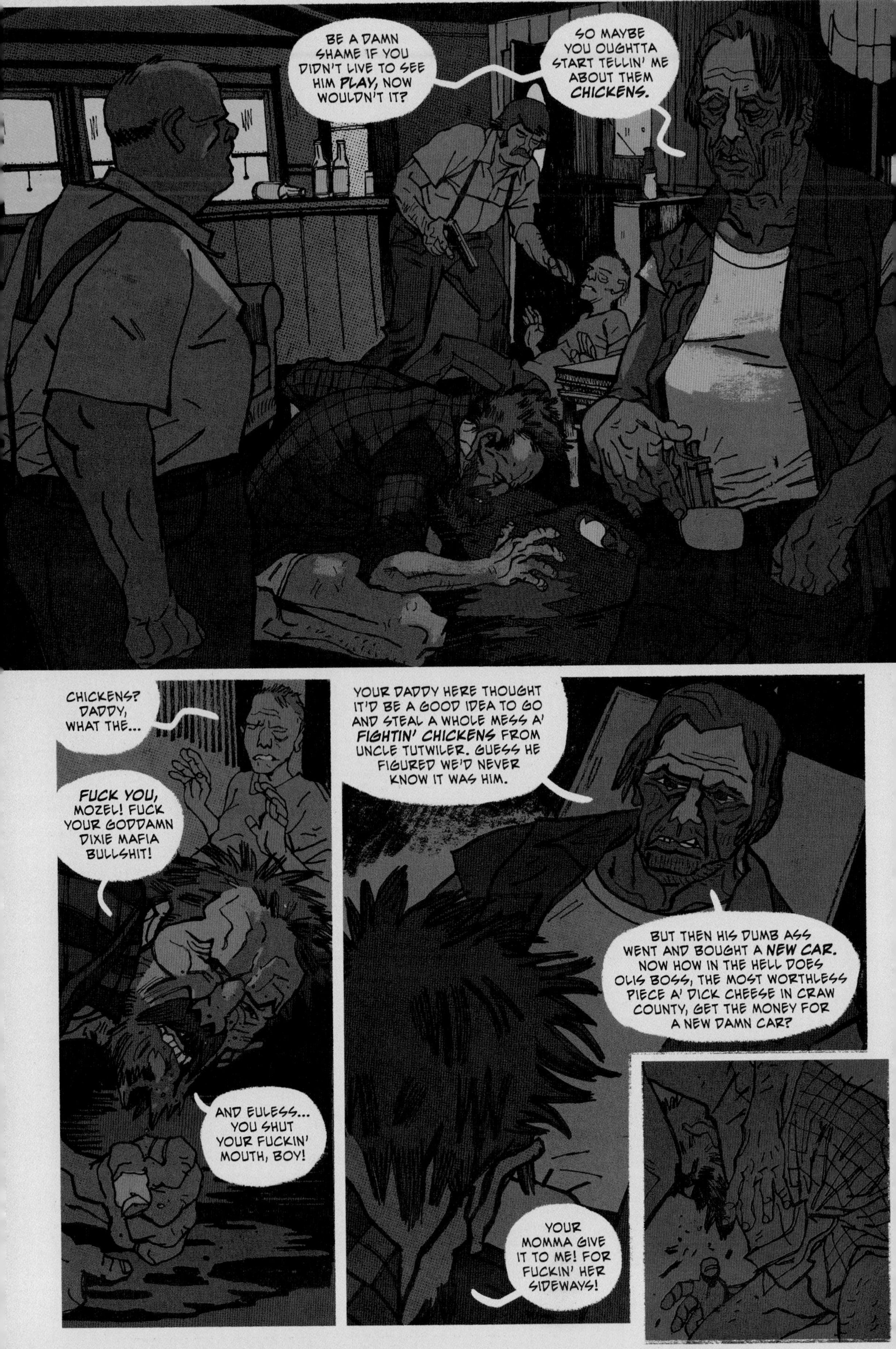
BE A DAMN SHAME IF YOU DIDN'T LIVE TO SEE HIM PLAY, NOW WOULDN'T IT?
SO MAYBE YOU OUGHTTA START TELLIN' ME ABOUT THEM CHICKENS.
CHICKENS? DADDY, WHAT THE...
FUCK YOU, MOZEL! FUCK YOUR GODDAMN DIXIE MAFIA BULLSHIT!
AND EULESS... YOU SHUT YOUR FUCKIN' MOUTH, BOY!
YOUR DADDY HERE THOUGHT IT'D BE A GOOD IDEA TO GO AND STEAL A WHOLE MESS A' FIGHTIN' CHICKENS FROM UNCLE TUTWILER. GUESS HE FIGURED WE'D NEVER KNOW IT WAS HIM.
BUT THEN HIS DUMB ASS WENT AND BOUGHT A NEW CAR. NOW HOW IN THE HELL DOES OLIS BOSS, THE MOST WORTHLESS PIECE A' DICK CHEESE IN CRAW COUNTY, GET THE MONEY FOR A NEW DAMN CAR?
YOUR MOMMA GIVE IT TO ME! FOR FUCKIN' HER SIDEWAYS!

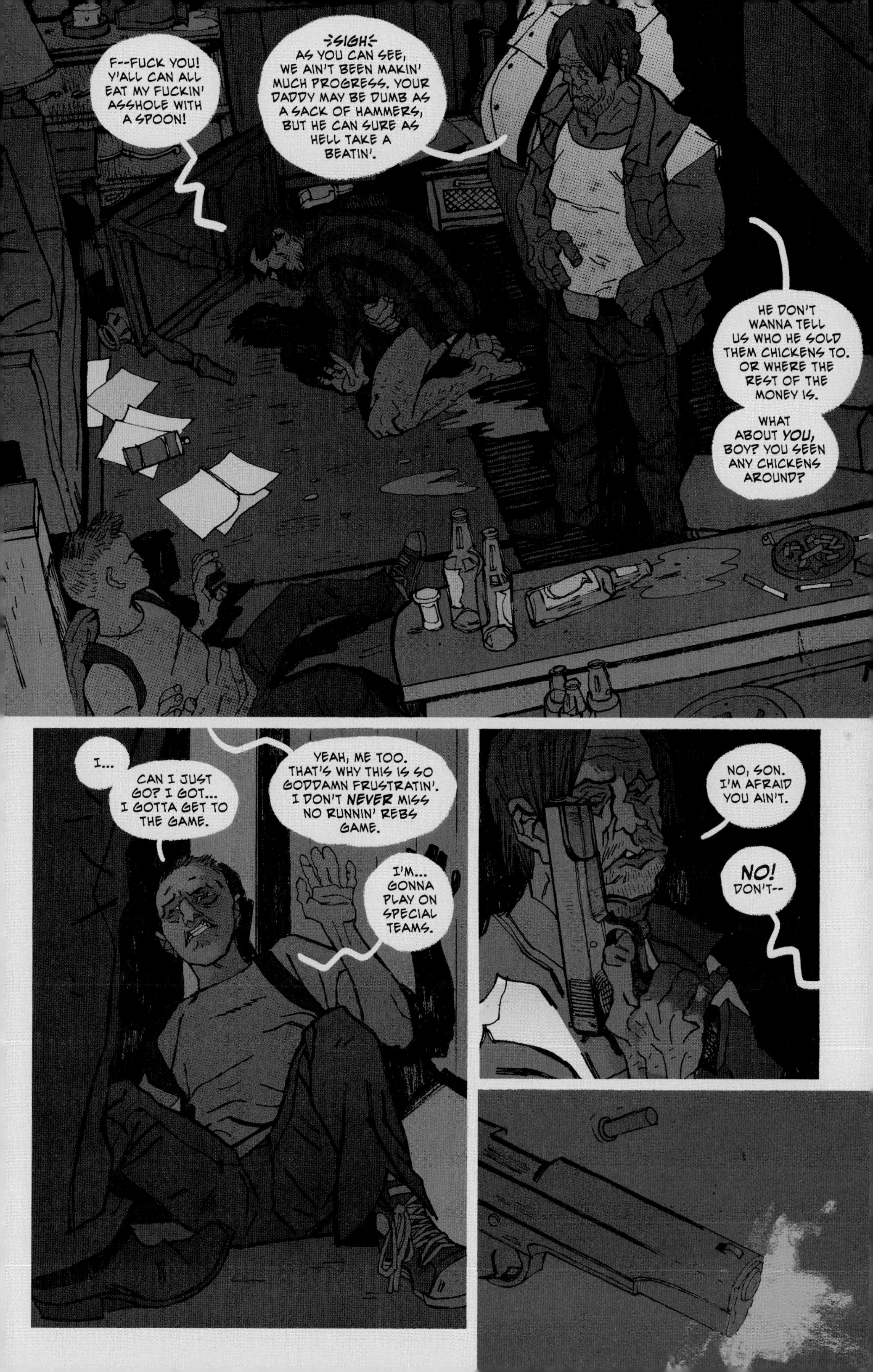
F--FUCK YOU! Y'ALL CAN ALL EAT MY FUCKIN' ASSHOLE WITH A SPOON!
SIGH
AS YOU CAN SEE, WE AIN'T BEEN MAKIN' MUCH PROGRESS. YOUR DADDY MAY BE DUMB AS A SACK OF HAMMERS, BUT HE CAN SURE AS HELL TAKE A BEATIN'.
HE DON'T WANNA TELL US WHO HE SOLD THEM CHICKENS TO. OR WHERE THE REST OF THE MONEY IS.
WHAT ABOUT YOU, BOY? YOU SEEN ANY CHICKENS AROUND?
I...
CAN I JUST GO? I GOT... I GOTTA GET TO THE GAME.
YEAH, ME TOO. THAT'S WHY THIS IS SO GODDAMN FRUSTRATIN'. I DON'T NEVER MISS NO RUNNIN' REBS GAME.
I'M... GONNA PLAY ON SPECIAL TEAMS.
NO, SON. I'M AFRAID YOU AIN'T.
NO! DON'T--

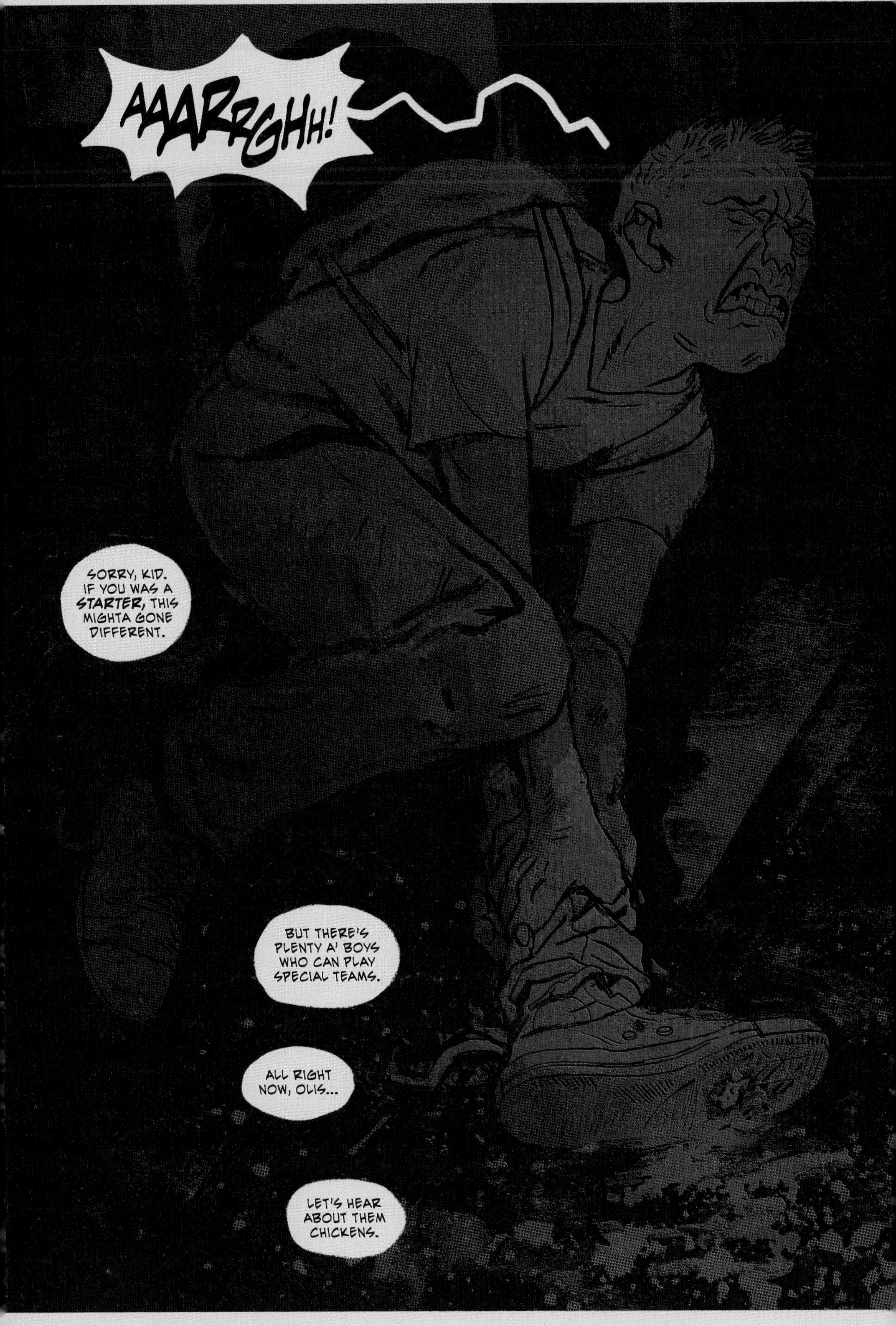
AAARRGHH!
SORRY, KID. IF YOU WAS A STARTER, THIS MIGHTA GONE DIFFERENT.
BUT THERE'S PLENTY A' BOYS WHO CAN PLAY SPECIAL TEAMS.
ALL RIGHT NOW, OLIS...
LET'S HEAR ABOUT THEM CHICKENS.

Chapter 7

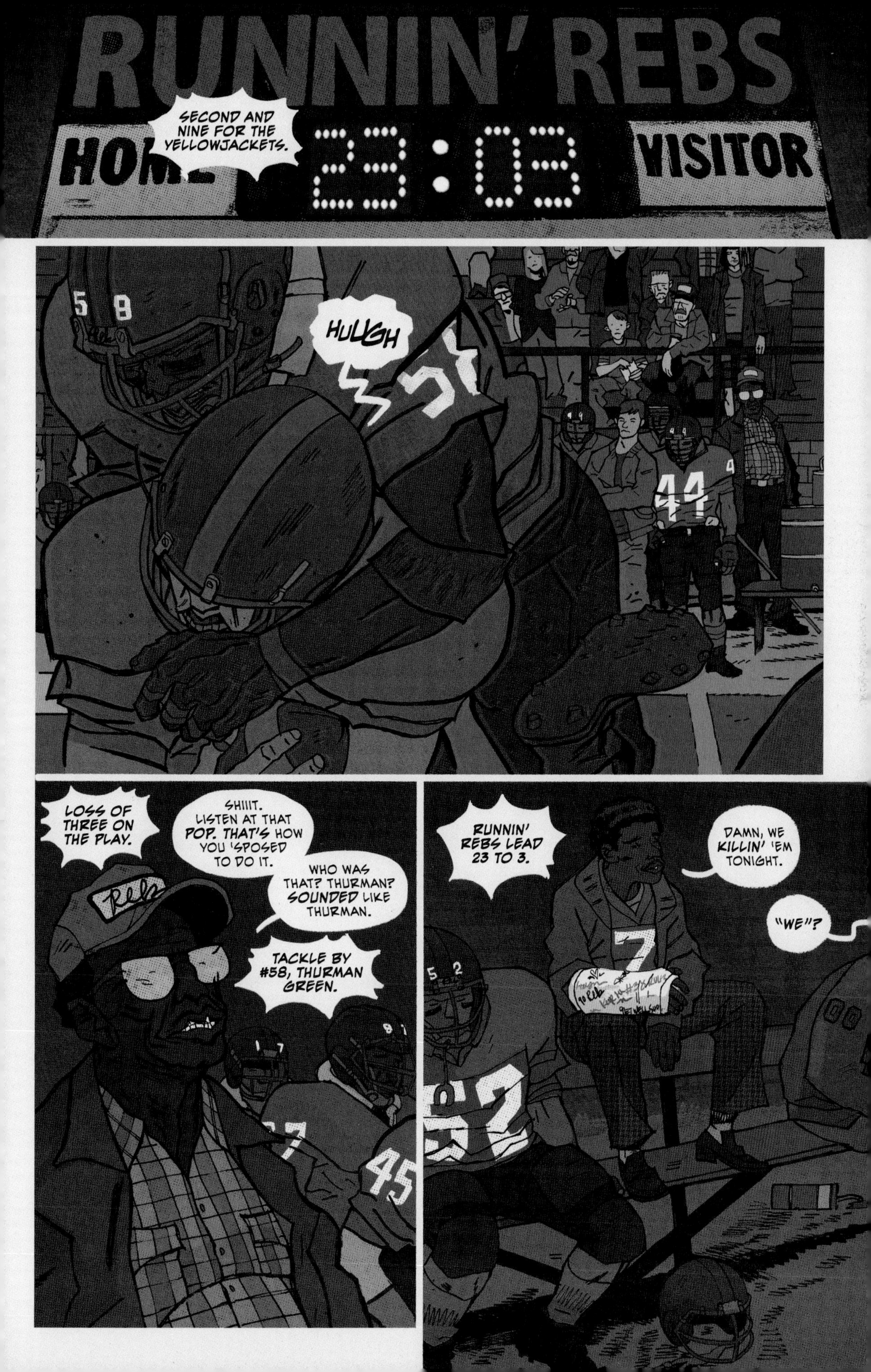

RUNNIN' REBS
HOME
23:03
VISITOR
SECOND AND NINE FOR THE YELLOWJACKETS.
HULUGH
LOSS OF THREE ON THE PLAY.
SHIIIT. LISTEN AT THAT POP. THAT'S HOW YOU 'SPOSED TO DO IT.
WHO WAS THAT? THURMAN? SOUNDED LIKE THURMAN.
TACKLE BY #58, THURMAN GREEN.
RUNNIN' REBS LEAD 23 TO 3.
DAMN, WE KILLIN' 'EM TONIGHT.
"WE"?

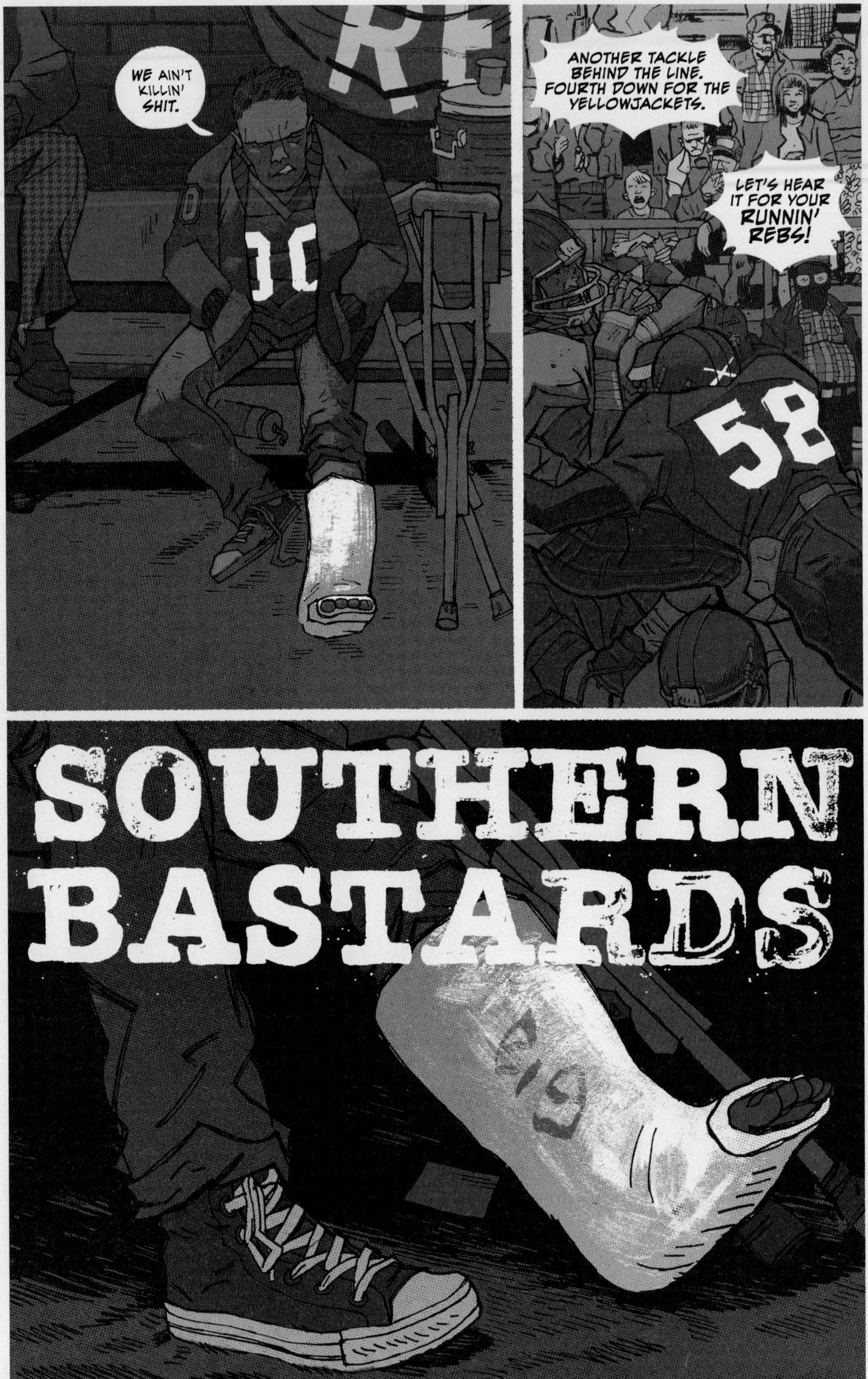
WE AIN'T KILLIN' SHIT.
ANOTHER TACKLE BEHIND THE LINE. FOURTH DOWN FOR THE YELLOWJACKETS.
LET'S HEAR IT FOR YOUR RUNNIN' REBS!
SOUTHERN BASTARDS

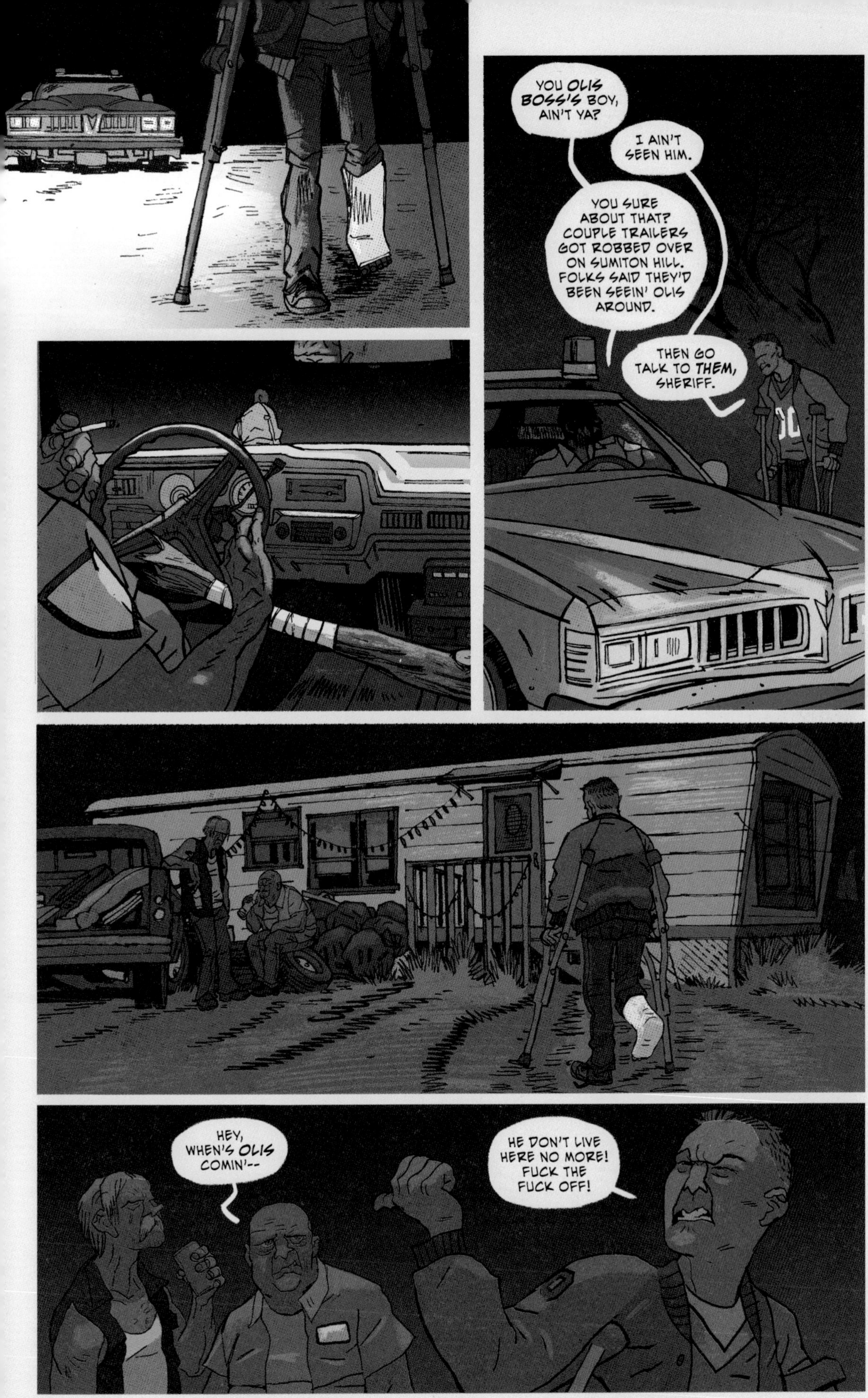

YOU OLIS BOSS'S BOY, AIN'T YA?
I AIN'T SEEN HIM.
YOU SURE ABOUT THAT? COUPLE TRAILERS GOT ROBBED OVER ON SUMITON HILL. FOLKS SAID THEY'D BEEN SEEIN' OLIS AROUND.
THEN GO TALK TO THEM, SHERIFF.
HEY, WHEN'S OLIS COMIN'--
HE DON'T LIVE HERE NO MORE! FUCK THE FUCK OFF!

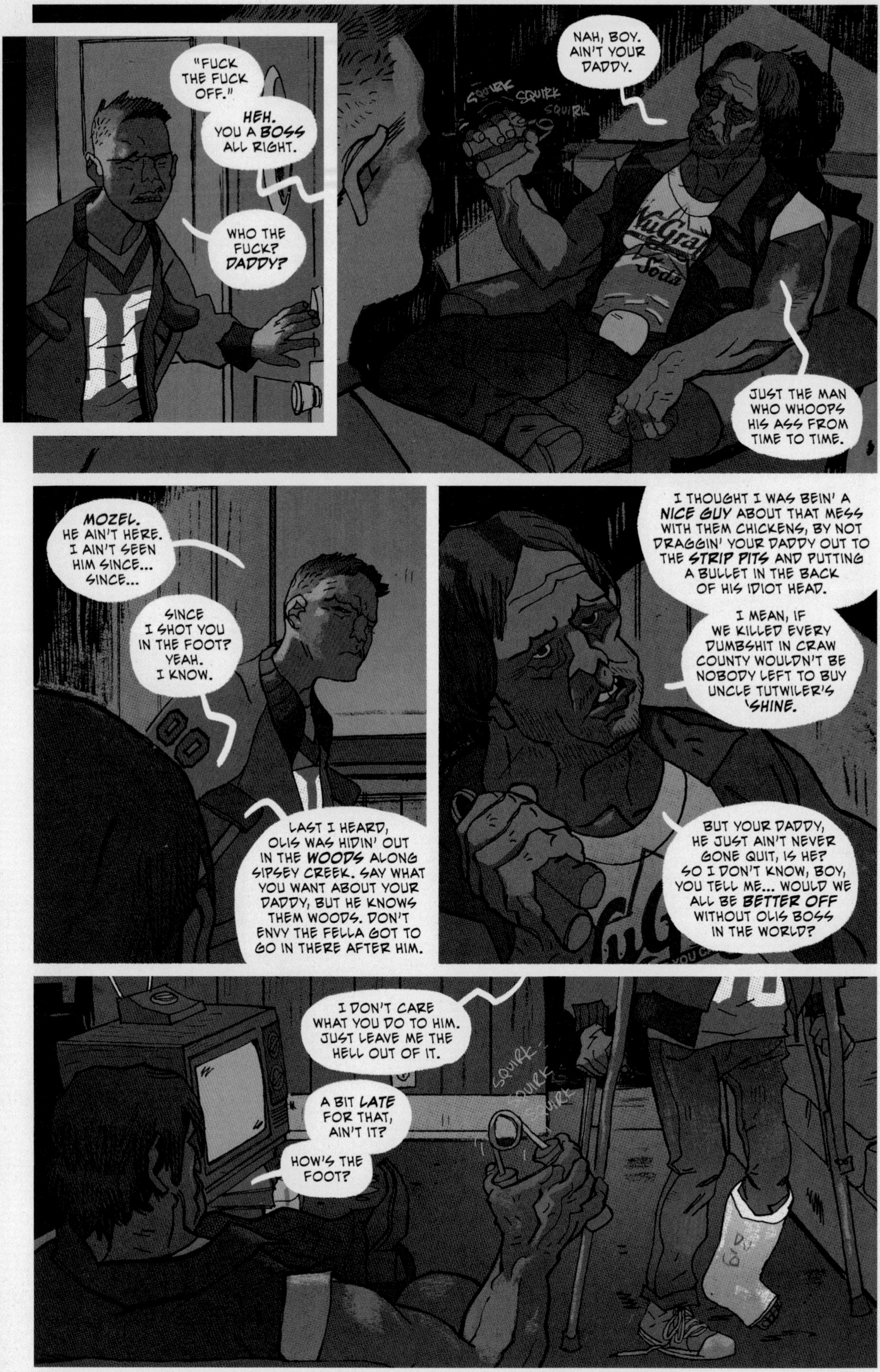
"FUCK THE FUCK OFF."
HEH. YOU A BOSS ALL RIGHT.
WHO THE FUCK? DADDY?
NAH, BOY. AIN'T YOUR DADDY.
SQUIRK SQUIRK SQUIRK
JUST THE MAN WHO WHOOPS HIS ASS FROM TIME TO TIME.
MOZEL. HE AIN'T HERE. I AIN'T SEEN HIM SINCE... SINCE...
SINCE I SHOT YOU IN THE FOOT? YEAH. I KNOW.
LAST I HEARD, OLIS WAS HIDIN' OUT IN THE WOODS ALONG SIPSEY CREEK. SAY WHAT YOU WANT ABOUT YOUR DADDY, BUT HE KNOWS THEM WOODS. DON'T ENVY THE FELLA GOT TO GO IN THERE AFTER HIM.
I THOUGHT I WAS BEIN' A NICE GUY ABOUT THAT MESS WITH THEM CHICKENS, BY NOT DRAGGIN' YOUR DADDY OUT TO THE STRIP PITS AND PUTTING A BULLET IN THE BACK OF HIS IDIOT HEAD.
I MEAN, IF WE KILLED EVERY DUMBSHIT IN CRAW COUNTY WOULDN'T BE NOBODY LEFT TO BUY UNCLE TUTWILER'S 'SHINE.
BUT YOUR DADDY, HE JUST AIN'T NEVER GONE QUIT, IS HE? SO I DON'T KNOW, BOY, YOU TELL ME... WOULD WE ALL BE BETTER OFF WITHOUT OLIS BOSS IN THE WORLD?
I DON'T CARE WHAT YOU DO TO HIM. JUST LEAVE ME THE HELL OUT OF IT.
SQUIRK SQUIRK SQUIRK
A BIT LATE FOR THAT, AIN'T IT?
HOW'S THE FOOT?

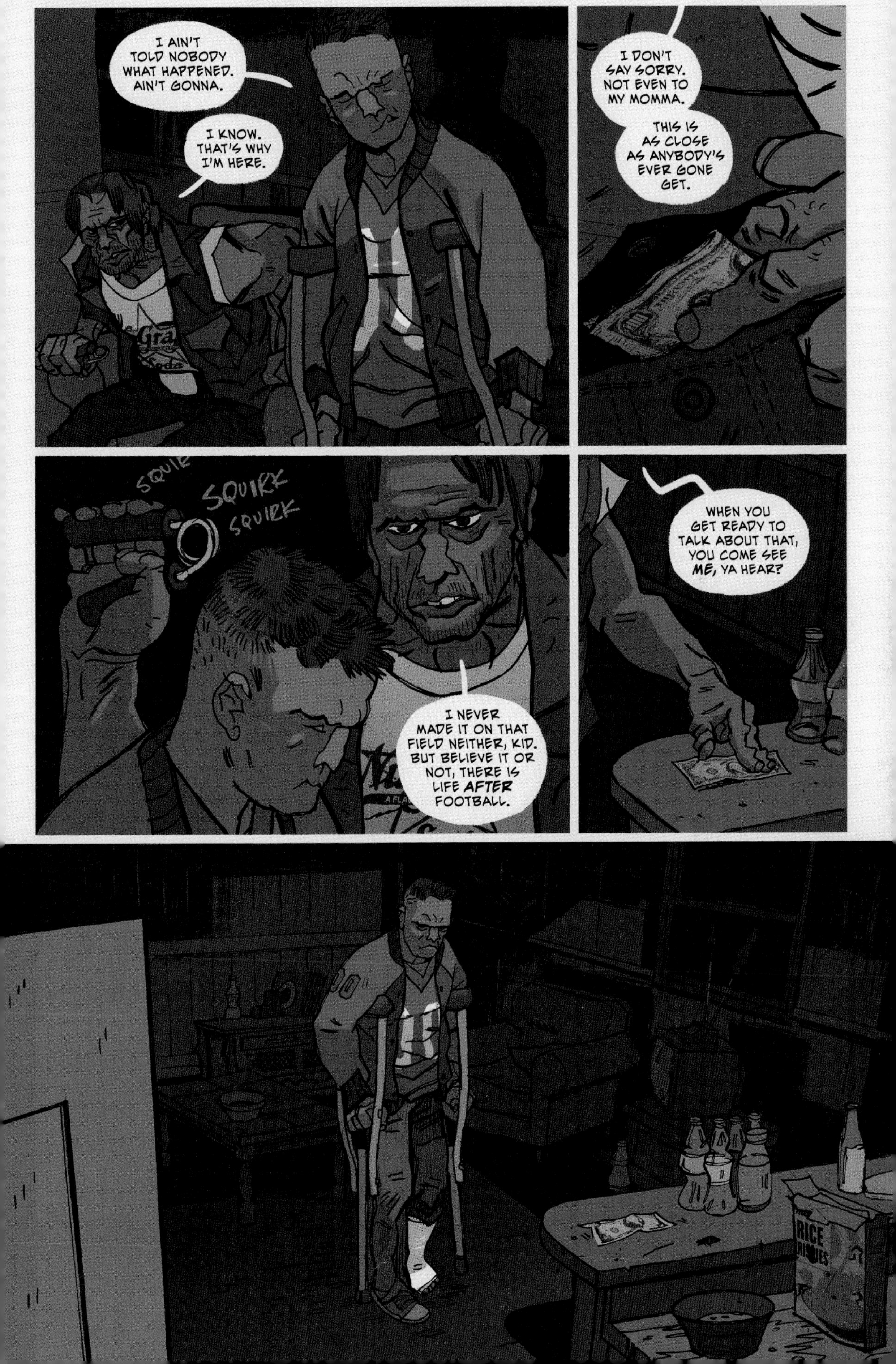
I AIN'T TOLD NOBODY WHAT HAPPENED. AIN'T GONNA.
I KNOW. THAT'S WHY I'M HERE.
I DON'T SAY SORRY. NOT EVEN TO MY MOMMA.
THIS IS AS CLOSE AS ANYBODY'S EVER GONE GET.
SQUIRK
SQUIRK
SQUIRK
I NEVER MADE IT ON THAT FIELD NEITHER, KID. BUT BELIEVE IT OR NOT, THERE IS LIFE AFTER FOOTBALL.
WHEN YOU GET READY TO TALK ABOUT THAT, YOU COME SEE ME, YA HEAR?
RICE

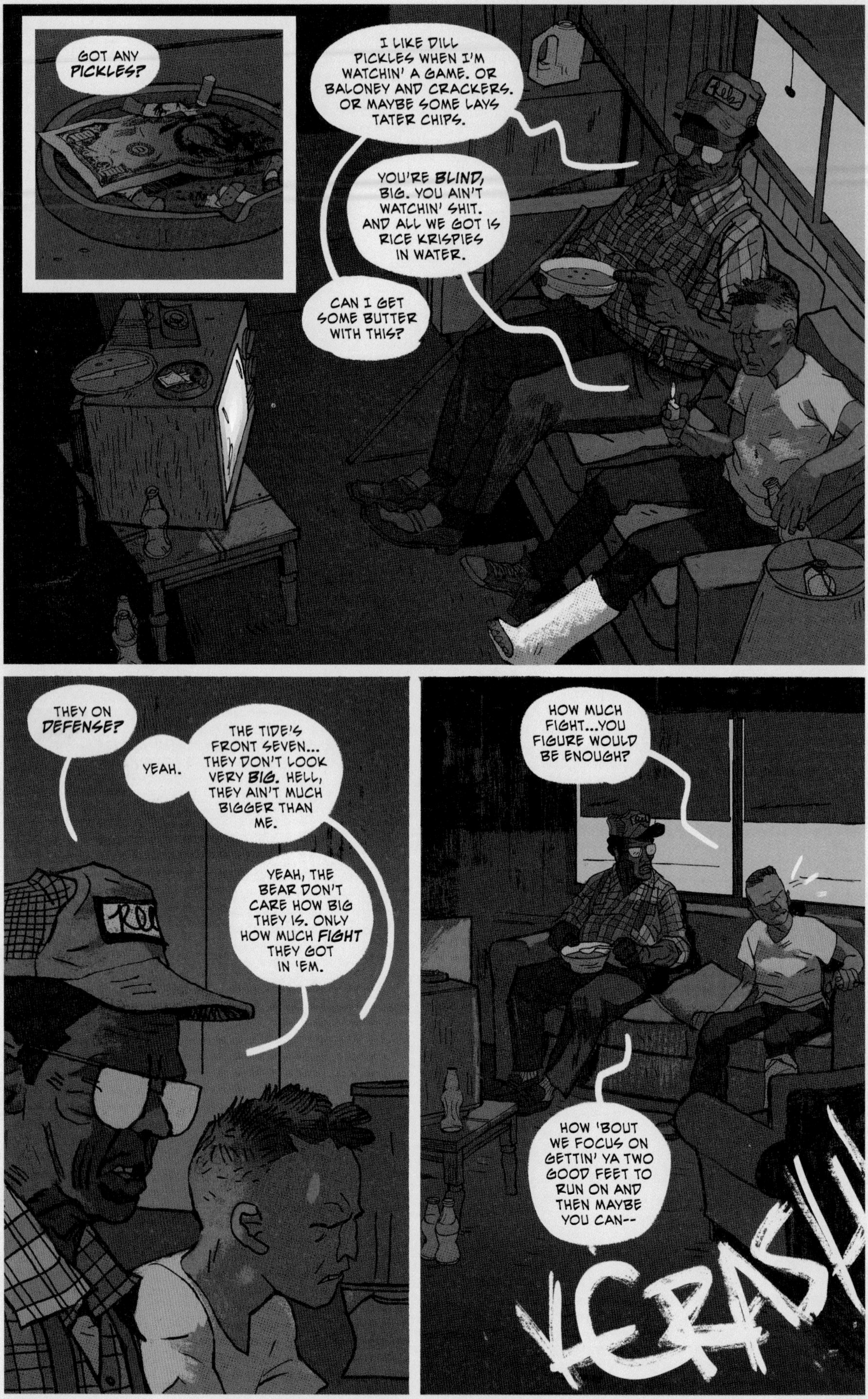
GOT ANY *PICKLES?*
I LIKE DILL PICKLES WHEN I'M WATCHIN' A GAME. OR BALONEY AND CRACKERS. OR MAYBE SOME LAYS TATER CHIPS.
YOU'RE **BLIND,** BIG. YOU AIN'T WATCHIN' SHIT. AND ALL WE GOT IS RICE KRISPIES IN WATER.
CAN I GET SOME BUTTER WITH THIS?
THEY ON *DEFENSE?*
YEAH.
THE TIDE'S FRONT SEVEN... THEY DON'T LOOK VERY **BIG.** HELL, THEY AIN'T MUCH BIGGER THAN ME.
YEAH, THE BEAR DON'T CARE HOW BIG THEY IS. ONLY HOW MUCH **FIGHT** THEY GOT IN 'EM.
HOW MUCH FIGHT...YOU FIGURE WOULD BE ENOUGH?
HOW 'BOUT WE FOCUS ON GETTIN' YA TWO GOOD FEET TO RUN ON AND THEN MAYBE YOU CAN--
KCRASH

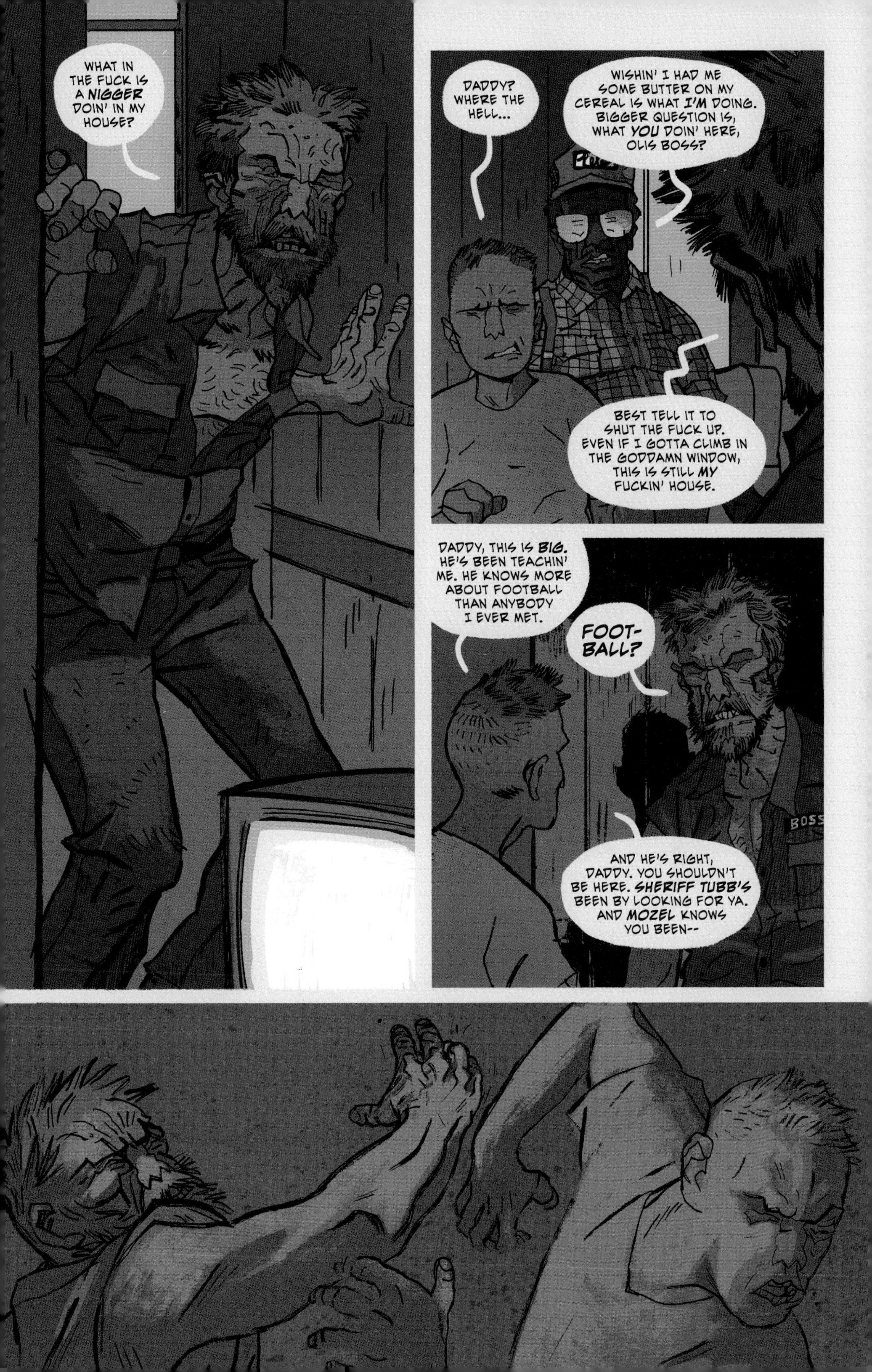
WHAT IN THE FUCK IS A NIGGER DOIN' IN MY HOUSE?
DADDY? WHERE THE HELL...
WISHIN' I HAD ME SOME BUTTER ON MY CEREAL IS WHAT I'M DOING. BIGGER QUESTION IS, WHAT YOU DOIN' HERE, OLIS BOSS?
BEST TELL IT TO SHUT THE FUCK UP. EVEN IF I GOTTA CLIMB IN THE GODDAMN WINDOW, THIS IS STILL MY FUCKIN' HOUSE.
DADDY, THIS IS BIG. HE'S BEEN TEACHIN' ME. HE KNOWS MORE ABOUT FOOTBALL THAN ANYBODY I EVER MET.
FOOT-BALL?
BOSS
AND HE'S RIGHT, DADDY. YOU SHOULDN'T BE HERE. SHERIFF TUBB'S BEEN BY LOOKING FOR YA. AND MOZEL KNOWS YOU BEEN--

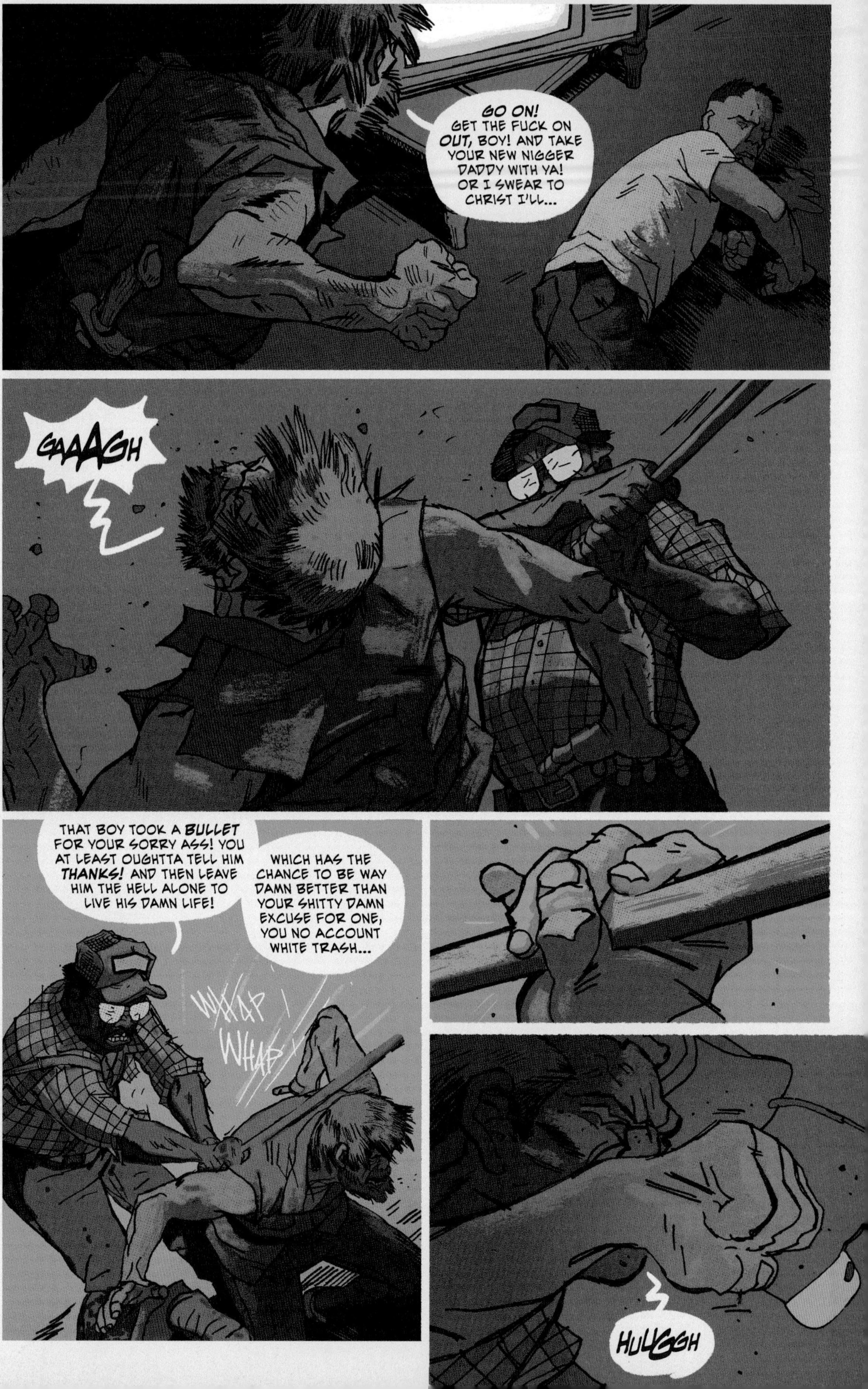
GO ON! GET THE FUCK ON OUT, BOY! AND TAKE YOUR NEW NIGGER DADDY WITH YA! OR I SWEAR TO CHRIST I'LL...
GAAAGH
THAT BOY TOOK A BULLET FOR YOUR SORRY ASS! YOU AT LEAST OUGHTTA TELL HIM THANKS! AND THEN LEAVE HIM THE HELL ALONE TO LIVE HIS DAMN LIFE!
WHICH HAS THE CHANCE TO BE WAY DAMN BETTER THAN YOUR SHITTY DAMN EXCUSE FOR ONE, YOU NO ACCOUNT WHITE TRASH...
WHAP
WHAP
HULGGH

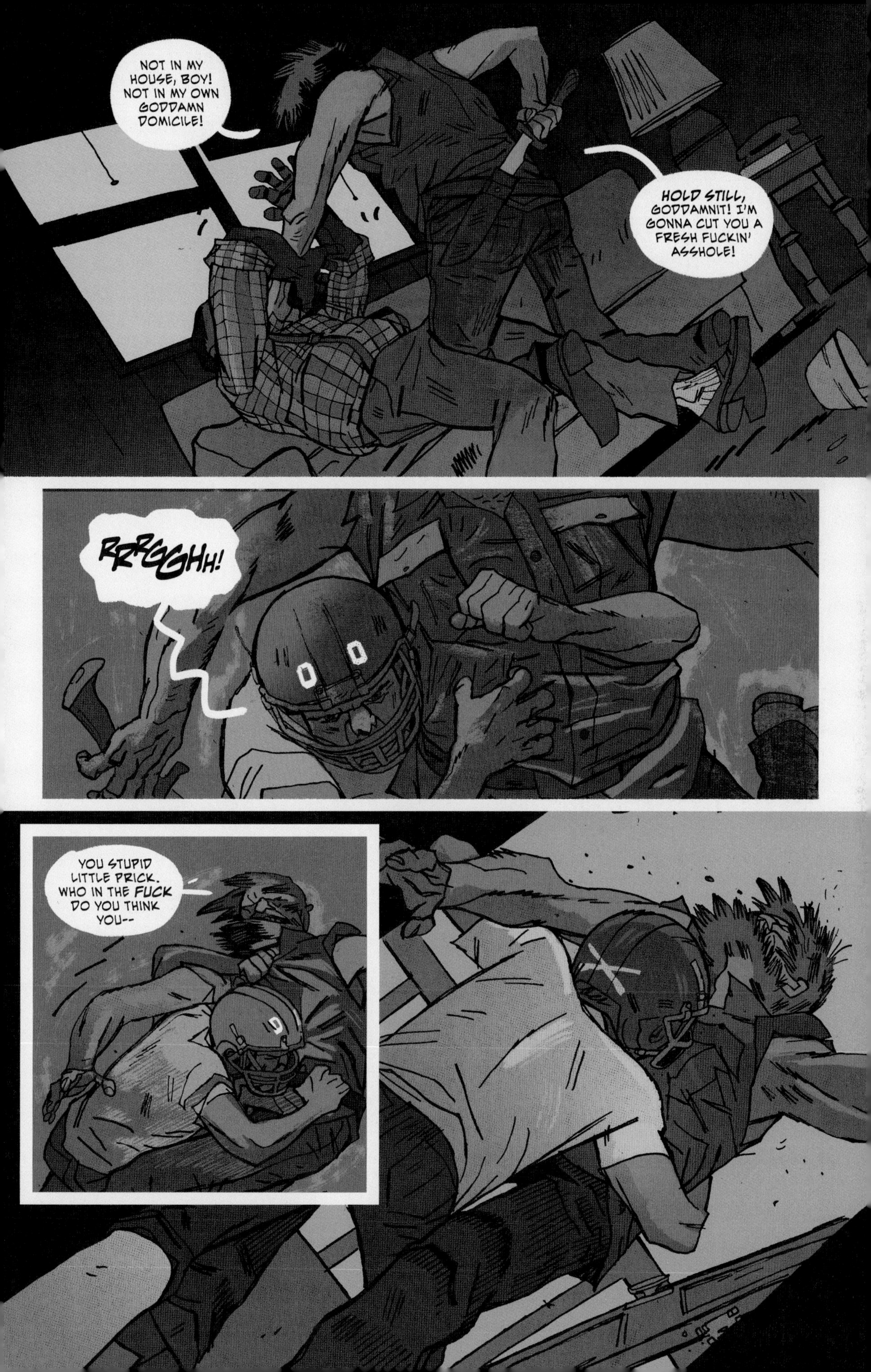
NOT IN MY HOUSE, BOY! NOT IN MY OWN GODDAMN DOMICILE!
HOLD STILL, GODDAMNIT! I'M GONNA CUT YOU A FRESH FUCKIN' ASSHOLE!
RRRGGHH!
YOU STUPID LITTLE PRICK. WHO IN THE FUCK DO YOU THINK YOU--

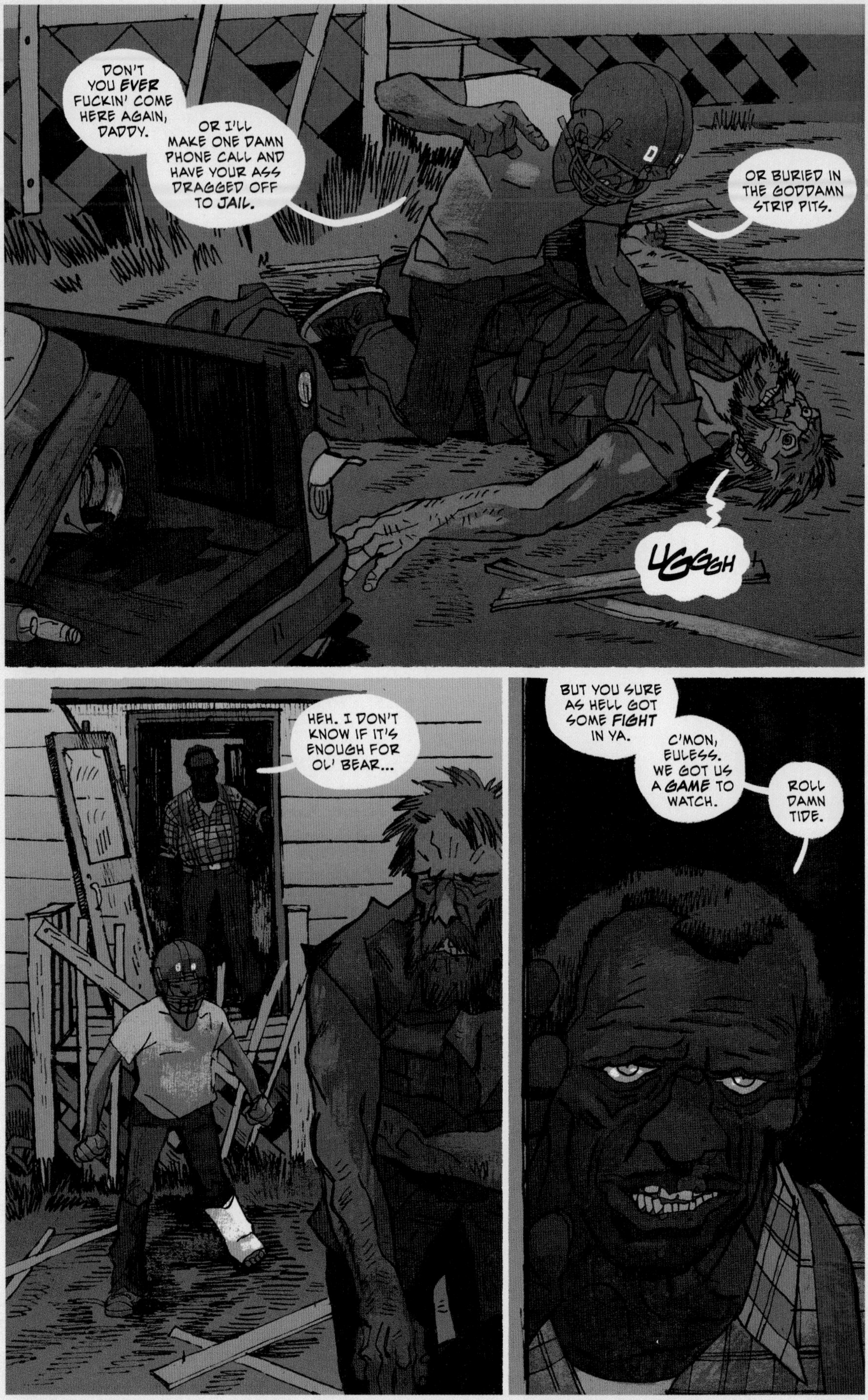
DON'T YOU EVER FUCKIN' COME HERE AGAIN, DADDY.
OR I'LL MAKE ONE DAMN PHONE CALL AND HAVE YOUR ASS DRAGGED OFF TO JAIL.
OR BURIED IN THE GODDAMN STRIP PITS.
UGGGH
HEH. I DON'T KNOW IF IT'S ENOUGH FOR OL' BEAR...
BUT YOU SURE AS HELL GOT SOME FIGHT IN YA.
C'MON, EULESS. WE GOT US A GAME TO WATCH.
ROLL DAMN TIDE.

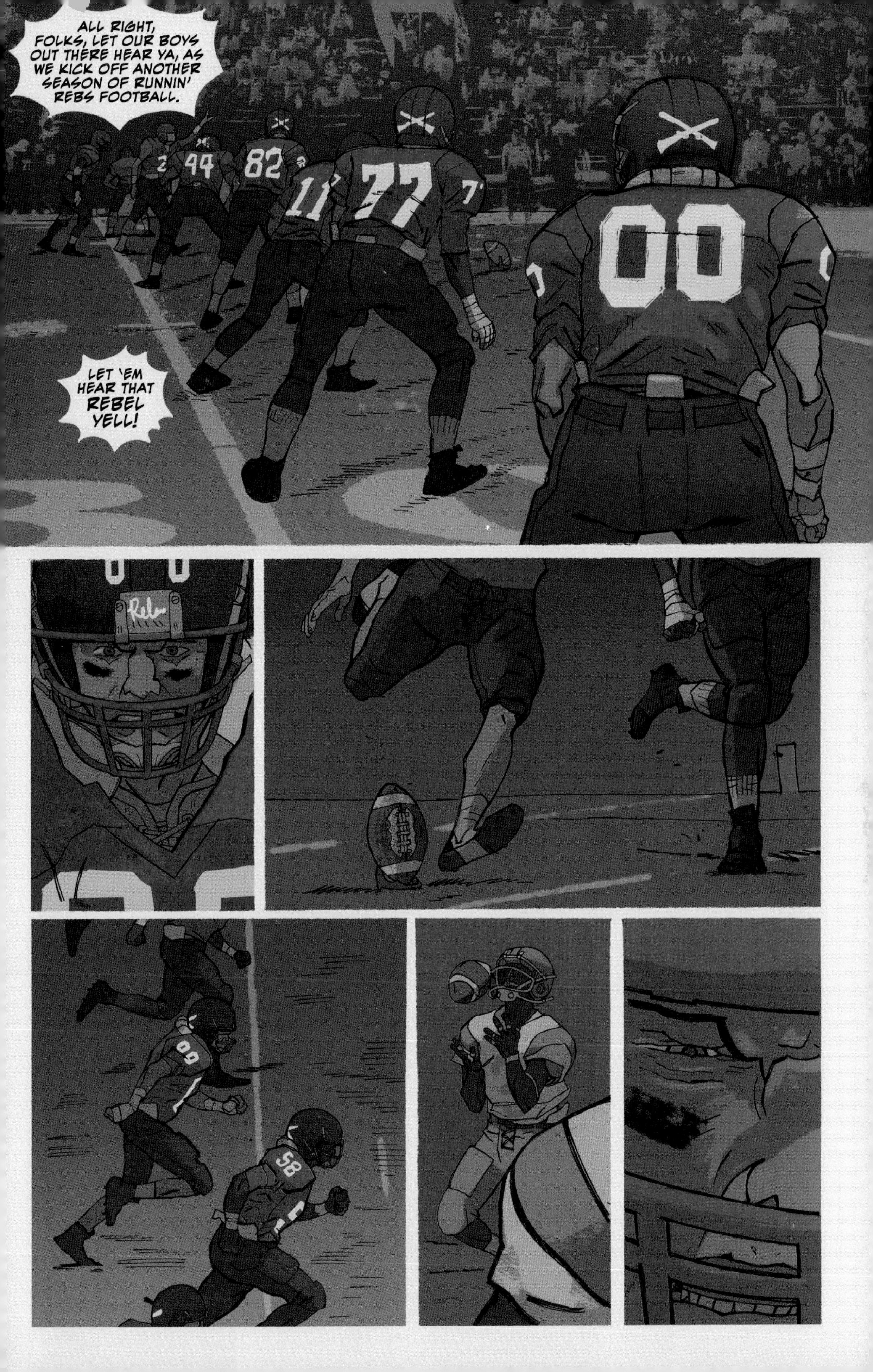
ALL RIGHT, FOLKS, LET OUR BOYS OUT THERE HEAR YA, AS WE KICK OFF ANOTHER SEASON OF RUNNIN' REBS FOOTBALL.
LET 'EM HEAR THAT REBEL YELL!

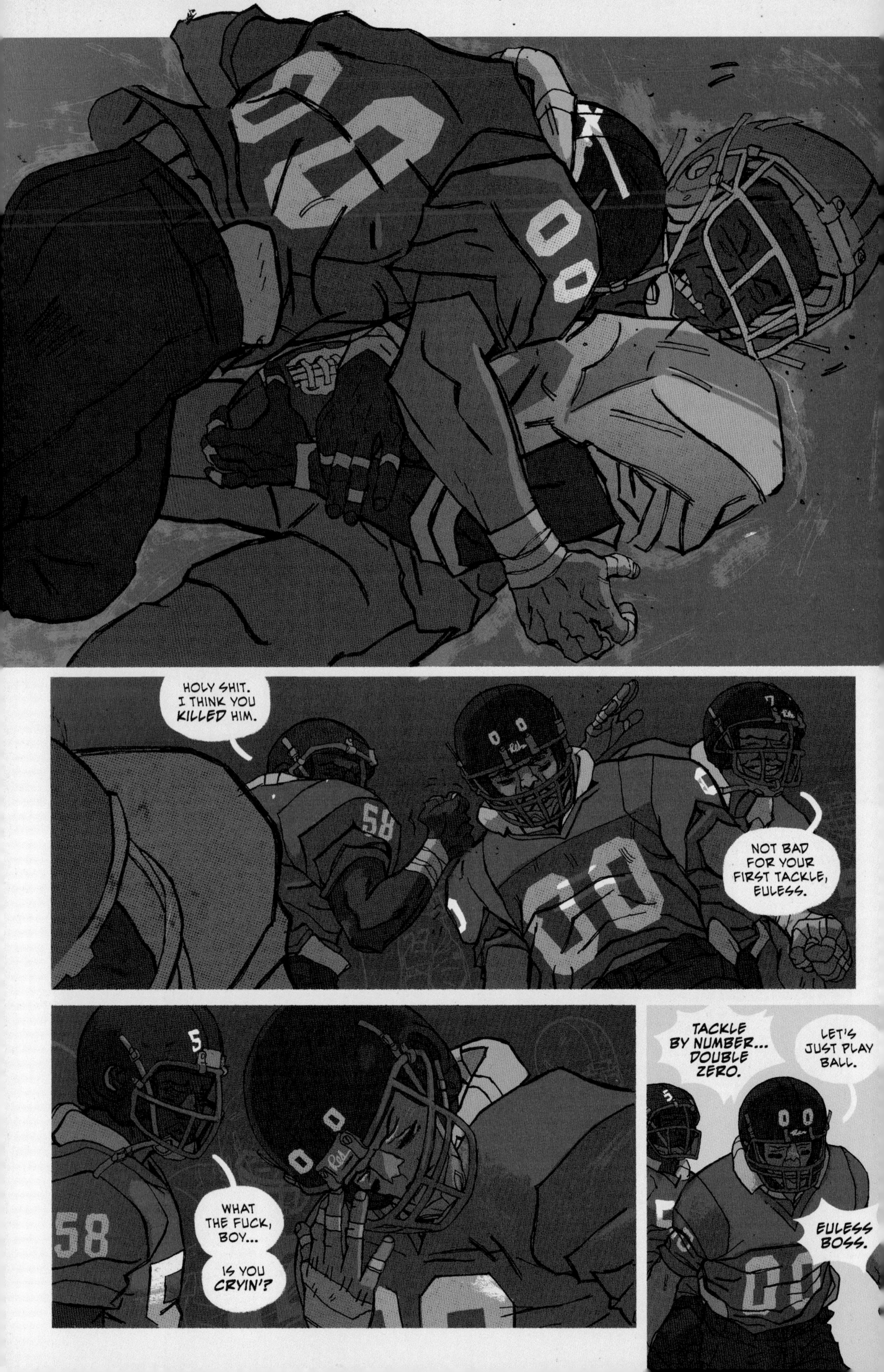
HOLY SHIT. I THINK YOU KILLED HIM.
NOT BAD FOR YOUR FIRST TACKLE, EULESS.
WHAT THE FUCK, BOY...
IS YOU CRYIN'?
TACKLE BY NUMBER... DOUBLE ZERO.
LET'S JUST PLAY BALL.
EULESS BOSS.

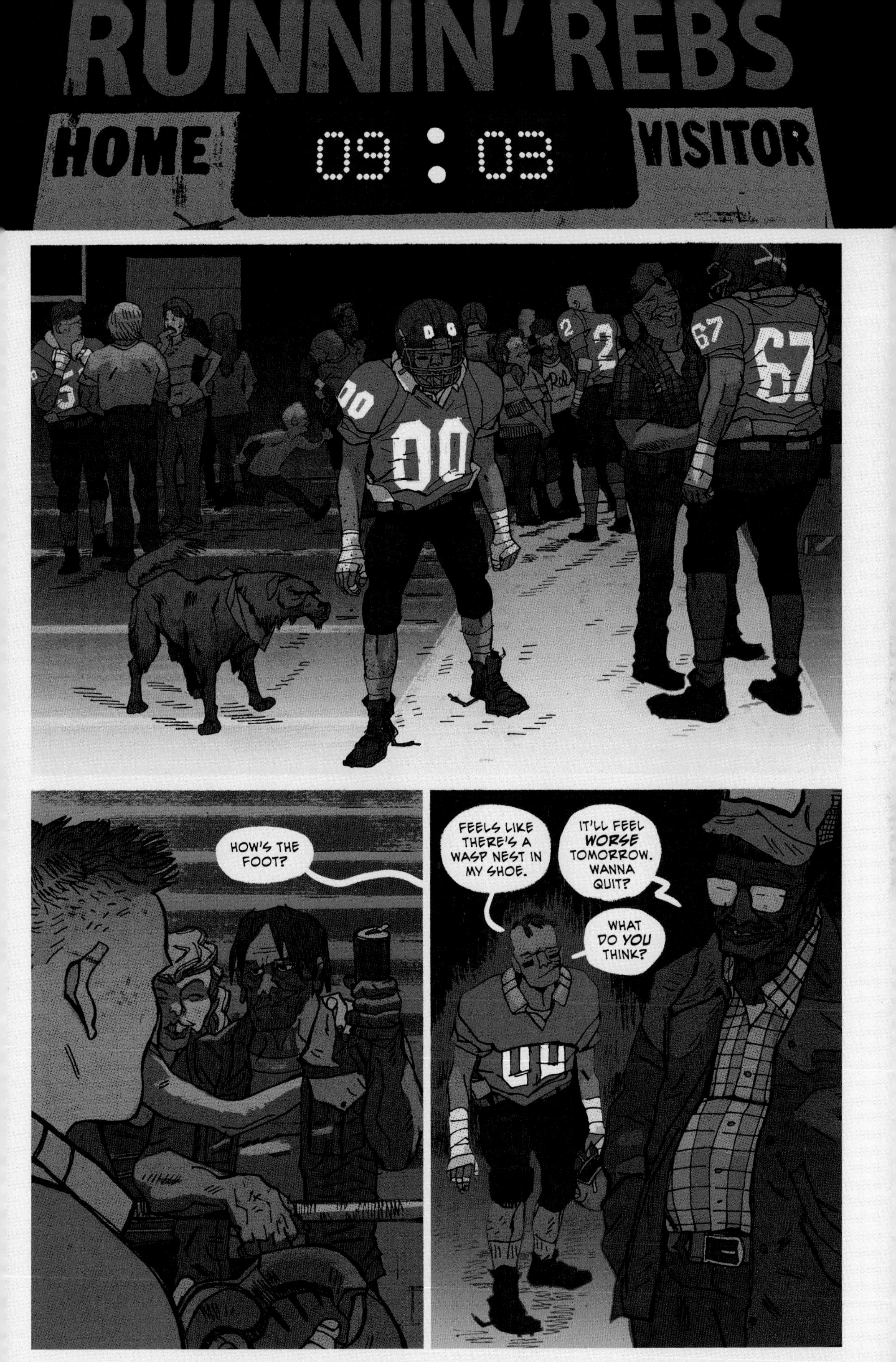
RUNNIN' REBS
HOME
09 : 03
VISITOR
HOW'S THE FOOT?
FEELS LIKE THERE'S A WASP NEST IN MY SHOE.
IT'LL FEEL WORSE TOMORROW. WANNA QUIT?
WHAT DO YOU THINK?

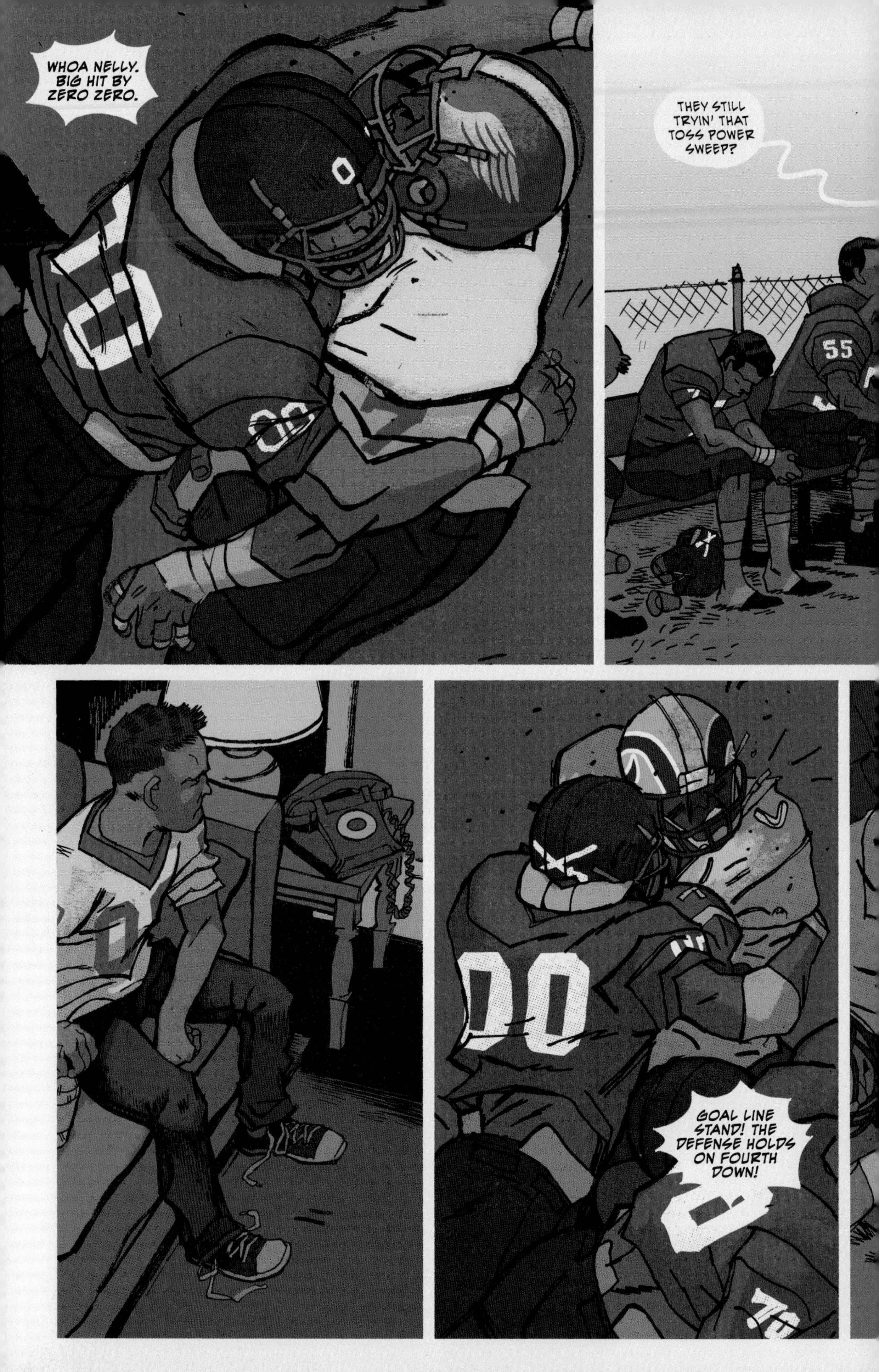
WHOA NELLY. BIG HIT BY ZERO ZERO.
THEY STILL TRYIN' THAT TOSS POWER SWEEP?
GOAL LINE STAND! THE DEFENSE HOLDS ON FOURTH DOWN!

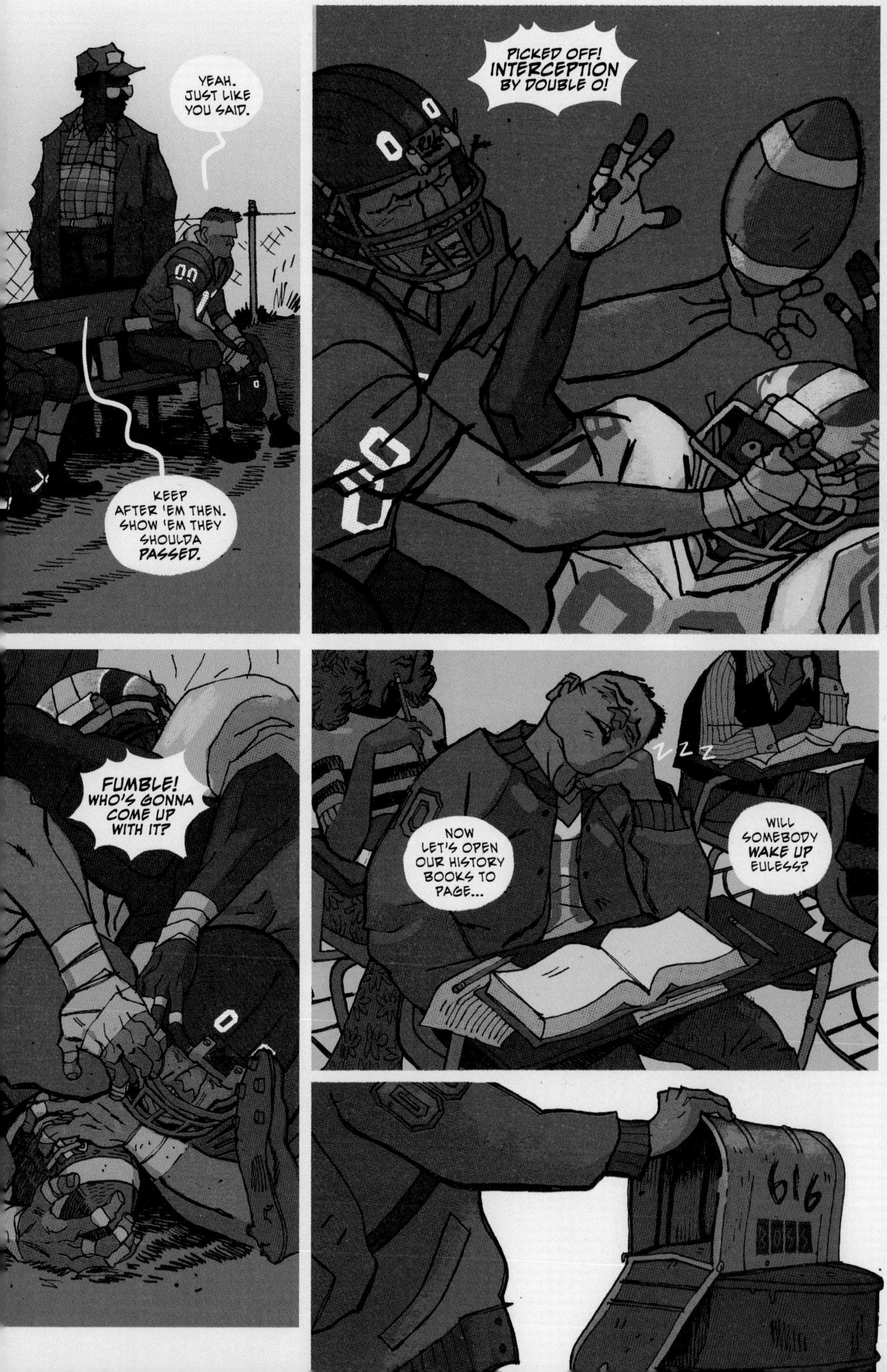
YEAH. JUST LIKE YOU SAID.
KEEP AFTER 'EM THEN. SHOW 'EM THEY SHOULDA PASSED.
PICKED OFF! INTERCEPTION BY DOUBLE O!
FUMBLE! WHO'S GONNA COME UP WITH IT?
Z Z Z
NOW LET'S OPEN OUR HISTORY BOOKS TO PAGE...
WILL SOMEBODY WAKE UP EULESS?
616

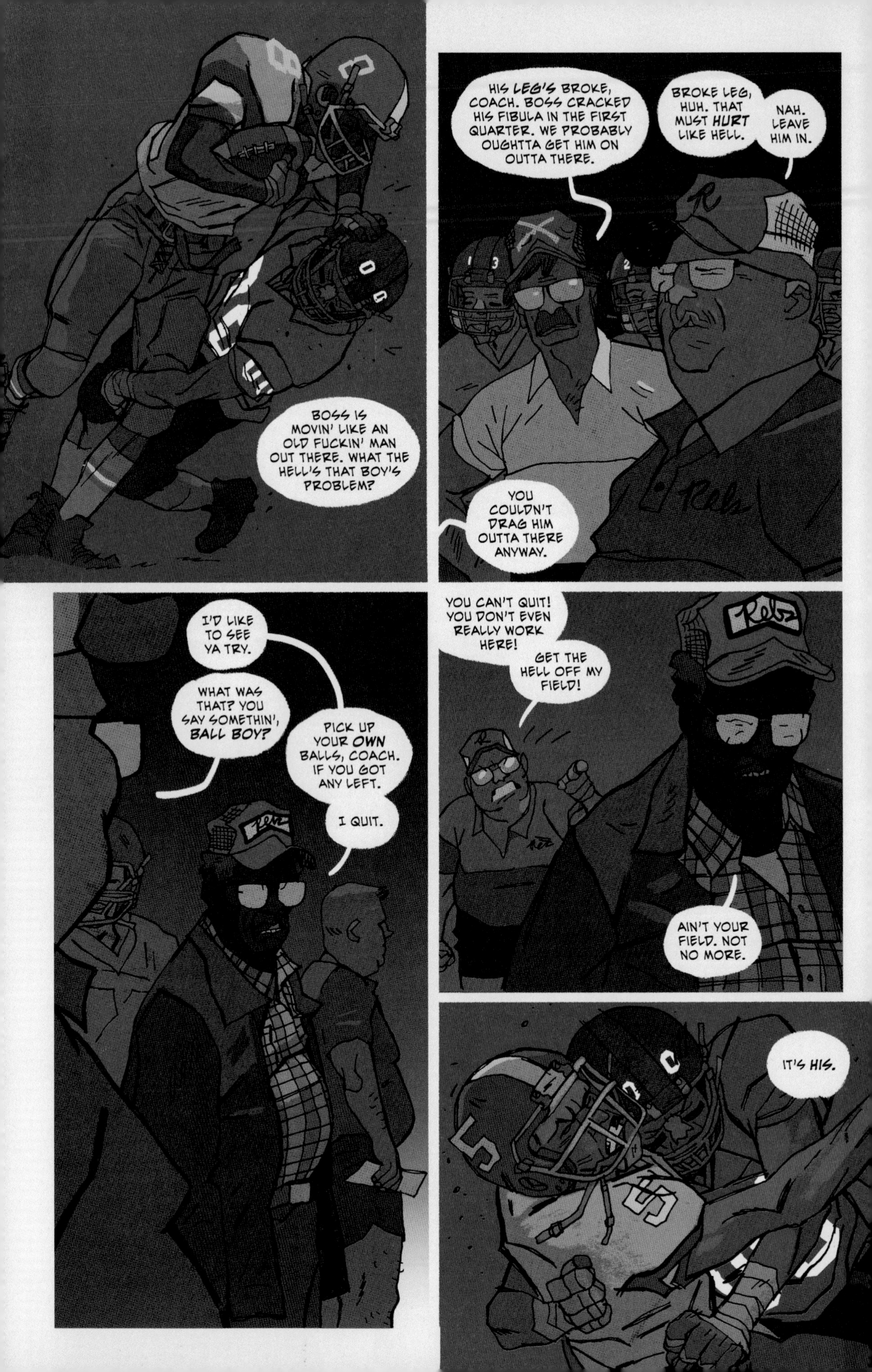
BOSS IS MOVIN' LIKE AN OLD FUCKIN' MAN OUT THERE. WHAT THE HELL'S THAT BOY'S PROBLEM?
HIS LEG'S BROKE, COACH. BOSS CRACKED HIS FIBULA IN THE FIRST QUARTER. WE PROBABLY OUGHTTA GET HIM ON OUTTA THERE.
BROKE LEG, HUH. THAT MUST HURT LIKE HELL.
NAH. LEAVE HIM IN.
YOU COULDN'T DRAG HIM OUTTA THERE ANYWAY.
I'D LIKE TO SEE YA TRY.
WHAT WAS THAT? YOU SAY SOMETHIN', BALL BOY?
PICK UP YOUR OWN BALLS, COACH. IF YOU GOT ANY LEFT.
I QUIT.
YOU CAN'T QUIT! YOU DON'T EVEN REALLY WORK HERE!
GET THE HELL OFF MY FIELD!
AIN'T YOUR FIELD. NOT NO MORE.
IT'S HIS.

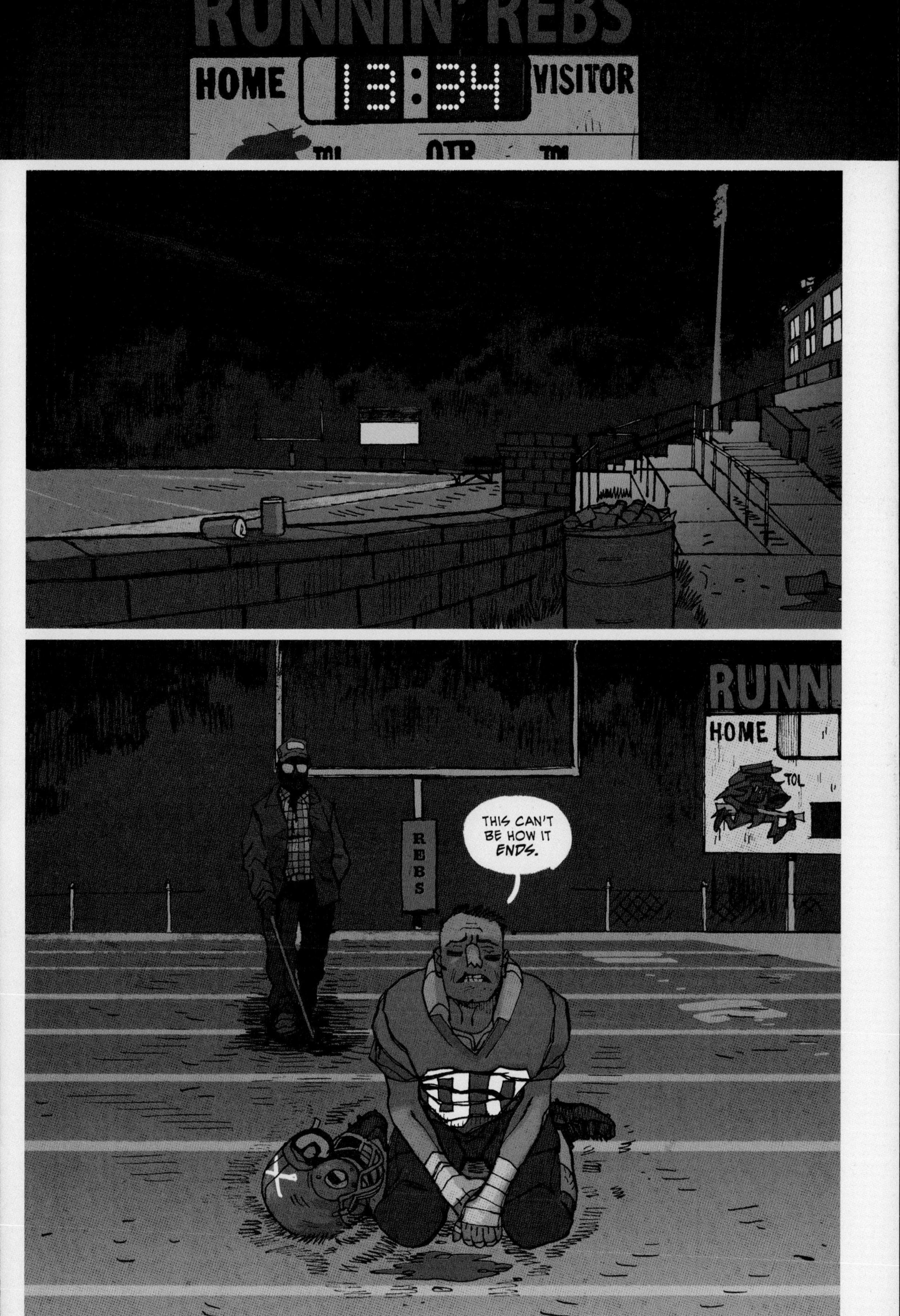
RUNNIN' REBS
HOME
13:34
VISITOR
RUNNIN
HOME
TOL
REBS
THIS CAN'T BE HOW IT ENDS.

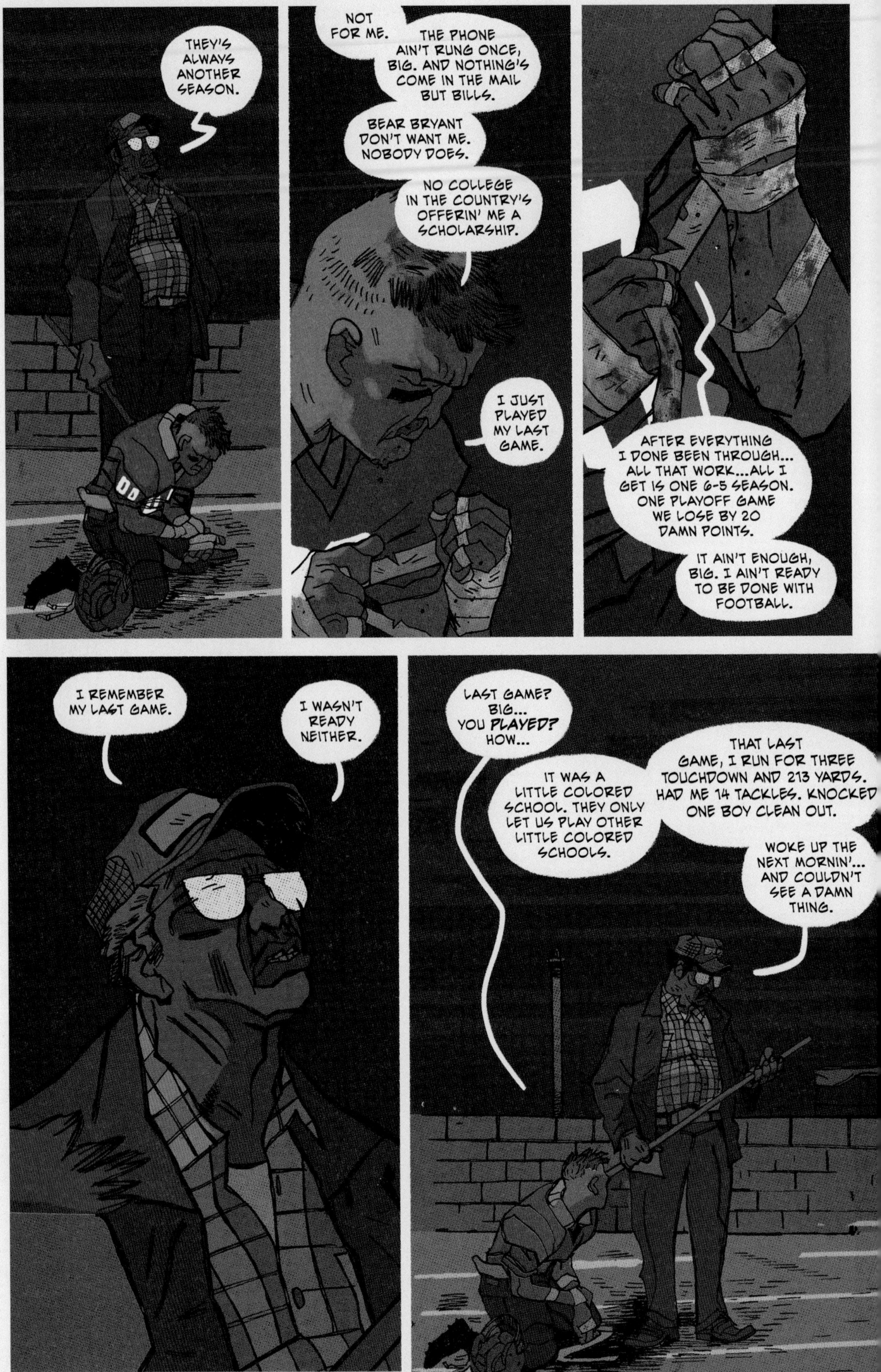
THEY'S ALWAYS ANOTHER SEASON.
NOT FOR ME.
THE PHONE AIN'T RUNG ONCE, BIG. AND NOTHING'S COME IN THE MAIL BUT BILLS.
BEAR BRYANT DON'T WANT ME. NOBODY DOES.
NO COLLEGE IN THE COUNTRY'S OFFERIN' ME A SCHOLARSHIP.
I JUST PLAYED MY LAST GAME.
AFTER EVERYTHING I DONE BEEN THROUGH... ALL THAT WORK...ALL I GET IS ONE 6-5 SEASON. ONE PLAYOFF GAME WE LOSE BY 20 DAMN POINTS.
IT AIN'T ENOUGH, BIG. I AIN'T READY TO BE DONE WITH FOOTBALL.
I REMEMBER MY LAST GAME.
I WASN'T READY NEITHER.
LAST GAME? BIG... YOU PLAYED? HOW...
IT WAS A LITTLE COLORED SCHOOL. THEY ONLY LET US PLAY OTHER LITTLE COLORED SCHOOLS.
THAT LAST GAME, I RUN FOR THREE TOUCHDOWN AND 213 YARDS. HAD ME 14 TACKLES. KNOCKED ONE BOY CLEAN OUT.
WOKE UP THE NEXT MORNIN'... AND COULDN'T SEE A DAMN THING.

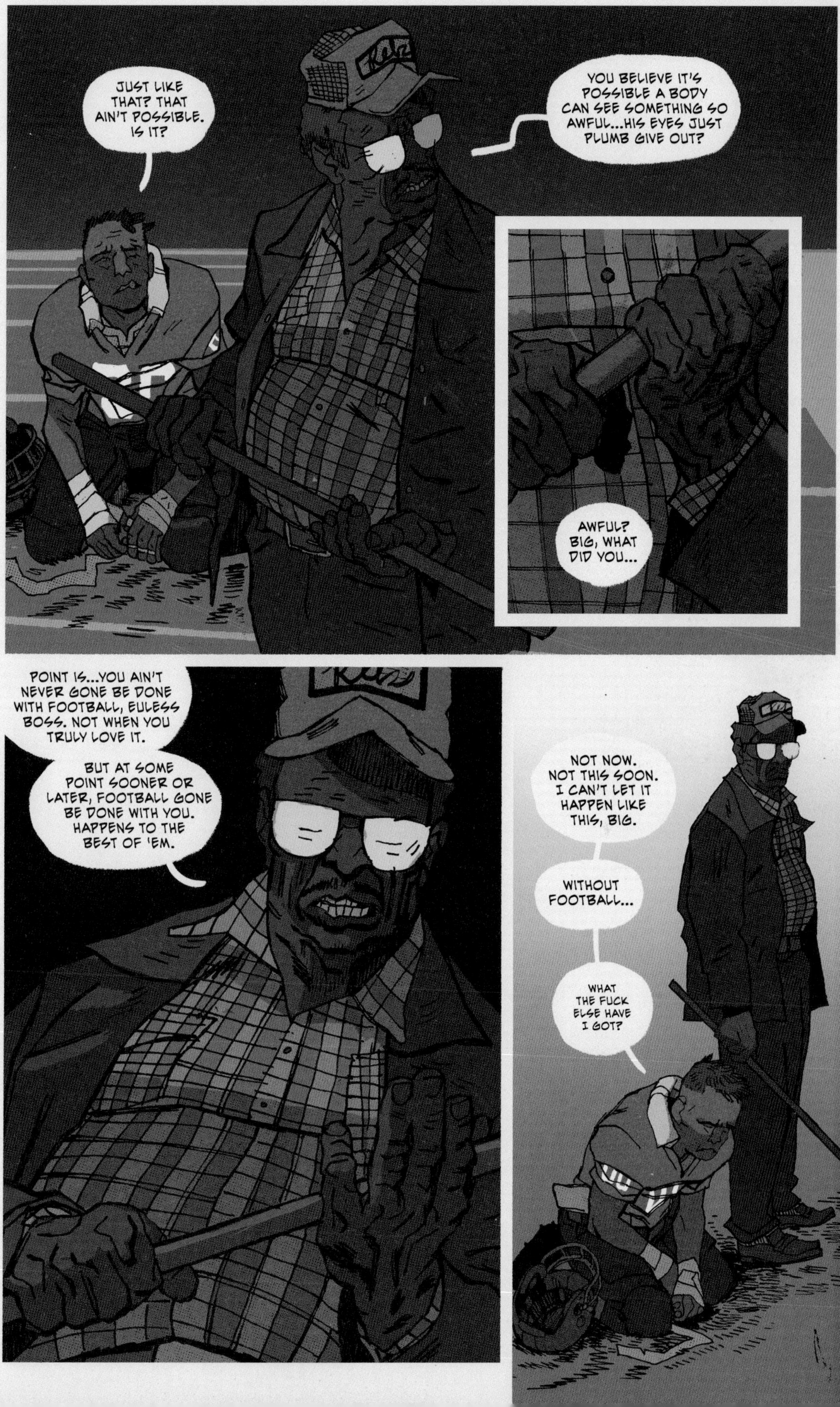
JUST LIKE THAT? THAT AIN'T POSSIBLE. IS IT?
YOU BELIEVE IT'S POSSIBLE A BODY CAN SEE SOMETHING SO AWFUL...HIS EYES JUST PLUMB GIVE OUT?
AWFUL? BIG, WHAT DID YOU...
POINT IS...YOU AIN'T NEVER GONE BE DONE WITH FOOTBALL, EULESS BOSS. NOT WHEN YOU TRULY LOVE IT.
BUT AT SOME POINT SOONER OR LATER, FOOTBALL GONE BE DONE WITH YOU. HAPPENS TO THE BEST OF 'EM.
NOT NOW. NOT THIS SOON. I CAN'T LET IT HAPPEN LIKE THIS, BIG.
WITHOUT FOOTBALL...
WHAT THE FUCK ELSE HAVE I GOT?

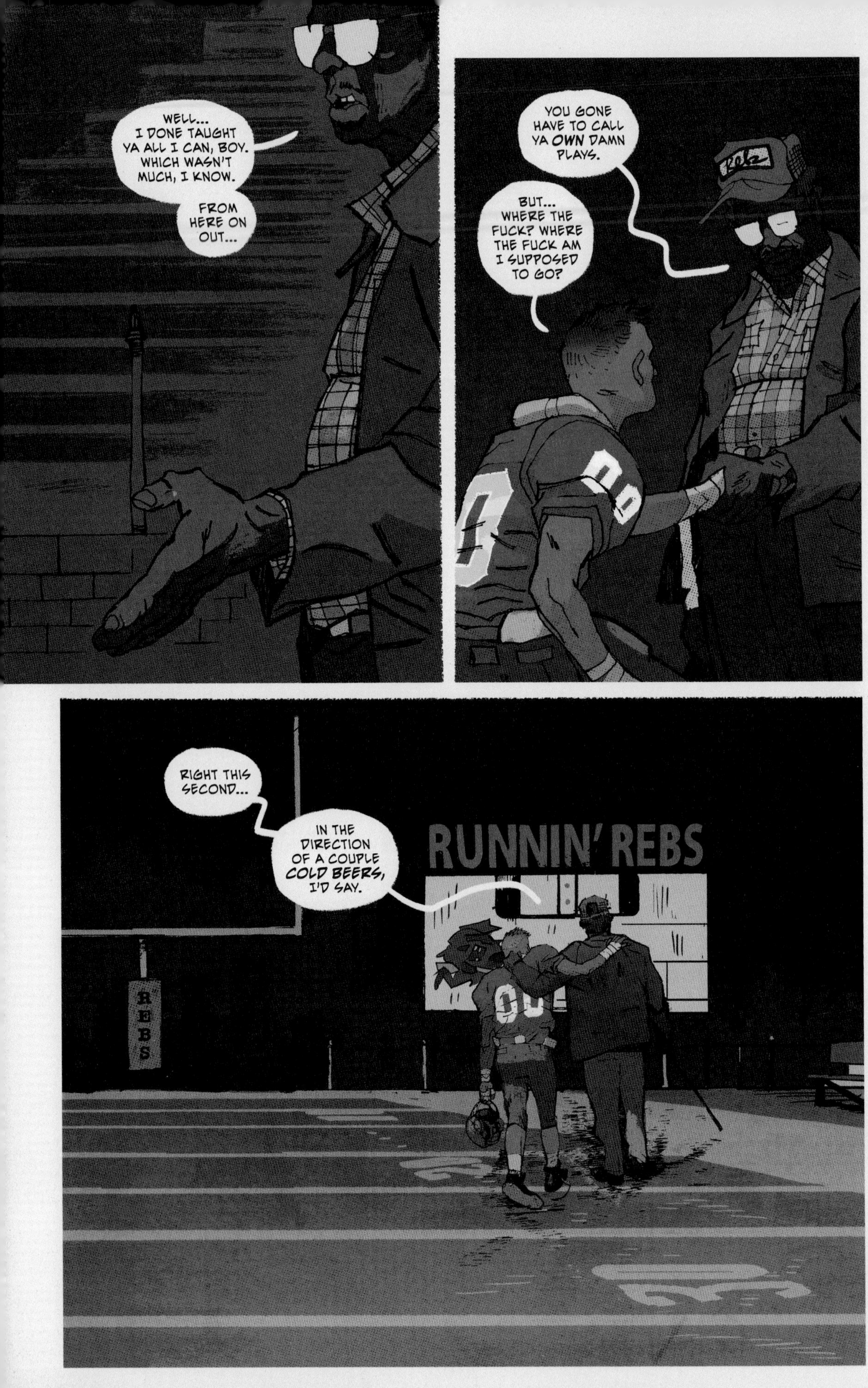
WELL... I DONE TAUGHT YA ALL I CAN, BOY. WHICH WASN'T MUCH, I KNOW.
FROM HERE ON OUT...
YOU GONE HAVE TO CALL YA OWN DAMN PLAYS.
BUT... WHERE THE FUCK? WHERE THE FUCK AM I SUPPOSED TO GO?
RIGHT THIS SECOND...
IN THE DIRECTION OF A COUPLE COLD BEERS, I'D SAY.
RUNNIN' REBS
REBS

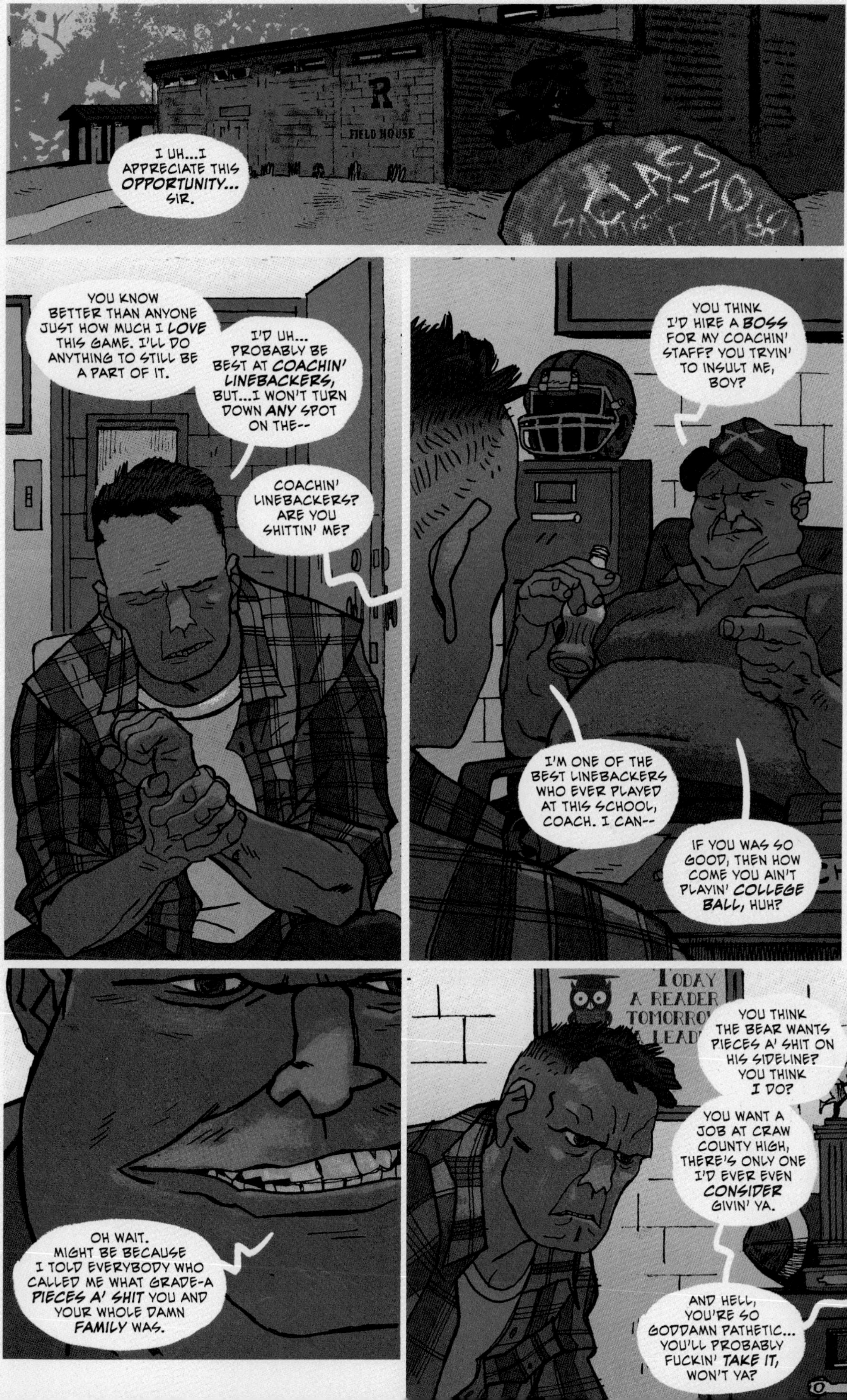
FIELD HOUSE
CLASS '70
I UH...I APPRECIATE THIS OPPORTUNITY... SIR.
YOU KNOW BETTER THAN ANYONE JUST HOW MUCH I LOVE THIS GAME. I'LL DO ANYTHING TO STILL BE A PART OF IT.
I'D UH... PROBABLY BE BEST AT COACHIN' LINEBACKERS, BUT...I WON'T TURN DOWN ANY SPOT ON THE--
COACHIN' LINEBACKERS? ARE YOU SHITTIN' ME?
YOU THINK I'D HIRE A BOSS FOR MY COACHIN' STAFF? YOU TRYIN' TO INSULT ME, BOY?
I'M ONE OF THE BEST LINEBACKERS WHO EVER PLAYED AT THIS SCHOOL, COACH. I CAN--
IF YOU WAS SO GOOD, THEN HOW COME YOU AIN'T PLAYIN' COLLEGE BALL, HUH?
OH WAIT. MIGHT BE BECAUSE I TOLD EVERYBODY WHO CALLED ME WHAT GRADE-A PIECES A' SHIT YOU AND YOUR WHOLE DAMN FAMILY WAS.
TODAY A READER TOMORROW A LEADER
YOU THINK THE BEAR WANTS PIECES A' SHIT ON HIS SIDELINE? YOU THINK I DO?
YOU WANT A JOB AT CRAW COUNTY HIGH, THERE'S ONLY ONE I'D EVER EVEN CONSIDER GIVIN' YA.
AND HELL, YOU'RE SO GODDAMN PATHETIC... YOU'LL PROBABLY FUCKIN' TAKE IT, WON'T YA?

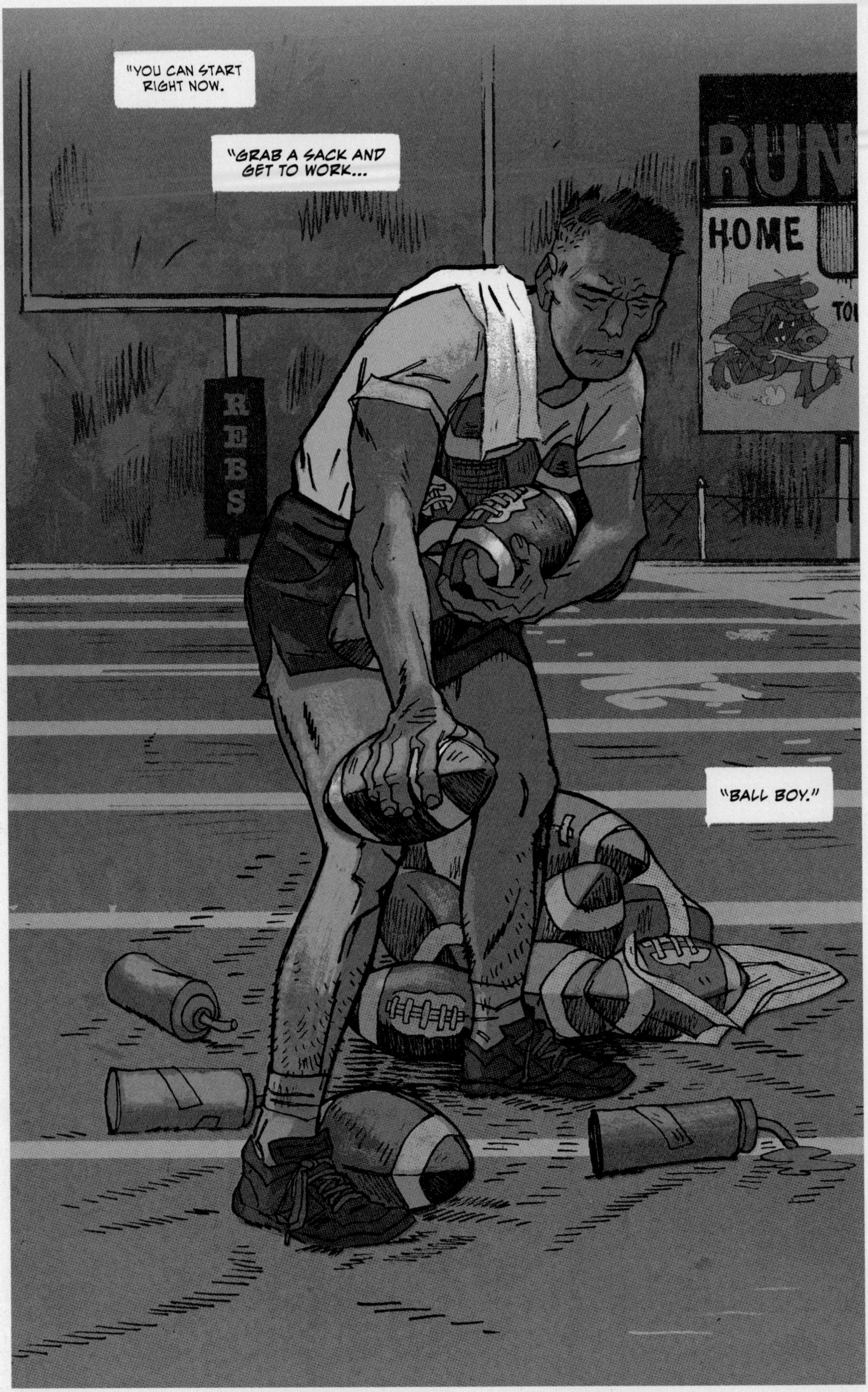
"YOU CAN START RIGHT NOW.
"GRAB A SACK AND GET TO WORK...
RUN
HOME
REBS
"BALL BOY."

Chapter 8

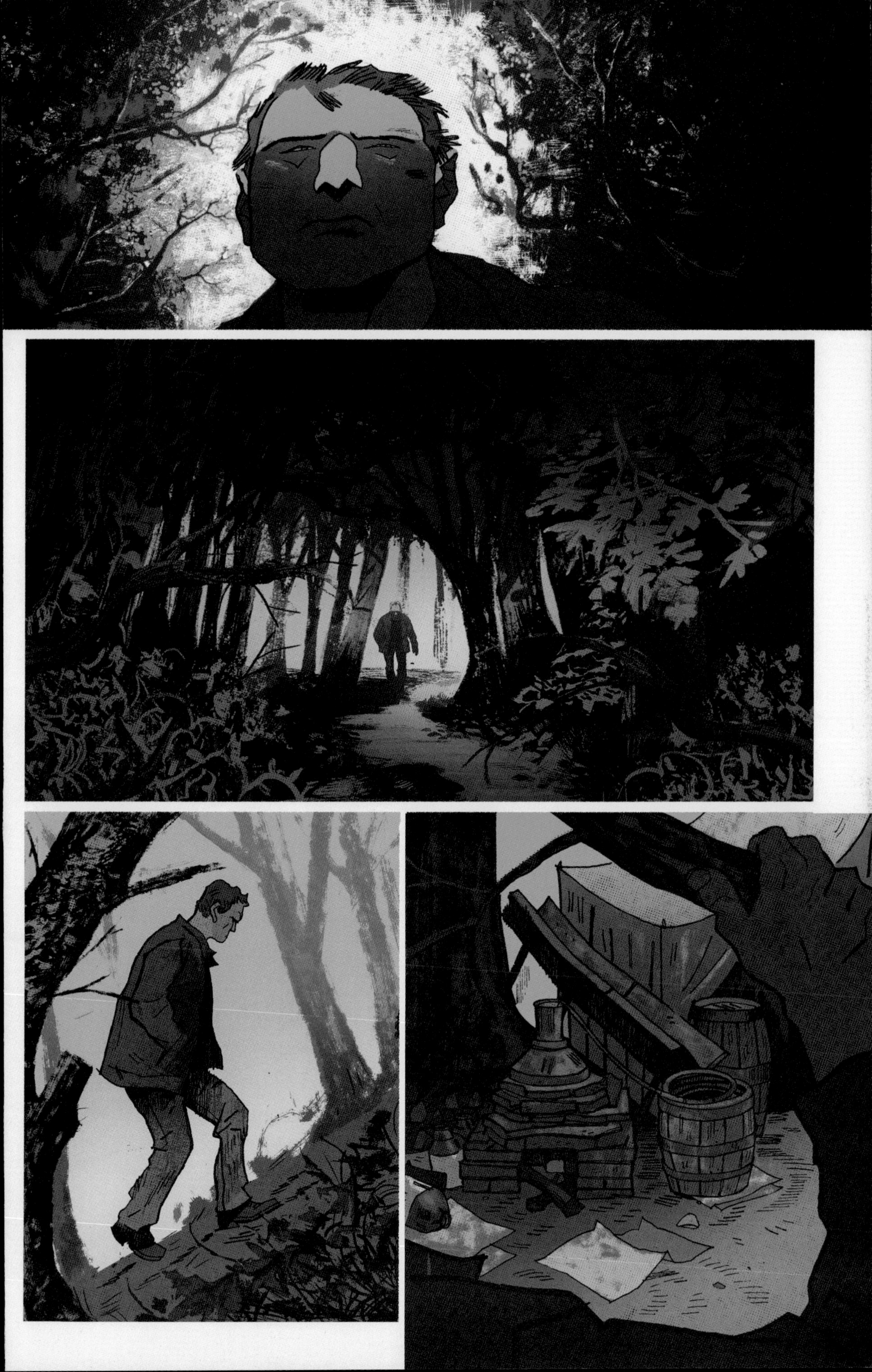

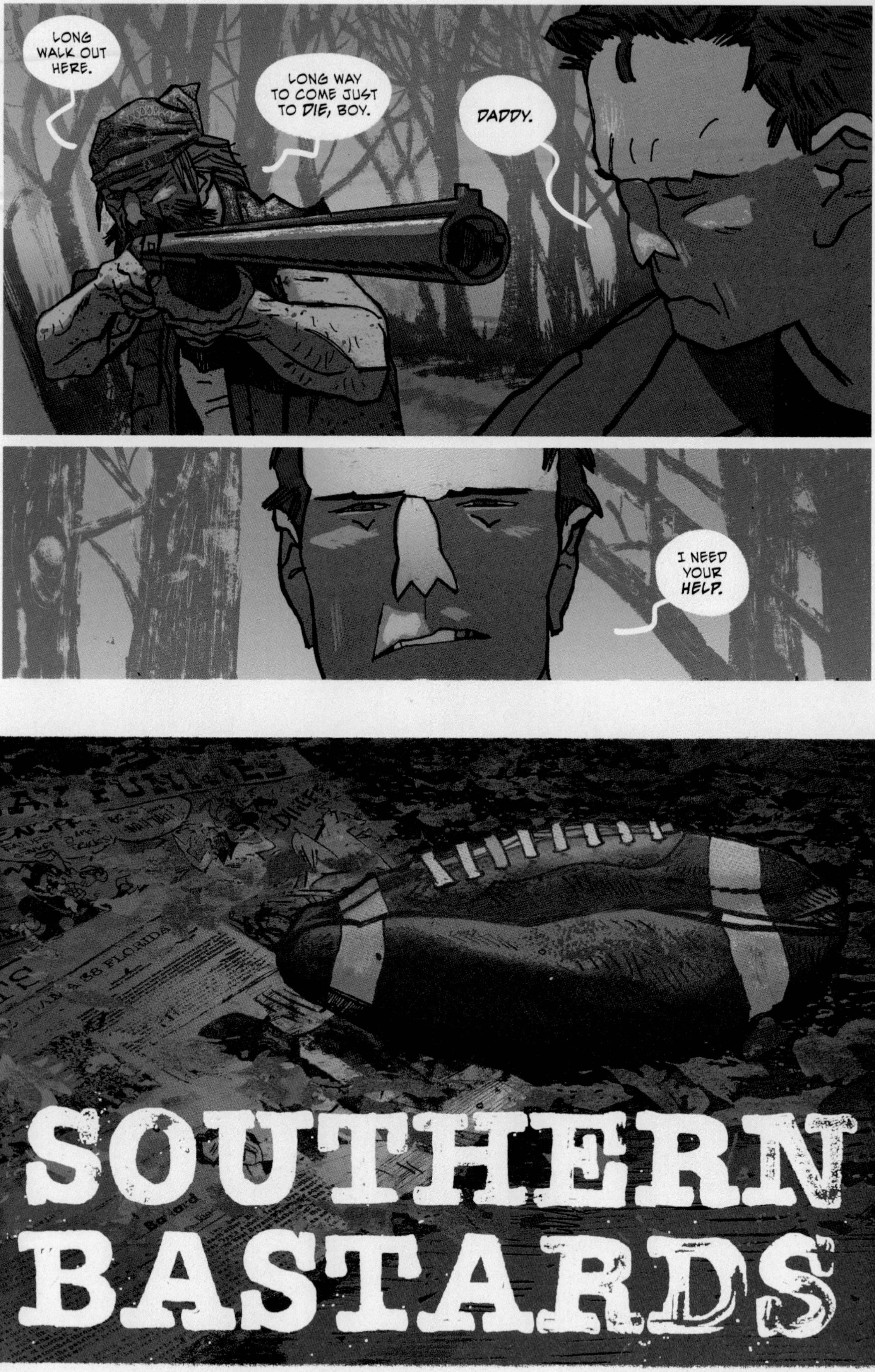
LONG WALK OUT HERE.
LONG WAY TO COME JUST TO DIE, BOY.
DADDY.
I NEED YOUR HELP.
SOUTHERN BASTARDS

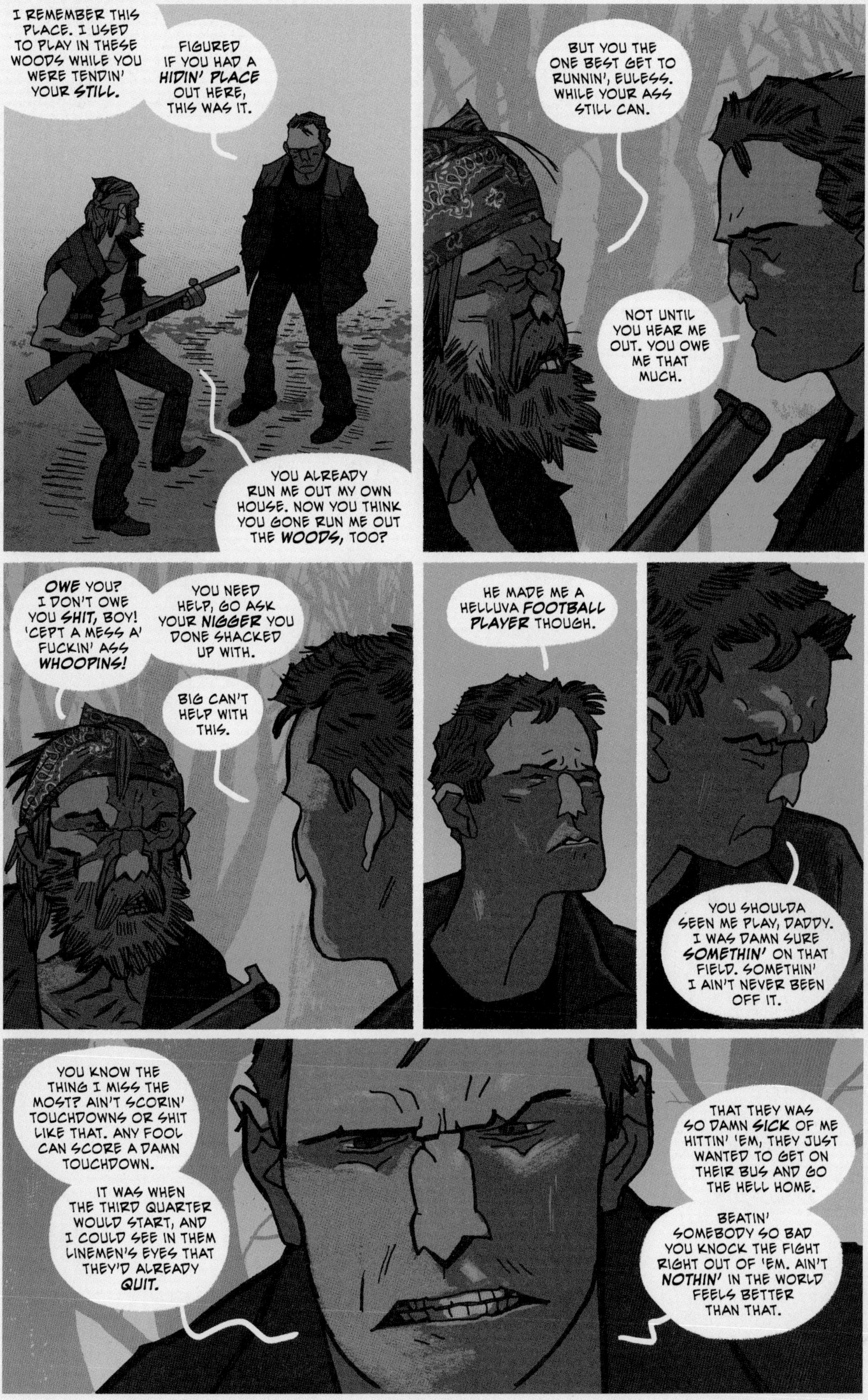
I REMEMBER THIS PLACE. I USED TO PLAY IN THESE WOODS WHILE YOU WERE TENDIN' YOUR STILL.
FIGURED IF YOU HAD A HIDIN' PLACE OUT HERE, THIS WAS IT.
YOU ALREADY RUN ME OUT MY OWN HOUSE. NOW YOU THINK YOU GONE RUN ME OUT THE WOODS, TOO?
BUT YOU THE ONE BEST GET TO RUNNIN', EULESS. WHILE YOUR ASS STILL CAN.
NOT UNTIL YOU HEAR ME OUT. YOU OWE ME THAT MUCH.
OWE YOU? I DON'T OWE YOU SHIT, BOY! 'CEPT A MESS A' FUCKIN' ASS WHOOPINS!
YOU NEED HELP, GO ASK YOUR NIGGER YOU DONE SHACKED UP WITH.
BIG CAN'T HELP WITH THIS.
HE MADE ME A HELLUVA FOOTBALL PLAYER THOUGH.
YOU SHOULDA SEEN ME PLAY, DADDY. I WAS DAMN SURE SOMETHIN' ON THAT FIELD. SOMETHIN' I AIN'T NEVER BEEN OFF IT.
YOU KNOW THE THING I MISS THE MOST? AIN'T SCORIN' TOUCHDOWNS OR SHIT LIKE THAT. ANY FOOL CAN SCORE A DAMN TOUCHDOWN.
IT WAS WHEN THE THIRD QUARTER WOULD START, AND I COULD SEE IN THEM LINEMEN'S EYES THAT THEY'D ALREADY QUIT.
THAT THEY WAS SO DAMN SICK OF ME HITTIN' 'EM, THEY JUST WANTED TO GET ON THEIR BUS AND GO THE HELL HOME.
BEATIN' SOMEBODY SO BAD YOU KNOCK THE FIGHT RIGHT OUT OF 'EM. AIN'T NOTHIN' IN THE WORLD FEELS BETTER THAN THAT.

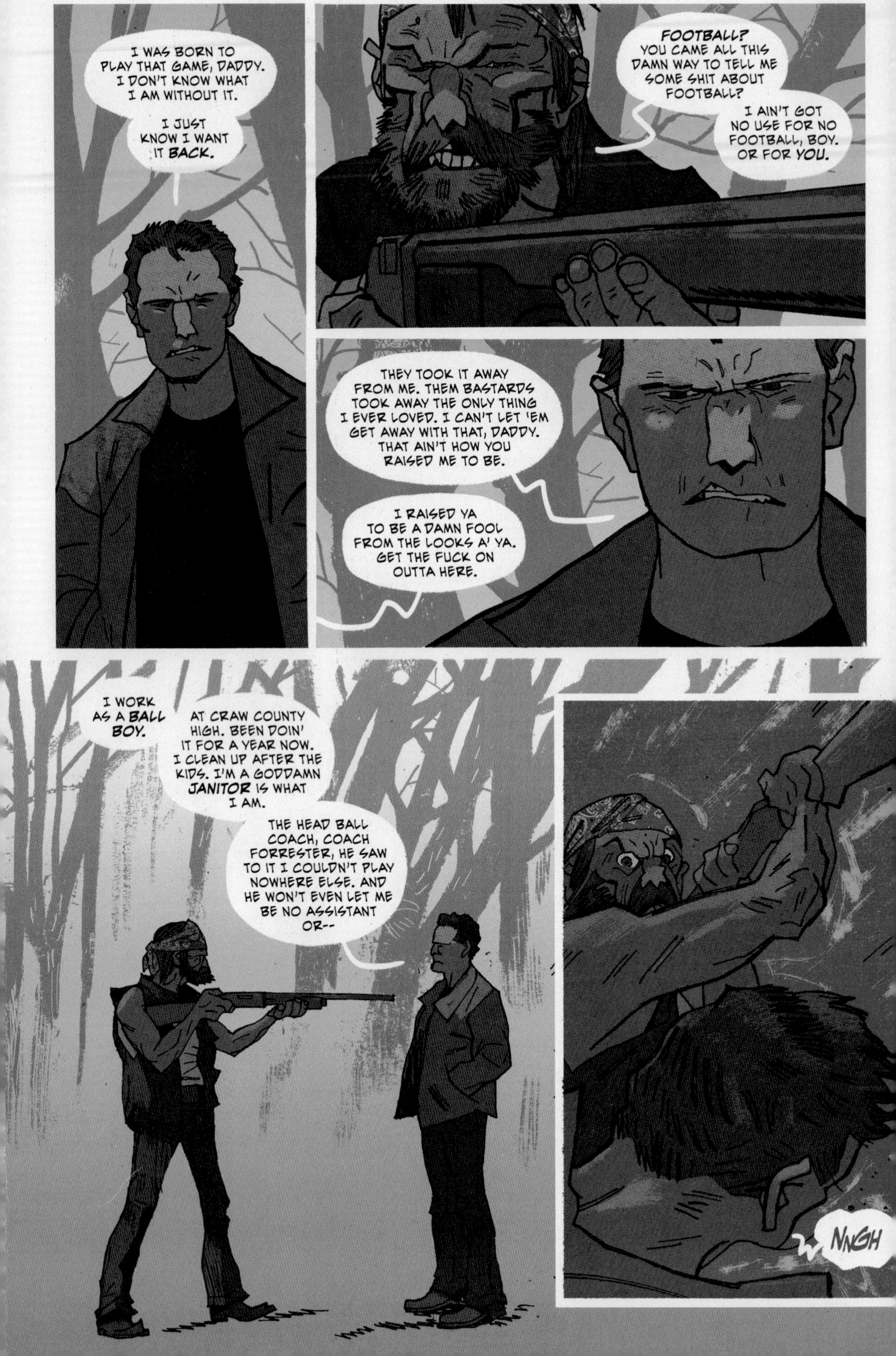
I WAS BORN TO PLAY THAT GAME, DADDY. I DON'T KNOW WHAT I AM WITHOUT IT.
I JUST KNOW I WANT IT BACK.
FOOTBALL? YOU CAME ALL THIS DAMN WAY TO TELL ME SOME SHIT ABOUT FOOTBALL?
I AIN'T GOT NO USE FOR NO FOOTBALL, BOY. OR FOR YOU.
THEY TOOK IT AWAY FROM ME. THEM BASTARDS TOOK AWAY THE ONLY THING I EVER LOVED. I CAN'T LET 'EM GET AWAY WITH THAT, DADDY. THAT AIN'T HOW YOU RAISED ME TO BE.
I RAISED YA TO BE A DAMN FOOL FROM THE LOOKS A' YA. GET THE FUCK ON OUTTA HERE.
I WORK AS A BALL BOY.
AT CRAW COUNTY HIGH. BEEN DOIN' IT FOR A YEAR NOW. I CLEAN UP AFTER THE KIDS. I'M A GODDAMN JANITOR IS WHAT I AM.
THE HEAD BALL COACH, COACH FORRESTER, HE SAW TO IT I COULDN'T PLAY NOWHERE ELSE. AND HE WON'T EVEN LET ME BE NO ASSISTANT OR--
NNGH

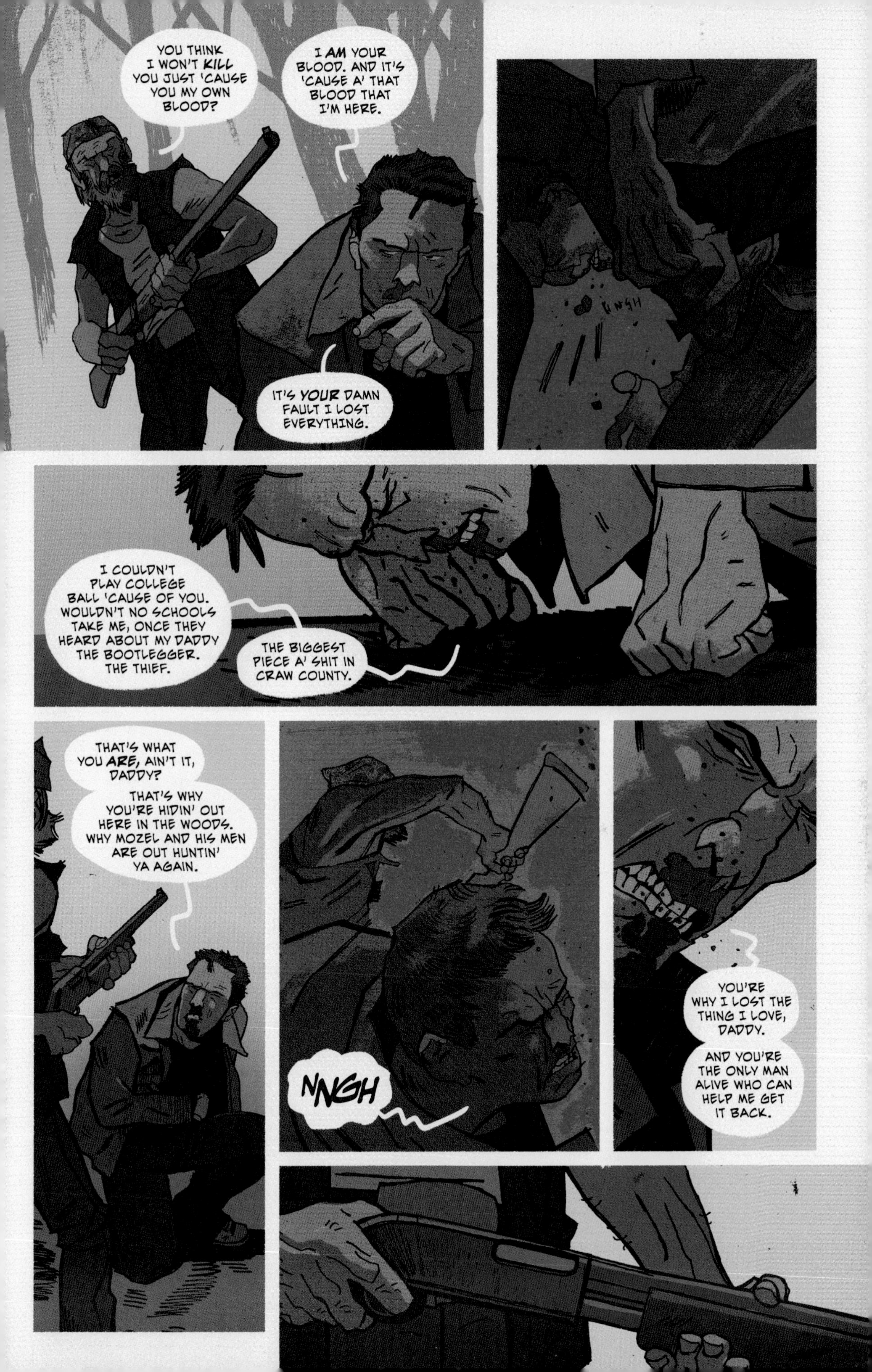
YOU THINK I WON'T KILL YOU JUST 'CAUSE YOU MY OWN BLOOD?
I AM YOUR BLOOD. AND IT'S 'CAUSE A' THAT BLOOD THAT I'M HERE.
IT'S YOUR DAMN FAULT I LOST EVERYTHING.
NNGH
I COULDN'T PLAY COLLEGE BALL 'CAUSE OF YOU. WOULDN'T NO SCHOOLS TAKE ME, ONCE THEY HEARD ABOUT MY DADDY THE BOOTLEGGER. THE THIEF.
THE BIGGEST PIECE A' SHIT IN CRAW COUNTY.
THAT'S WHAT YOU ARE, AIN'T IT, DADDY?
THAT'S WHY YOU'RE HIDIN' OUT HERE IN THE WOODS. WHY MOZEL AND HIS MEN ARE OUT HUNTIN' YA AGAIN.
NNGH
YOU'RE WHY I LOST THE THING I LOVE, DADDY.
AND YOU'RE THE ONLY MAN ALIVE WHO CAN HELP ME GET IT BACK.

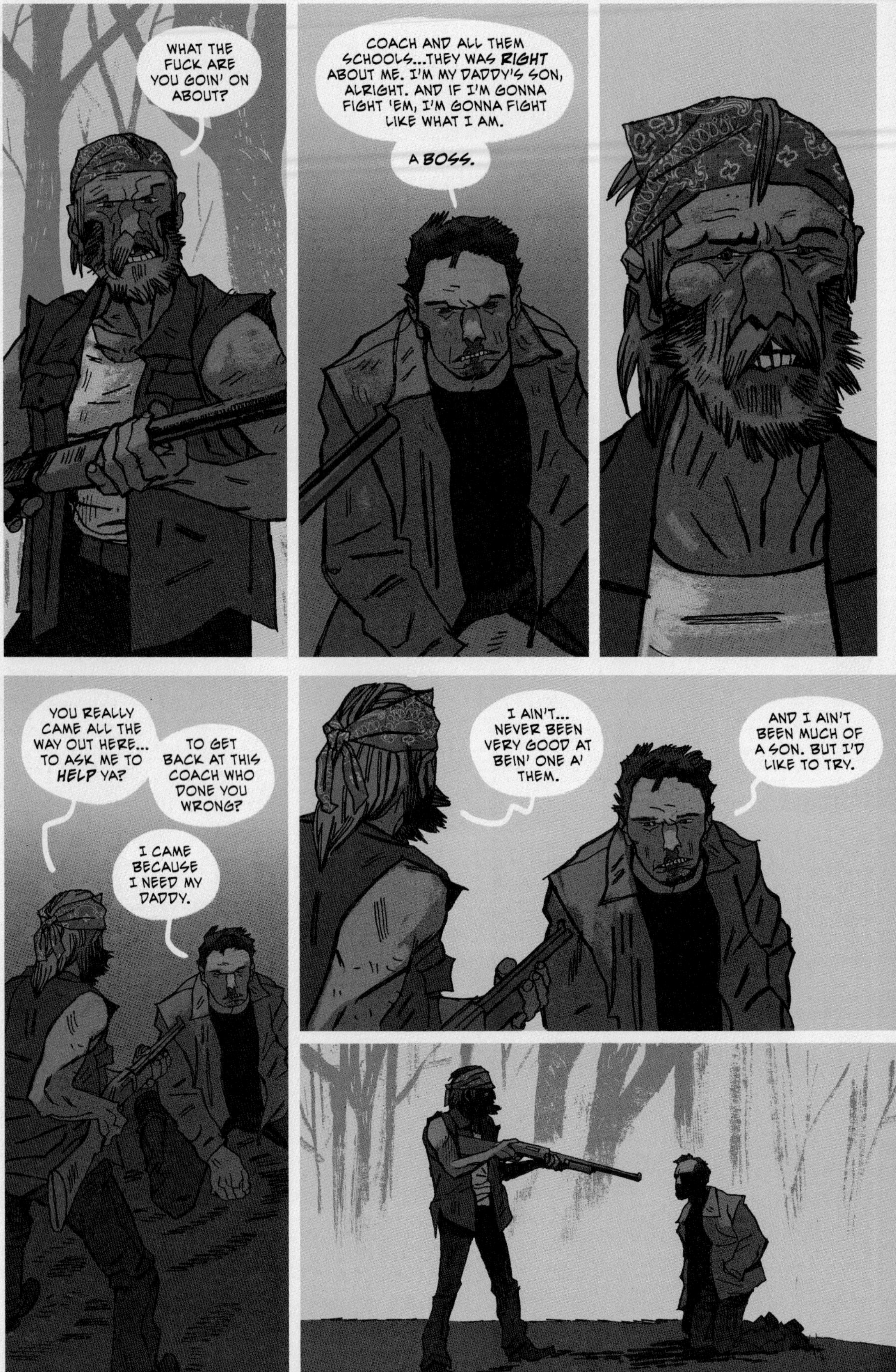
WHAT THE FUCK ARE YOU GOIN' ON ABOUT?
COACH AND ALL THEM SCHOOLS...THEY WAS RIGHT ABOUT ME. I'M MY DADDY'S SON, ALRIGHT. AND IF I'M GONNA FIGHT 'EM, I'M GONNA FIGHT LIKE WHAT I AM.
A BOSS.
YOU REALLY CAME ALL THE WAY OUT HERE... TO ASK ME TO HELP YA?
TO GET BACK AT THIS COACH WHO DONE YOU WRONG?
I CAME BECAUSE I NEED MY DADDY.
I AIN'T... NEVER BEEN VERY GOOD AT BEIN' ONE A' THEM.
AND I AIN'T BEEN MUCH OF A SON. BUT I'D LIKE TO TRY.

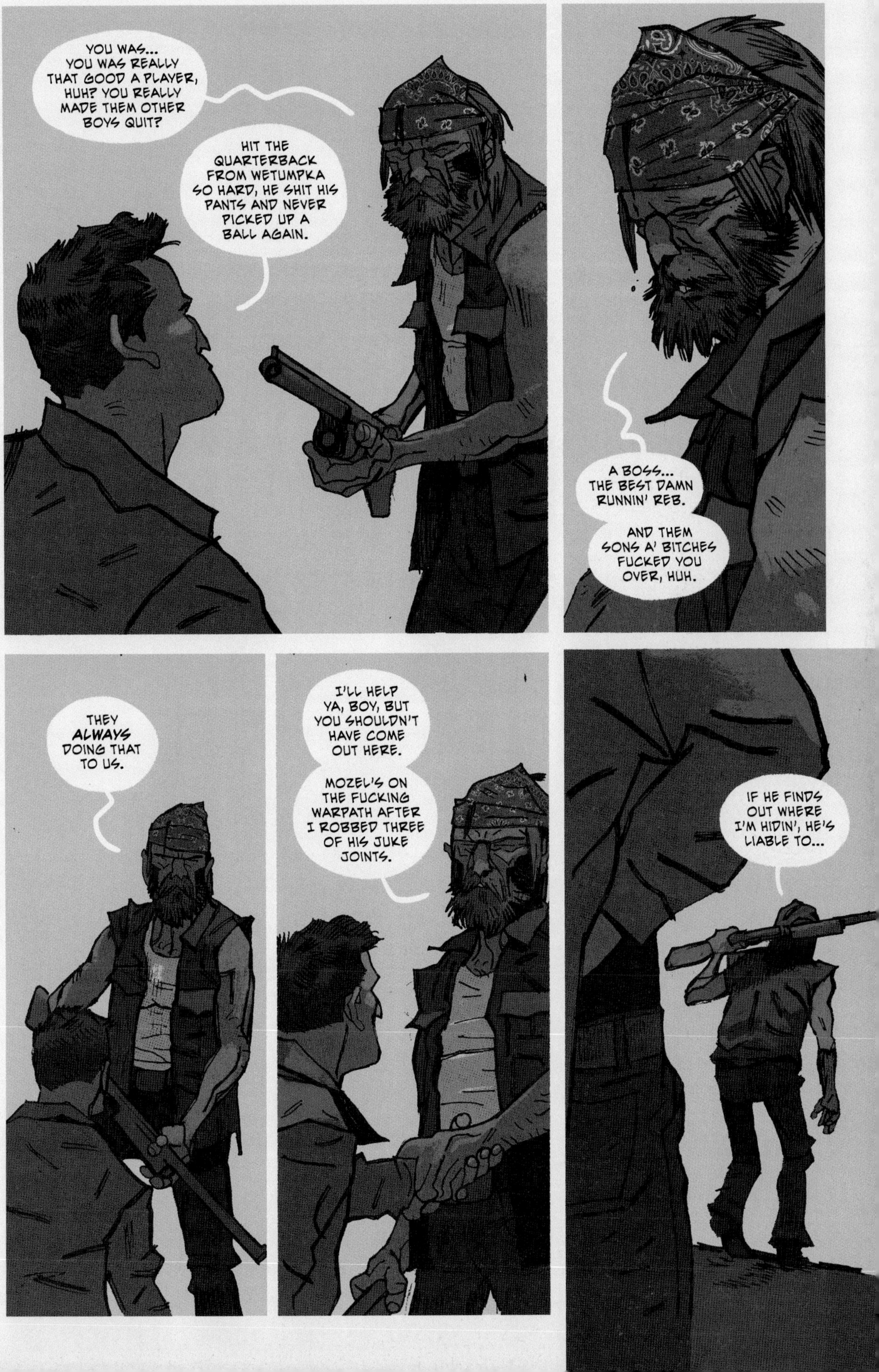
YOU WAS... YOU WAS REALLY THAT GOOD A PLAYER, HUH? YOU REALLY MADE THEM OTHER BOYS QUIT?
HIT THE QUARTERBACK FROM WETUMPKA SO HARD, HE SHIT HIS PANTS AND NEVER PICKED UP A BALL AGAIN.
A BOSS... THE BEST DAMN RUNNIN' REB.
AND THEM SONS A' BITCHES FUCKED YOU OVER, HUH.
THEY ALWAYS DOING THAT TO US.
I'LL HELP YA, BOY, BUT YOU SHOULDN'T HAVE COME OUT HERE.
MOZEL'S ON THE FUCKING WARPATH AFTER I ROBBED THREE OF HIS JUKE JOINTS.
IF HE FINDS OUT WHERE I'M HIDIN', HE'S LIABLE TO...

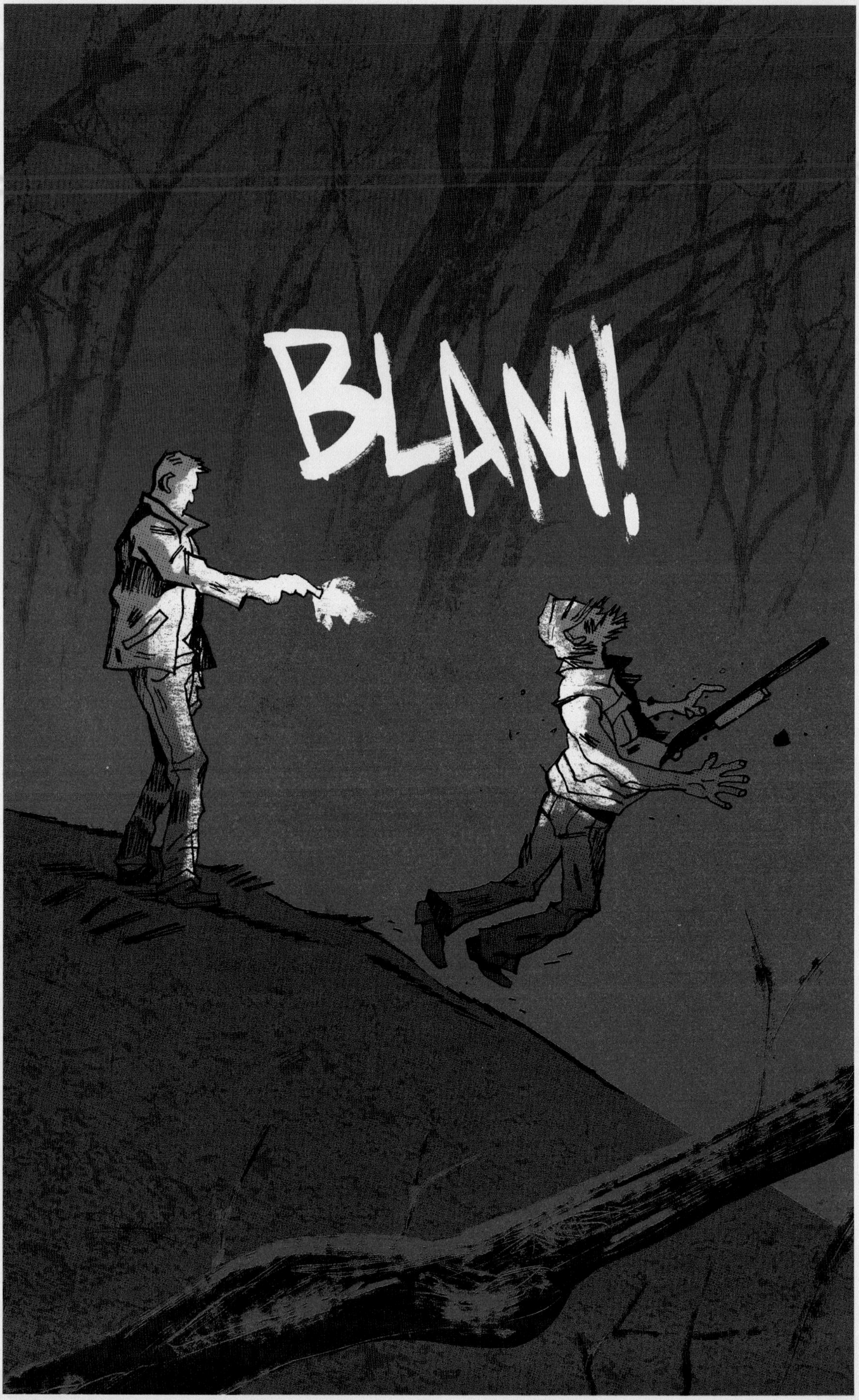
BLAM!

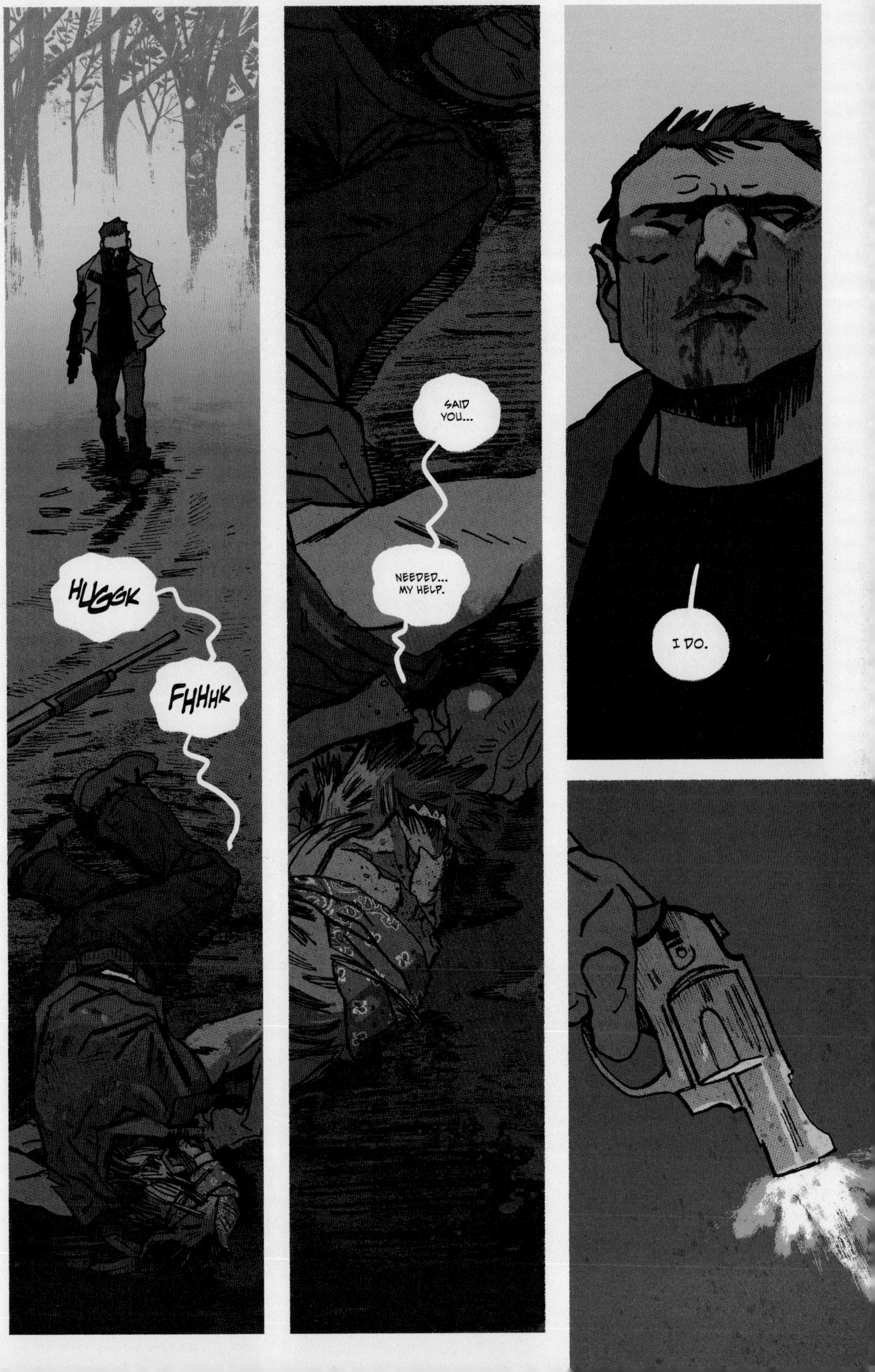
HUGGK
FHHHK
SAID YOU...
NEEDED... MY HELP.
I DO.

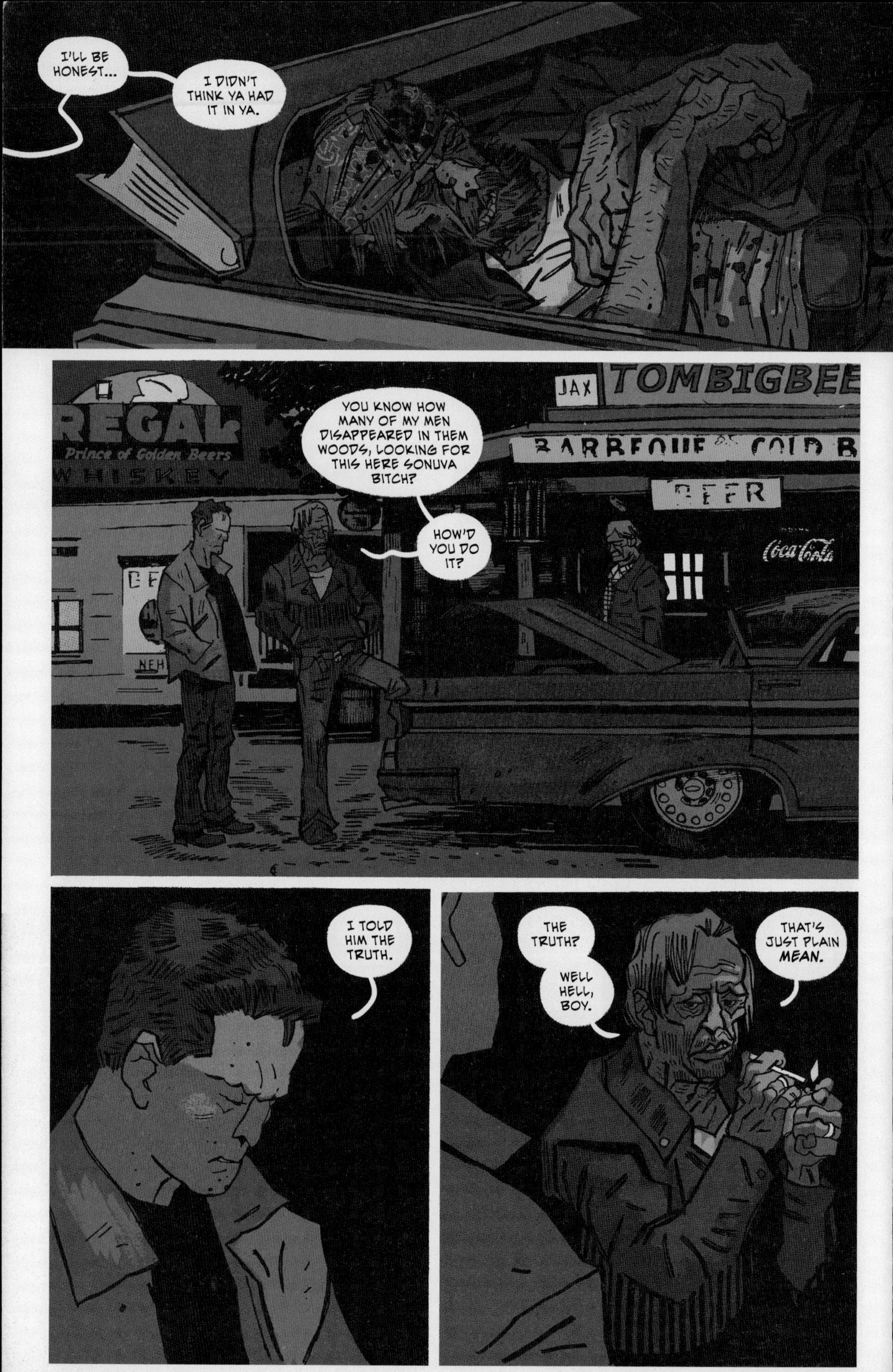
I'LL BE HONEST...
I DIDN'T THINK YA HAD IT IN YA.
REGAL
Prince of Golden Beers
WHISKEY
JAX
TOMBIGBEE
Coca-Cola
YOU KNOW HOW MANY OF MY MEN DISAPPEARED IN THEM WOODS, LOOKING FOR THIS HERE SONUVA BITCH?
HOW'D YOU DO IT?
I TOLD HIM THE TRUTH.
THE TRUTH?
WELL HELL, BOY.
THAT'S JUST PLAIN **MEAN.**

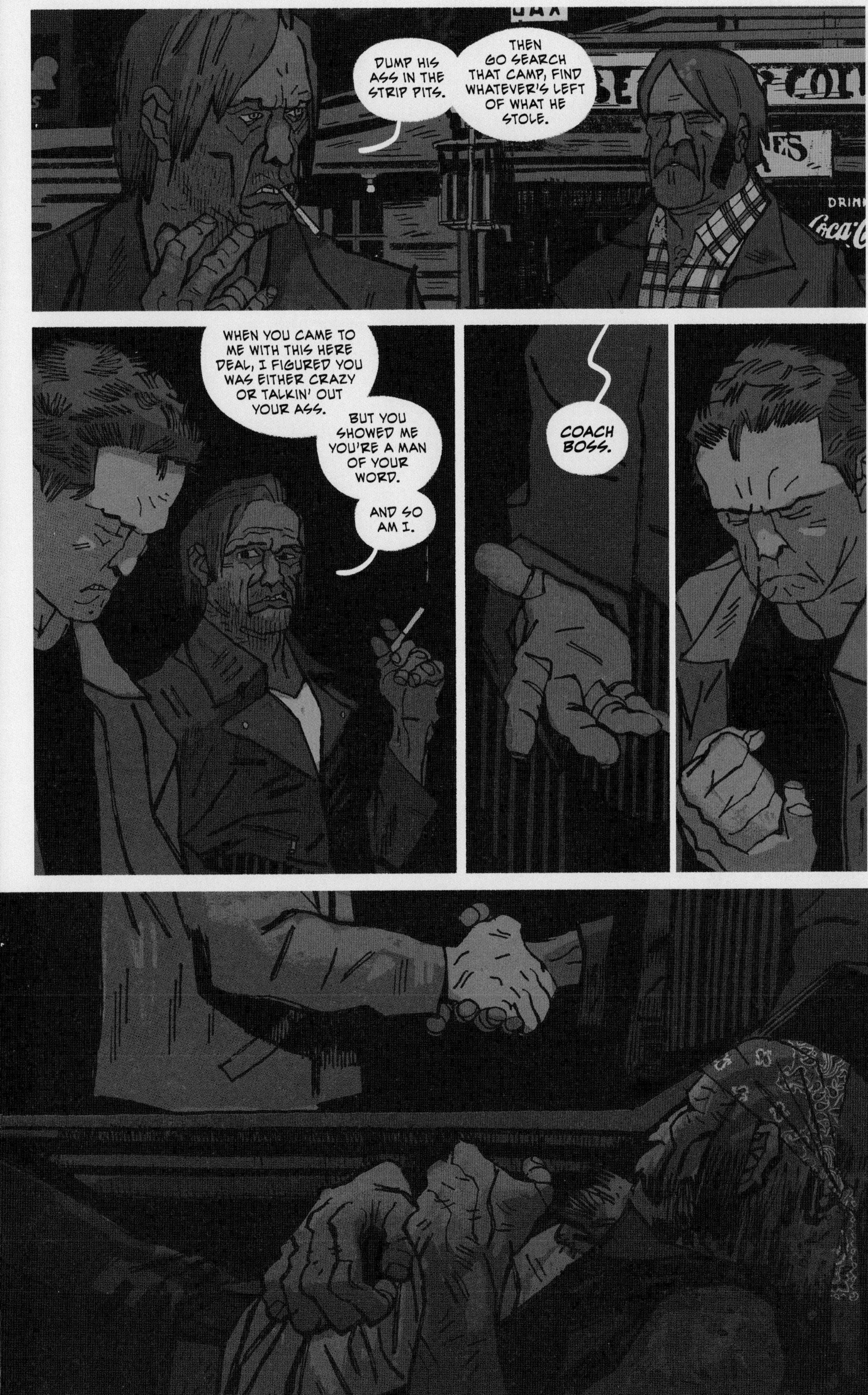
DUMP HIS ASS IN THE STRIP PITS.
THEN GO SEARCH THAT CAMP, FIND WHATEVER'S LEFT OF WHAT HE STOLE.
DRINK
Coca-Co
WHEN YOU CAME TO ME WITH THIS HERE DEAL, I FIGURED YOU WAS EITHER CRAZY OR TALKIN' OUT YOUR ASS.
BUT YOU SHOWED ME YOU'RE A MAN OF YOUR WORD.
AND SO AM I.
COACH BOSS.

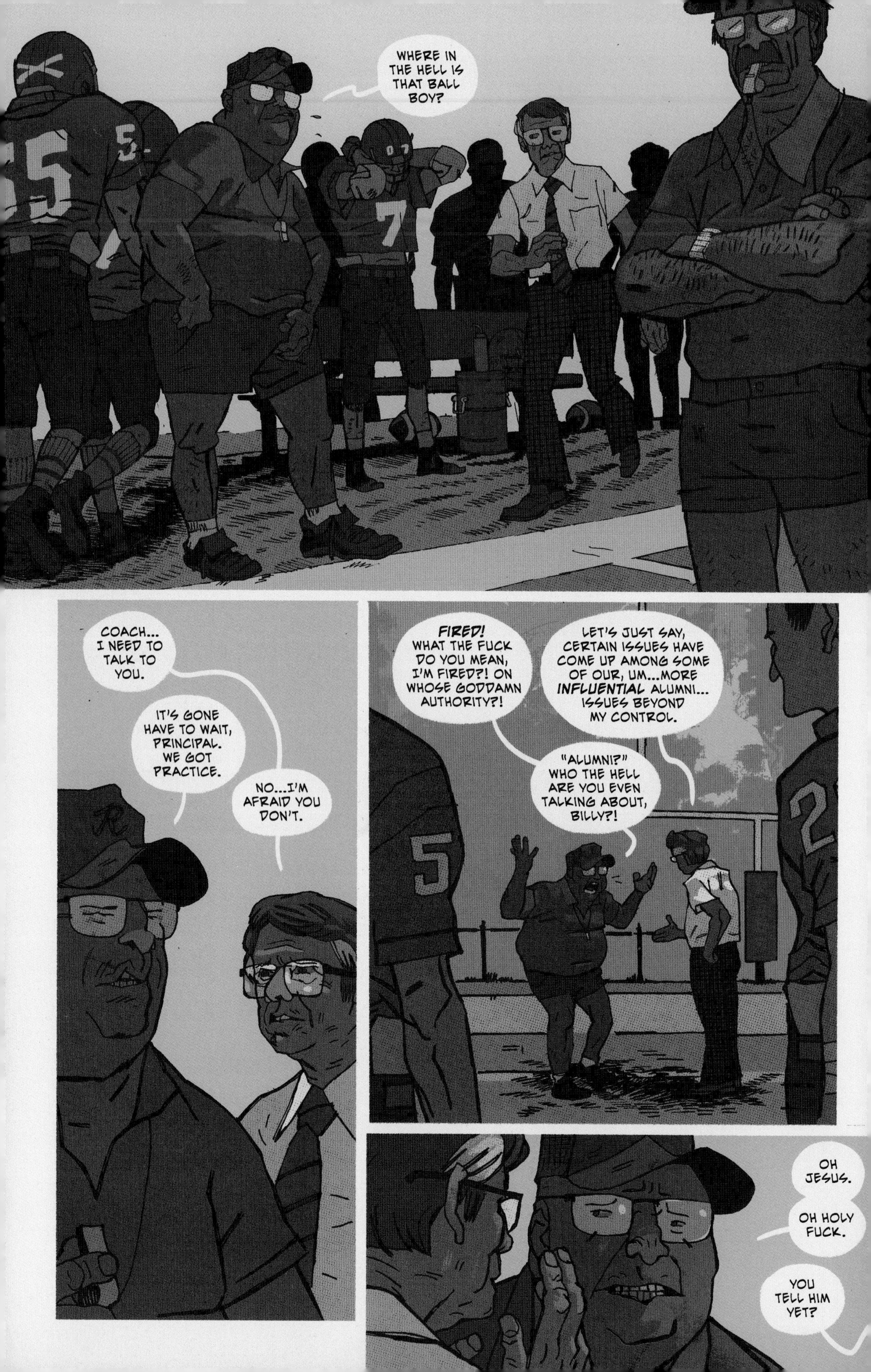

WHERE IN THE HELL IS THAT BALL BOY?
COACH... I NEED TO TALK TO YOU.
IT'S GONE HAVE TO WAIT, PRINCIPAL. WE GOT PRACTICE.
NO...I'M AFRAID YOU DON'T.
FIRED! WHAT THE FUCK DO YOU MEAN, I'M FIRED?! ON WHOSE GODDAMN AUTHORITY?!
LET'S JUST SAY, CERTAIN ISSUES HAVE COME UP AMONG SOME OF OUR, UM...MORE INFLUENTIAL ALUMNI... ISSUES BEYOND MY CONTROL.
"ALUMNI?" WHO THE HELL ARE YOU EVEN TALKING ABOUT, BILLY?!
OH JESUS.
OH HOLY FUCK.
YOU TELL HIM YET?

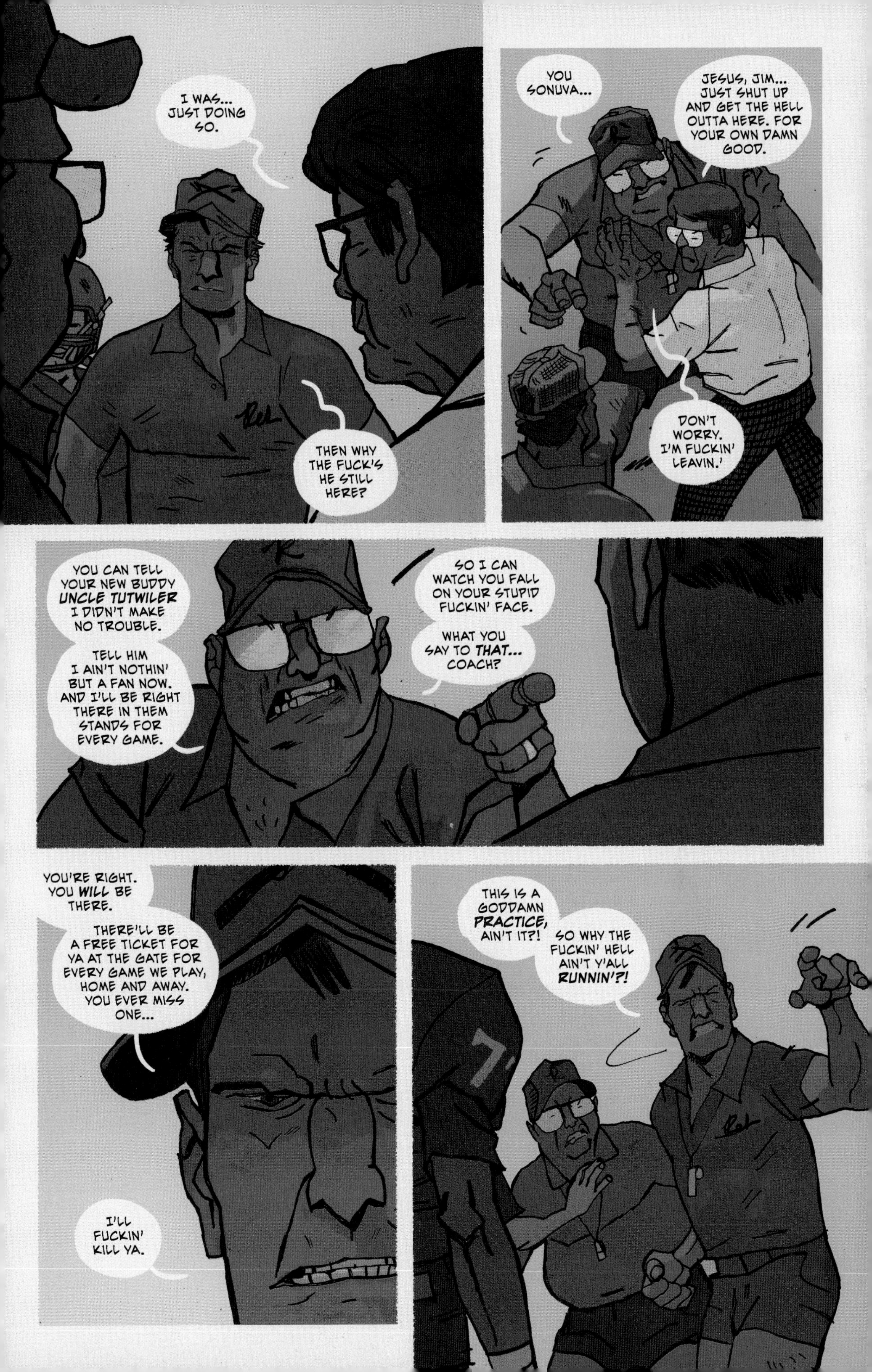
I WAS... JUST DOING SO.
THEN WHY THE FUCK'S HE STILL HERE?
YOU SONUVA...
JESUS, JIM... JUST SHUT UP AND GET THE HELL OUTTA HERE. FOR YOUR OWN DAMN GOOD.
DON'T WORRY. I'M FUCKIN' LEAVIN.'
YOU CAN TELL YOUR NEW BUDDY *UNCLE TUTWILER* I DIDN'T MAKE NO TROUBLE.
TELL HIM I AIN'T NOTHIN' BUT A FAN NOW. AND I'LL BE RIGHT THERE IN THEM STANDS FOR EVERY GAME.
SO I CAN WATCH YOU FALL ON YOUR STUPID FUCKIN' FACE.
WHAT YOU SAY TO **THAT...** COACH?
YOU'RE RIGHT. YOU **WILL** BE THERE.
THERE'LL BE A FREE TICKET FOR YA AT THE GATE FOR EVERY GAME WE PLAY, HOME AND AWAY. YOU EVER MISS ONE...
I'LL FUCKIN' KILL YA.
THIS IS A GODDAMN **PRACTICE**, AIN'T IT?!
SO WHY THE FUCKIN' HELL AIN'T Y'ALL ***RUNNIN'?!***

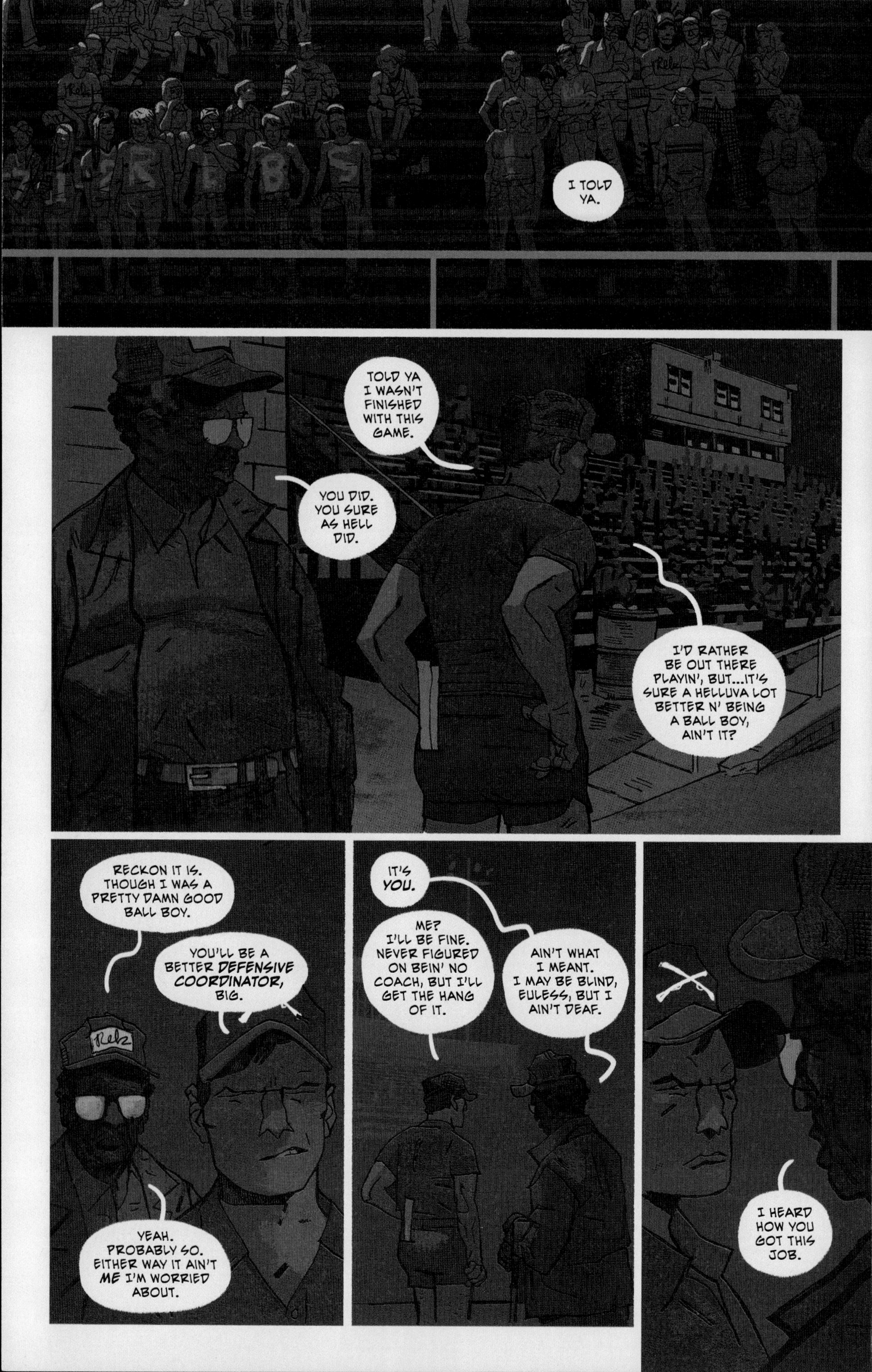
I TOLD YA.
TOLD YA I WASN'T FINISHED WITH THIS GAME.
YOU DID. YOU SURE AS HELL DID.
I'D RATHER BE OUT THERE PLAYIN', BUT...IT'S SURE A HELLUVA LOT BETTER N' BEING A BALL BOY, AIN'T IT?
RECKON IT IS. THOUGH I WAS A PRETTY DAMN GOOD BALL BOY.
YOU'LL BE A BETTER DEFENSIVE COORDINATOR, BIG.
YEAH. PROBABLY SO. EITHER WAY IT AIN'T ME I'M WORRIED ABOUT.
IT'S YOU.
ME? I'LL BE FINE. NEVER FIGURED ON BEIN' NO COACH, BUT I'LL GET THE HANG OF IT.
AIN'T WHAT I MEANT. I MAY BE BLIND, EULESS, BUT I AIN'T DEAF.
I HEARD HOW YOU GOT THIS JOB.

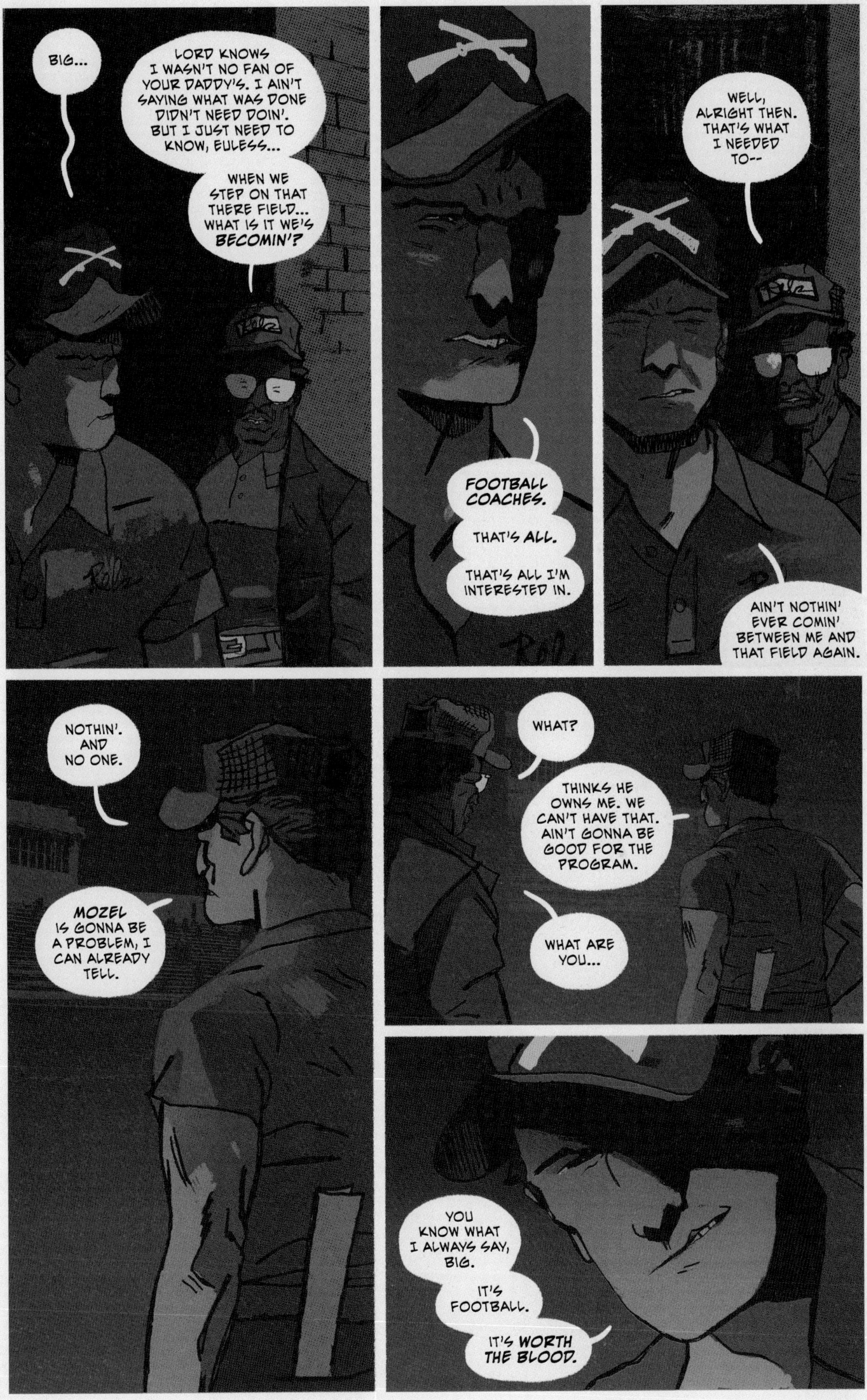
BIG...
LORD KNOWS I WASN'T NO FAN OF YOUR DADDY'S. I AIN'T SAYING WHAT WAS DONE DIDN'T NEED DOIN'. BUT I JUST NEED TO KNOW, EULESS...
WHEN WE STEP ON THAT THERE FIELD... WHAT IS IT WE'S BECOMIN'?
FOOTBALL COACHES.
THAT'S ALL.
THAT'S ALL I'M INTERESTED IN.
WELL, ALRIGHT THEN. THAT'S WHAT I NEEDED TO--
AIN'T NOTHIN' EVER COMIN' BETWEEN ME AND THAT FIELD AGAIN.
NOTHIN'. AND NO ONE.
MOZEL IS GONNA BE A PROBLEM, I CAN ALREADY TELL.
WHAT?
THINKS HE OWNS ME. WE CAN'T HAVE THAT. AIN'T GONNA BE GOOD FOR THE PROGRAM.
WHAT ARE YOU...
YOU KNOW WHAT I ALWAYS SAY, BIG.
IT'S FOOTBALL.
IT'S WORTH THE BLOOD.

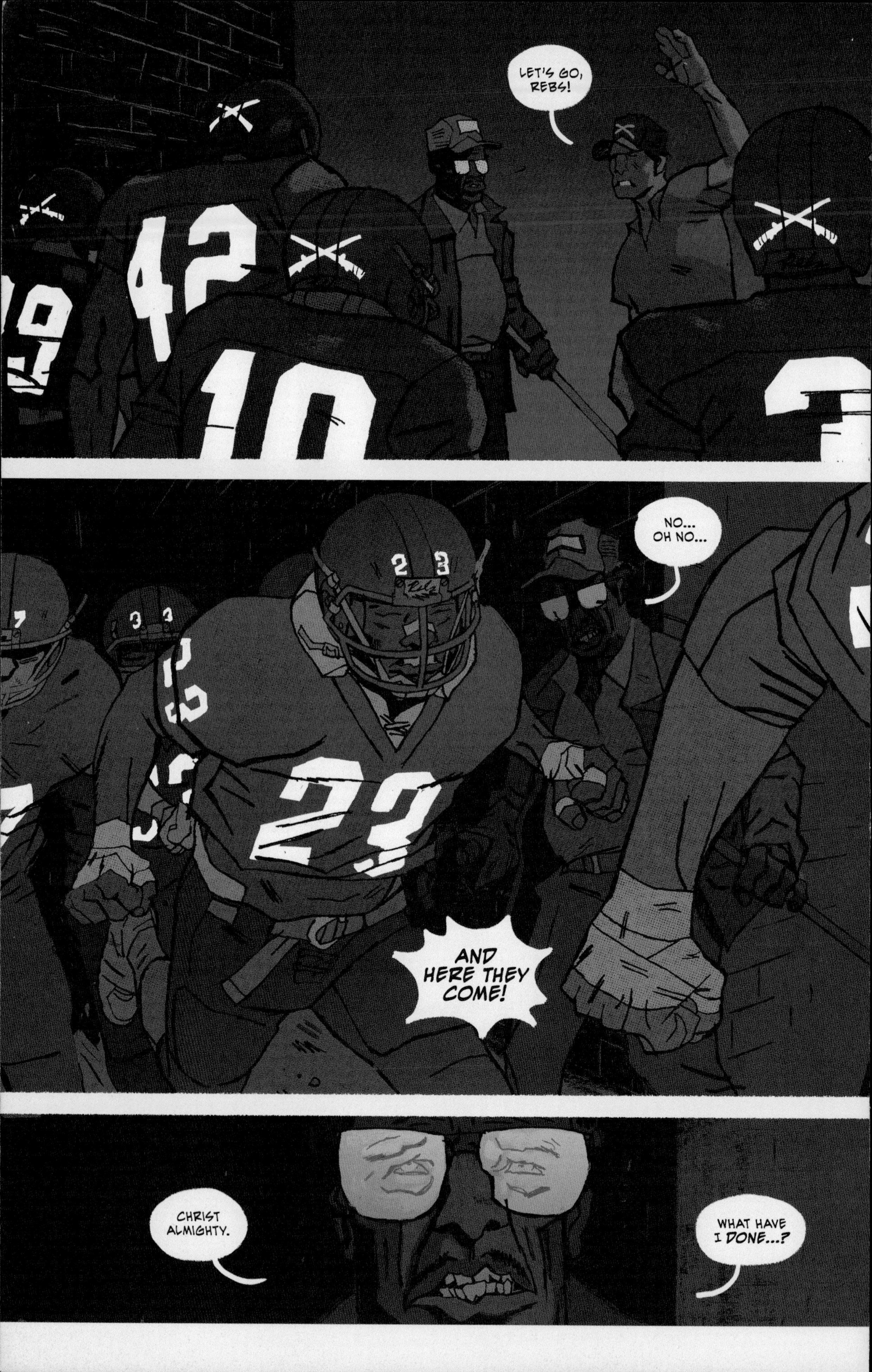

LET'S GO, REBS!
NO... OH NO...
AND HERE THEY COME!
CHRIST ALMIGHTY.
WHAT HAVE I DONE...?

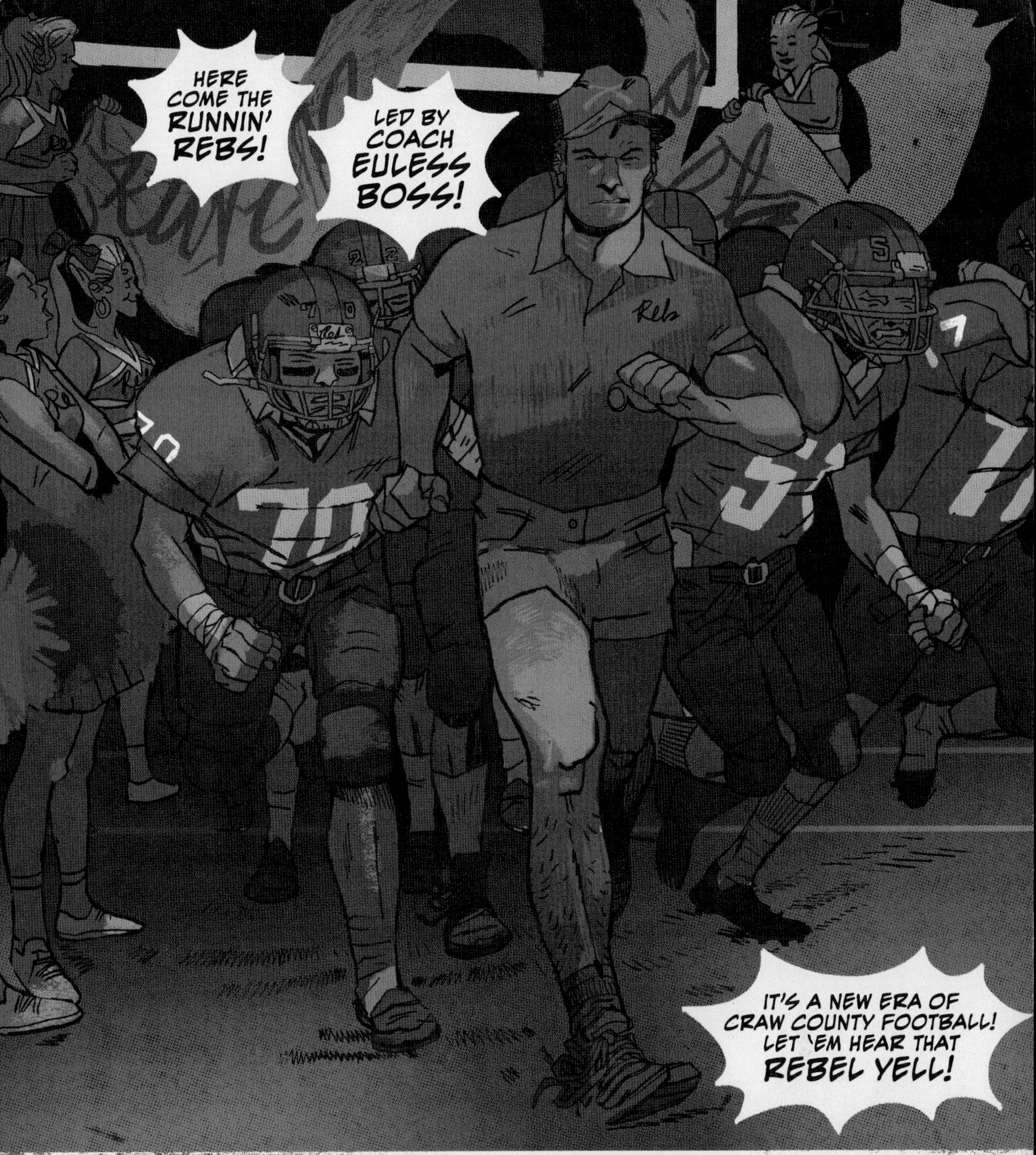
HERE COME THE RUNNIN' REBS!
LED BY COACH EULESS BOSS!
IT'S A NEW ERA OF CRAW COUNTY FOOTBALL! LET 'EM HEAR THAT REBEL YELL!

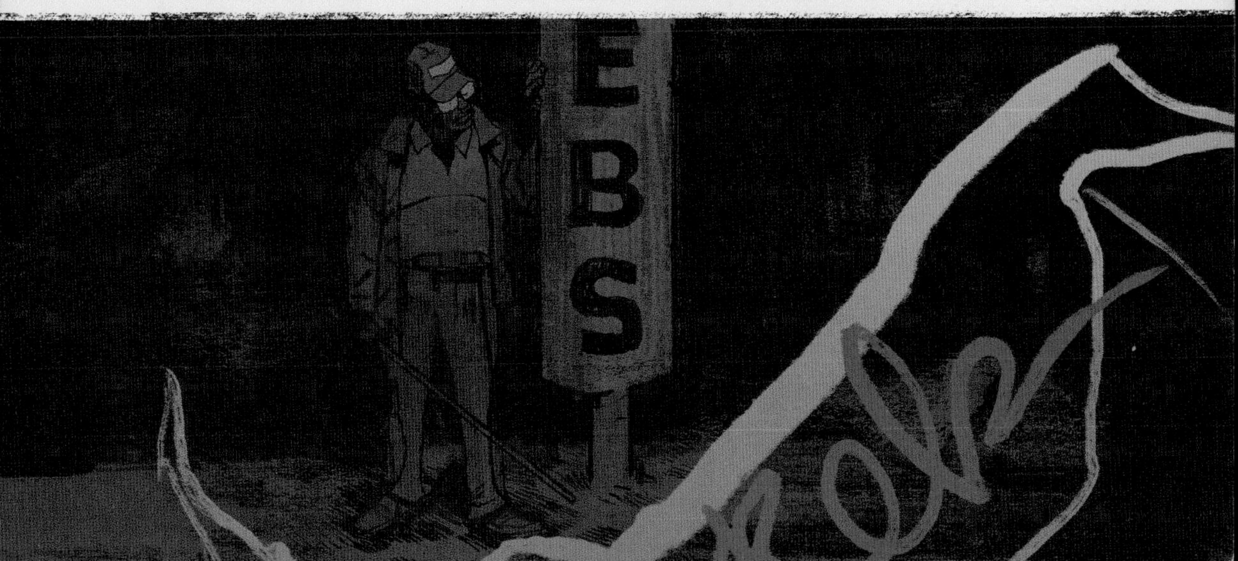
EBS

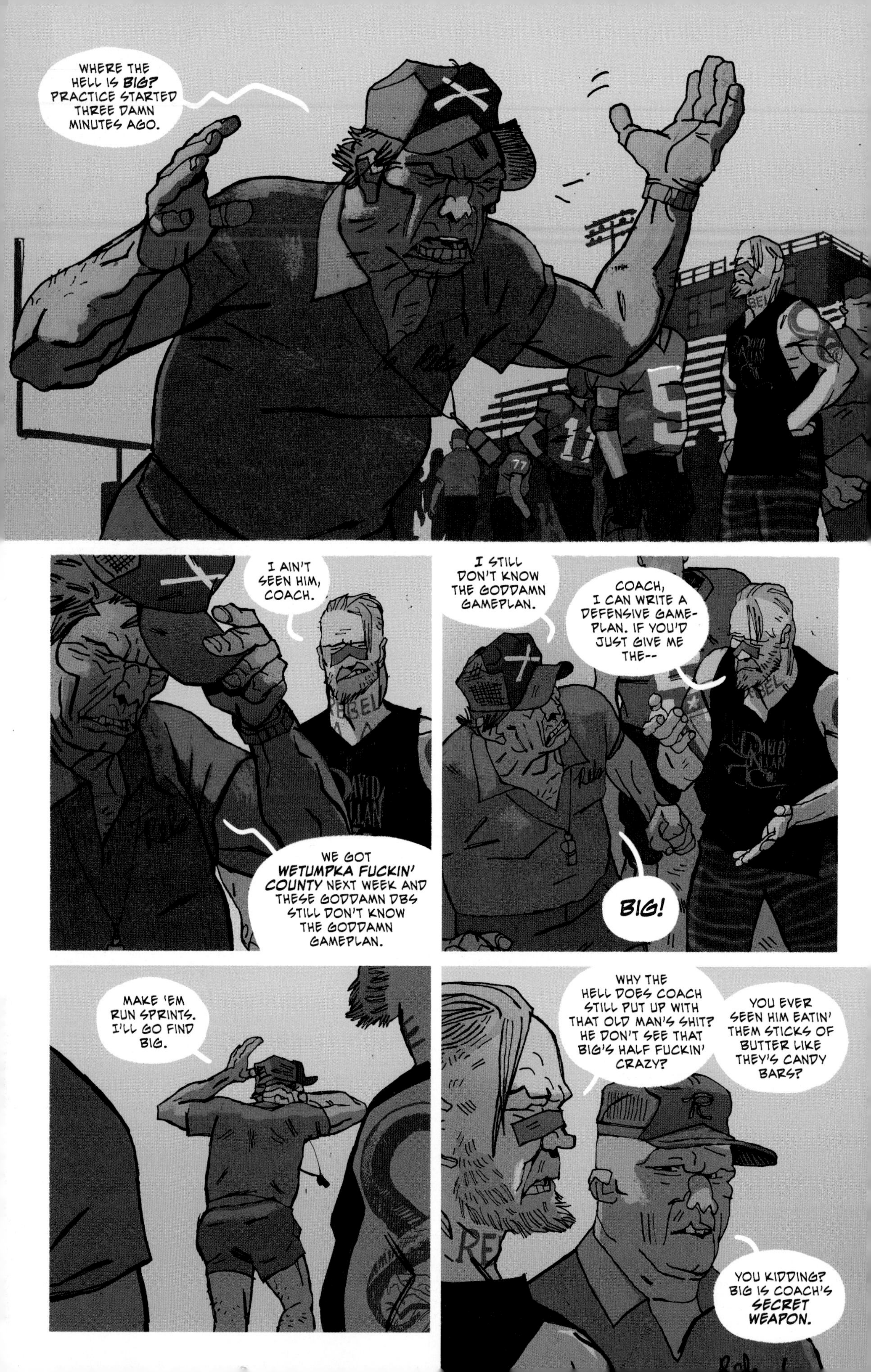
WHERE THE HELL IS **BIG?** PRACTICE STARTED THREE DAMN MINUTES AGO.
I AIN'T SEEN HIM, COACH.
WE GOT ***WETUMPKA FUCKIN' COUNTY*** NEXT WEEK AND THESE GODDAMN DBS STILL DON'T KNOW THE GODDAMN GAMEPLAN.
I STILL DON'T KNOW THE GODDAMN GAMEPLAN.
COACH, I CAN WRITE A DEFENSIVE GAME-PLAN. IF YOU'D JUST GIVE ME THE--
BIG!
MAKE 'EM RUN SPRINTS. I'LL GO FIND BIG.
WHY THE HELL DOES COACH STILL PUT UP WITH THAT OLD MAN'S SHIT? HE DON'T SEE THAT BIG'S HALF FUCKIN' CRAZY?
YOU EVER SEEN HIM EATIN' THEM STICKS OF BUTTER LIKE THEY'S CANDY BARS?
YOU KIDDING? BIG IS COACH'S ***SECRET WEAPON.***

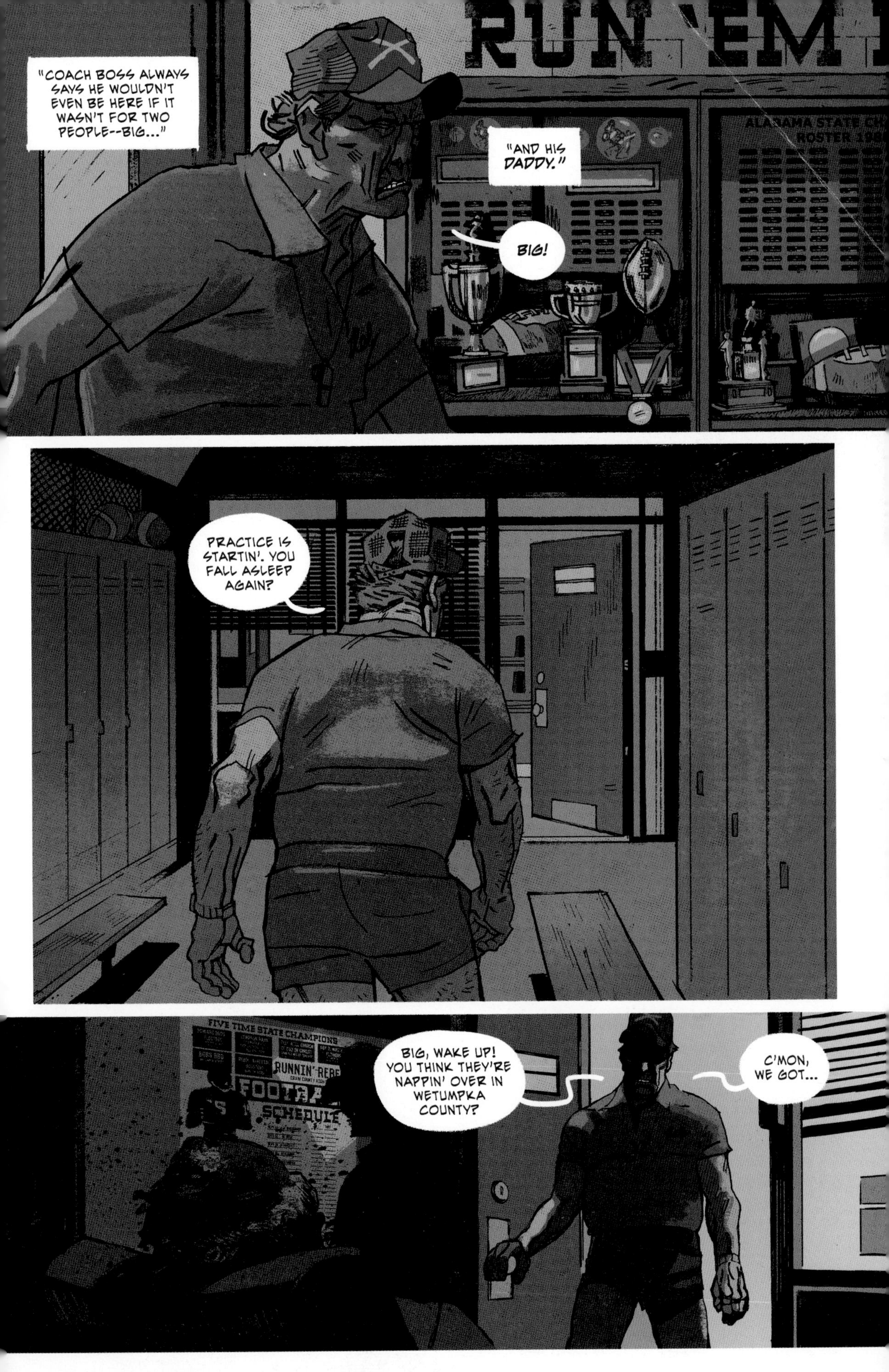
"COACH BOSS ALWAYS SAYS HE WOULDN'T EVEN BE HERE IF IT WASN'T FOR TWO PEOPLE--BIG..."
"AND HIS DADDY."
BIG!
PRACTICE IS STARTIN'. YOU FALL ASLEEP AGAIN?
FIVE TIME STATE CHAMPIONS
SCHEDULE
BIG, WAKE UP! YOU THINK THEY'RE NAPPIN' OVER IN WETUMPKA COUNTY?
C'MON, WE GOT...

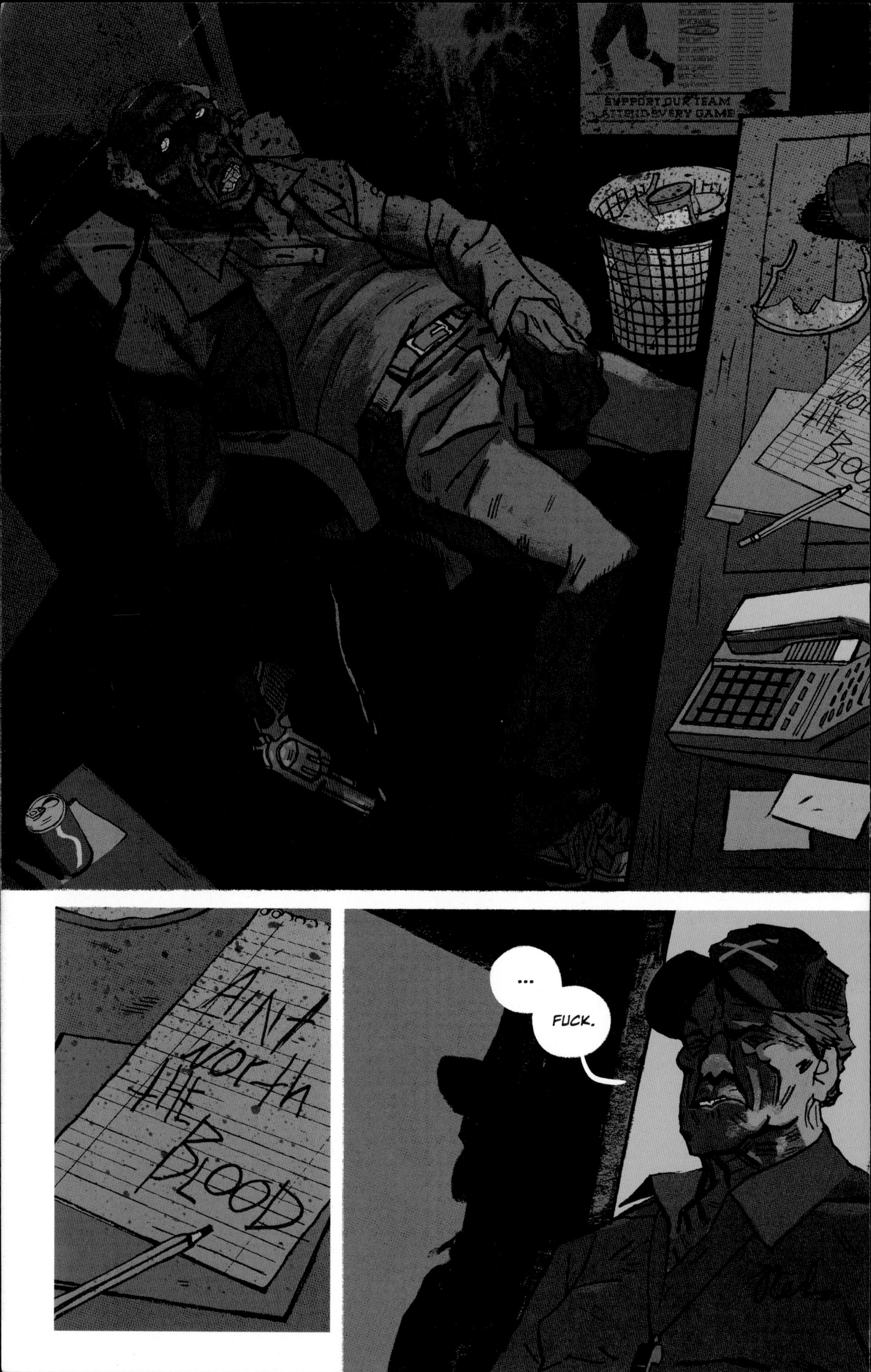
SUPPORT OUR TEAM
ATTEND EVERY GAME
Aint worth THE BLOOD
...
FUCK.

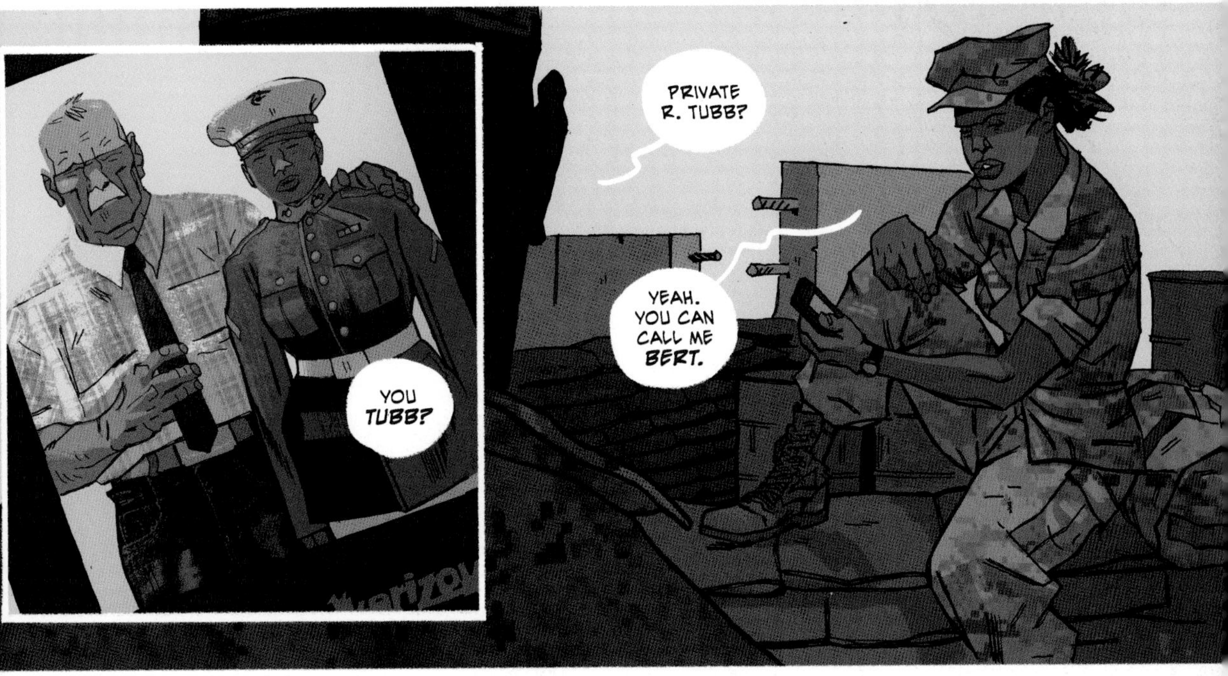
YOU *TUBB?*
PRIVATE R. TUBB?
YEAH. YOU CAN CALL ME **BERT.**

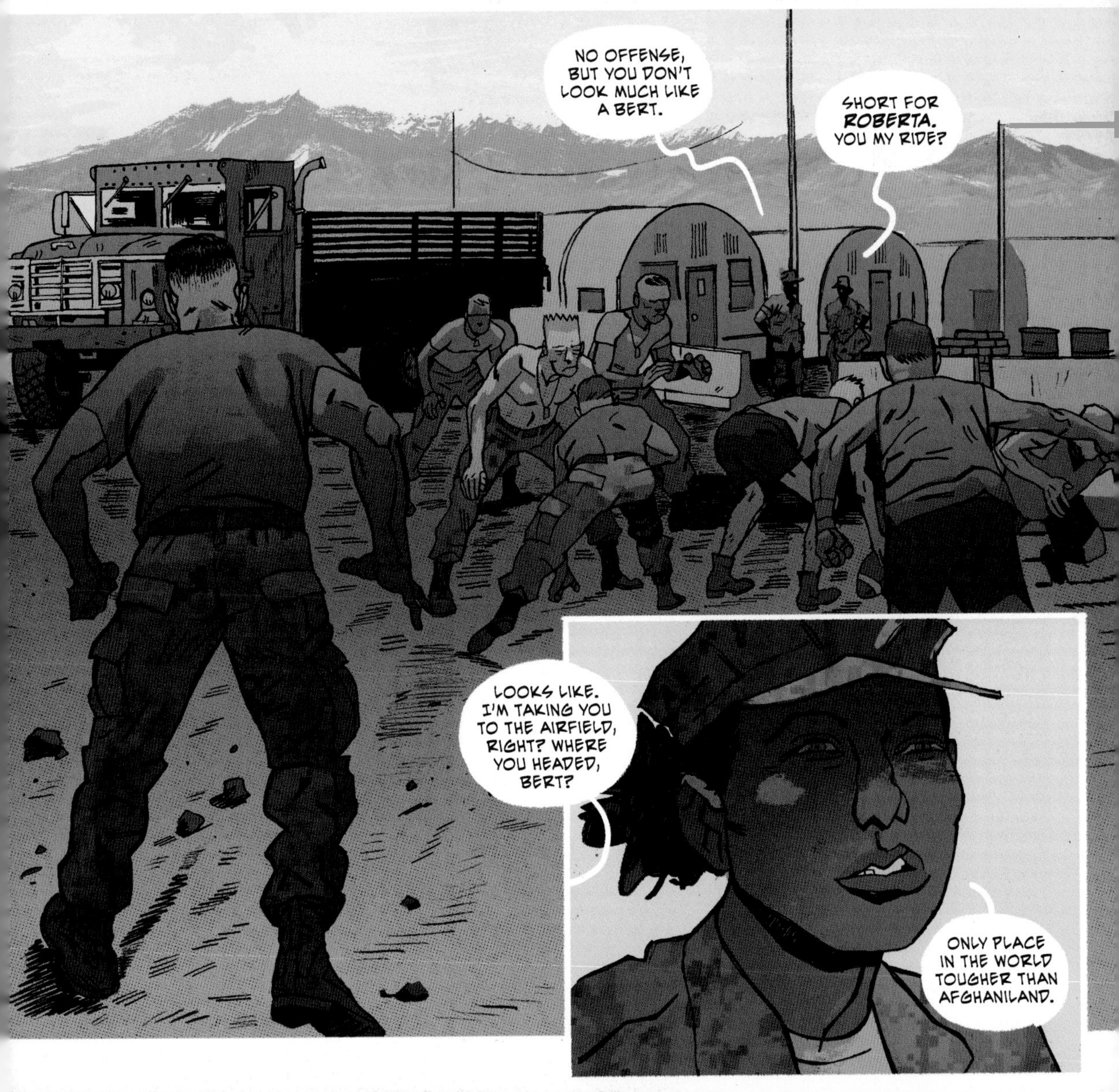
NO OFFENSE, BUT YOU DON'T LOOK MUCH LIKE A BERT.
SHORT FOR **ROBERTA.** YOU MY RIDE?
LOOKS LIKE. I'M TAKING YOU TO THE AIRFIELD, RIGHT? WHERE YOU HEADED, BERT?
ONLY PLACE IN THE WORLD TOUGHER THAN AFGHANILAND.

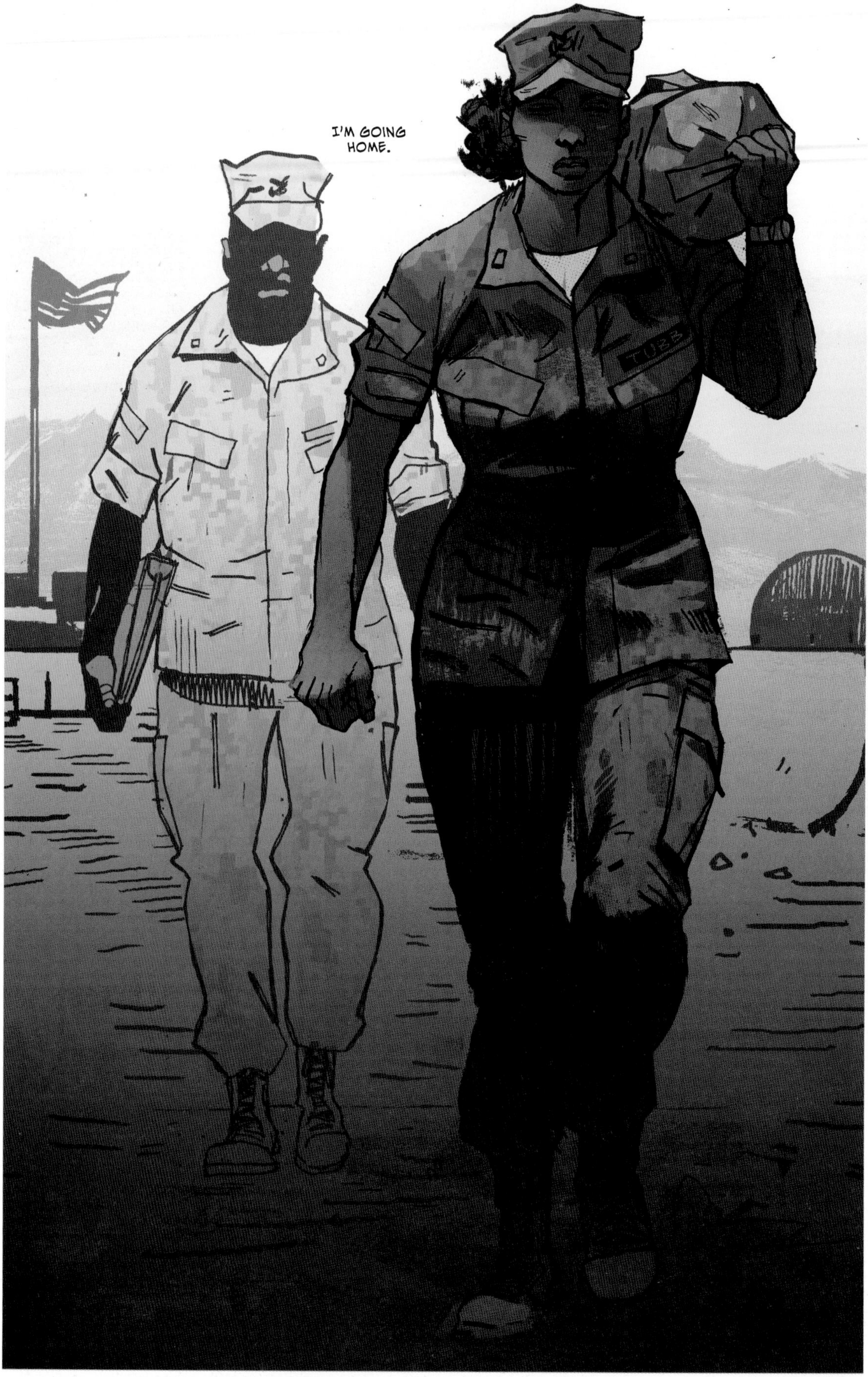
I'M GOING HOME.
TUBB

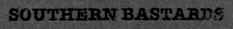

SOUTHERN BASTARDS

COVER GALLERY
& SKETCHBOOK

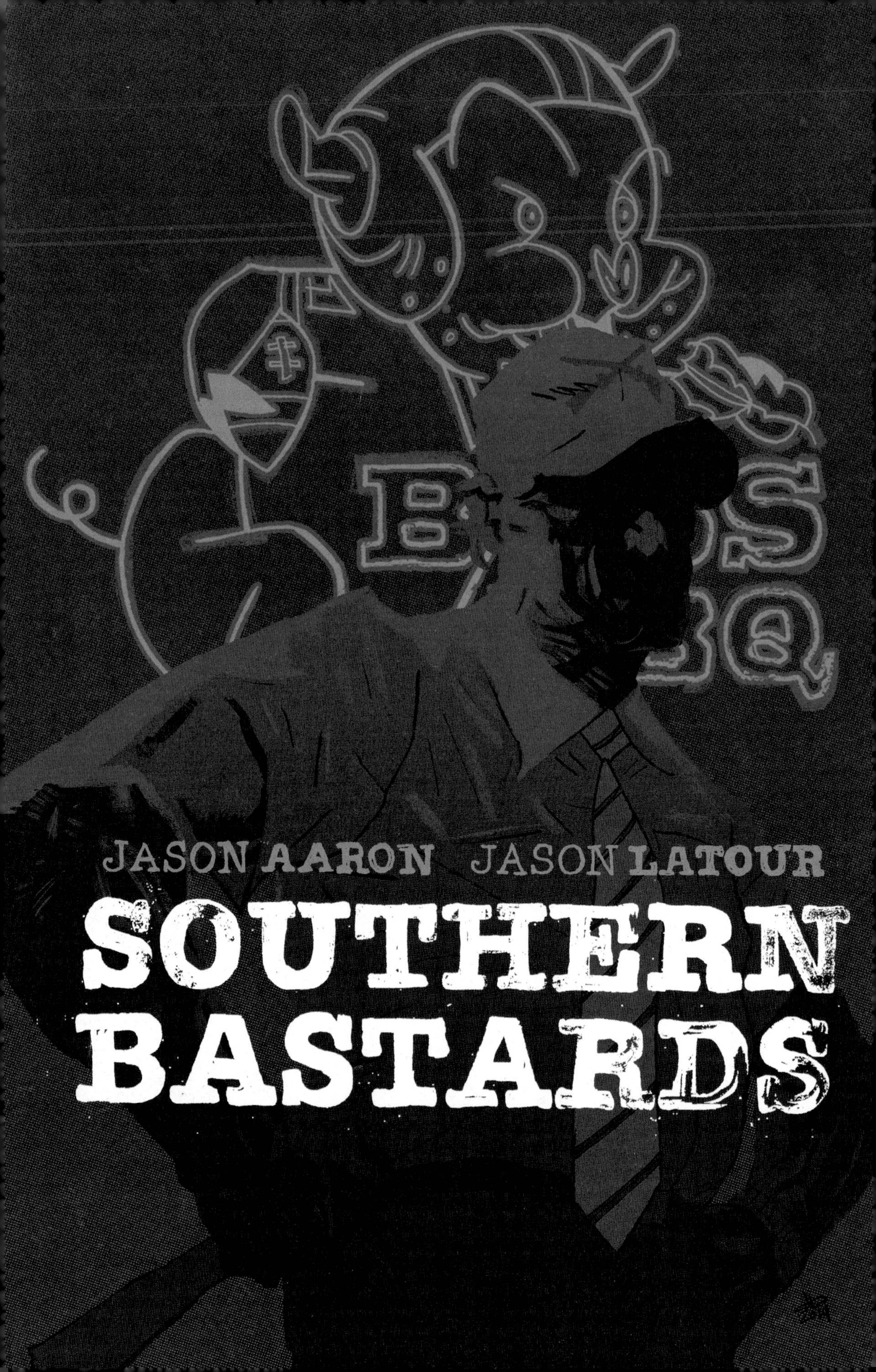
JASON AARON JASON LATOUR
SOUTHERN
BASTARDS

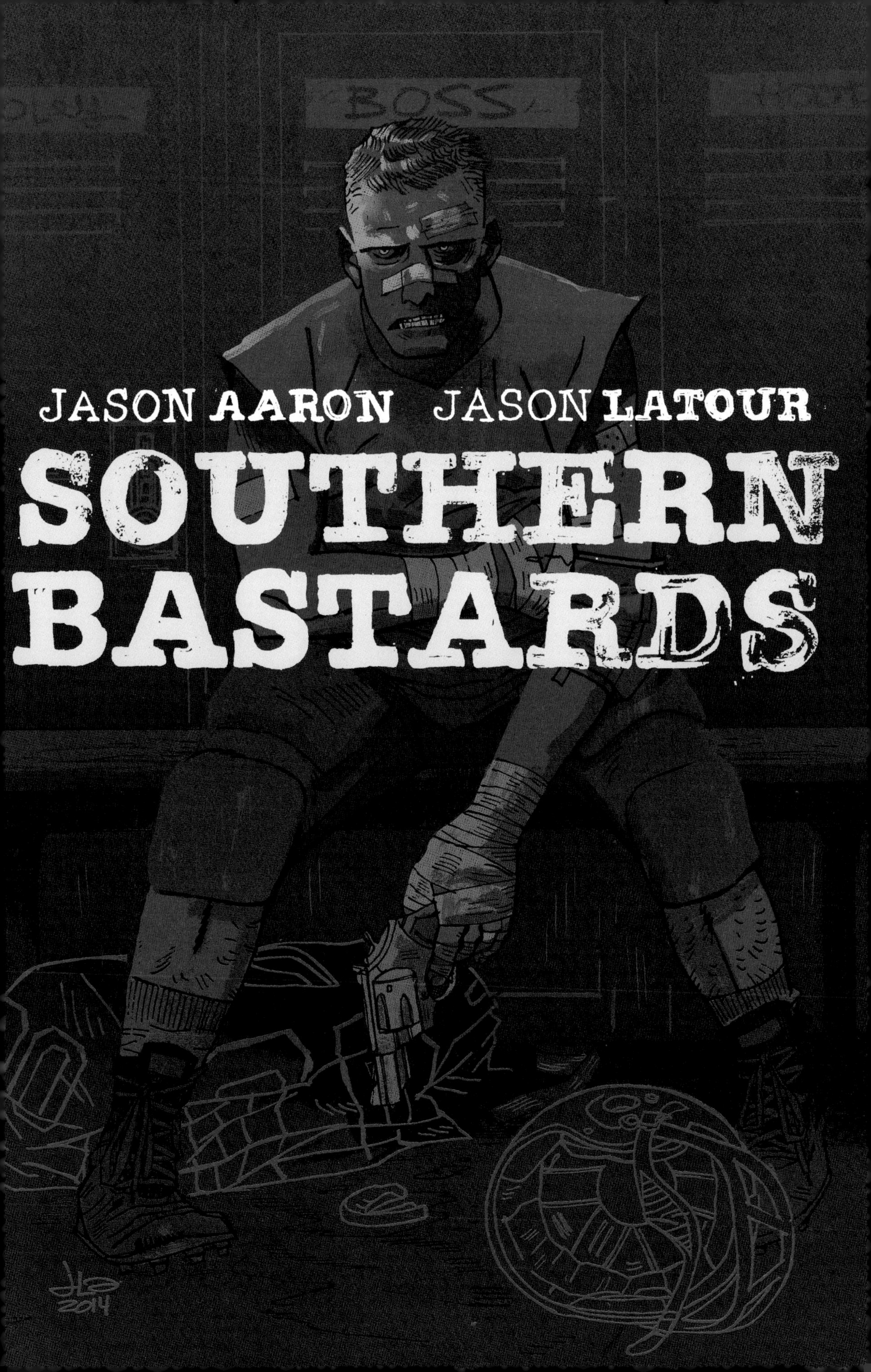
BOSS
JASON AARON JASON LATOUR
SOUTHERN
BASTARDS
2014

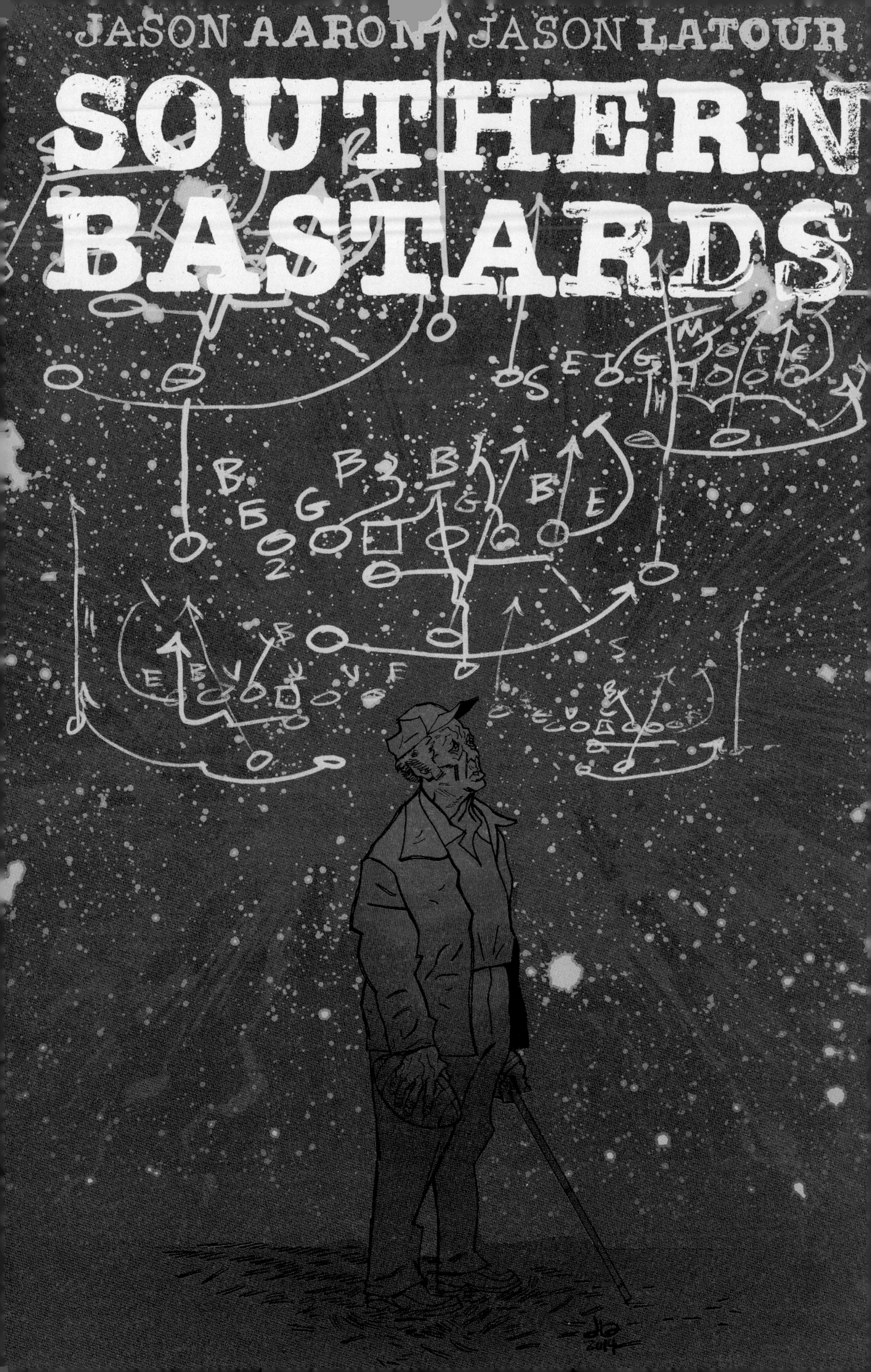
JASON AARON JASON LATOUR
SOUTHERN BASTARDS

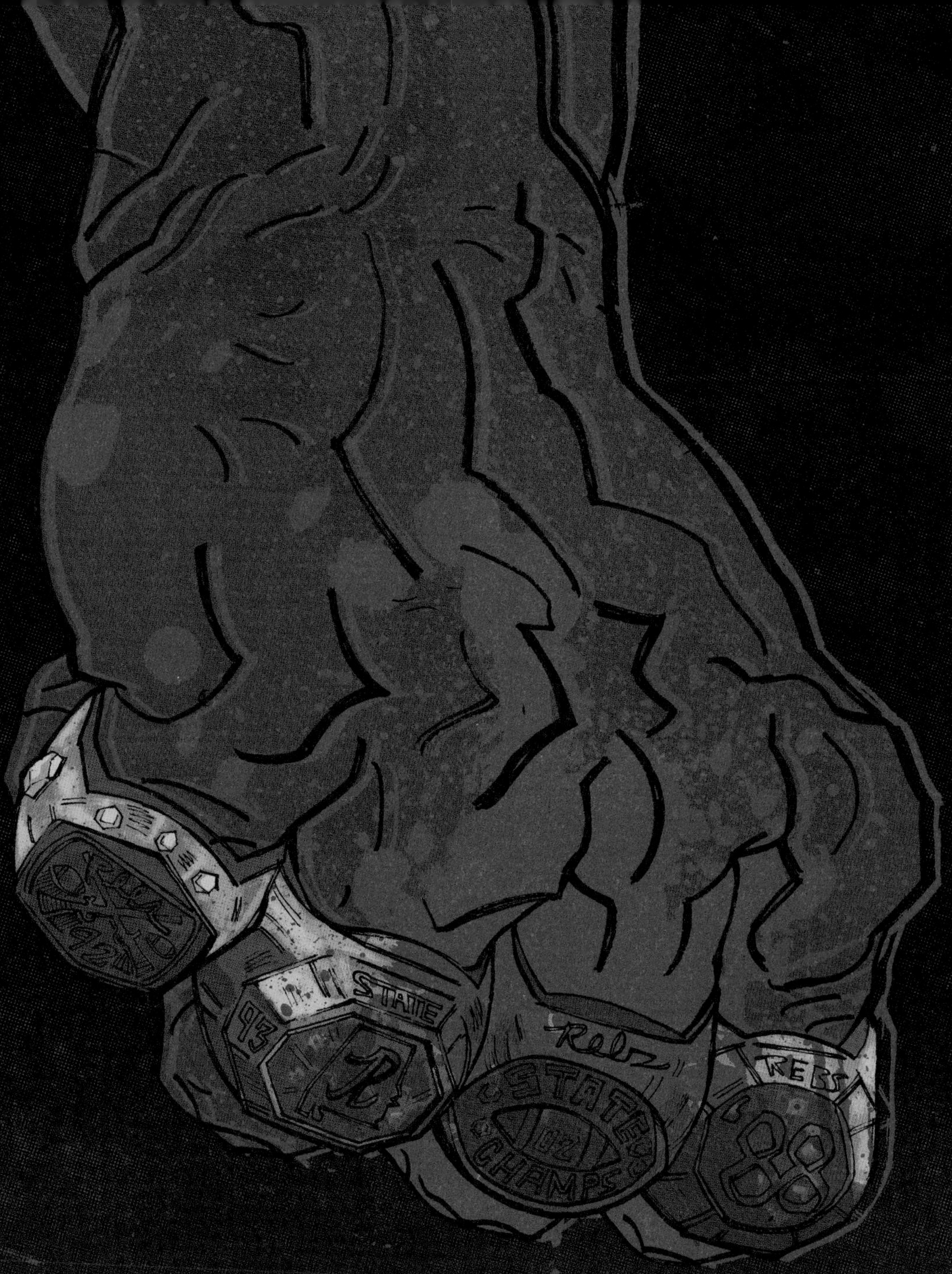
STATE
93
STATE
02
CHAMPS
REBS
88

JASON AARON JASON LATOUR

SOUTHERN BASTARDS

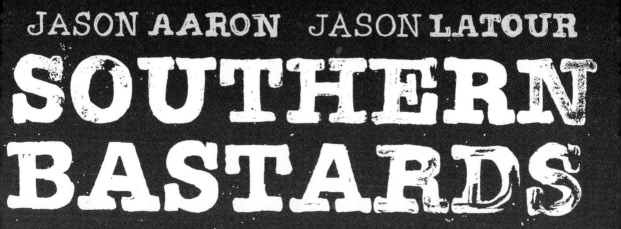

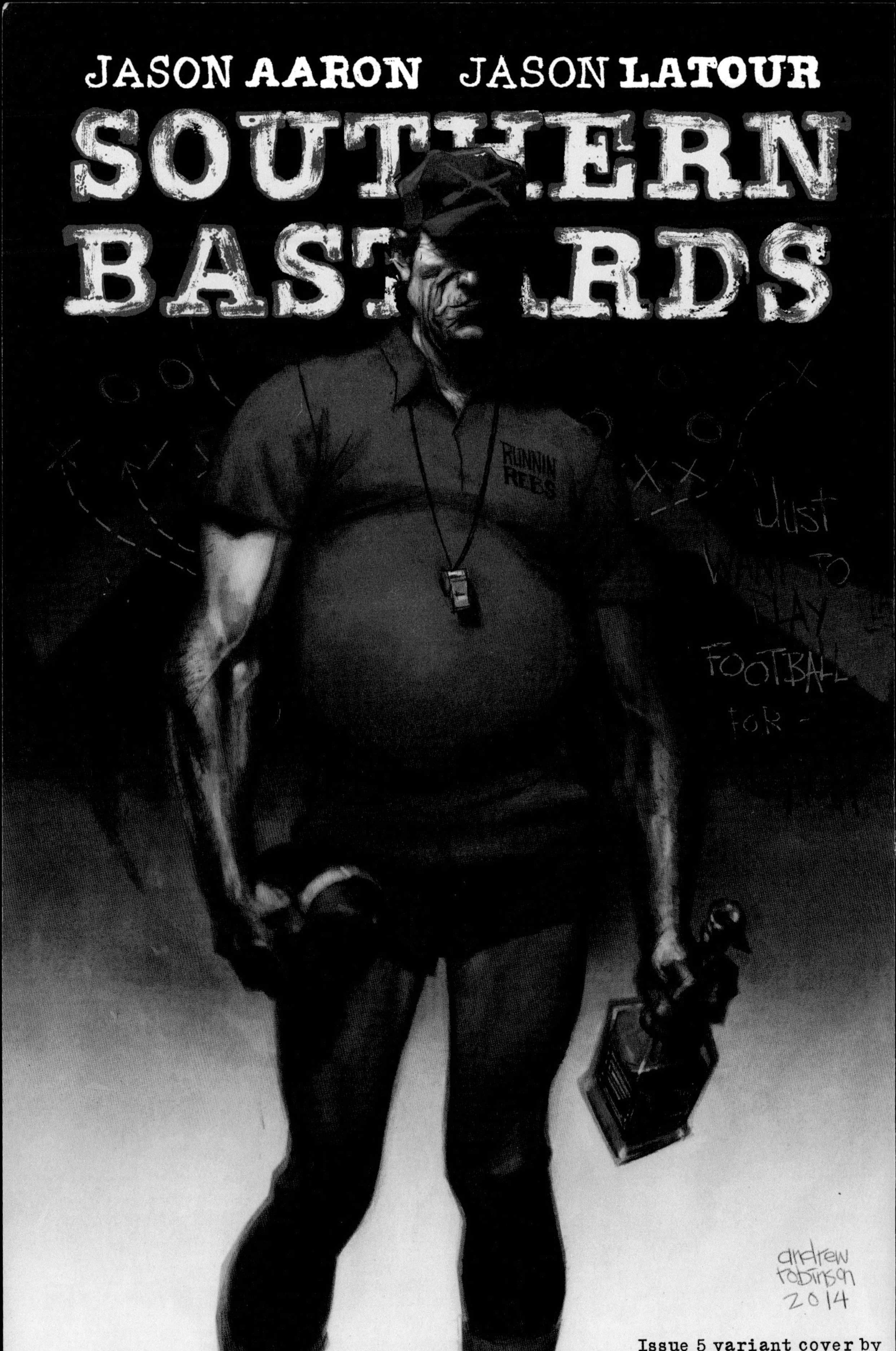
JASON AARON JASON LATOUR
SOUTHERN BASTARDS
RUNNIN REBS
JUST WANT TO PLAY FOOTBALL FOR -
andrew robinson 2014

Issue 5 variant cover by
ANDREW ROBINSON

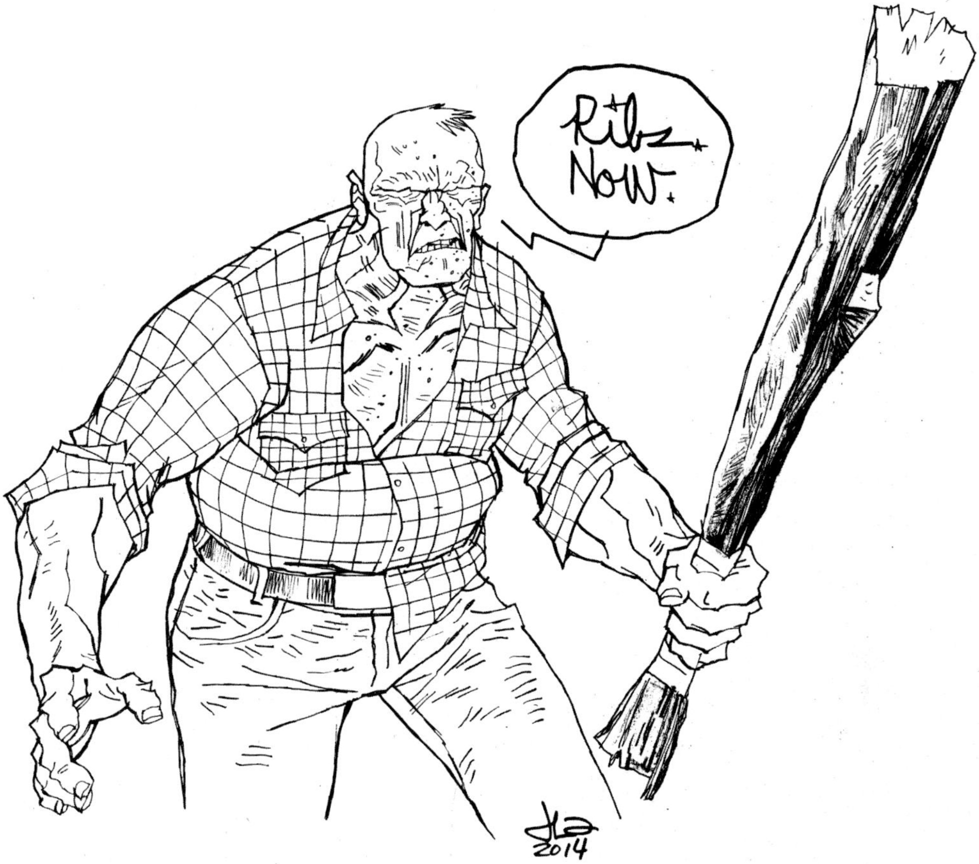
Ribz Now.
JLA 2014

"FRIENDLY FARMS" prelims from issue 8.

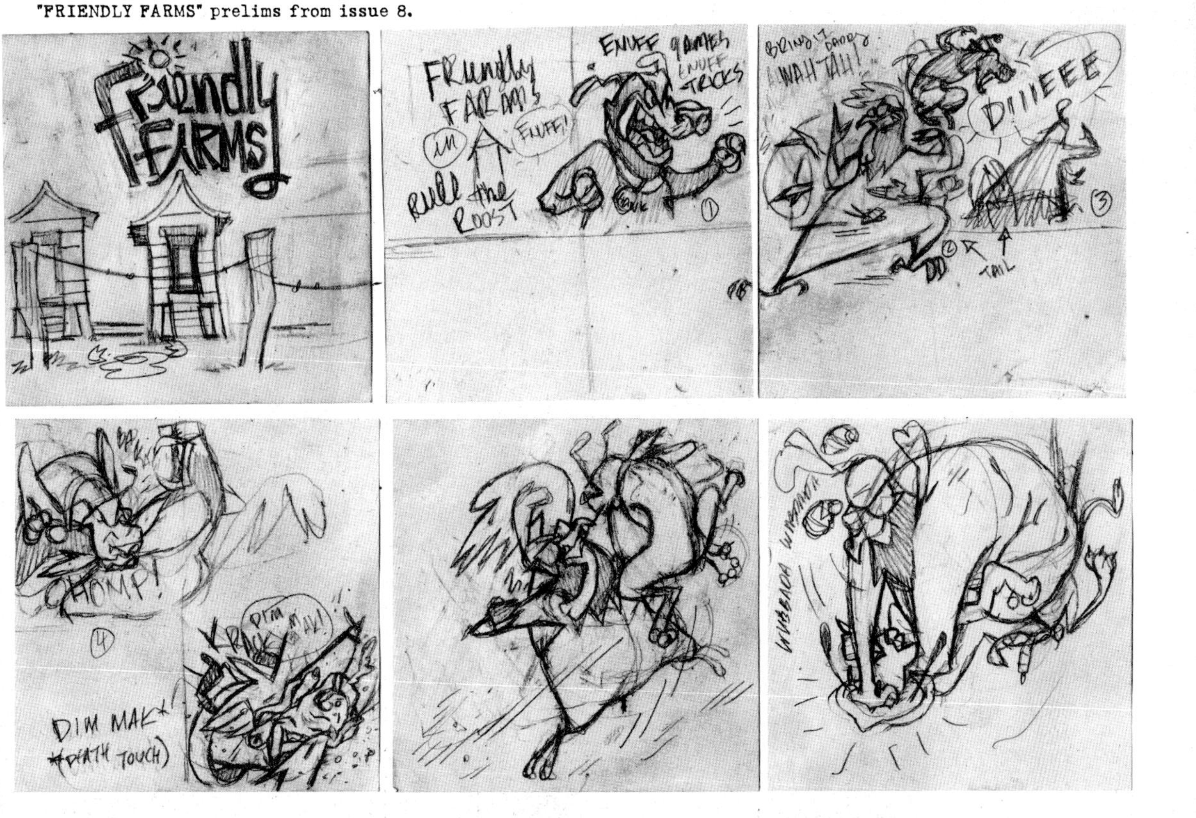
Friendly FARMS
ENUFF games ENUFF TRICKS
RULE the ROOST
ENUFF!
DIIIEEE
TAIL
CHOMP!
DIM MAK!
DIM MAK*
(*DEATH TOUCH)

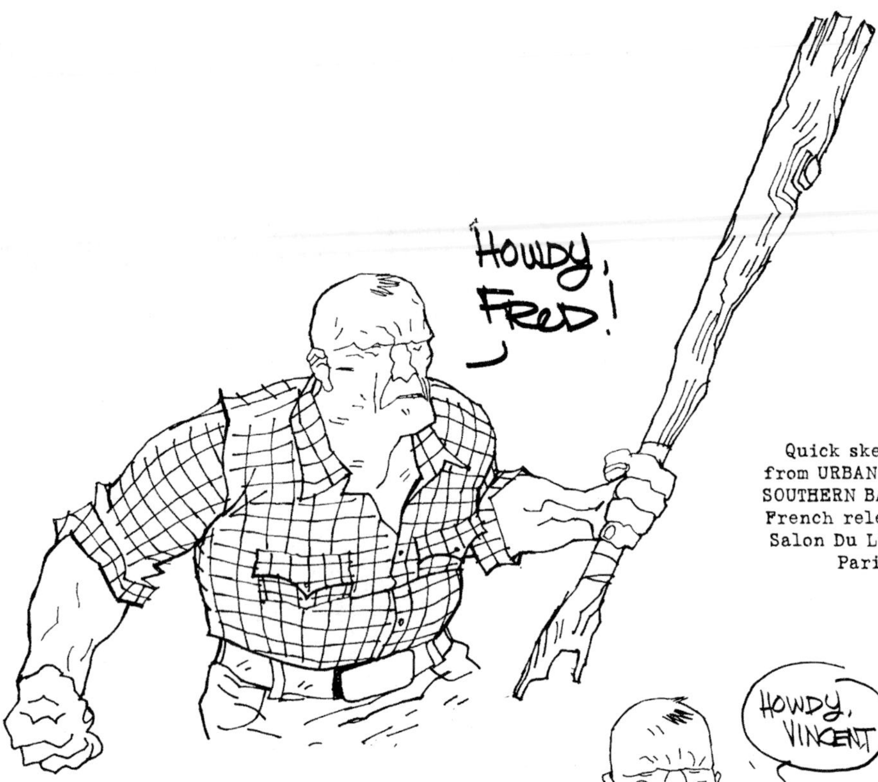
HOWDY, FRED!

Quick sketches
from URBAN COMICS
SOUTHERN BASTARDS
French release at
Salon Du Livre de
Paris

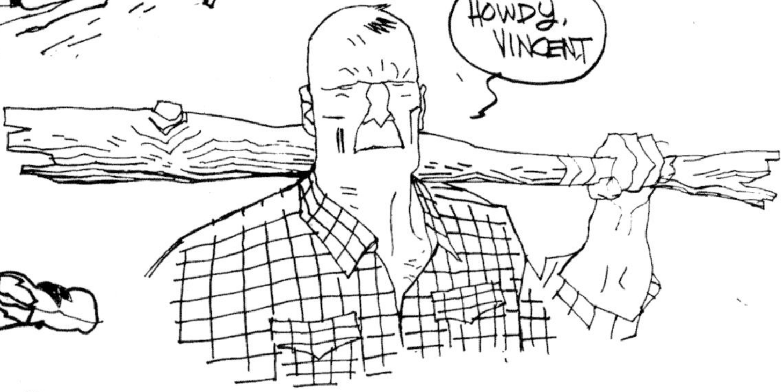
HOWDY, VINCENT

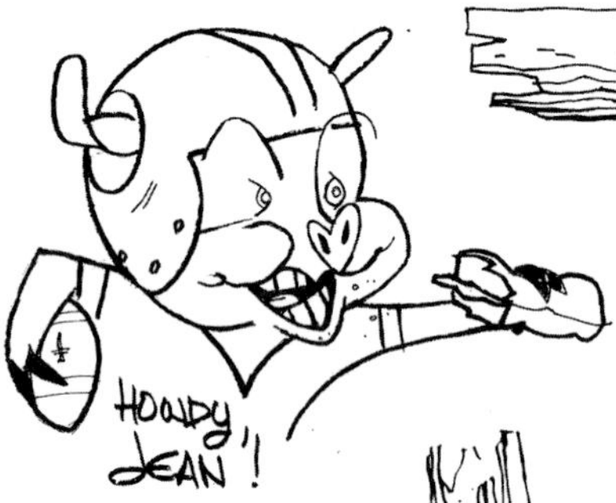
HOWDY JEAN!

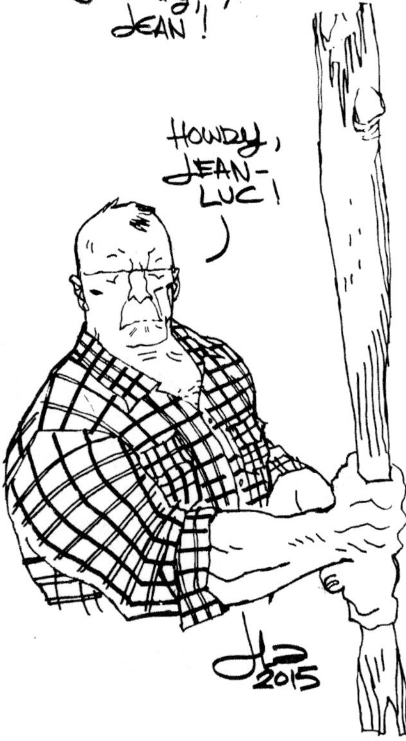
HOWDY, JEAN-LUC!
2015

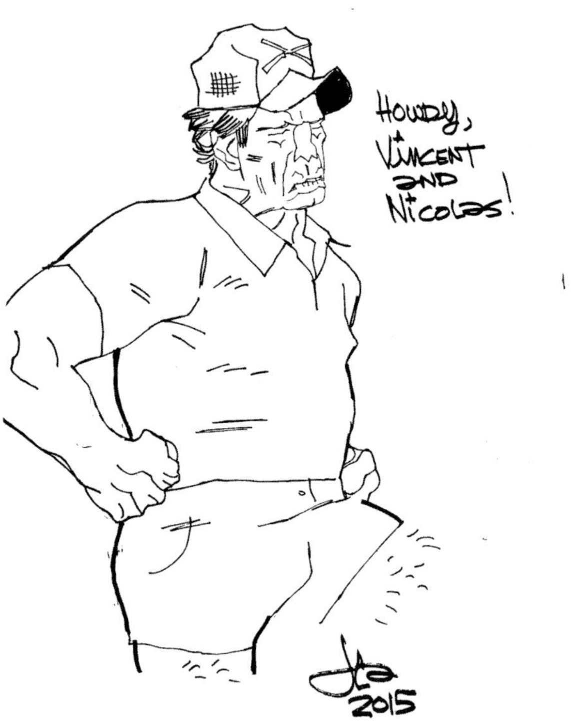
HOWDY, VINCENT AND NICOLAS!
2015

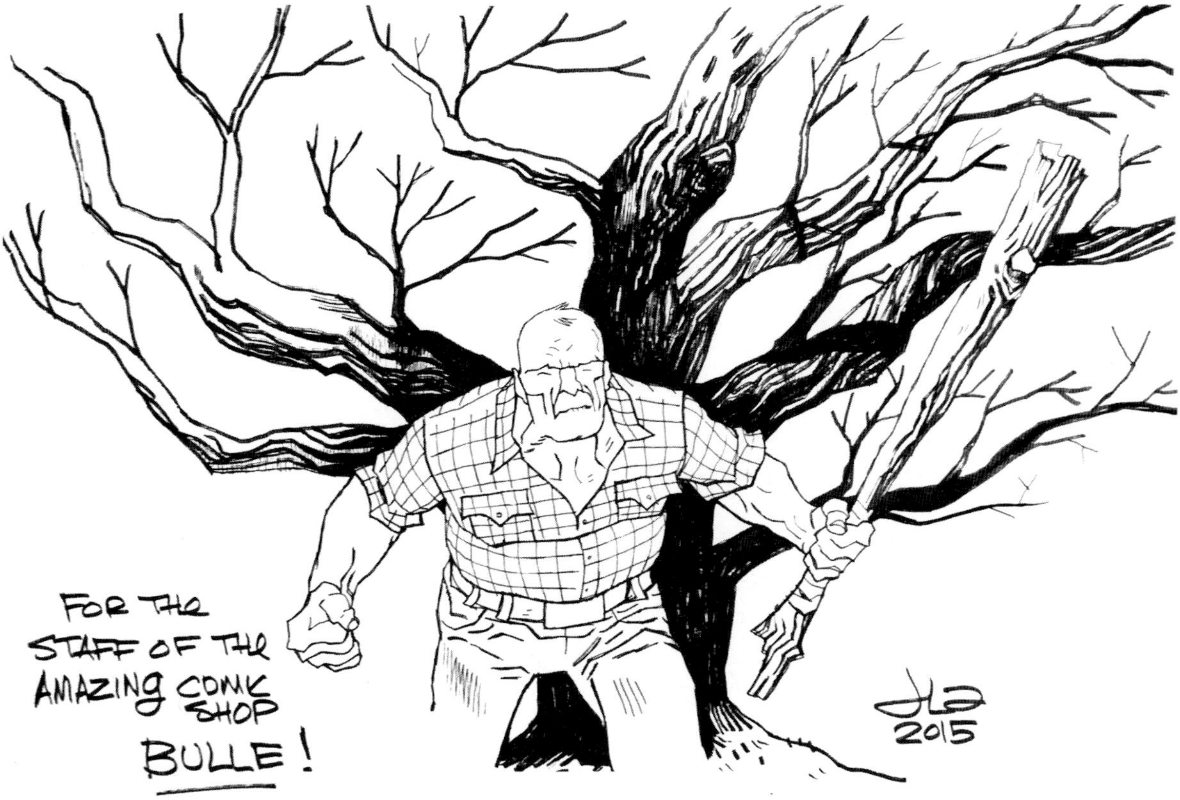
FOR THE
STAFF OF THE
AMAZING COMIC SHOP
BULLE!
2015

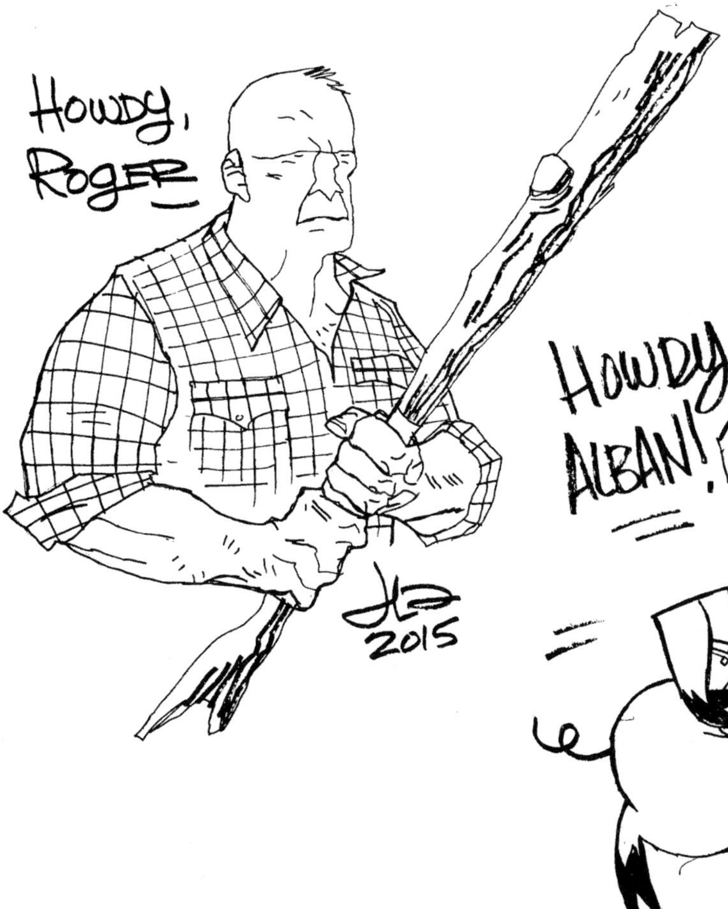
HOWDY,
ROGER
2015

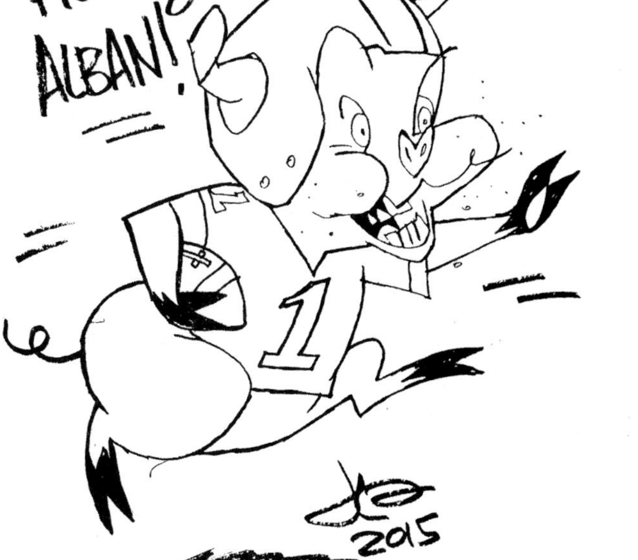
HOWDY,
ALBAN!
1
2015

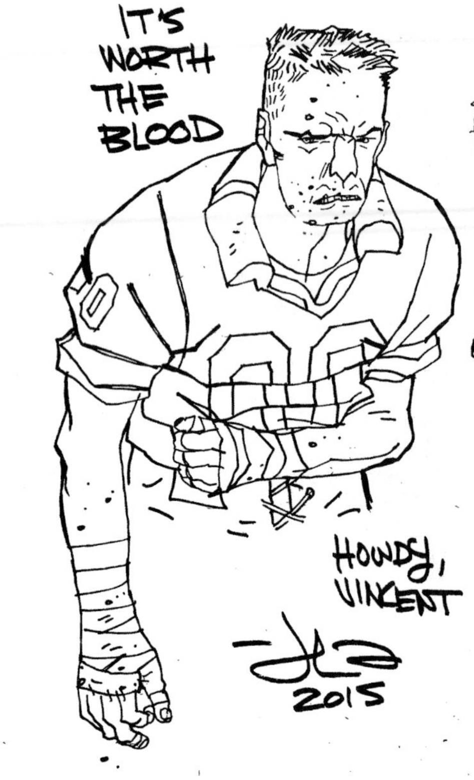
IT'S WORTH THE BLOOD
HOWDY, VINCENT
2015
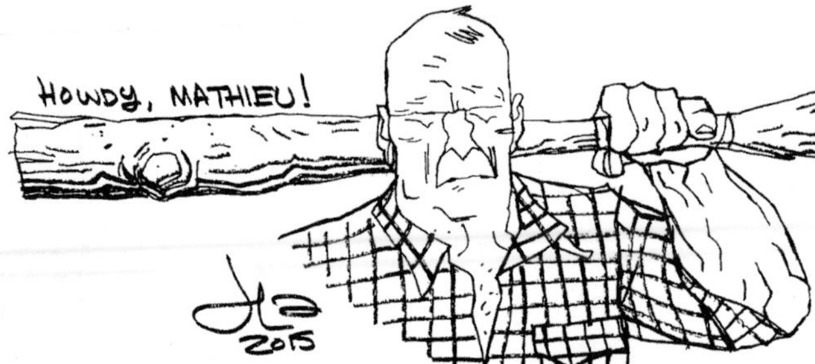
HOWDY, MATHIEU!
2015
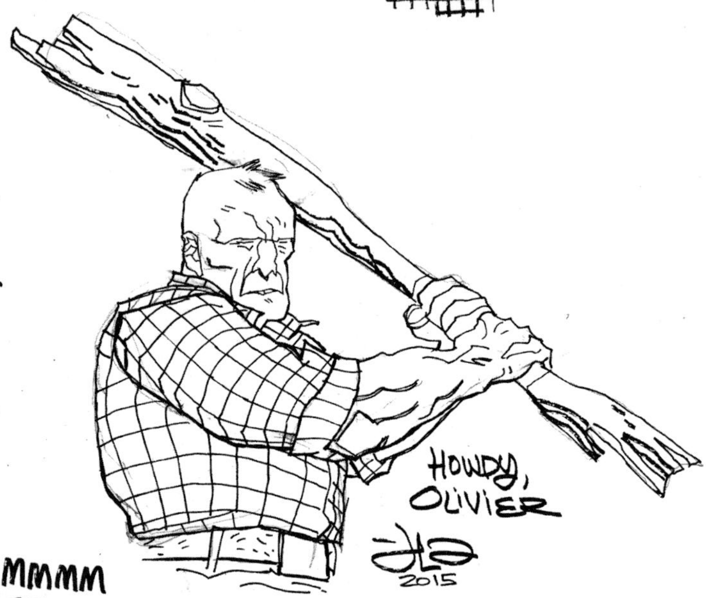
HOWDY, OLIVIER
2015
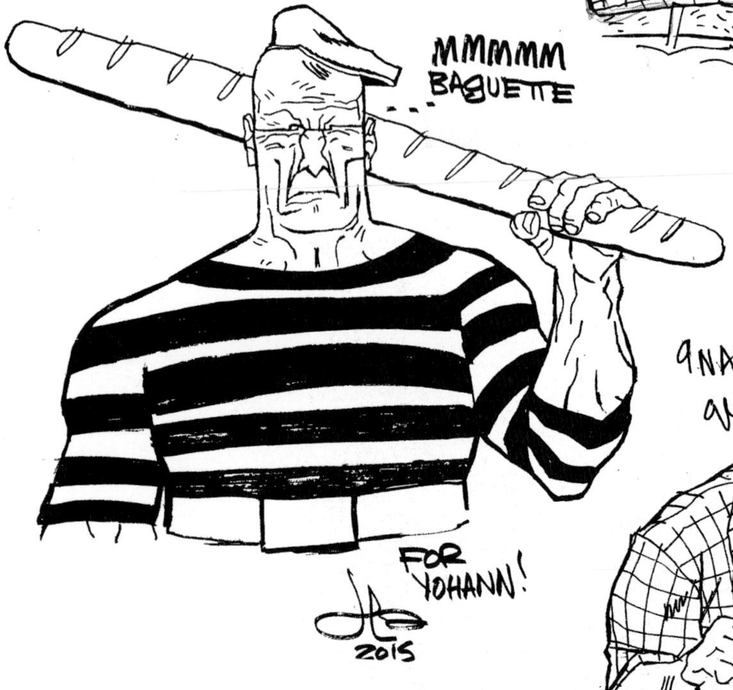
MMMMM ... BAGUETTE
FOR YOHANN!
2015
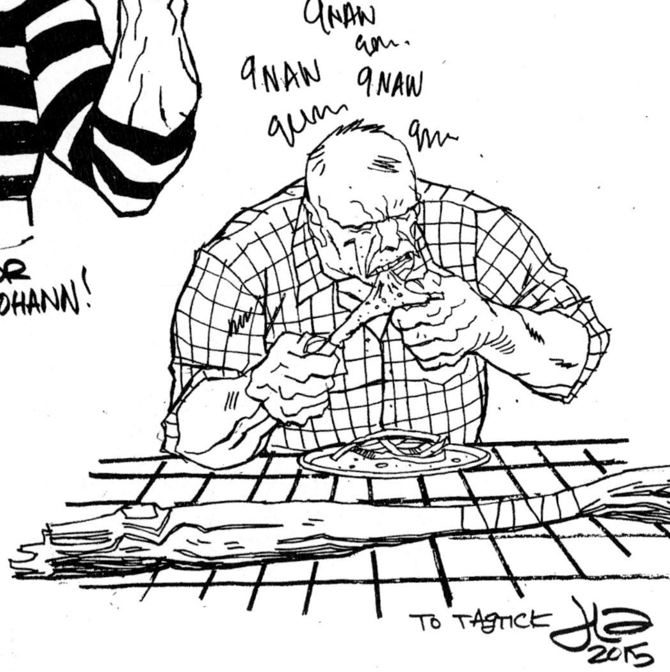
GNAW
GNAW
GNAW
2015

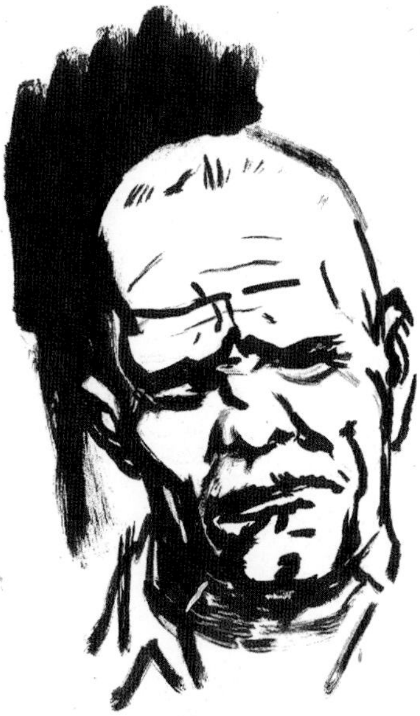

PAUL AZACETA

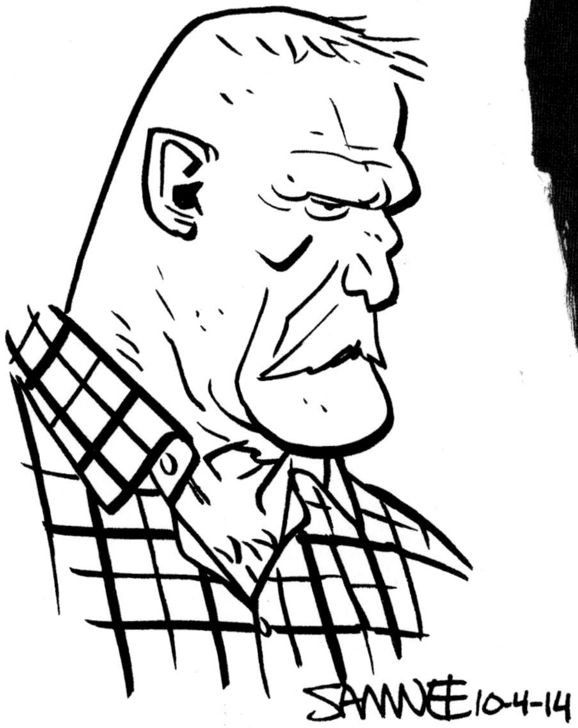
SAMNEE 10-4-14

CHRIS SAMNEE

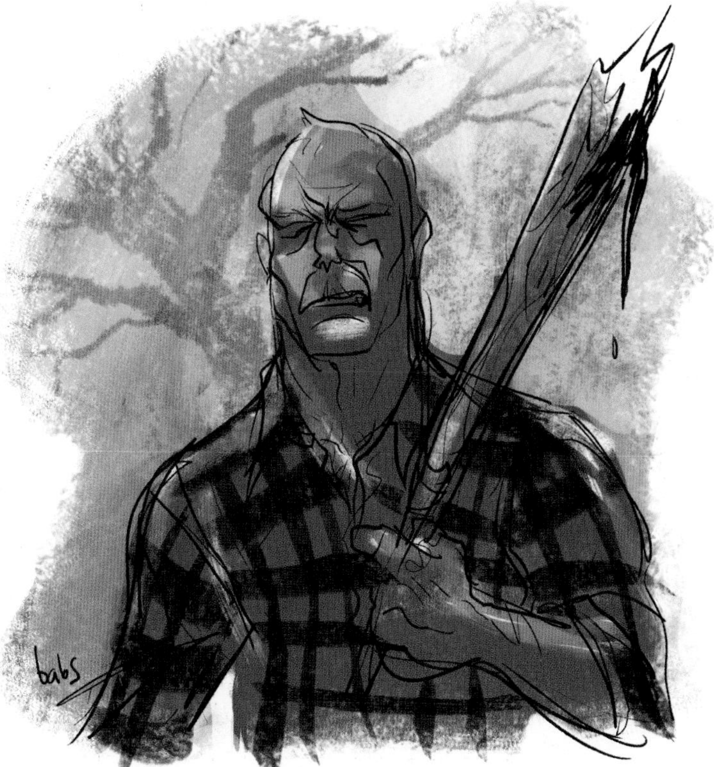
babs

BABS TARR

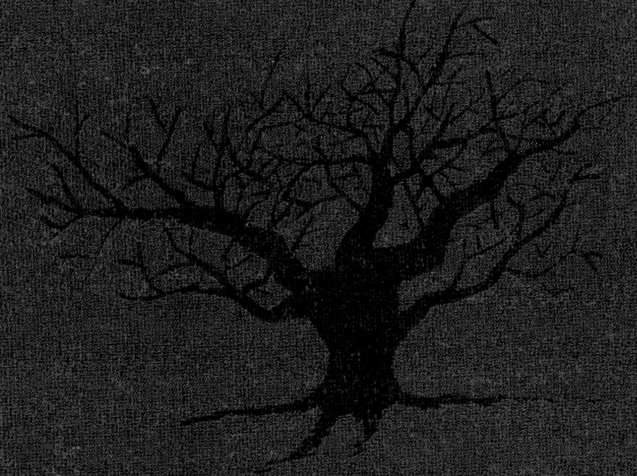

SOUTHERN BASTARDS

coming soon...

Volume 3: HOMECOMING